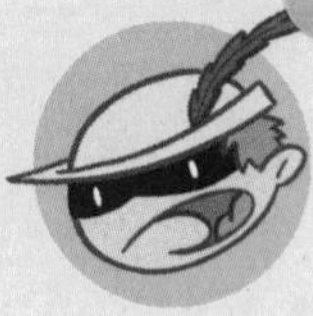

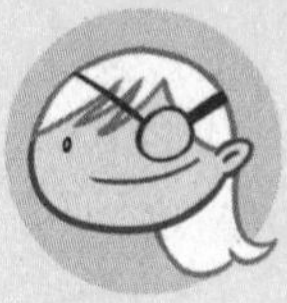

tiny titans

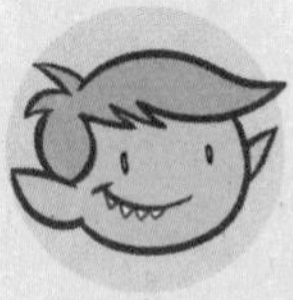

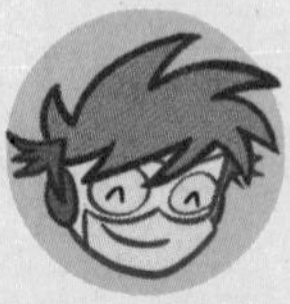

welcome to the Treehouse

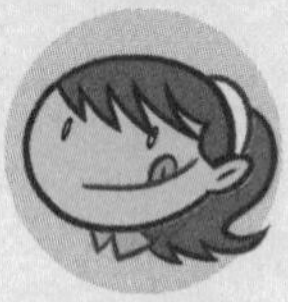

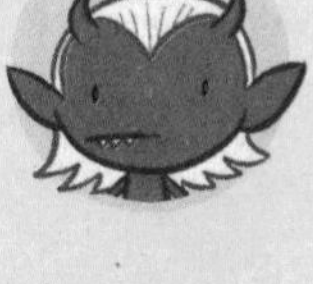

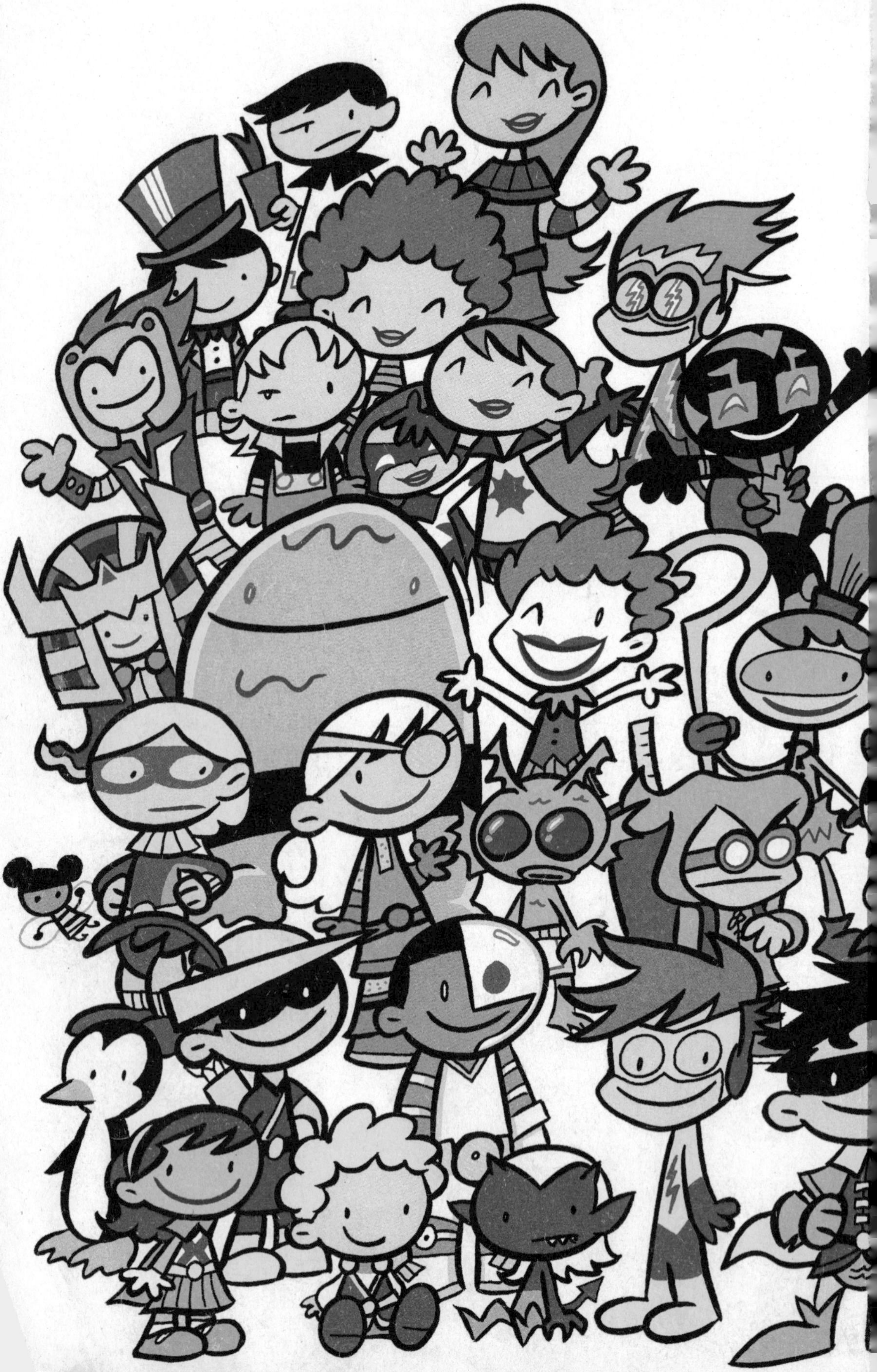

tiny titans

welcome to the Treehouse

Art Baltazar & Franco
Writers

Art Baltazar
Artist

Nick J. Napolitano (Issues #1 & 2)
Art Baltazar (Issues #3-6)
Letterers

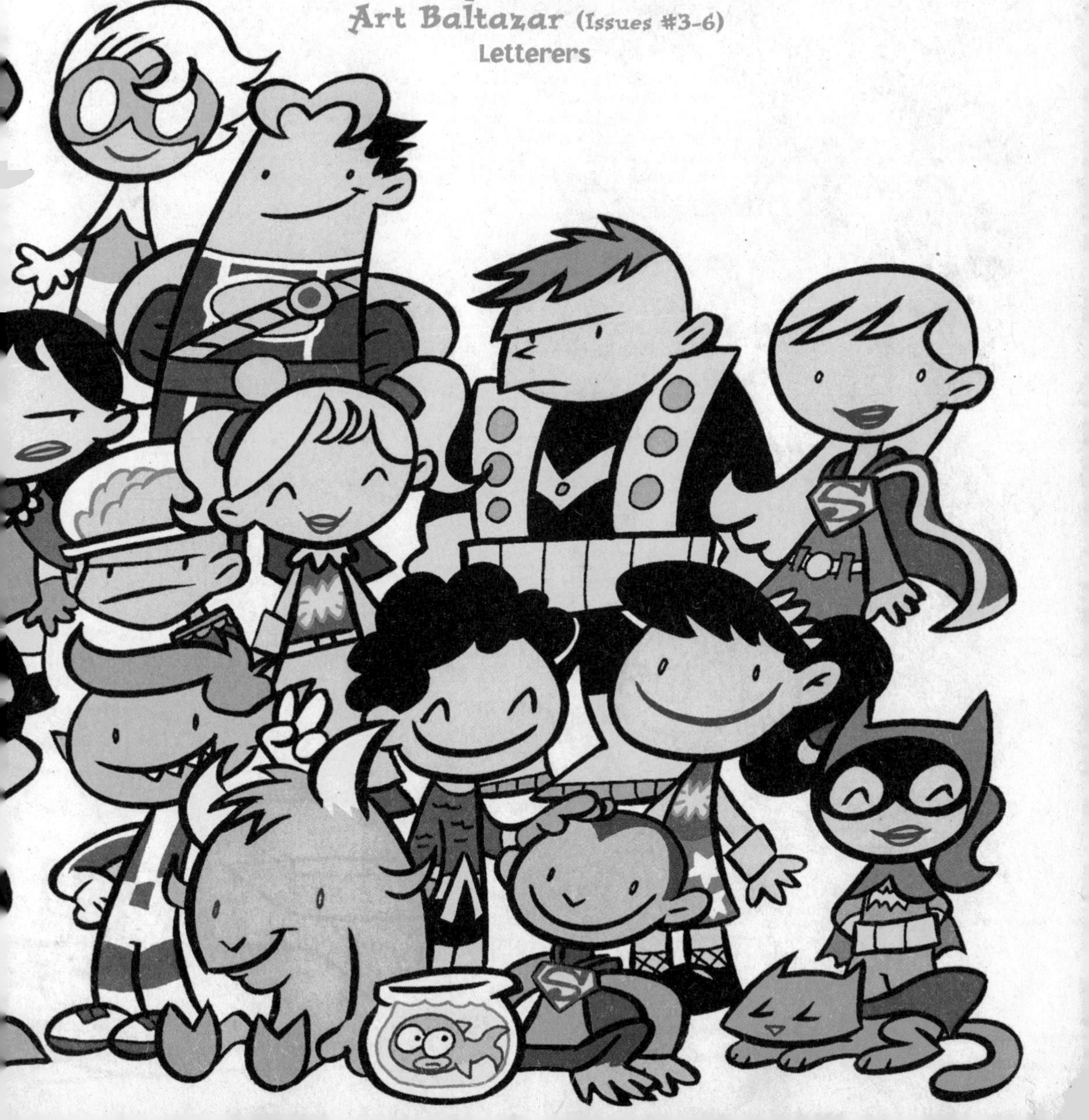

Jann Jones Editor – Original Series **Stephanie Buscema** Assistant Editor – Original Series
JEB WOODARD Group Editor – Collected Editions **Sean Mackiewicz** Editor **STEVE COOK** Design Director – Books

Bob Harras Senior VP – Editor-in-Chief, DC Comics
PAT McCALLUM Executive Editor, DC Comics

DIANE NELSON President
DAN DiDIO Publisher **JIM LEE** Publisher
GEOFF JOHNS President & Chief Creative Officer
AMIT DESAI Executive VP – Business & Marketing Strategy, Direct to Consumer & Global Franchise Management
SAM ADES Senior VP & General Manager, Digital Services **BOBBIE CHASE** VP & Executive Editor, Young Reader & Talent Development
MARK CHIARELLO Senior VP – Art, Design & Collected Editions **JOHN CUNNINGHAM** Senior VP – Sales & Trade Marketing
ANNE DePIES Senior VP – Business Strategy, Finance & Administration **DON FALLETTI** VP – Manufacturing Operations
LAWRENCE GANEM VP – Editorial Administration & Talent Relations **ALISON GILL** Senior VP – Manufacturing & Operations
HANK KANALZ Senior VP – Editorial Strategy & Administration **JAY KOGAN** VP – Legal Affairs
JACK MAHAN VP – Business Affairs **NICK J. NAPOLITANO** VP – Manufacturing Administration
EDDIE SCANNELL VP – Consumer Marketing **COURTNEY SIMMONS** Senior VP – Publicity & Communications
JIM (SKI) SOKOLOWSKI VP – Comic Book Specialty Sales & Trade Marketing
NANCY SPEARS VP – Mass, Book, Digital Sales & Trade Marketing
MICHELE R. WELLS VP – Content Strategy

Cover by Art Baltazar.
TINY TITANS: WELCOME TO THE TREEHOUSE
Published by DC Comics. Cover, text and compilation Copyright © 2009 DC Comics. All Rights Reserved.
Originally published in single magazine form in TINY TITANS 1-6. Copyright © 2008 DC Comics. All Rights Reserved. All characters, their distinctive likenesses and related elements featured in this publication are trademarks of DC Comics. The stories, characters and incidents featured in this publication are entirely fictional. DC Comics does not read or accept unsolicited submissions of ideas, stories or artwork.

DC Comics, 2900 West Alameda Ave., Burbank, CA 91505.
A Warner Bros. Entertainment Company
Printed by Transcontinental Interglobe, Beauceville, QC, Canada. 2/2/18. Tenth Printing.
ISBN: 978-1-4012-2078-5

Library of Congress Cataloging-in-Publication Data

Baltazar, Art.
Tiny titans. Welcome to the treehouse / Art Baltazar and Franco
p. cm.
"Contains material originally published in magazine form as Tiny Titans #1-6"–T. p. verso.
Summary: " The young superheroes begin a new school year. The teachers are super villains, the field trips are out of the world, and their playground must be protected from the Fearsome Five."– Provided by publisher.
ISBN 978-1-4012-2078-5 (pbk.)
1. Graphic novels. [1. Graphic novels. 2. Superheroes–Fiction.] I.
Aureliani, Franco, ill. II. Title.
———
741.5'973–dc23
2009281352

PEFC Certified
Printed on paper from
sustainably managed
forests and controlled
sources
PEFC/01-31-106   www.pefc.org

This Label only applies to the text section

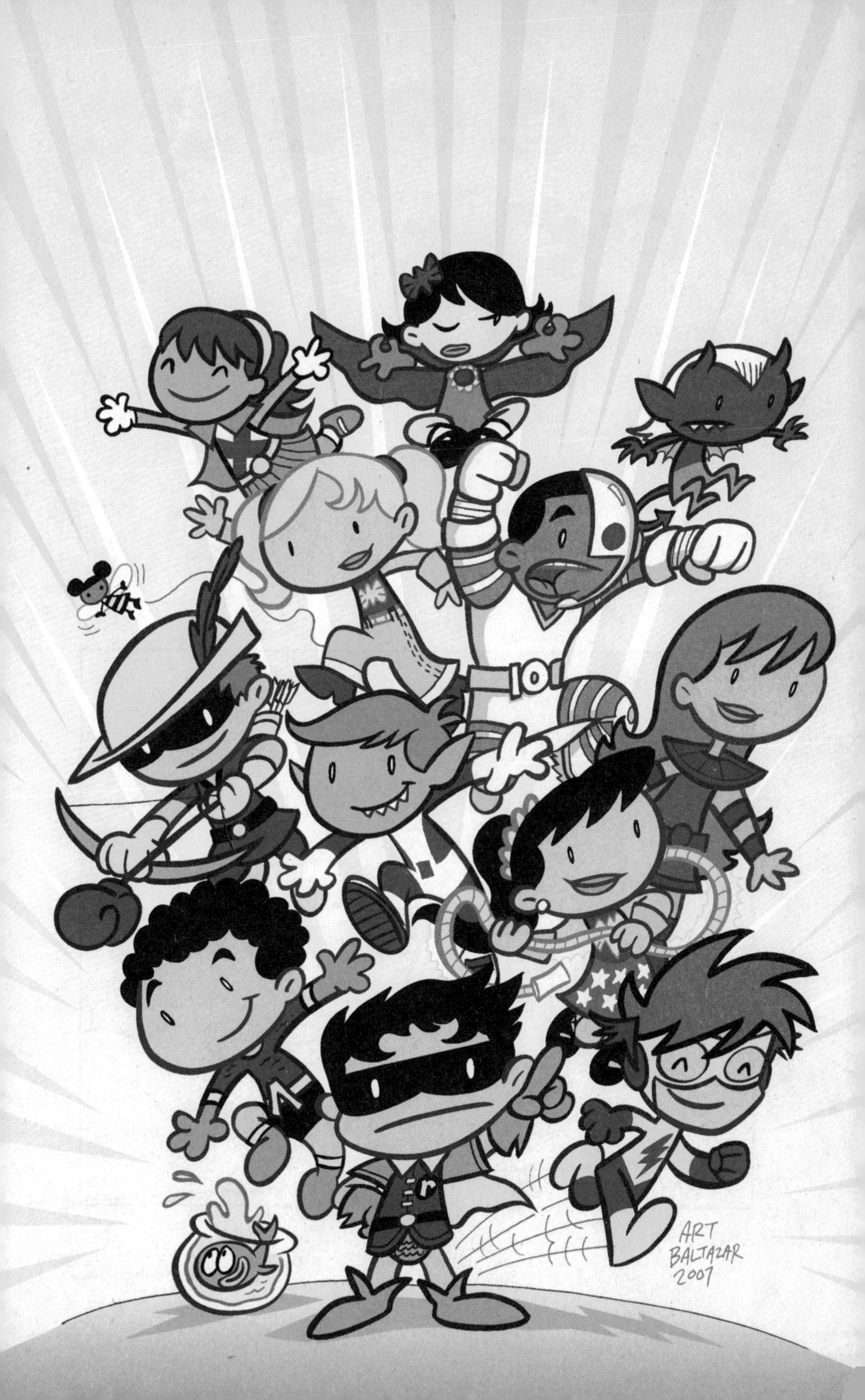
ART
BALTAZAR
2007

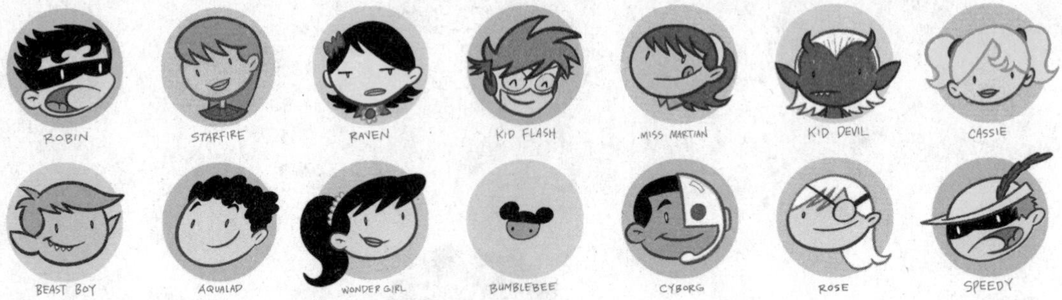
ROBIN
STARFIRE
RAVEN
KID FLASH
MISS MARTIAN
KID DEVIL
CASSIE
BEAST BOY
AQUALAD
WONDER GIRL
BUMBLEBEE
CYBORG
ROSE
SPEEDY

tiny titans

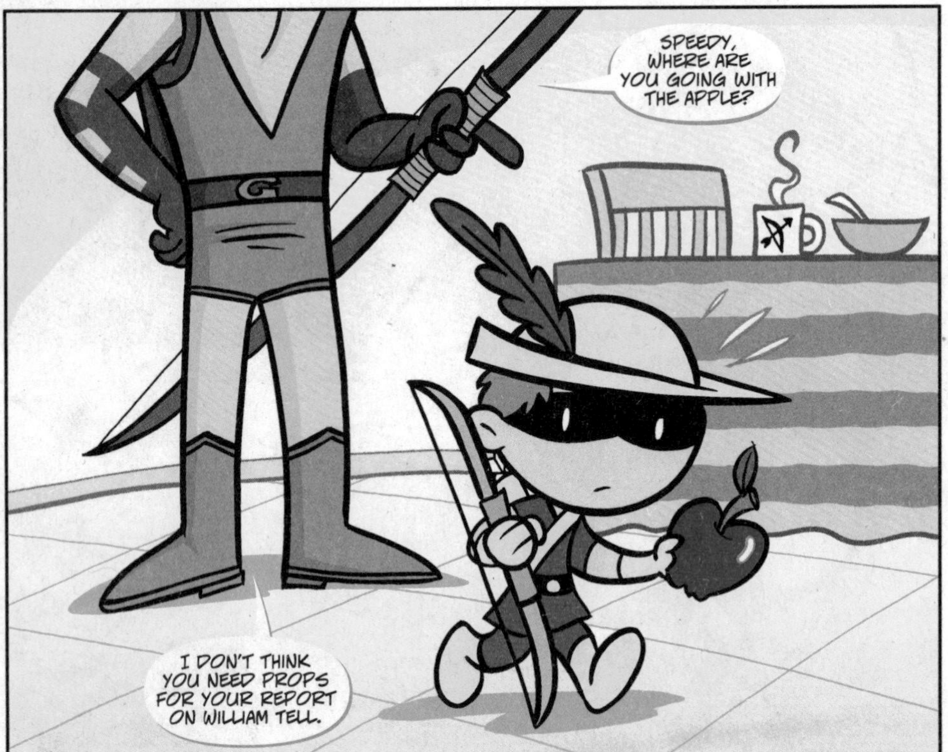
SPEEDY, WHERE ARE YOU GOING WITH THE APPLE?
I DON'T THINK YOU NEED PROPS FOR YOUR REPORT ON WILLIAM TELL.

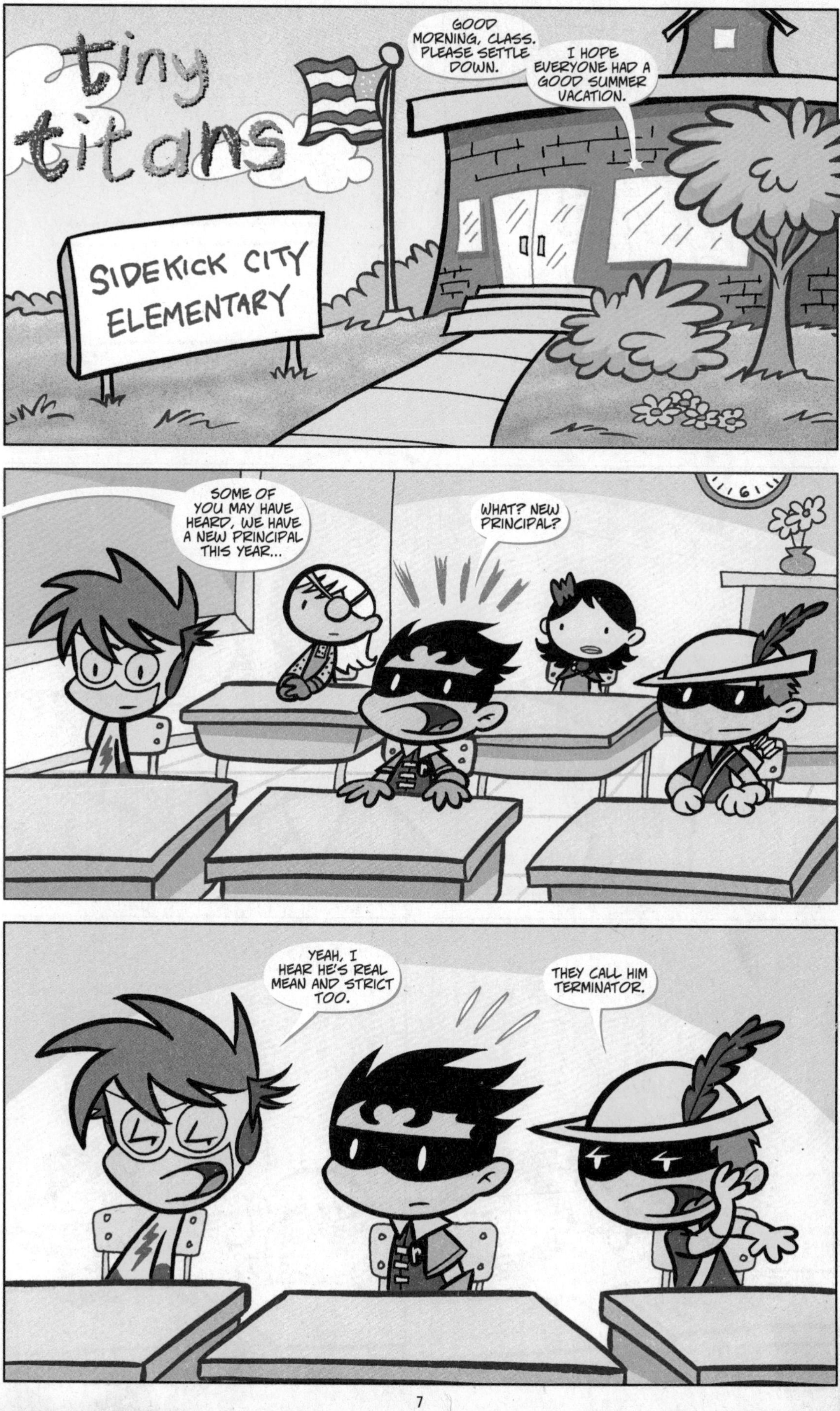
tiny titans
SIDEKICK CITY ELEMENTARY
GOOD MORNING, CLASS. PLEASE SETTLE DOWN.
I HOPE EVERYONE HAD A GOOD SUMMER VACATION.
SOME OF YOU MAY HAVE HEARD, WE HAVE A NEW PRINCIPAL THIS YEAR...
WHAT? NEW PRINCIPAL?
YEAH, I HEAR HE'S REAL MEAN AND STRICT TOO.
THEY CALL HIM TERMINATOR.

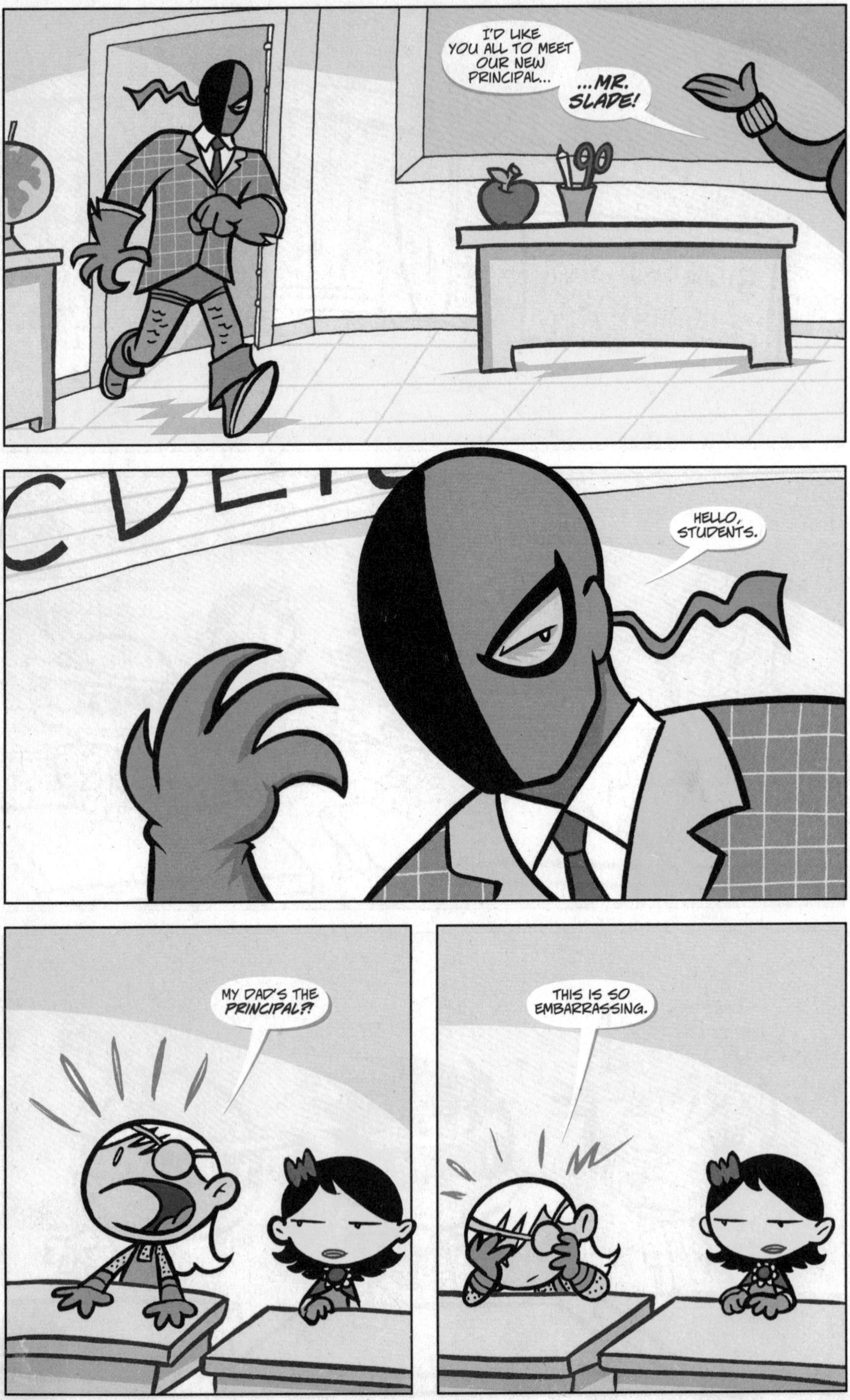
I'D LIKE YOU ALL TO MEET OUR NEW PRINCIPAL...
...MR. SLADE!
HELLO, STUDENTS.
MY DAD'S THE PRINCIPAL?!
THIS IS SO EMBARRASSING.

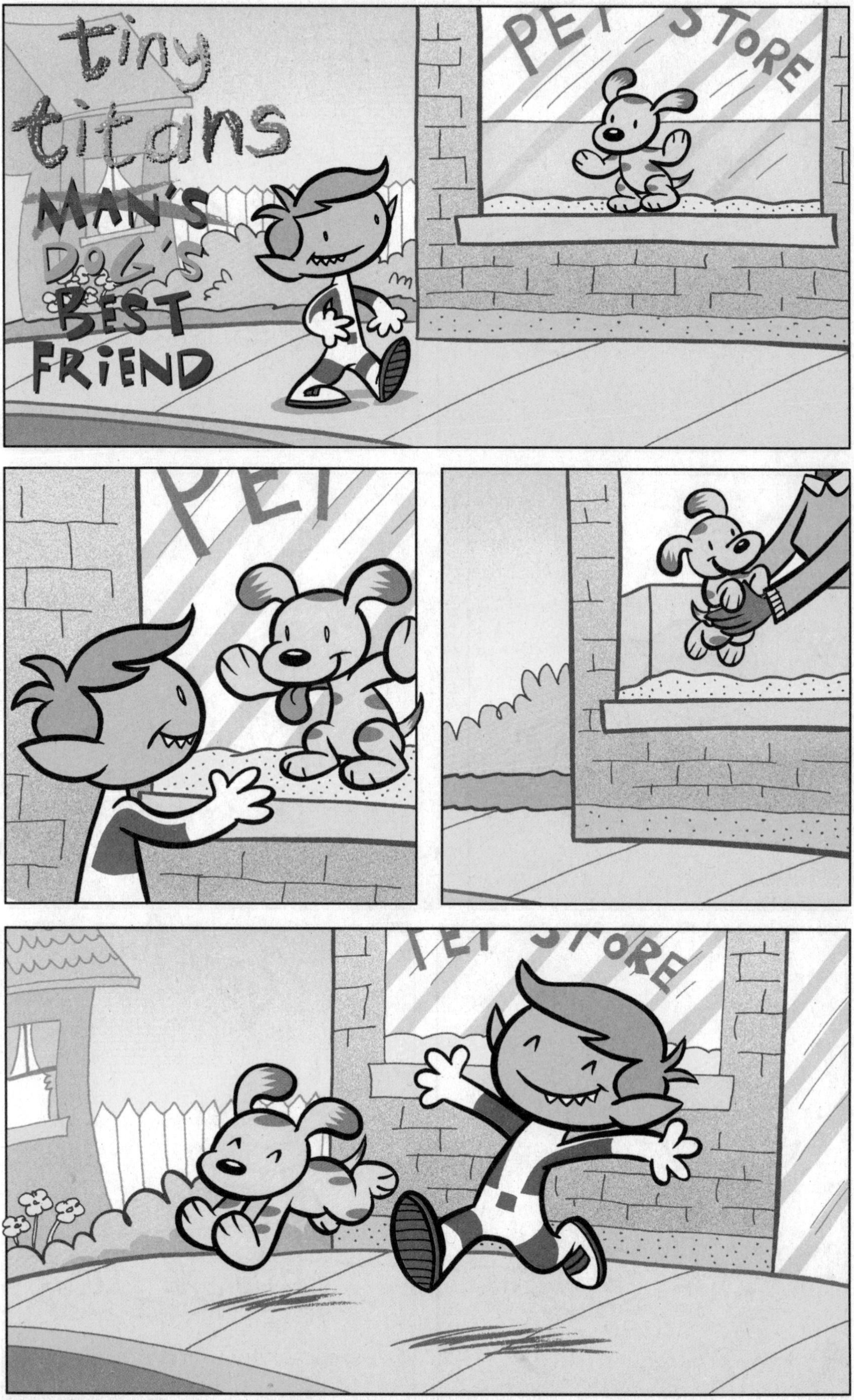
tiny titans
~~MAN'S~~ DOG'S BEST FRIEND
PET STORE

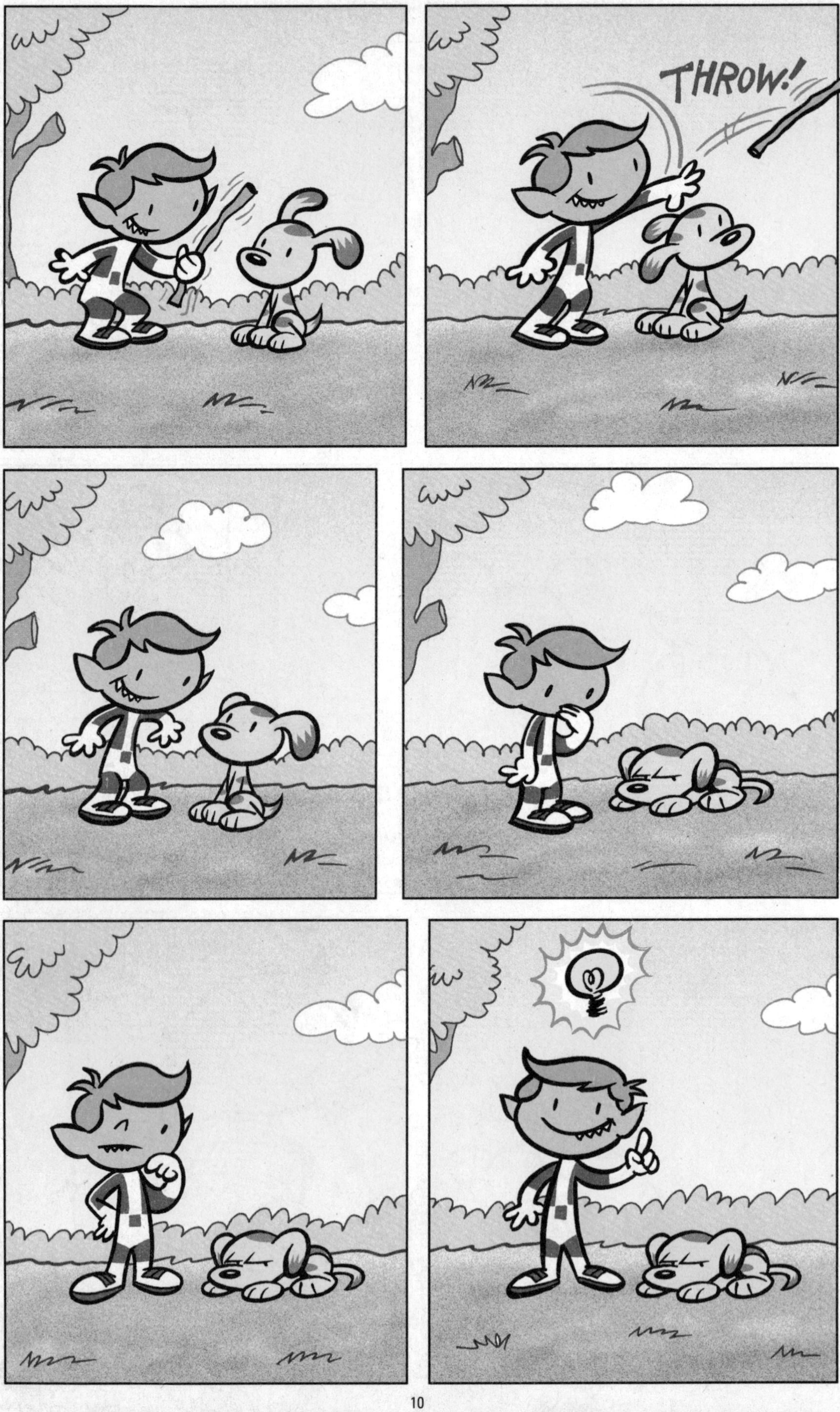
THROW!

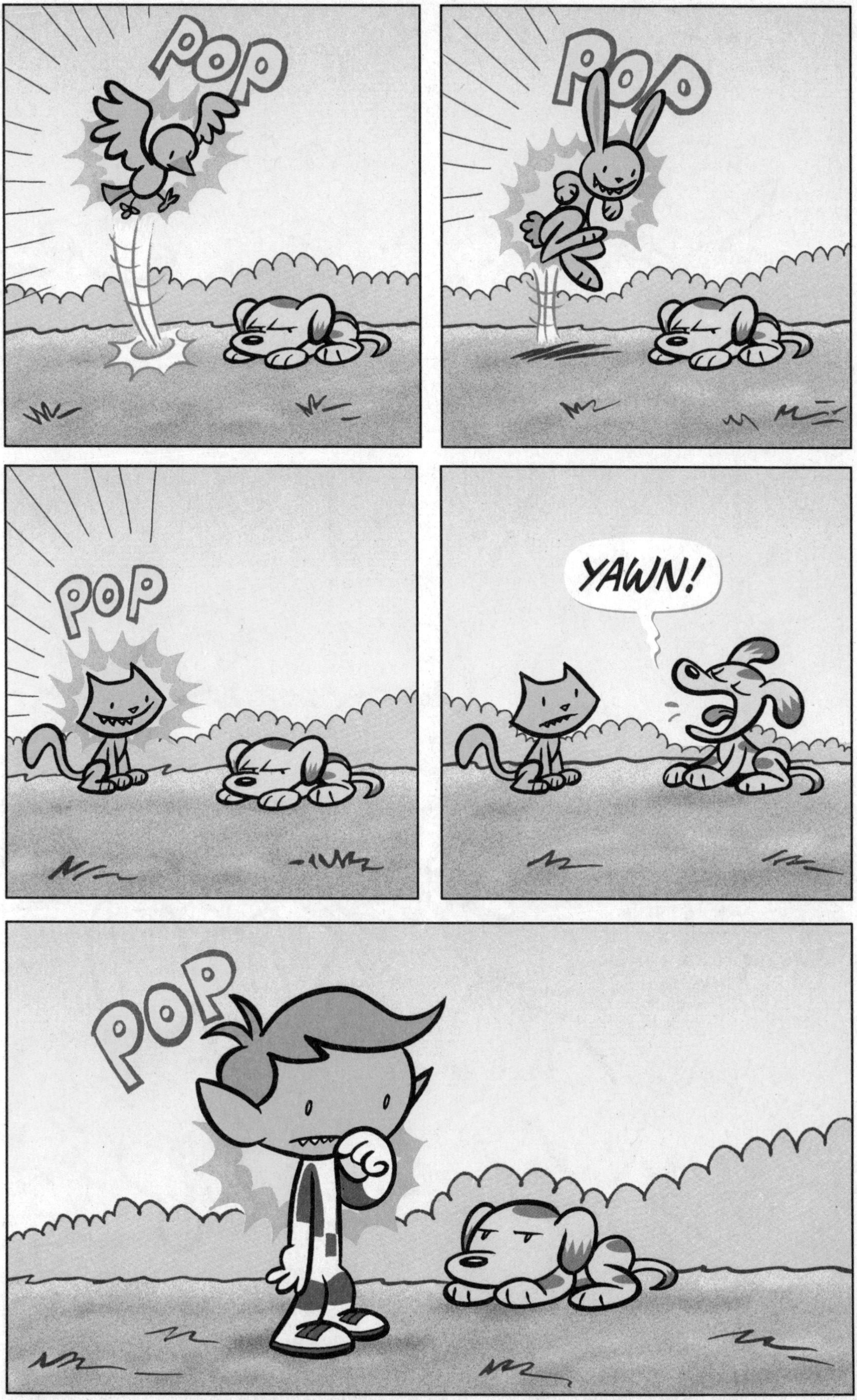
POP
POP
POP
YAWN!
POP

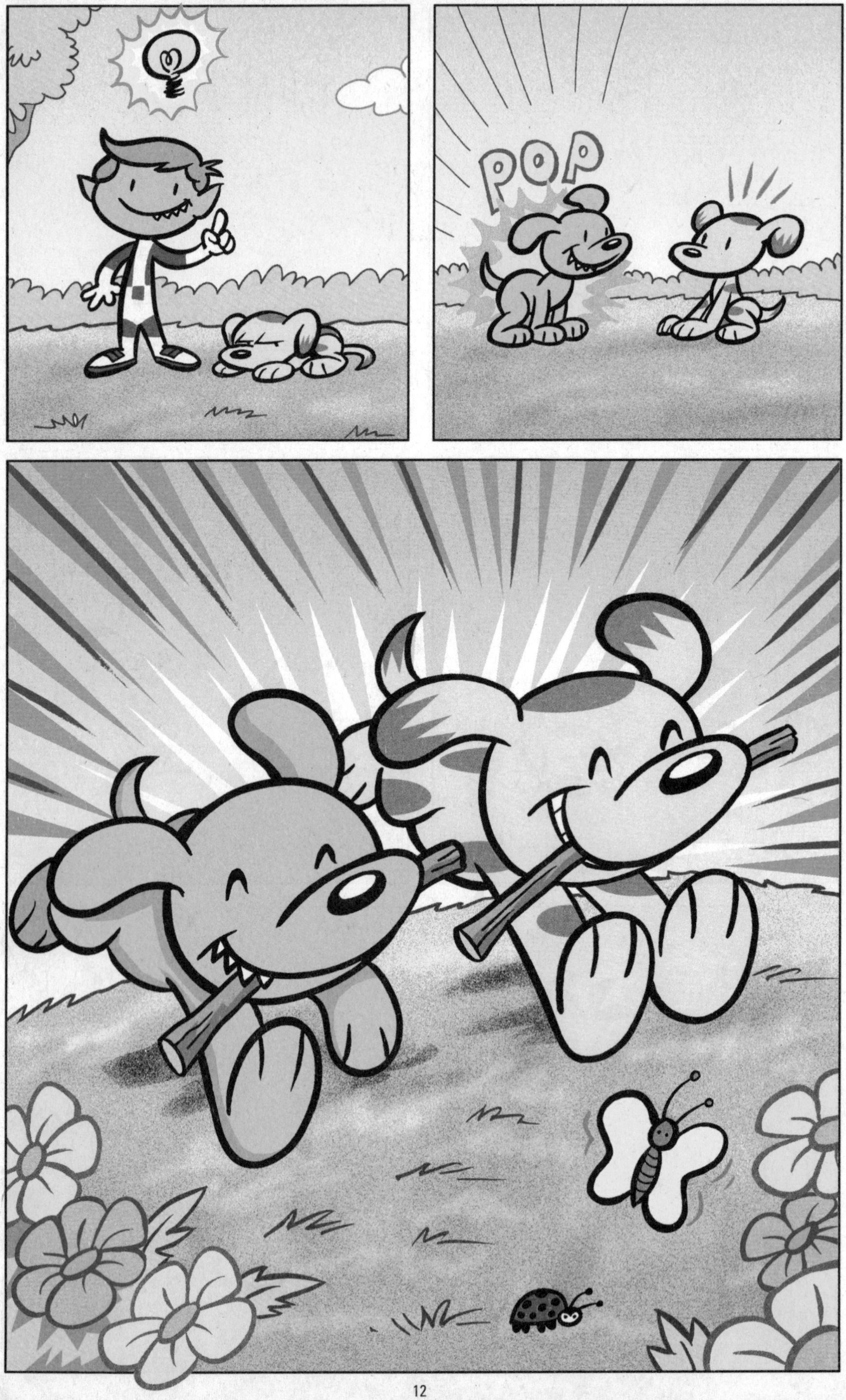
POP

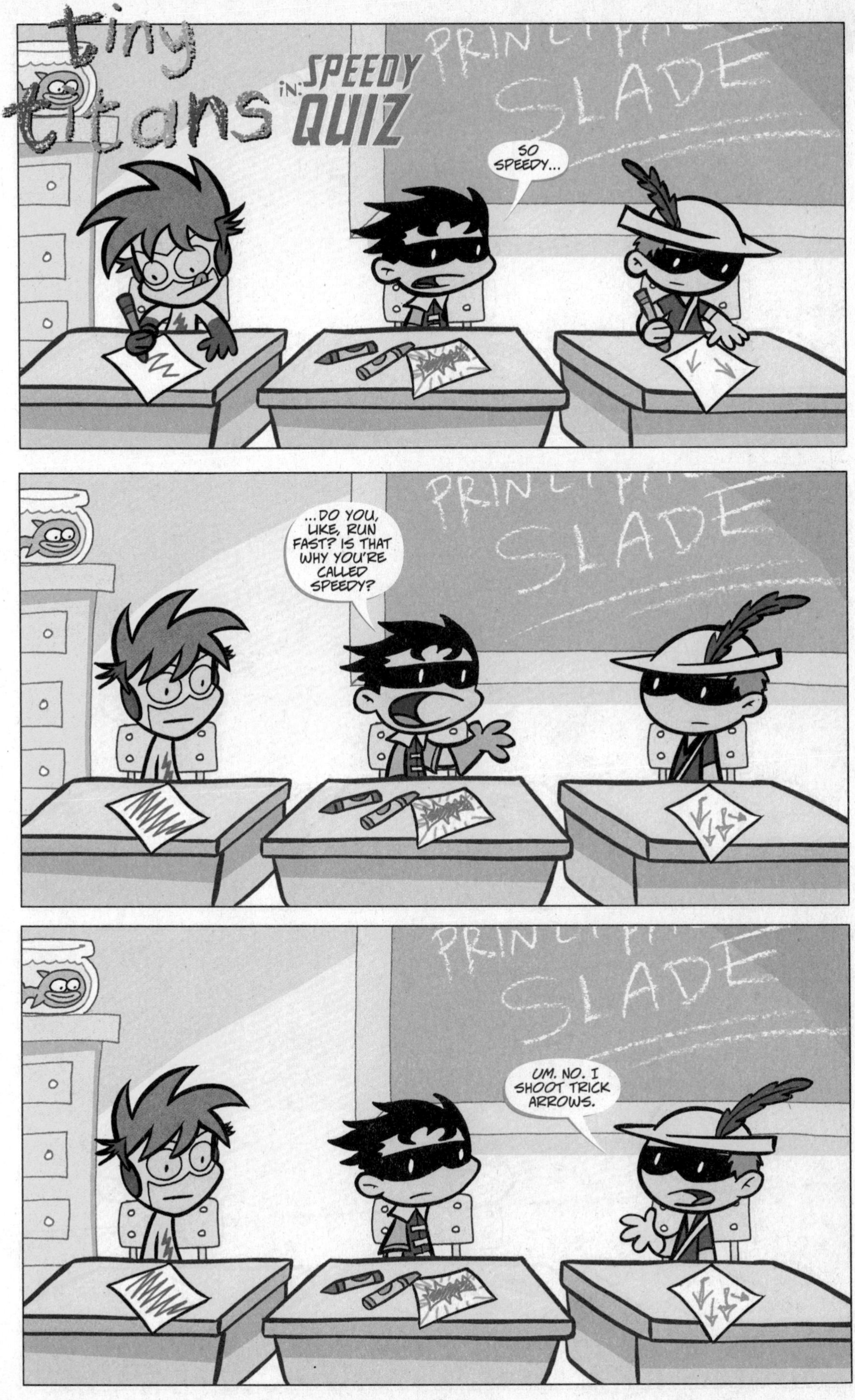
tiny titans
in: SPEEDY QUIZ
PRINCIPAL SLADE
SO SPEEDY...
...DO YOU, LIKE, RUN FAST? IS THAT WHY YOU'RE CALLED SPEEDY?
UM. NO. I SHOOT TRICK ARROWS.

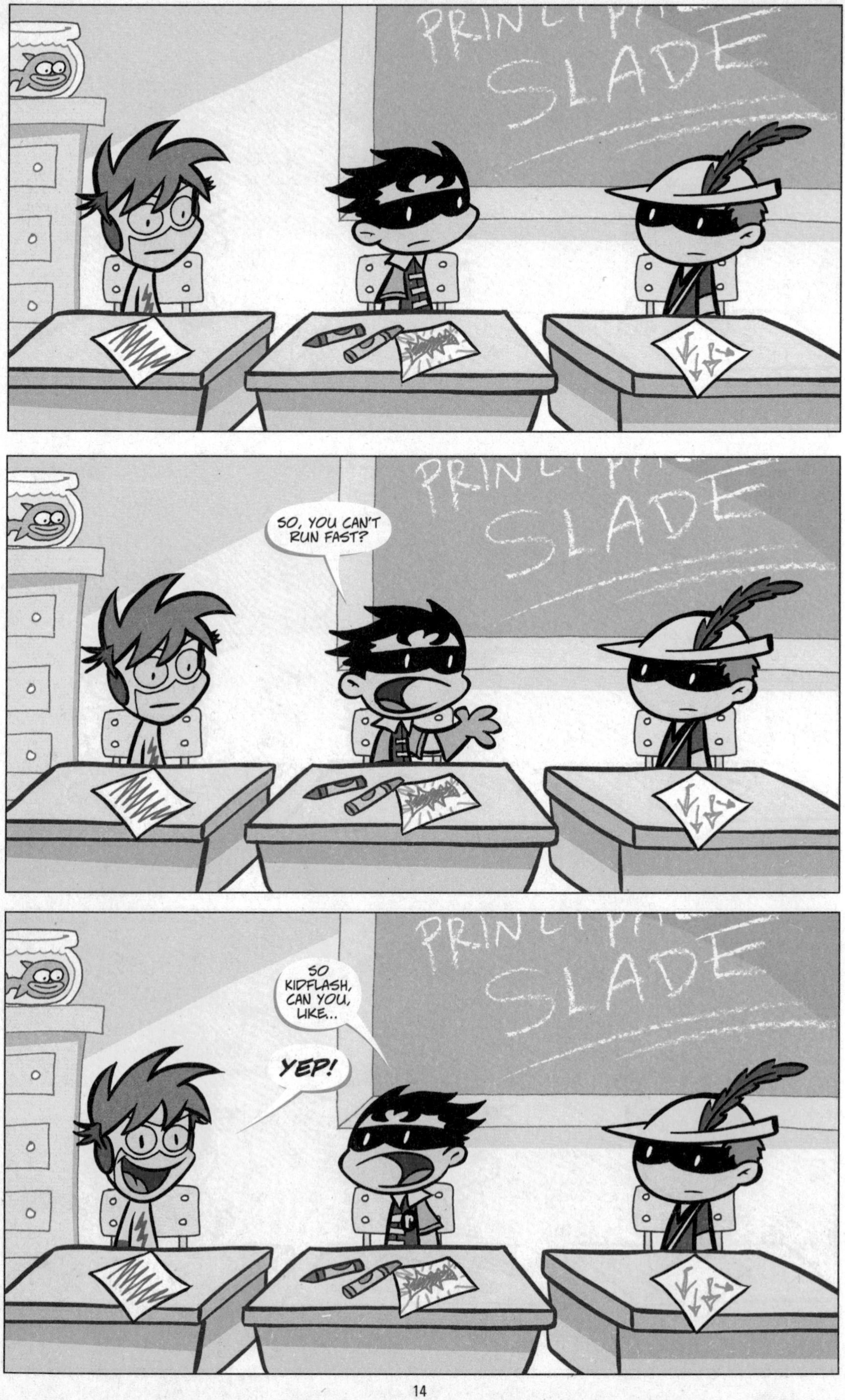
SLADE
SO, YOU CAN'T RUN FAST?
SO KIDFLASH, CAN YOU, LIKE...
YEP!

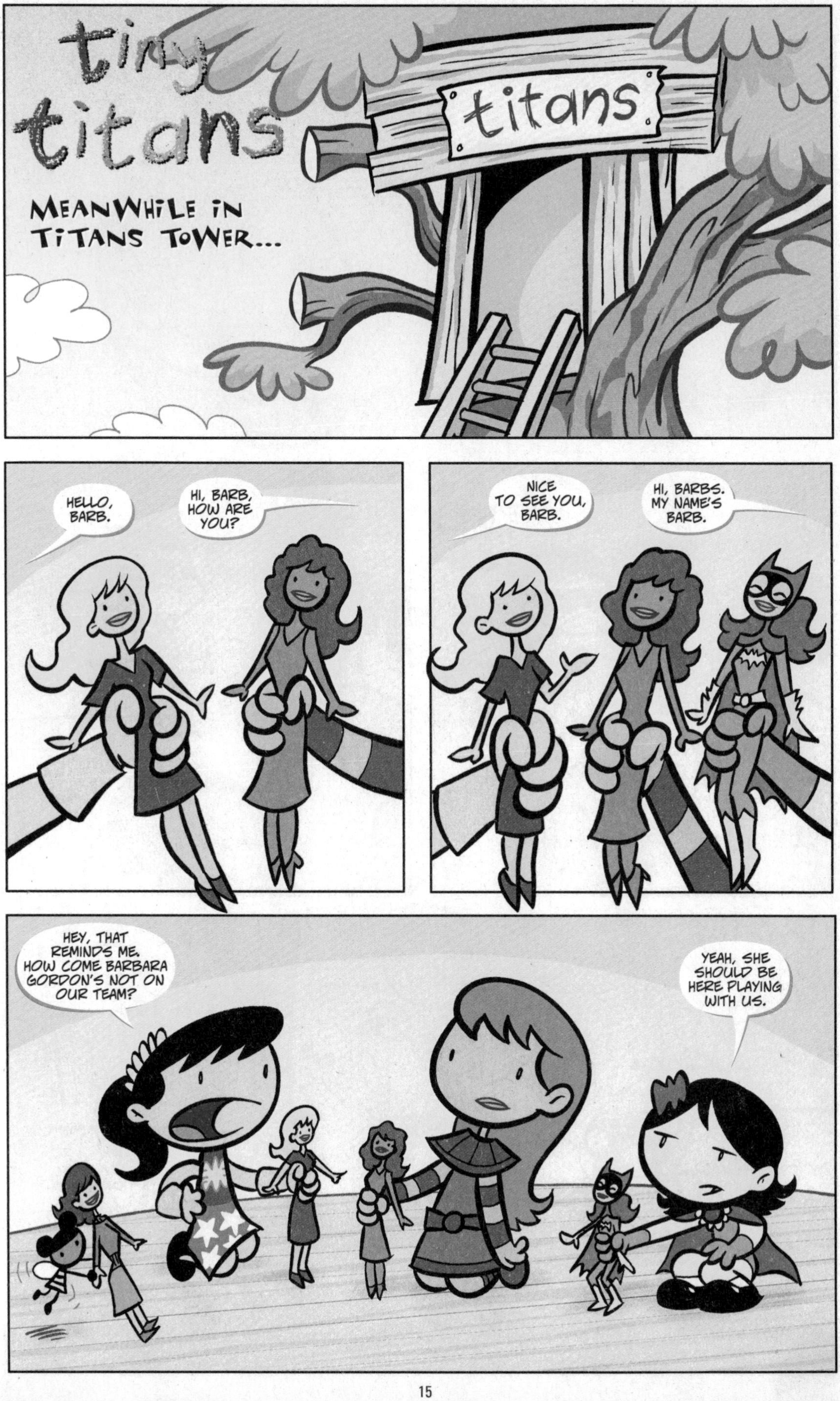
tiny titans
titans
MEANWHILE IN TITANS TOWER...
HELLO, BARB.
HI, BARB, HOW ARE YOU?
NICE TO SEE YOU, BARB.
HI, BARBS. MY NAME'S BARB.
HEY, THAT REMINDS ME. HOW COME BARBARA GORDON'S NOT ON OUR TEAM?
YEAH, SHE SHOULD BE HERE PLAYING WITH US.

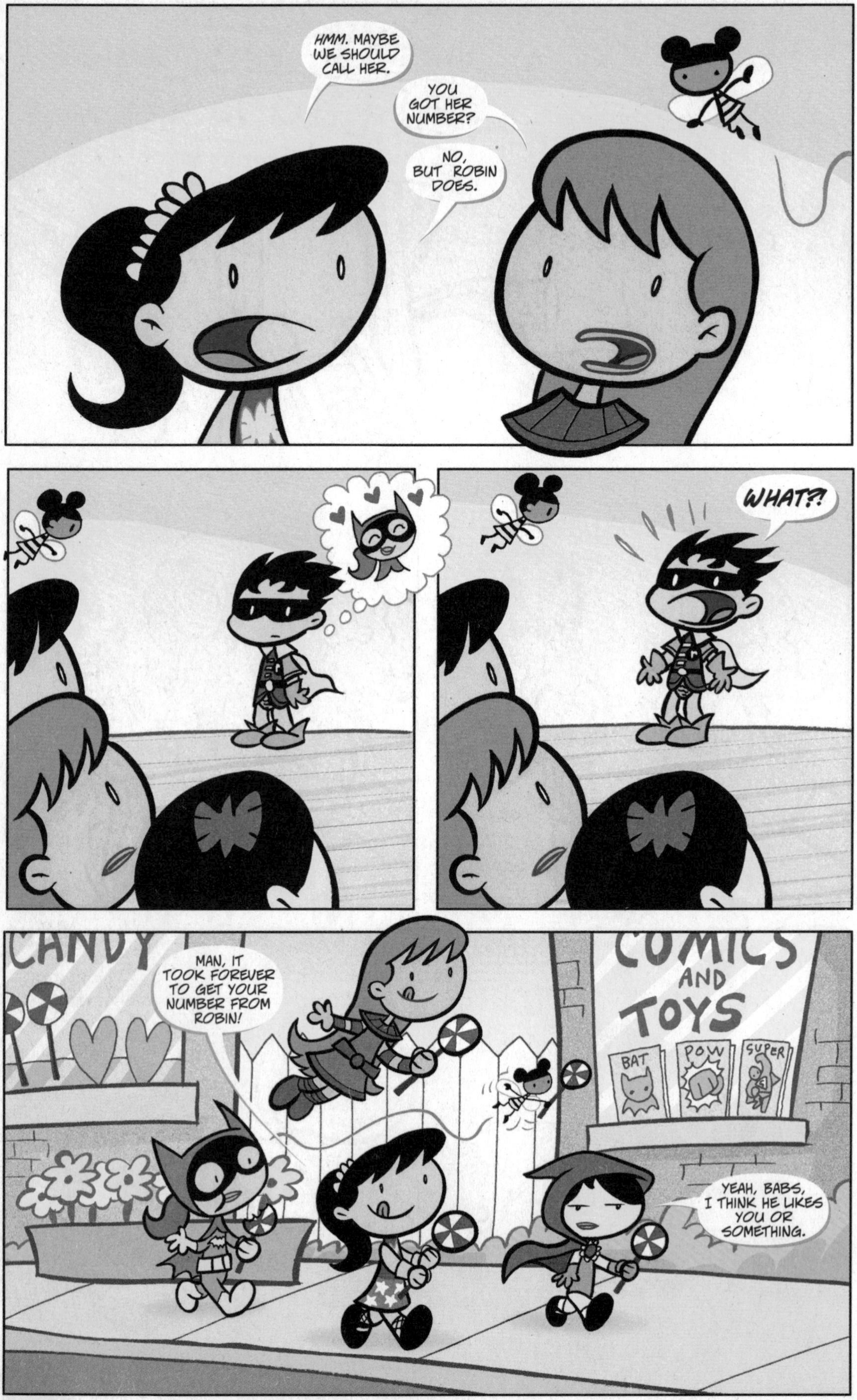
HMM. MAYBE WE SHOULD CALL HER.
YOU GOT HER NUMBER?
NO, BUT ROBIN DOES.
WHAT?!
MAN, IT TOOK FOREVER TO GET YOUR NUMBER FROM ROBIN!
YEAH, BABS, I THINK HE LIKES YOU OR SOMETHING.
CANDY
COMICS AND TOYS
BAT
POW
SUPER

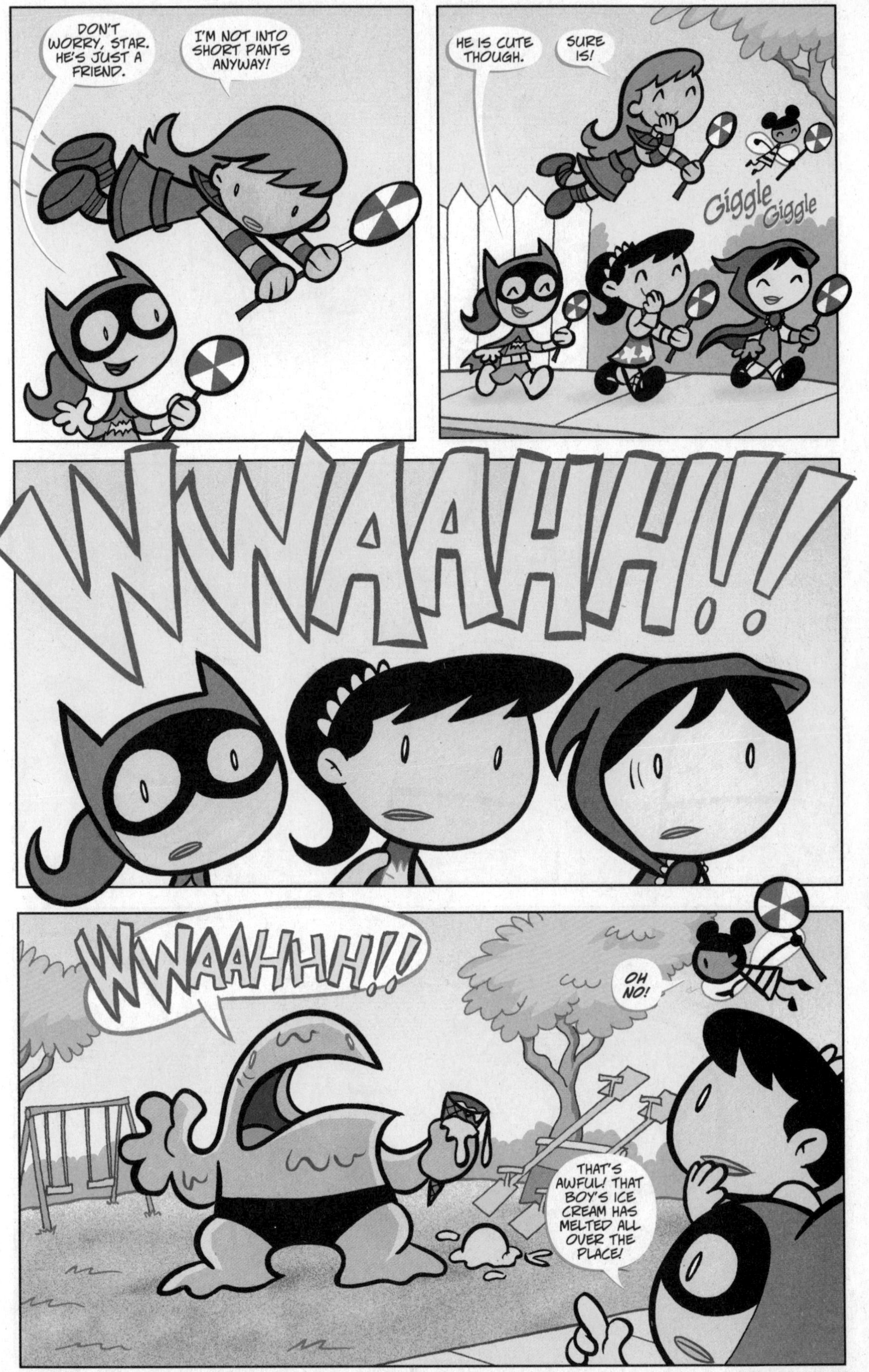

DON'T WORRY, STAR. HE'S JUST A FRIEND.
I'M NOT INTO SHORT PANTS ANYWAY!
HE IS CUTE THOUGH.
SURE IS!
Giggle Giggle
WWAAHH!!
WWAAHHH!!
OH NO!
THAT'S AWFUL! THAT BOY'S ICE CREAM HAS MELTED ALL OVER THE PLACE!

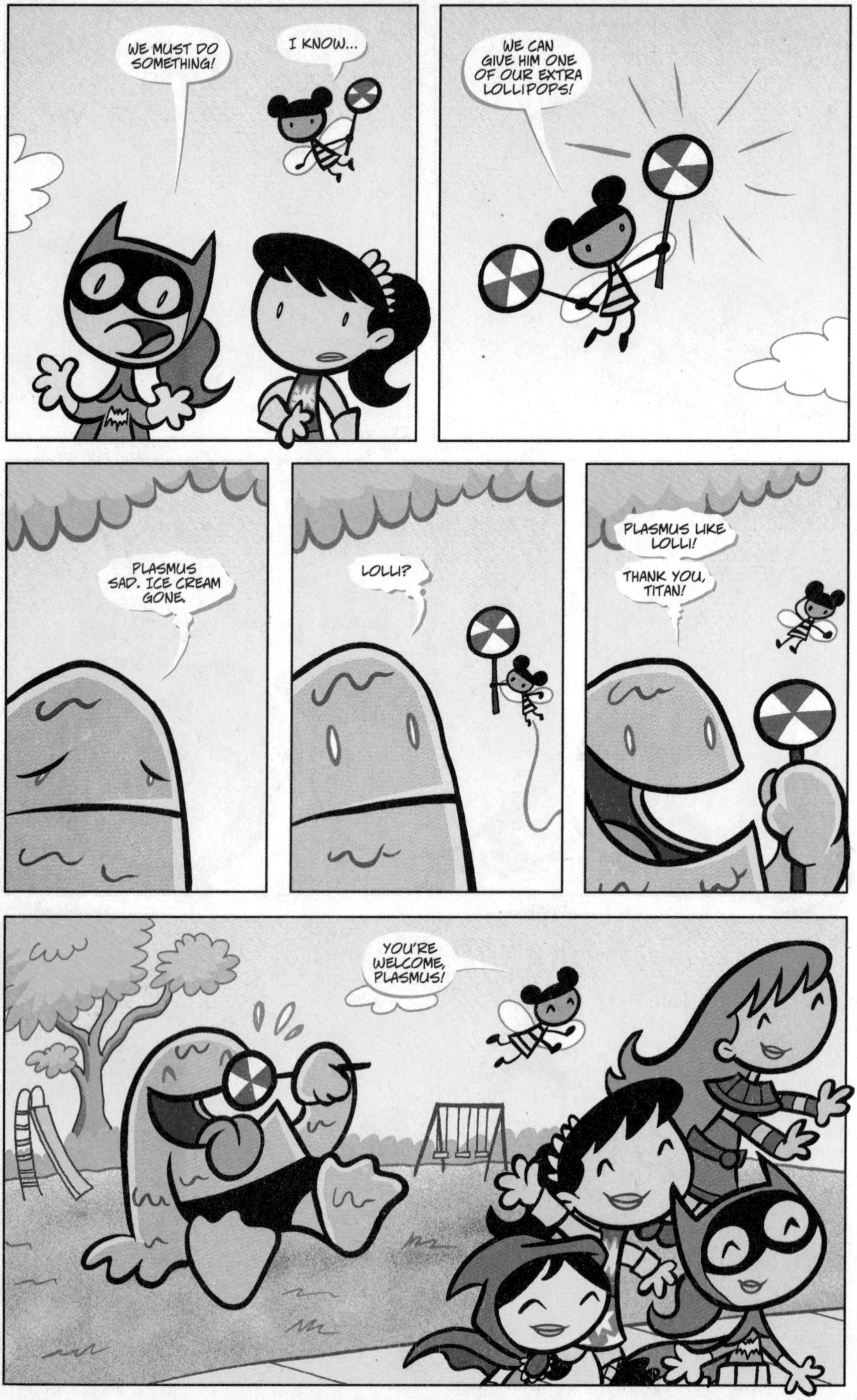
WE MUST DO SOMETHING!
I KNOW...
WE CAN GIVE HIM ONE OF OUR EXTRA LOLLIPOPS!
PLASMUS SAD. ICE CREAM GONE.
LOLLI?
PLASMUS LIKE LOLLI!
THANK YOU, TITAN!
YOU'RE WELCOME, PLASMUS!

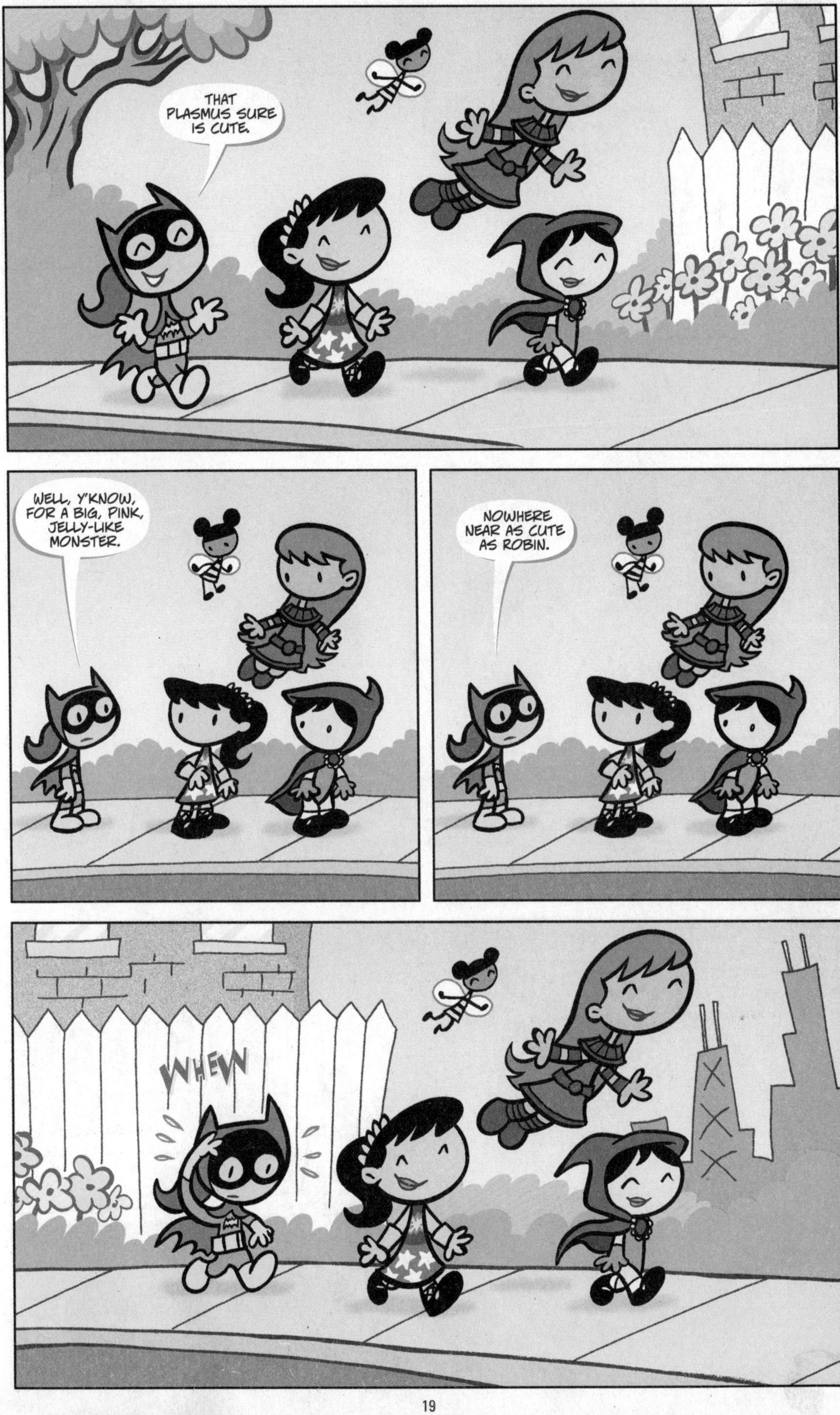
THAT PLASMUS SURE IS CUTE.
WELL, Y'KNOW, FOR A BIG, PINK, JELLY-LIKE MONSTER.
NOWHERE NEAR AS CUTE AS ROBIN.
WHEW

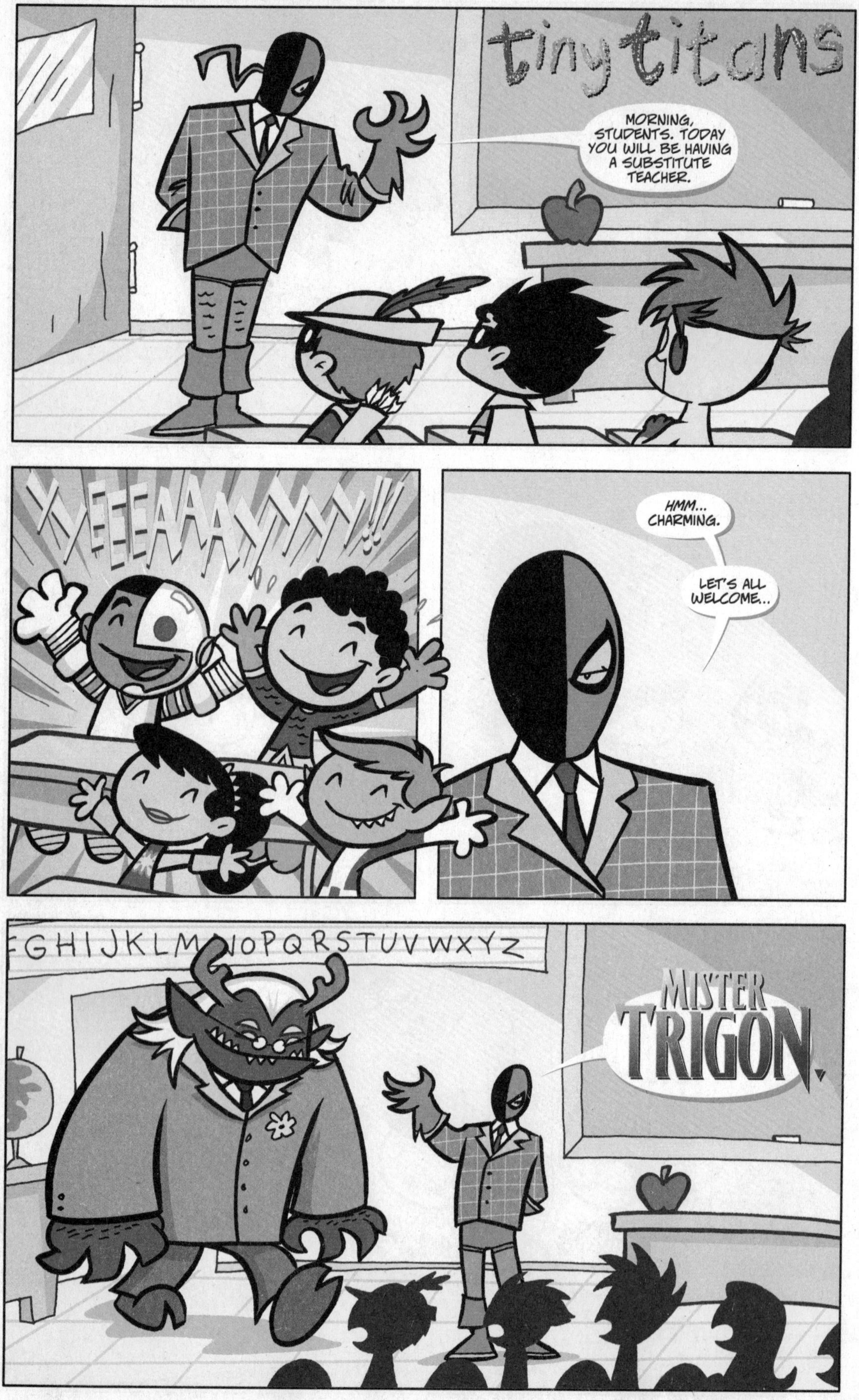
tiny titans
MORNING, STUDENTS. TODAY YOU WILL BE HAVING A SUBSTITUTE TEACHER.
YYEEEAAAYYYY!!!
HMM... CHARMING.
LET'S ALL WELCOME...
FGHIJKLMNOPQRSTUVWXYZ
MISTER TRIGON.

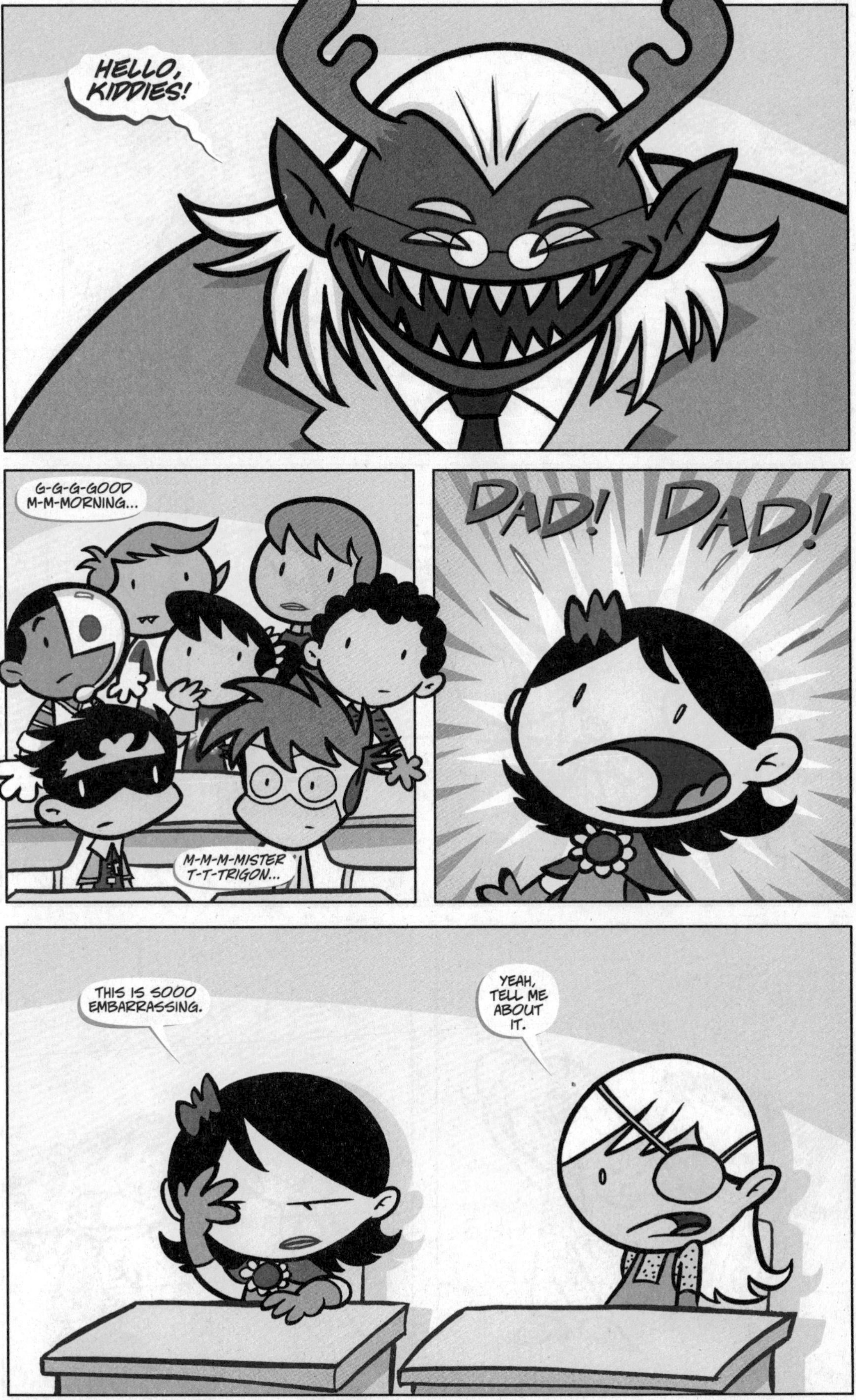
HELLO, KIDDIES!
G-G-G-GOOD M-M-MORNING...
M-M-M-MISTER T-T-TRIGON...
DAD! DAD!
THIS IS SOOO EMBARRASSING.
YEAH, TELL ME ABOUT IT.

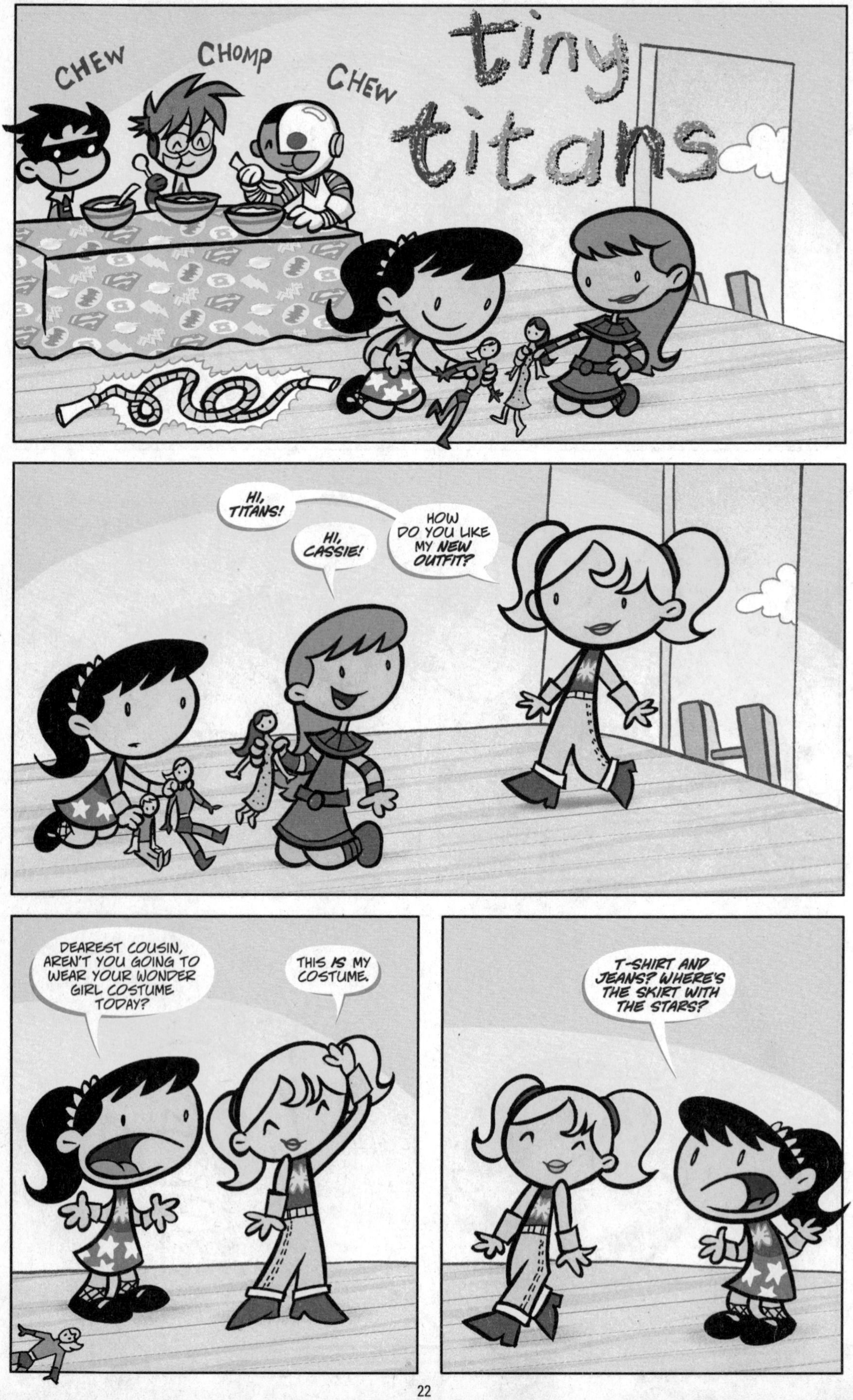
CHEW
CHOMP
CHEW
tiny titans
HI, TITANS!
HI, CASSIE!
HOW DO YOU LIKE MY NEW OUTFIT?
DEAREST COUSIN, AREN'T YOU GOING TO WEAR YOUR WONDER GIRL COSTUME TODAY?
THIS IS MY COSTUME.
T-SHIRT AND JEANS? WHERE'S THE SKIRT WITH THE STARS?

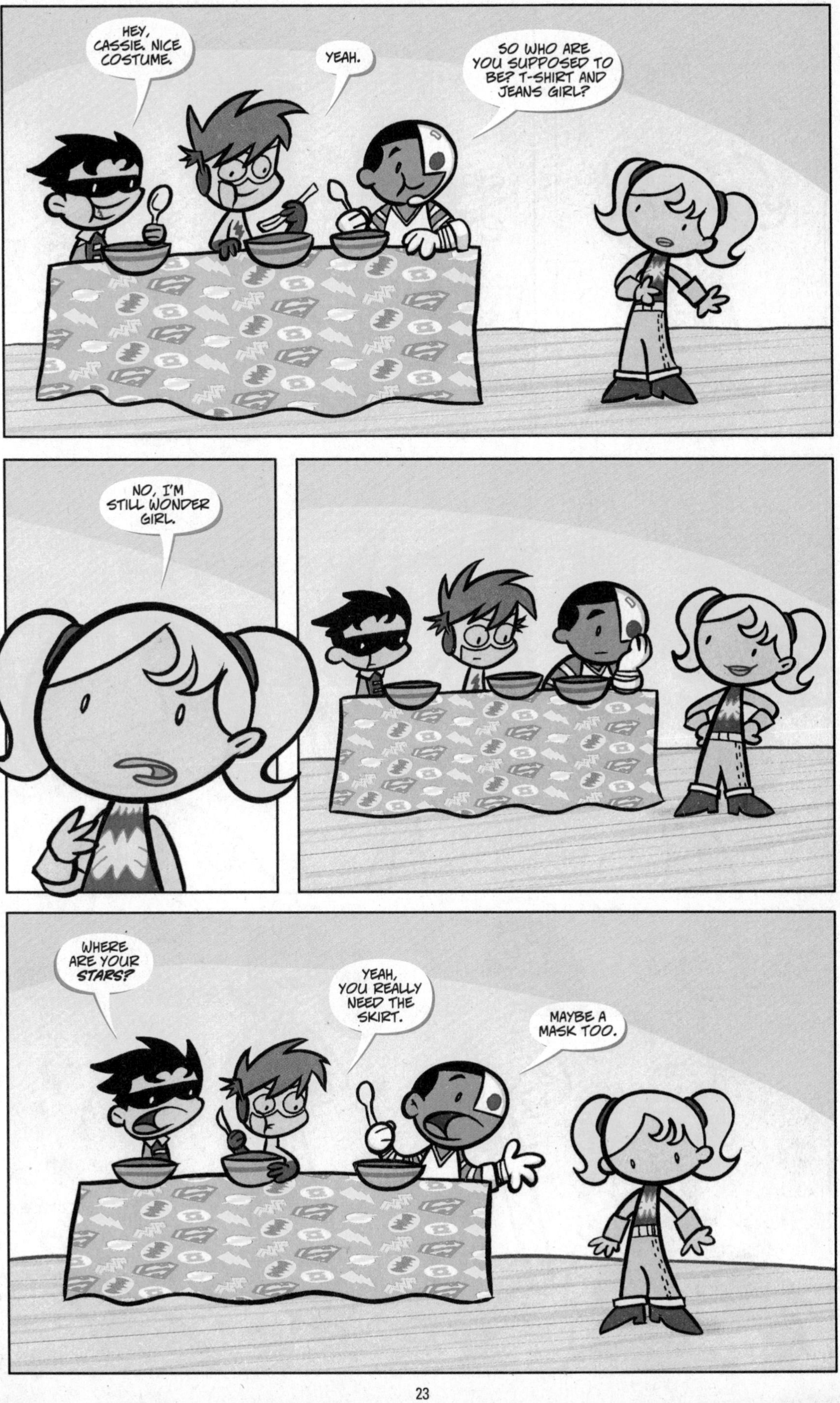
HEY, CASSIE. NICE COSTUME.
YEAH.
SO WHO ARE YOU SUPPOSED TO BE? T-SHIRT AND JEANS GIRL?
NO, I'M STILL WONDER GIRL.
WHERE ARE YOUR STARS?
YEAH, YOU REALLY NEED THE SKIRT.
MAYBE A MASK TOO.

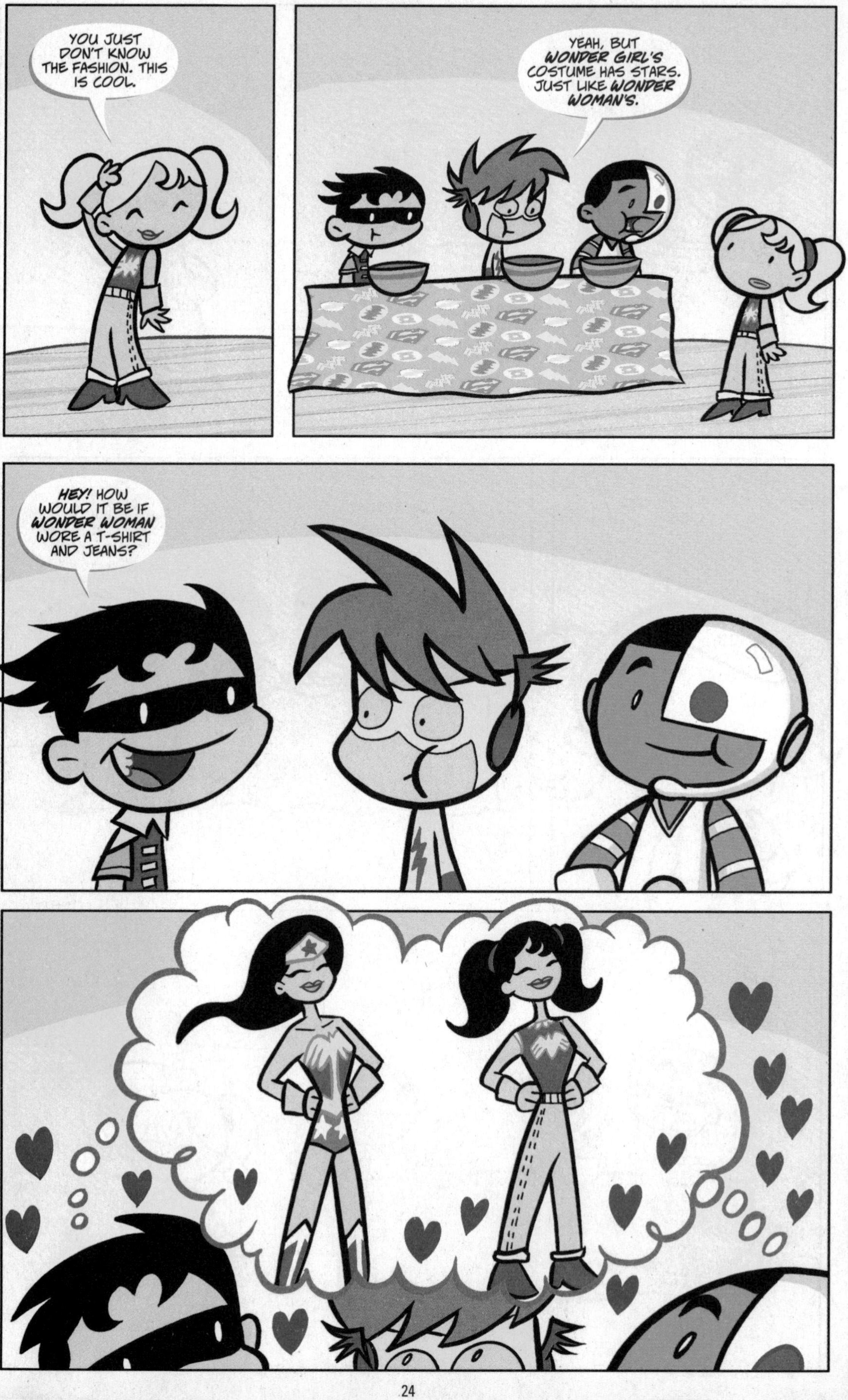
YOU JUST DON'T KNOW THE FASHION. THIS IS COOL.
YEAH, BUT WONDER GIRL'S COSTUME HAS STARS. JUST LIKE WONDER WOMAN'S.
HEY! HOW WOULD IT BE IF WONDER WOMAN WORE A T-SHIRT AND JEANS?

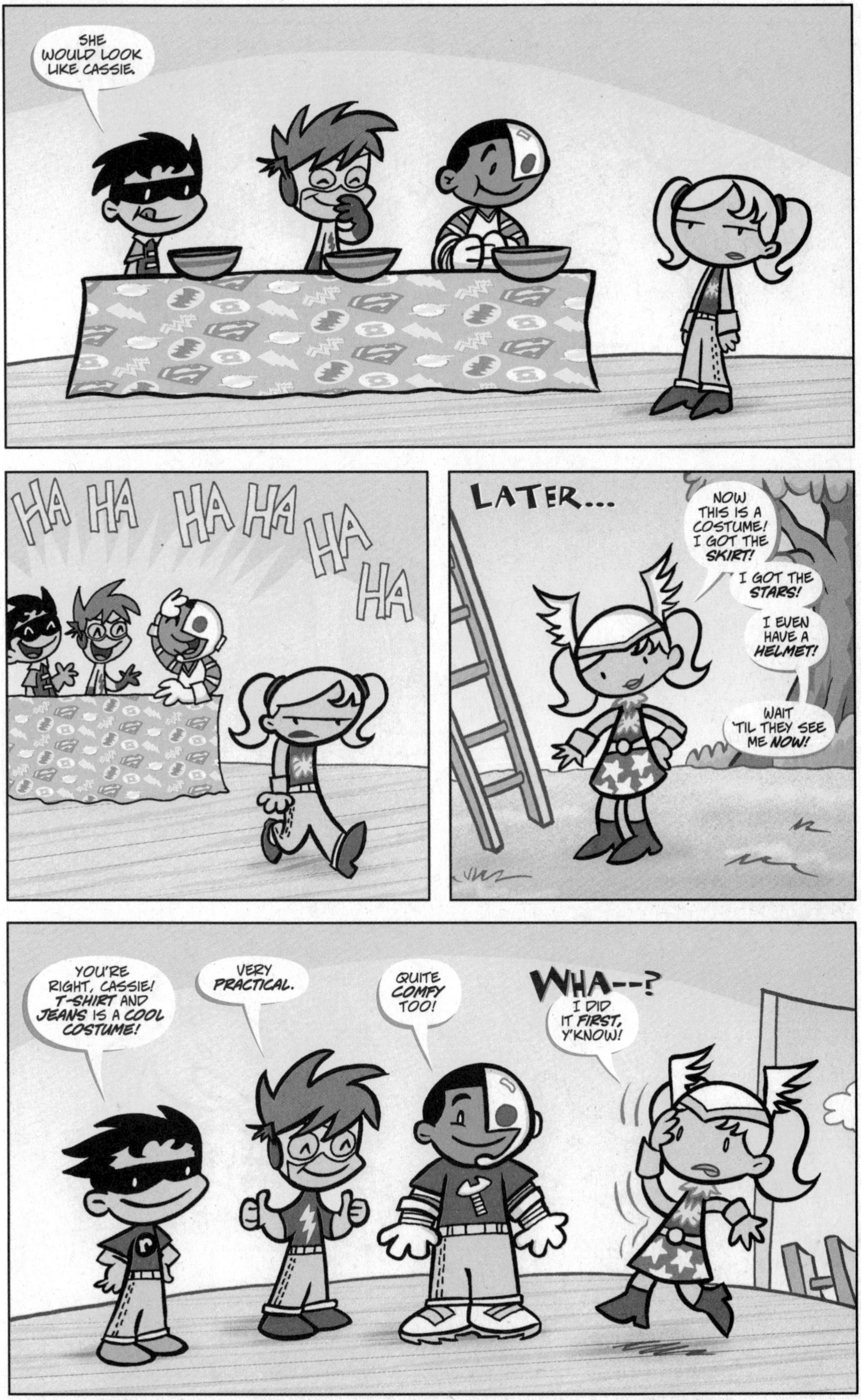
SHE WOULD LOOK LIKE CASSIE.
HA HA HA HA HA HA
LATER...
NOW THIS IS A COSTUME! I GOT THE SKIRT!
I GOT THE STARS!
I EVEN HAVE A HELMET!
WAIT 'TIL THEY SEE ME NOW!
YOU'RE RIGHT, CASSIE! T-SHIRT AND JEANS IS A COOL COSTUME!
VERY PRACTICAL.
QUITE COMFY TOO!
WHA--?
I DID IT FIRST, Y'KNOW!

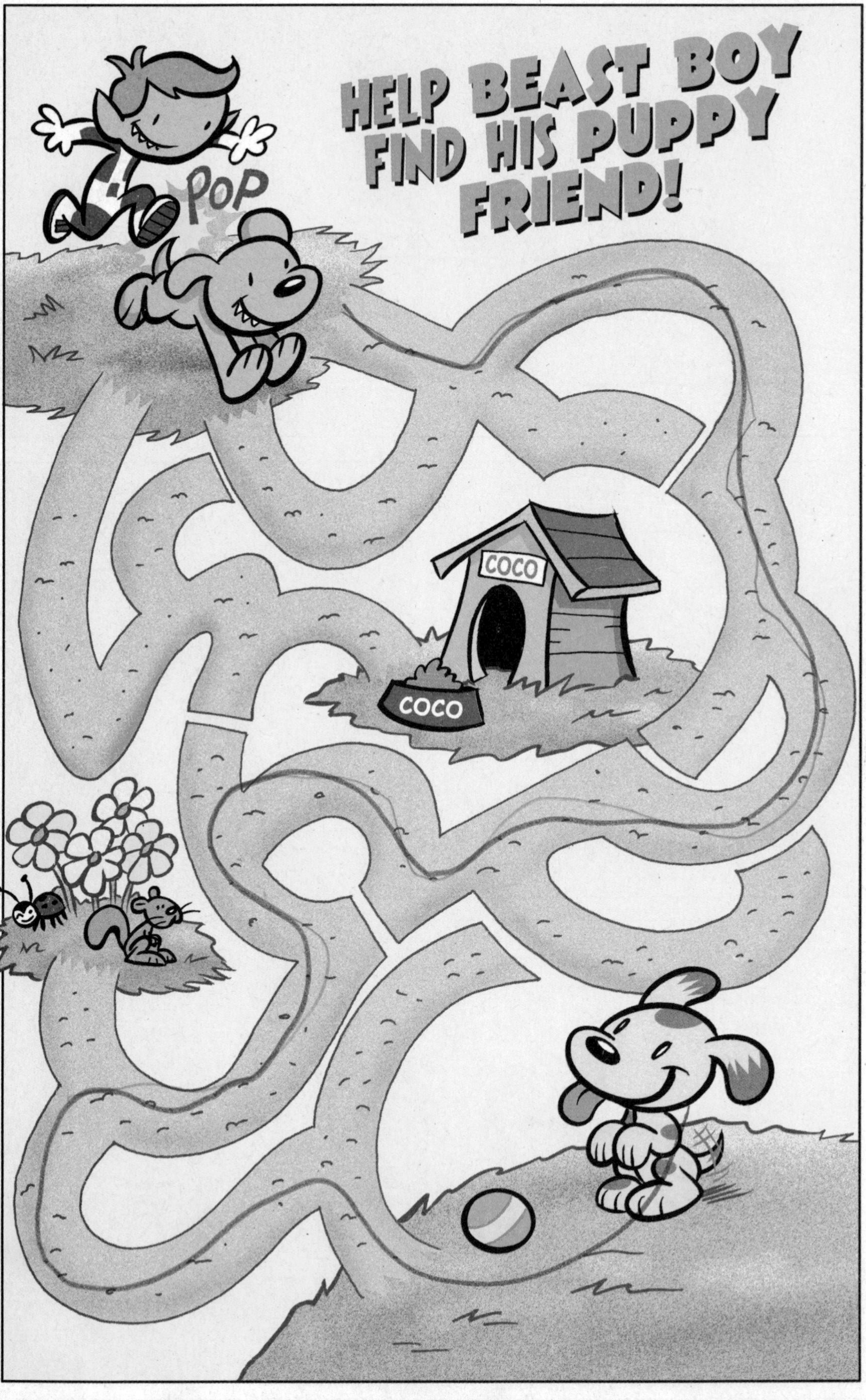
HELP BEAST BOY FIND HIS PUPPY FRIEND!
POP
COCO
COCO

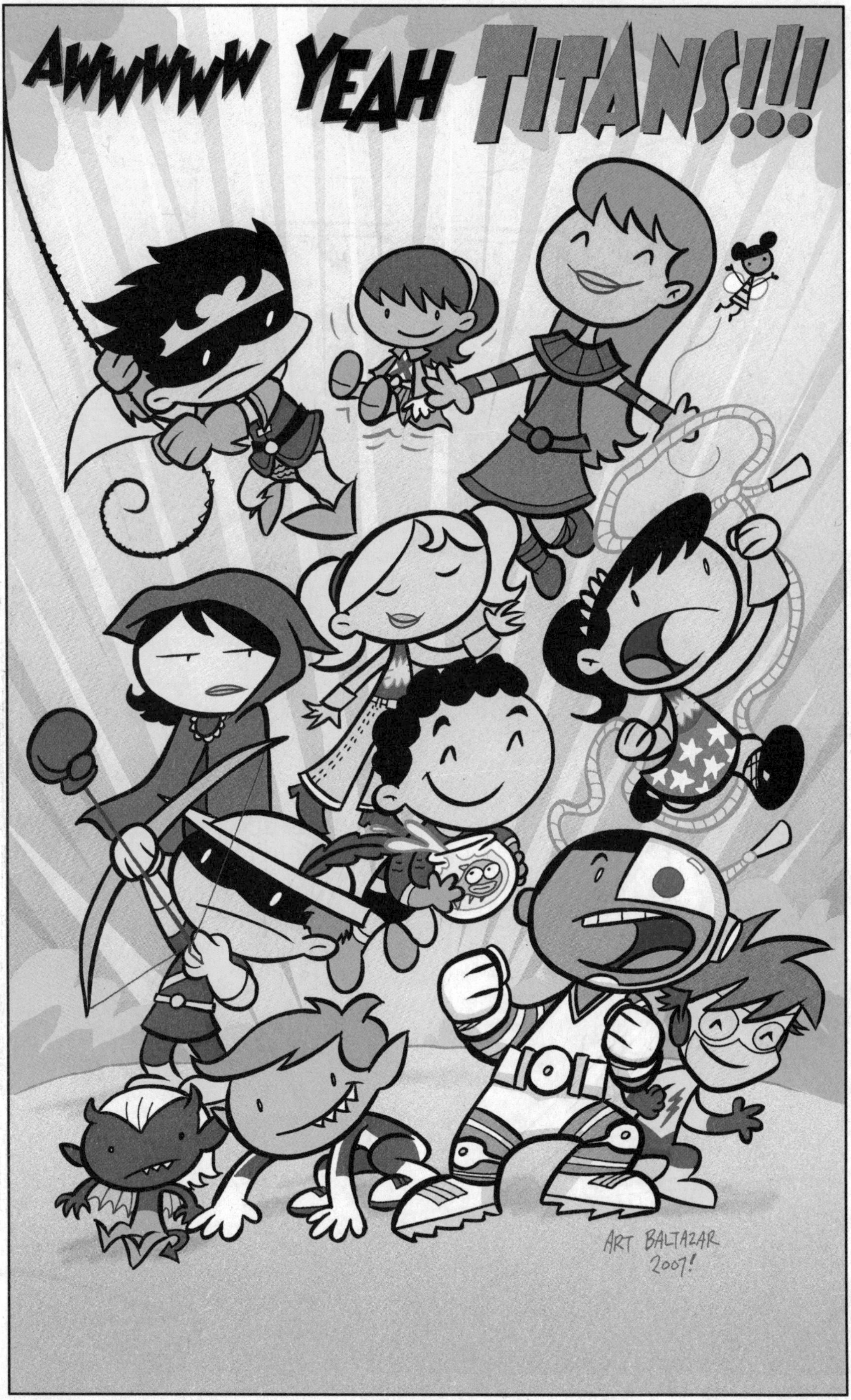
AWWWWW YEAH TITANS!!!
ART BALTAZAR 2007!

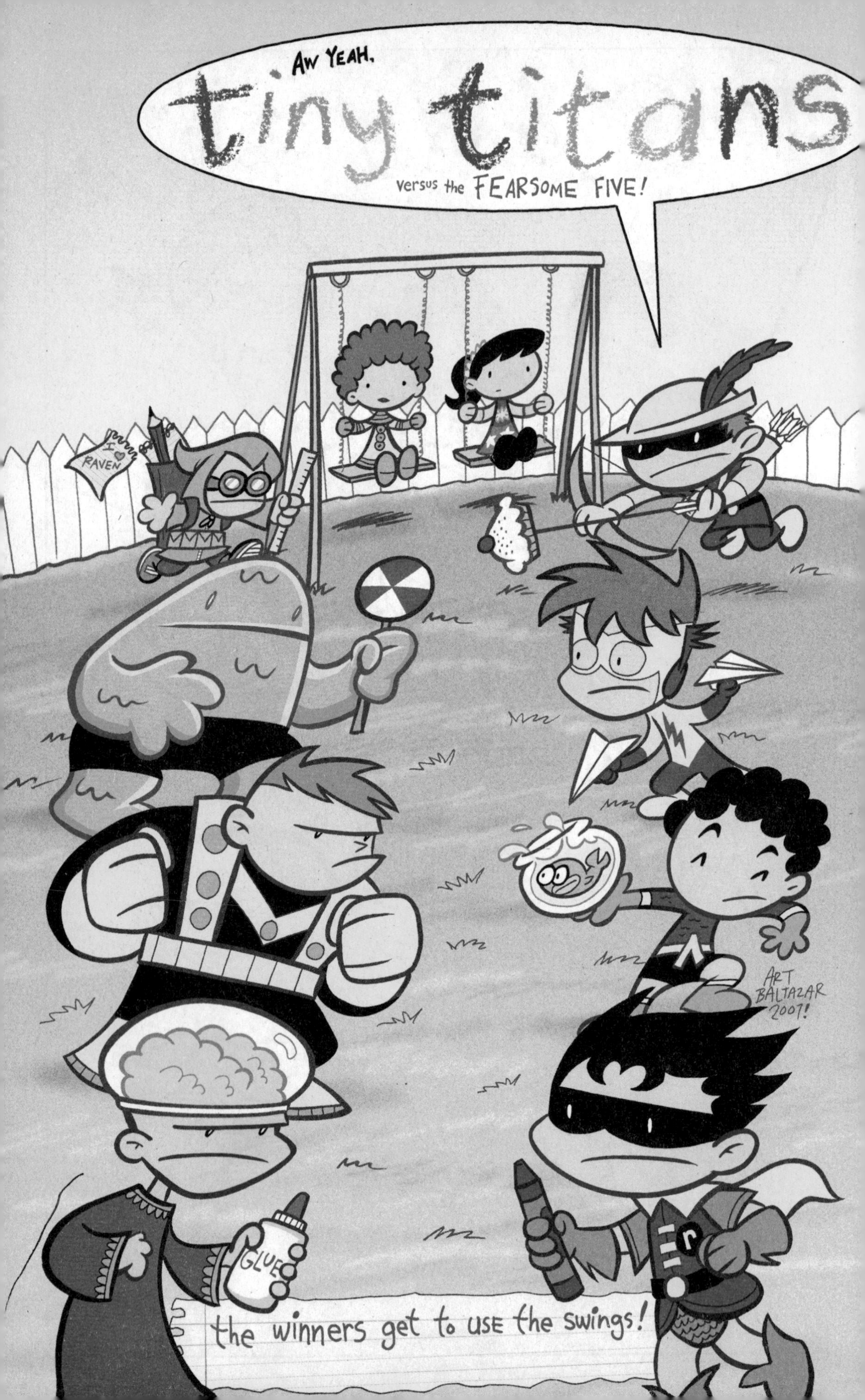
AW YEAH,
tiny titans
versus the FEARSOME FIVE!
I ♥ RAVEN
GLUE
ART BALTAZAR 2007!
the winners get to use the swings!

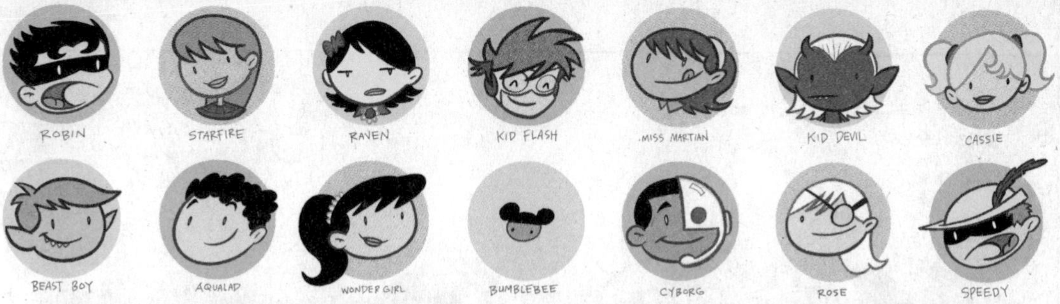
ROBIN
STARFIRE
RAVEN
KID FLASH
MISS MARTIAN
KID DEVIL
CASSIE
BEAST BOY
AQUALAD
WONDER GIRL
BUMBLEBEE
CYBORG
ROSE
SPEEDY

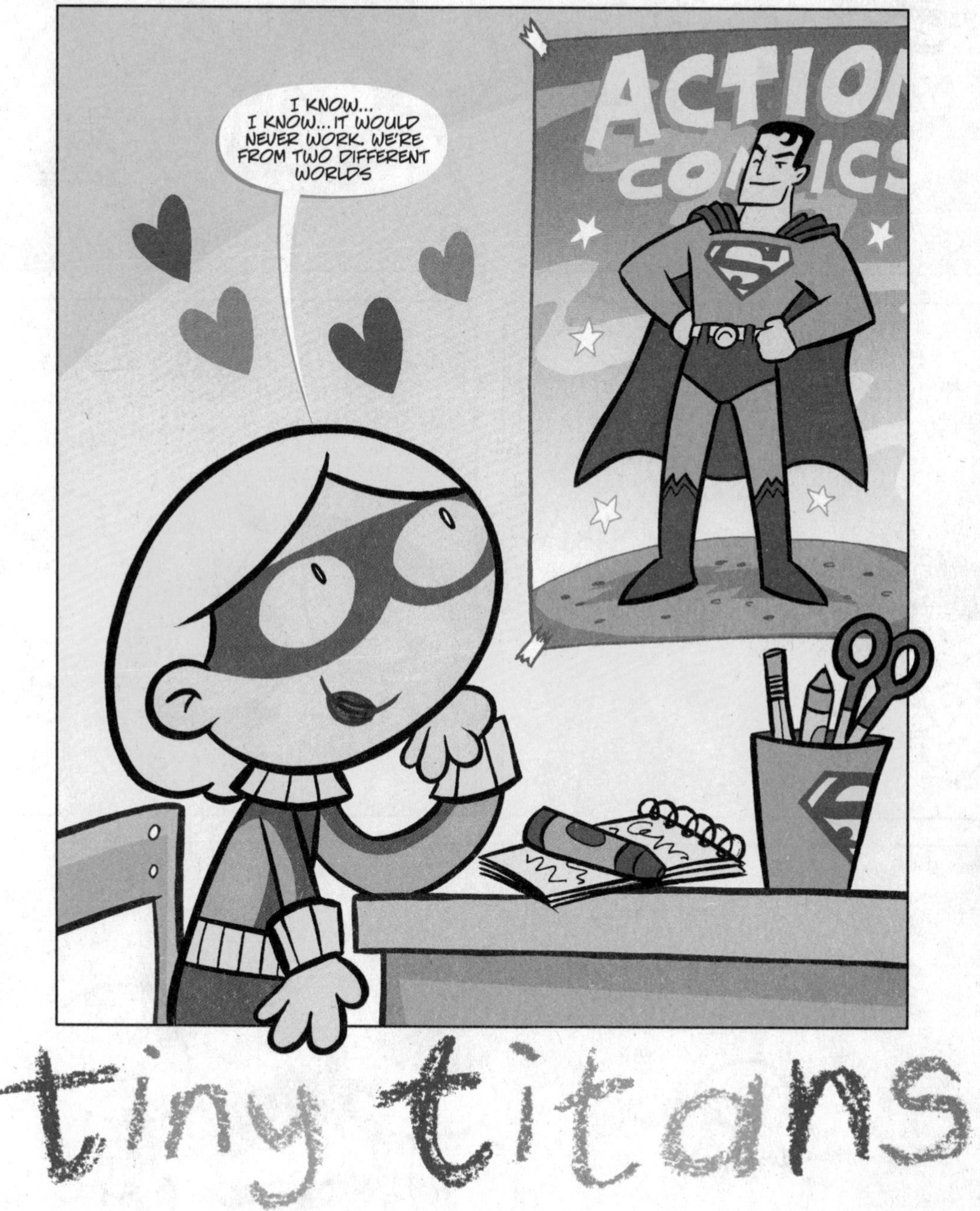
I KNOW... I KNOW... IT WOULD NEVER WORK. WE'RE FROM TWO DIFFERENT WORLDS

tiny titans

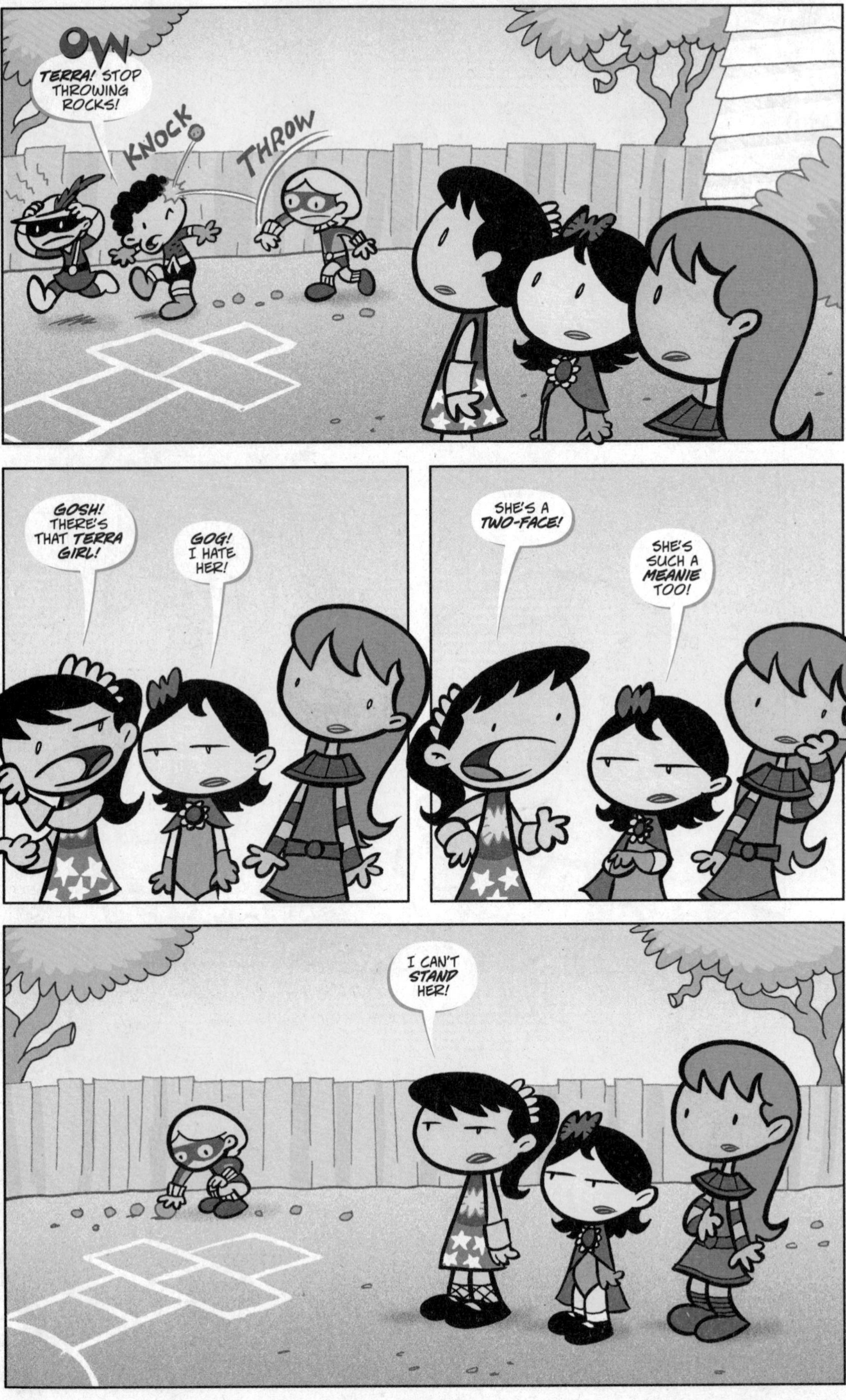
OW
TERRA! STOP THROWING ROCKS!
KNOCK
THROW
GOSH! THERE'S THAT TERRA GIRL!
GOG! I HATE HER!
SHE'S A TWO-FACE!
SHE'S SUCH A MEANIE TOO!
I CAN'T STAND HER!

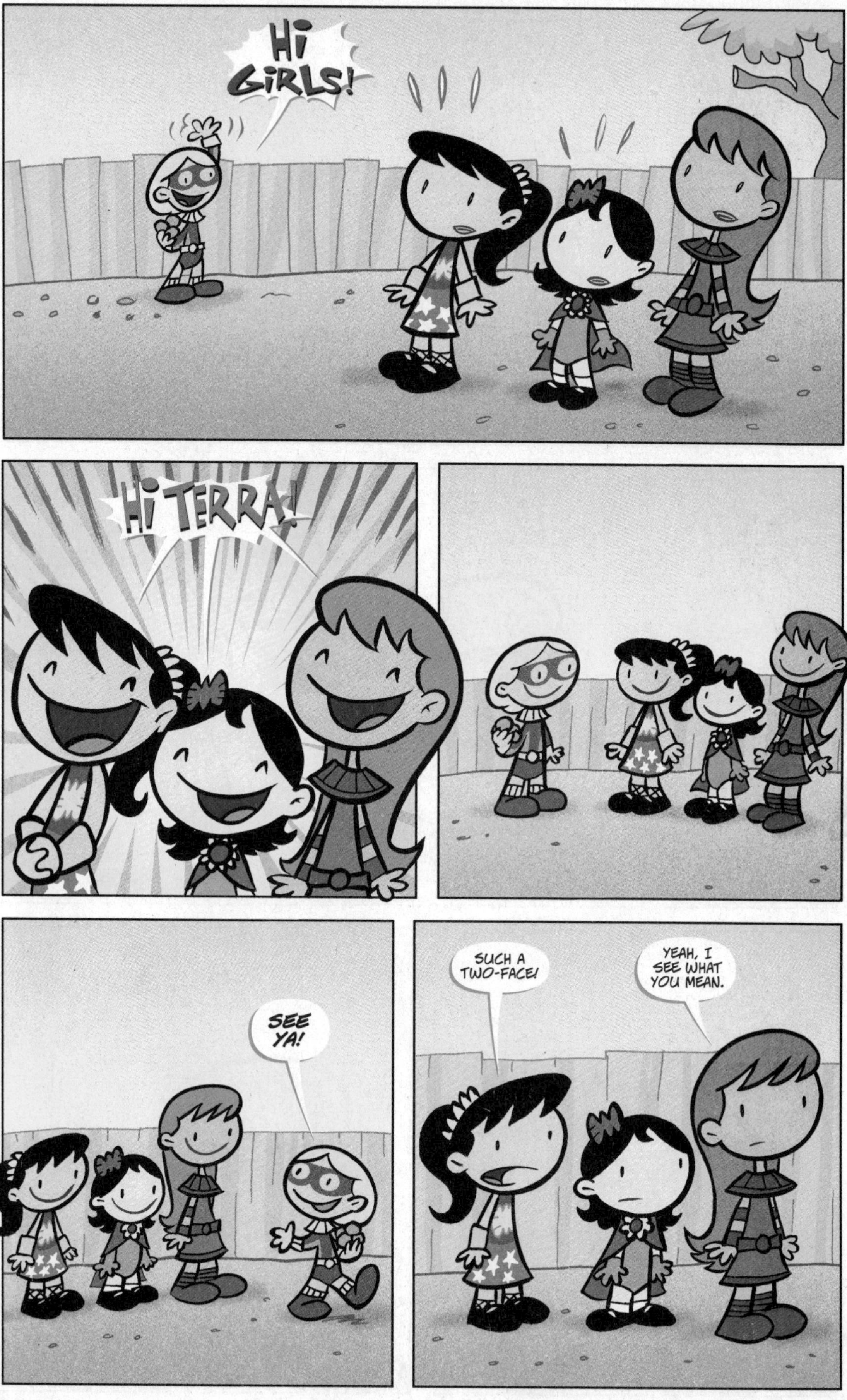
HI GIRLS!
HI TERRA!
SEE YA!
SUCH A TWO-FACE!
YEAH, I SEE WHAT YOU MEAN.

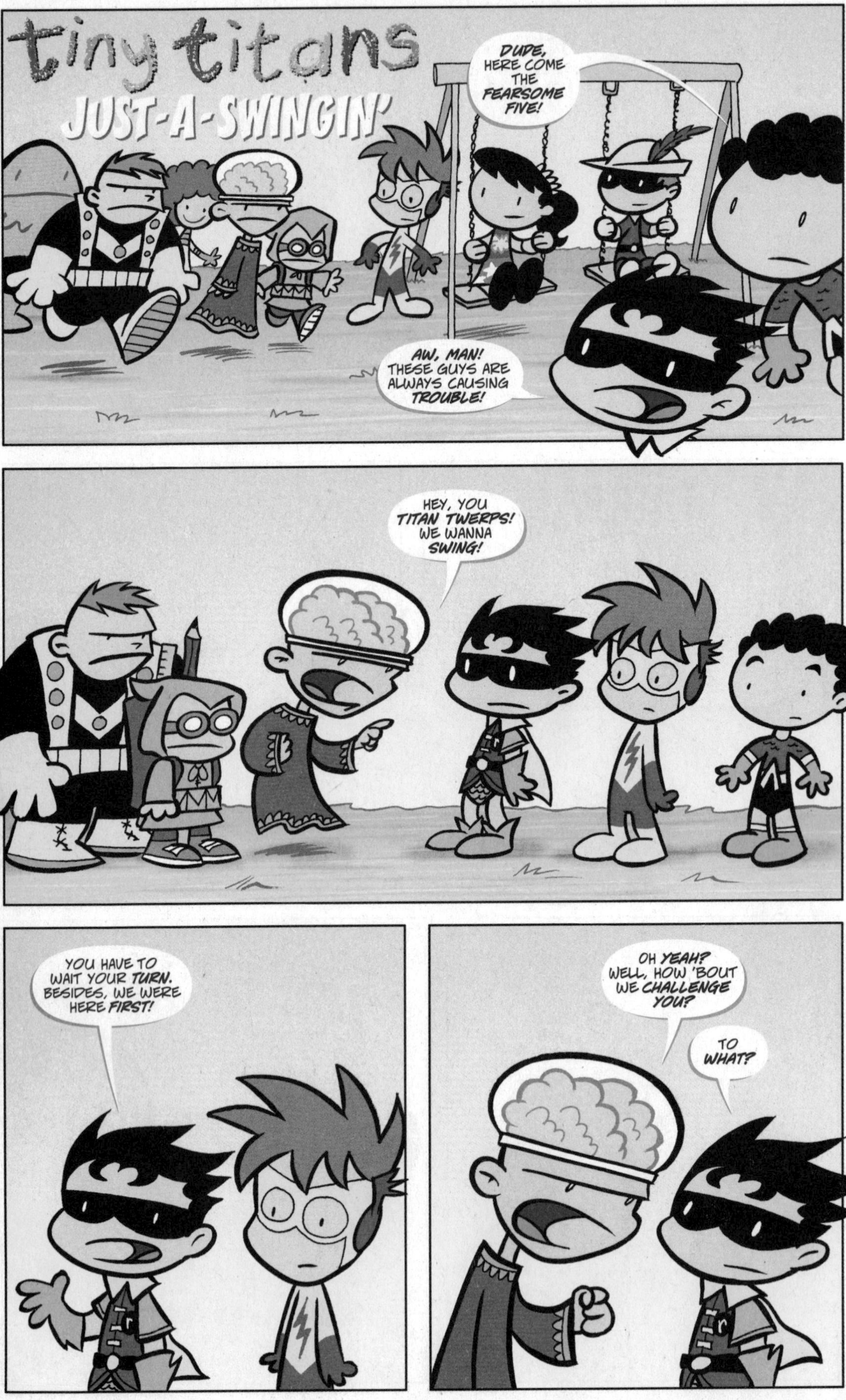
tiny titans
JUST-A-SWINGIN'
DUDE, HERE COME THE FEARSOME FIVE!
AW, MAN! THESE GUYS ARE ALWAYS CAUSING TROUBLE!
HEY, YOU TITAN TWERPS! WE WANNA SWING!
YOU HAVE TO WAIT YOUR TURN. BESIDES, WE WERE HERE FIRST!
OH YEAH? WELL, HOW 'BOUT WE CHALLENGE YOU?
TO WHAT?

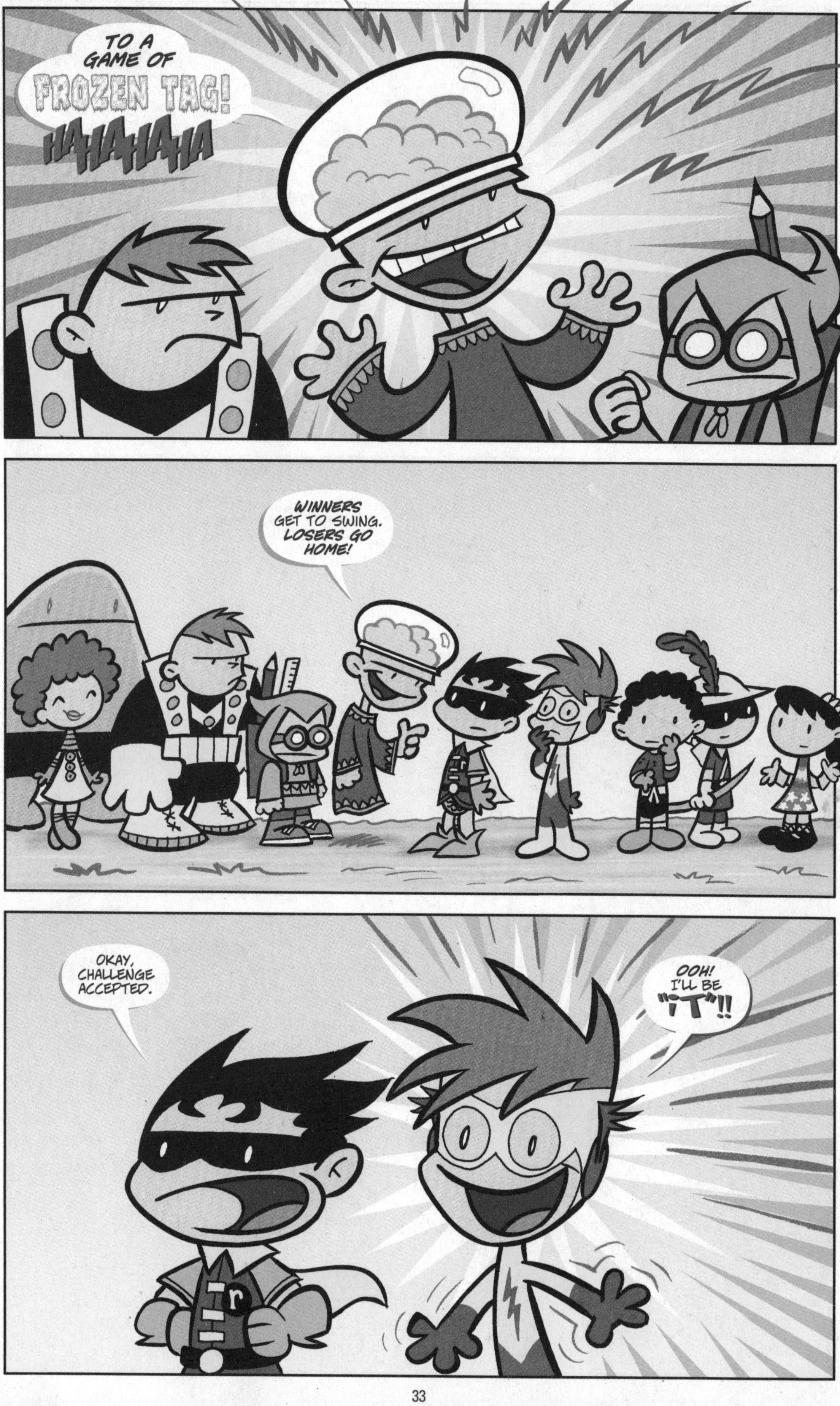
TO A GAME OF FROZEN TAG!
HAHAHAHA
WINNERS GET TO SWING. LOSERS GO HOME!
OKAY, CHALLENGE ACCEPTED.
OOH! I'LL BE "IT"!!

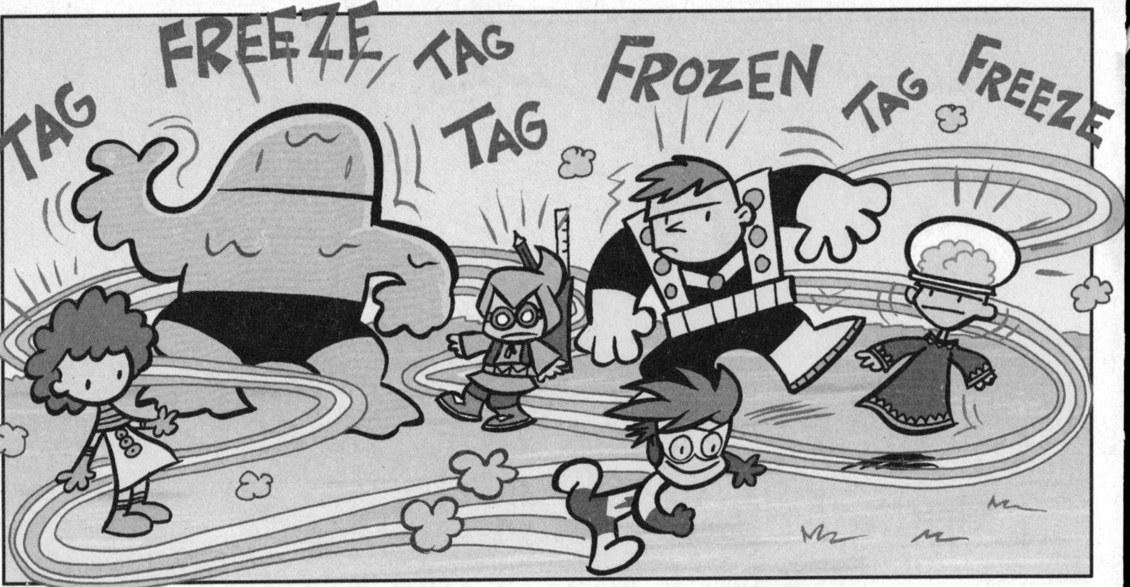
TAG
FREEZE
TAG
TAG
FROZEN
TAG
FREEZE

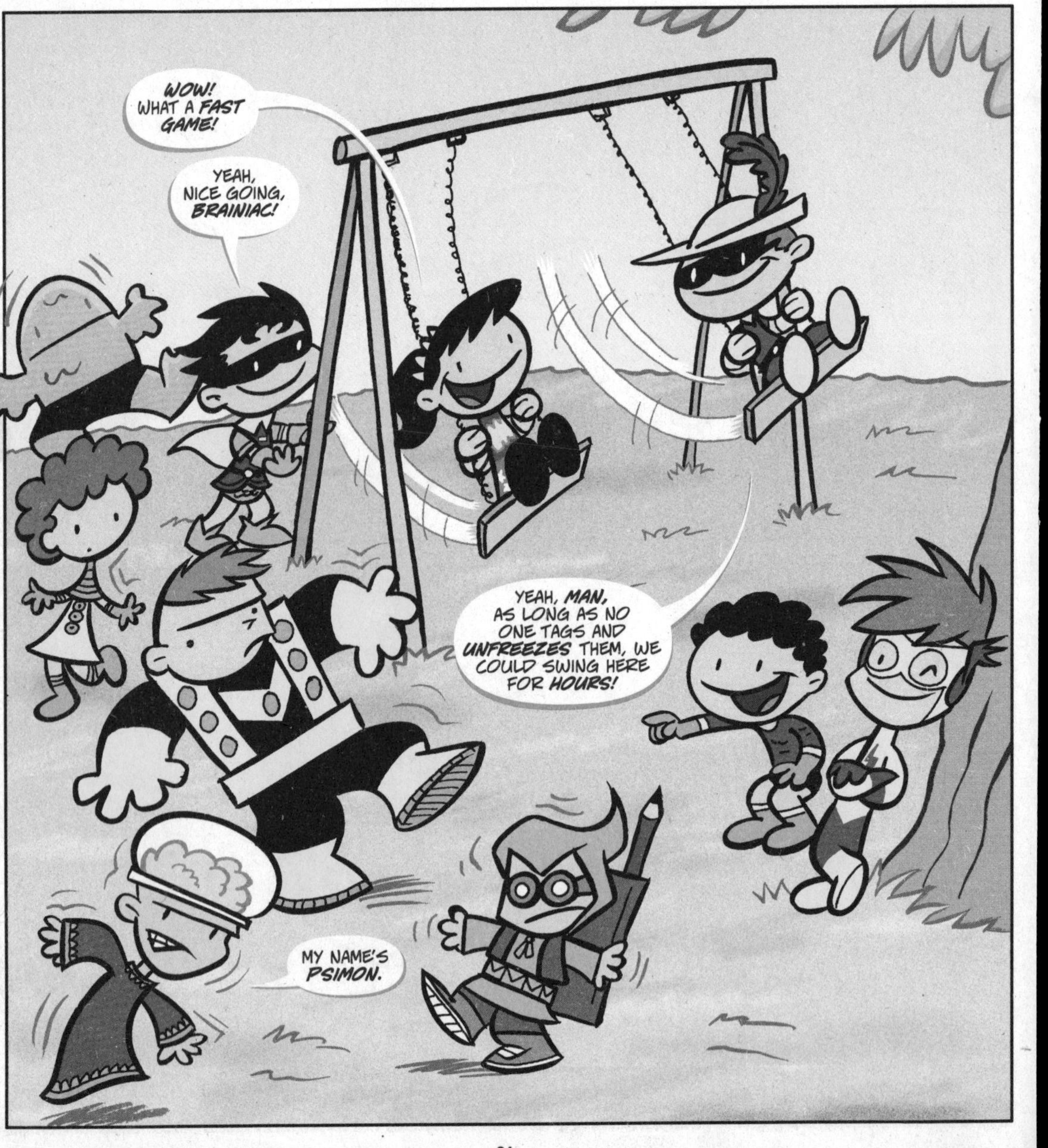
WOW! WHAT A FAST GAME!
YEAH, NICE GOING, BRAINIAC!
YEAH, MAN, AS LONG AS NO ONE TAGS AND UNFREEZES THEM, WE COULD SWING HERE FOR HOURS!
MY NAME'S PSIMON.

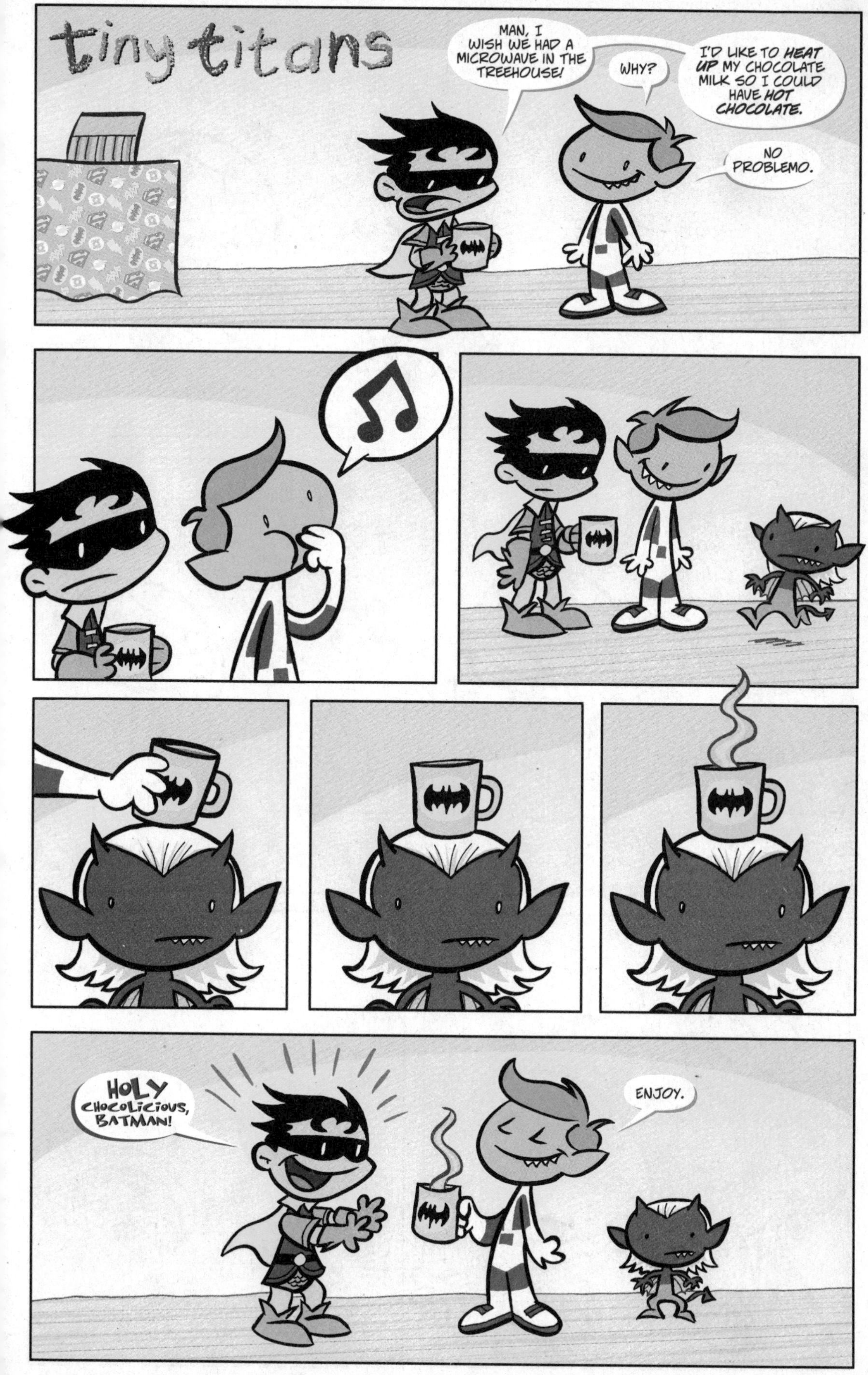
tiny titans
MAN, I WISH WE HAD A MICROWAVE IN THE TREEHOUSE!
WHY?
I'D LIKE TO HEAT UP MY CHOCOLATE MILK SO I COULD HAVE HOT CHOCOLATE.
NO PROBLEMO.
HOLY CHOCOLICIOUS, BATMAN!
ENJOY.

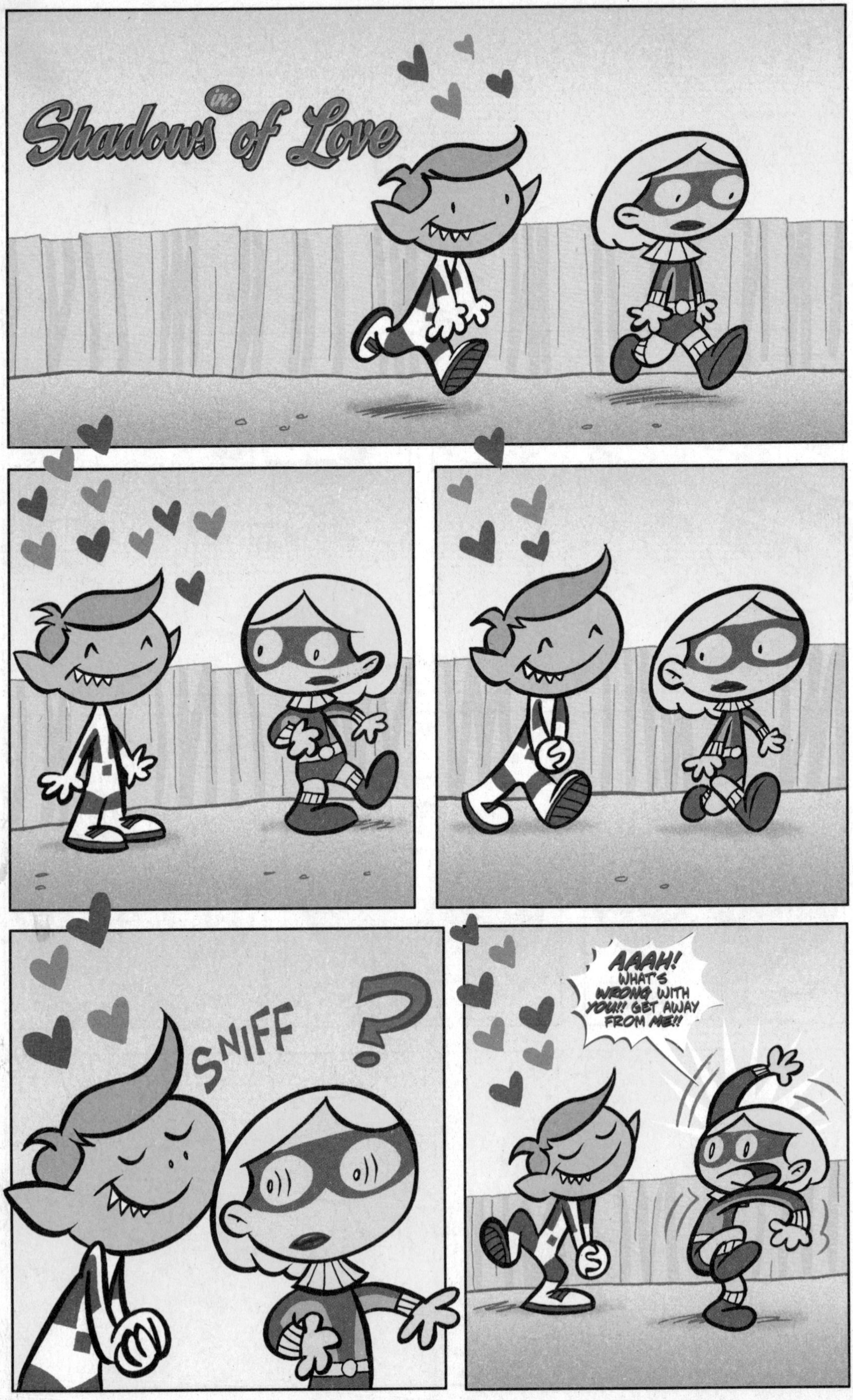
in:
Shadows of Love
SNIFF
AAAH! WHAT'S WRONG WITH YOU!! GET AWAY FROM ME!!

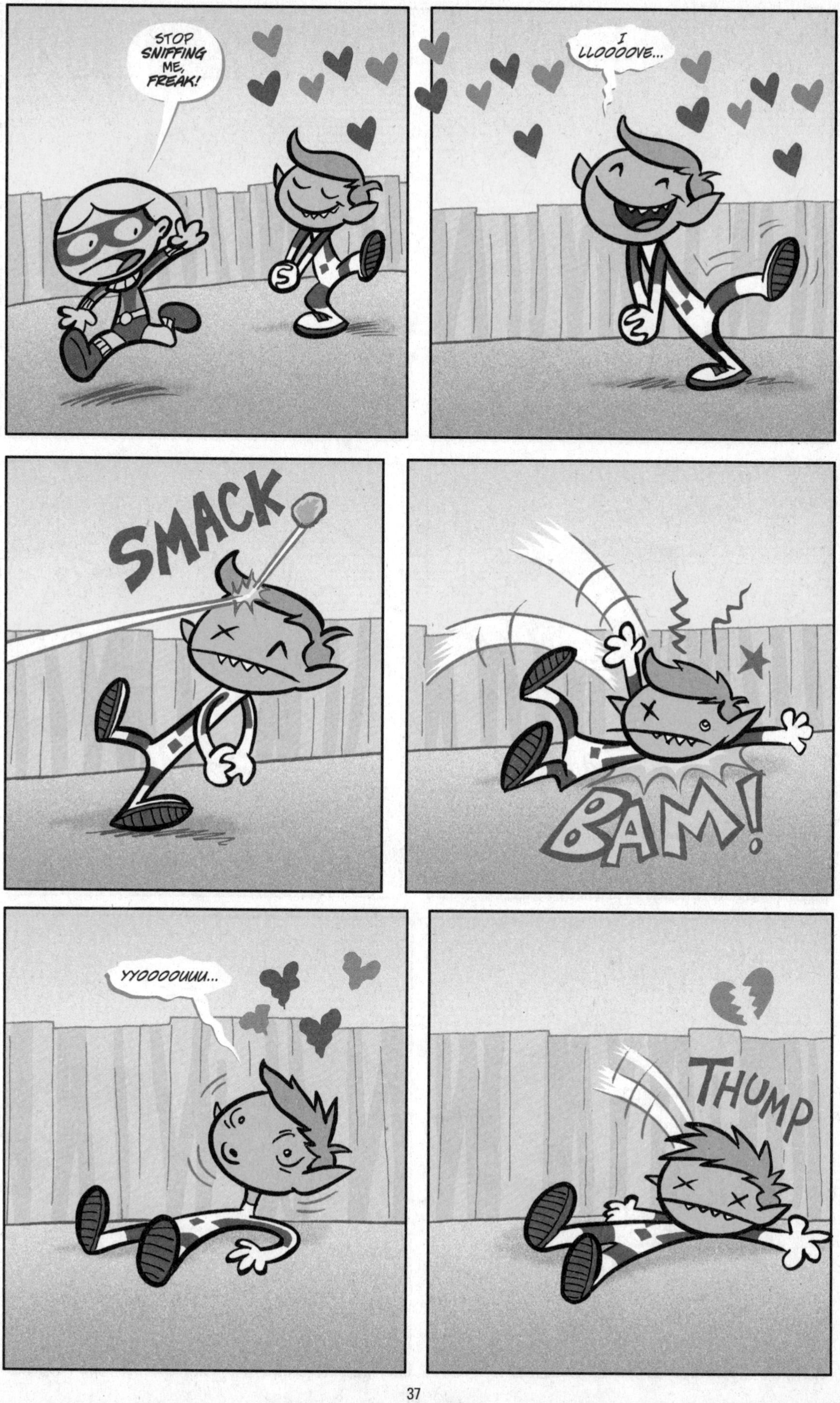
STOP SNIFFING ME, FREAK!
I LLOOOOVE...
SMACK
BAM!
YYOOOOUUU...
THUMP

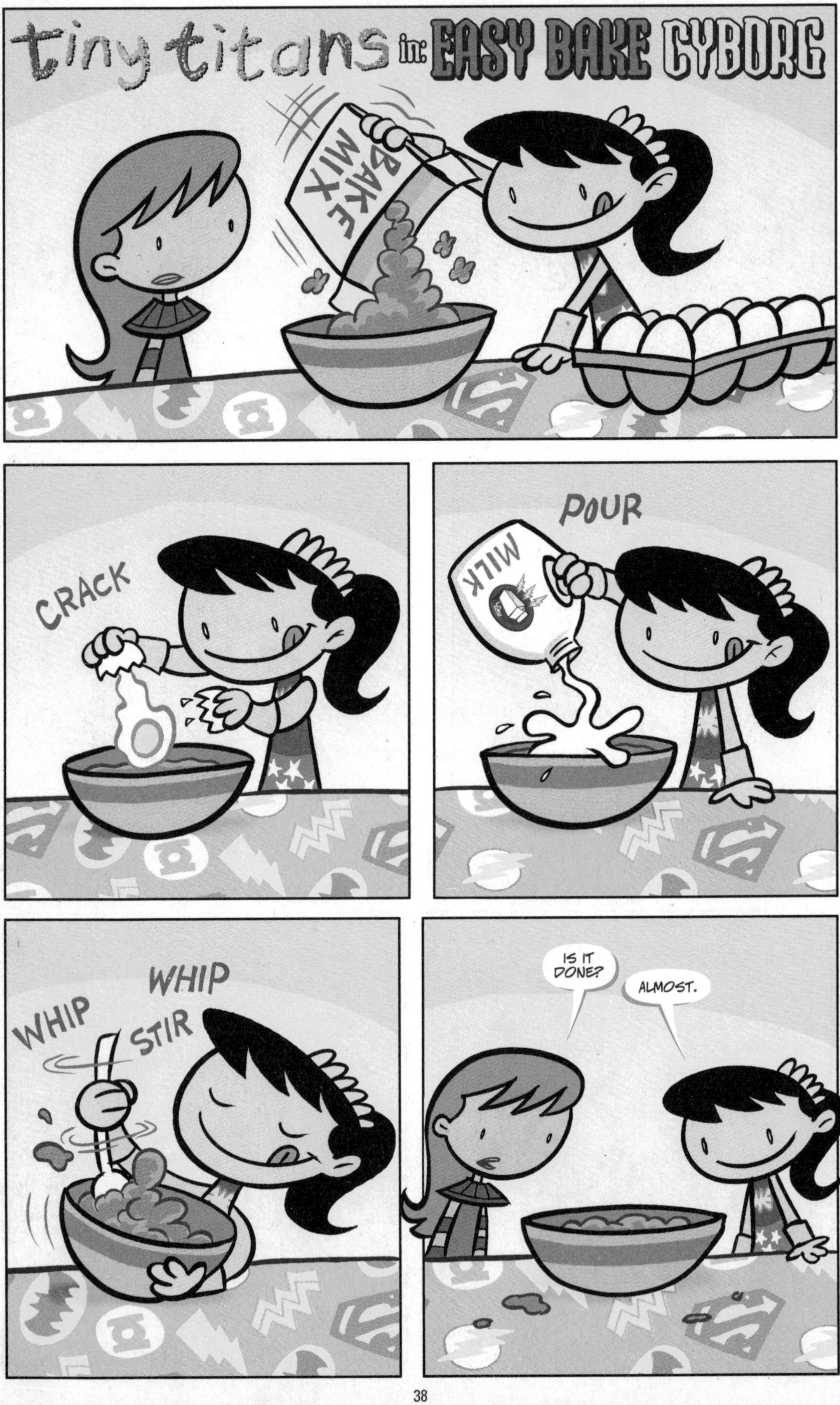
tiny titans in: EASY BAKE CYBORG
BAKE MIX
CRACK
POUR
MILK
WHIP
WHIP
STIR
IS IT DONE?
ALMOST.

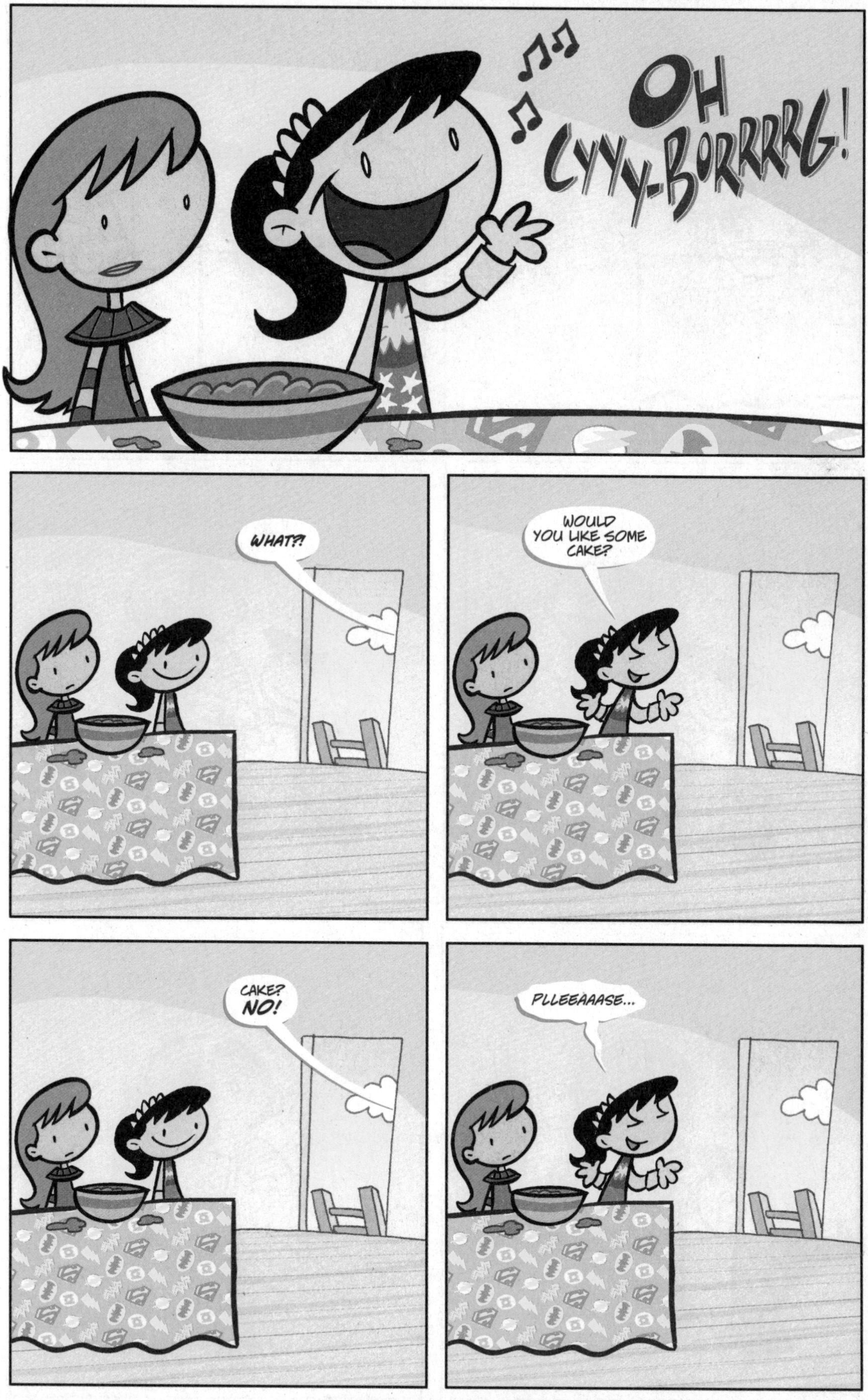
OH CYYY-BORRRRG!
WHAT?!
WOULD YOU LIKE SOME CAKE?
CAKE? NO!
PLLEEAAAASE...

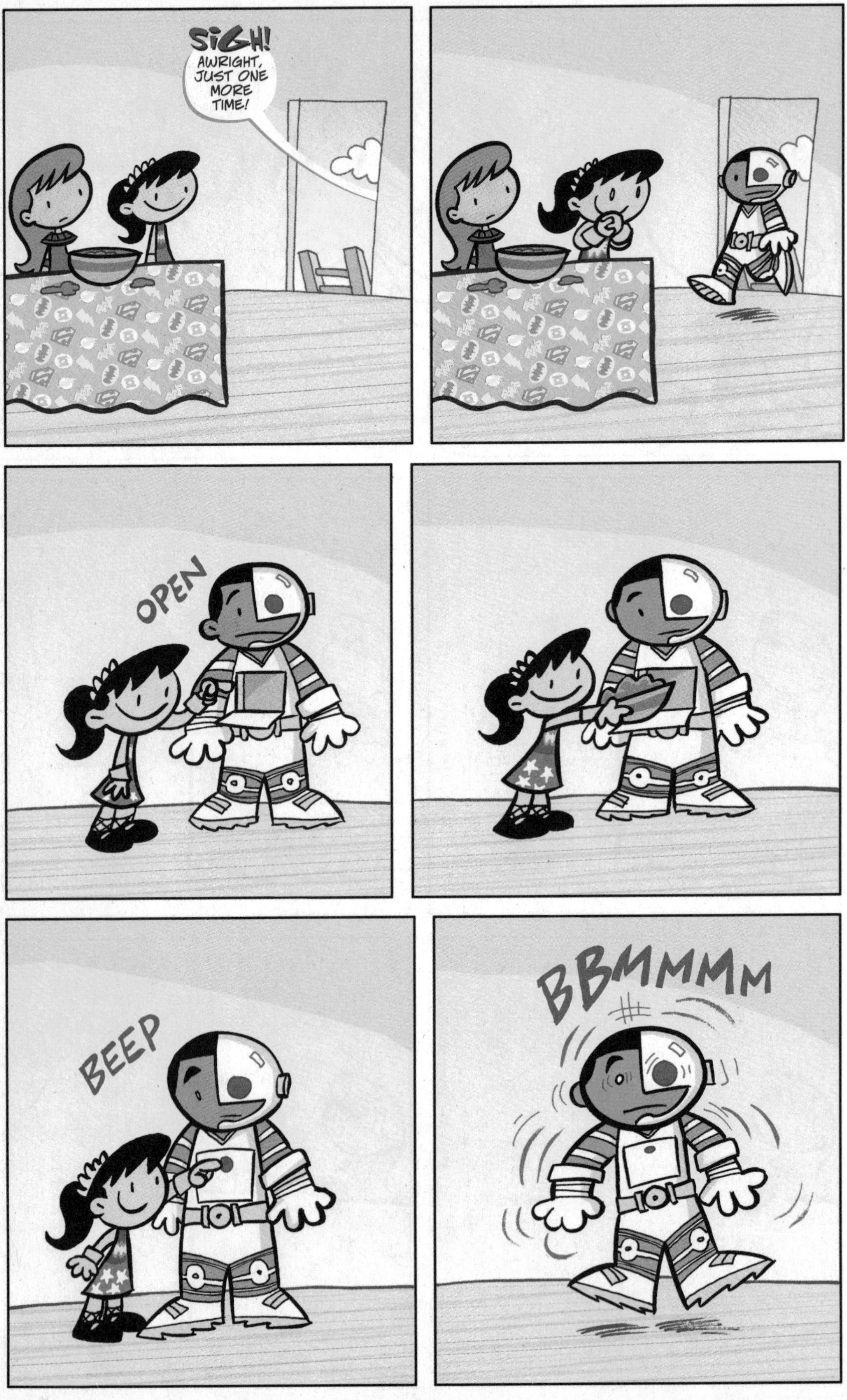
SIGH!
AWRIGHT, JUST ONE MORE TIME!
OPEN
BEEP
BBMMMM

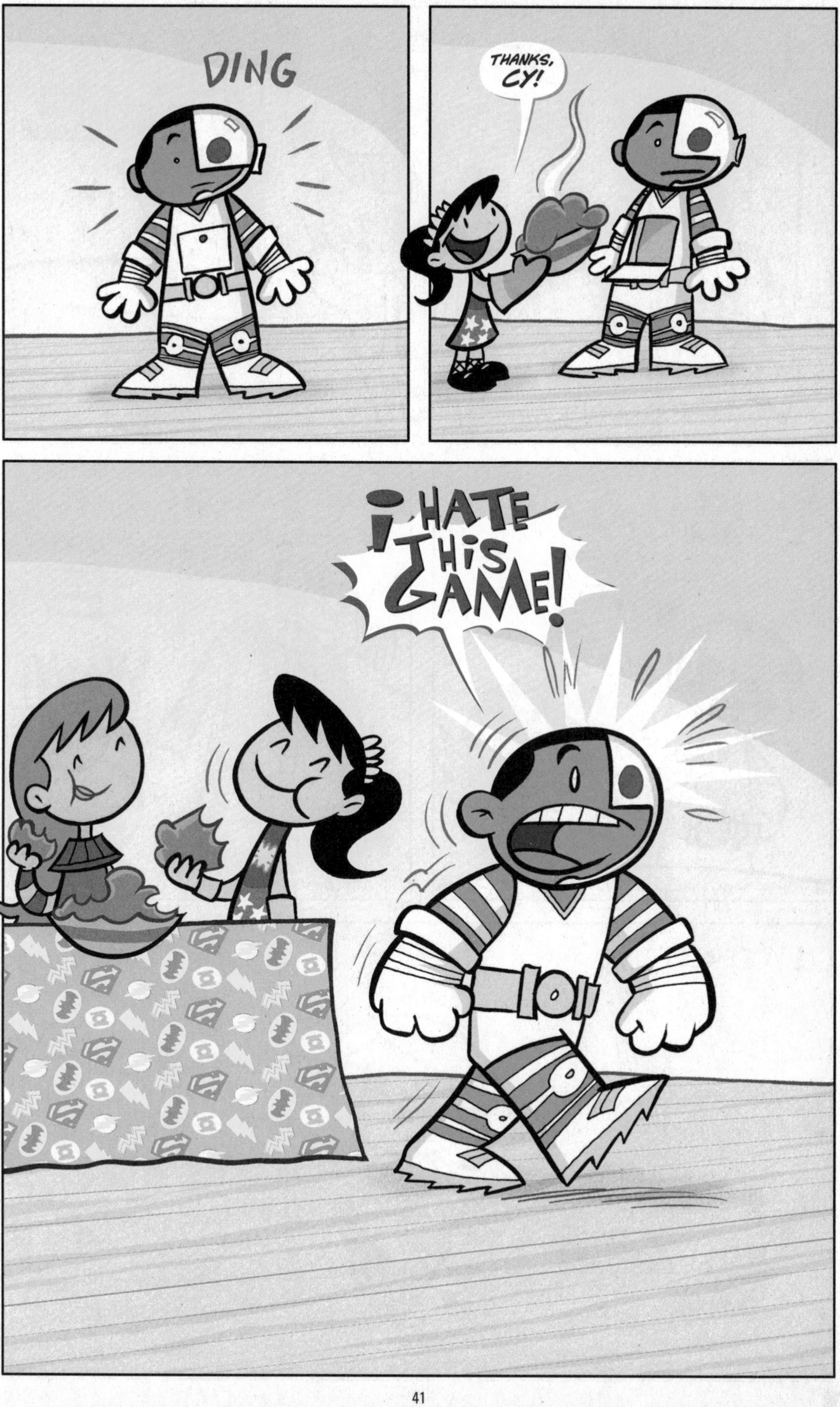
DING
THANKS, CY!
I HATE THIS GAME!

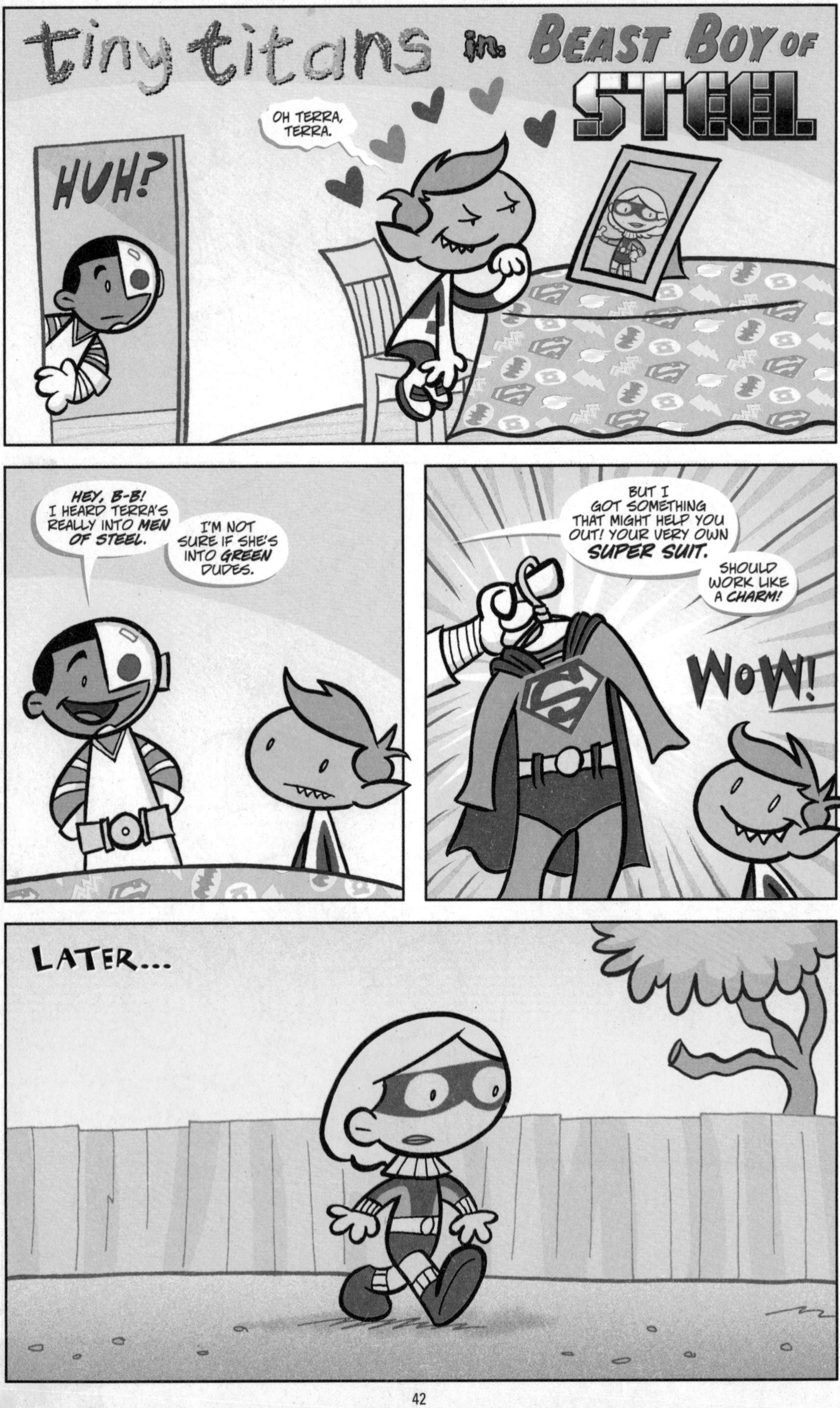
tiny titans in: BEAST BOY OF STEEL
OH TERRA, TERRA.
HUH?
HEY, B-B! I HEARD TERRA'S REALLY INTO MEN OF STEEL.
I'M NOT SURE IF SHE'S INTO GREEN DUDES.
BUT I GOT SOMETHING THAT MIGHT HELP YOU OUT! YOUR VERY OWN SUPER SUIT.
SHOULD WORK LIKE A CHARM!
WOW!
LATER...

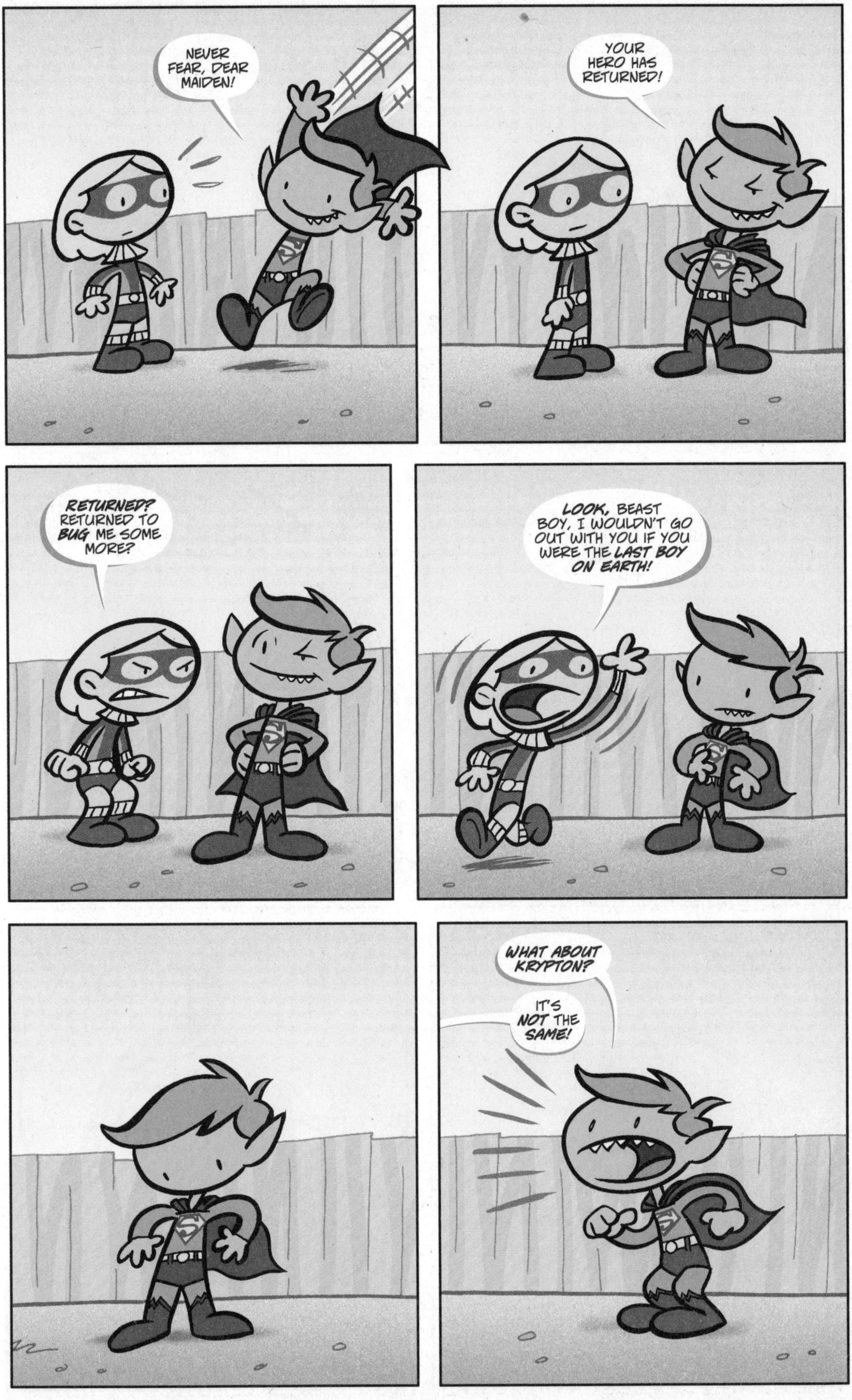
NEVER FEAR, DEAR MAIDEN!
YOUR HERO HAS RETURNED!
RETURNED? RETURNED TO BUG ME SOME MORE?
LOOK, BEAST BOY, I WOULDN'T GO OUT WITH YOU IF YOU WERE THE LAST BOY ON EARTH!
WHAT ABOUT KRYPTON?
IT'S NOT THE SAME!

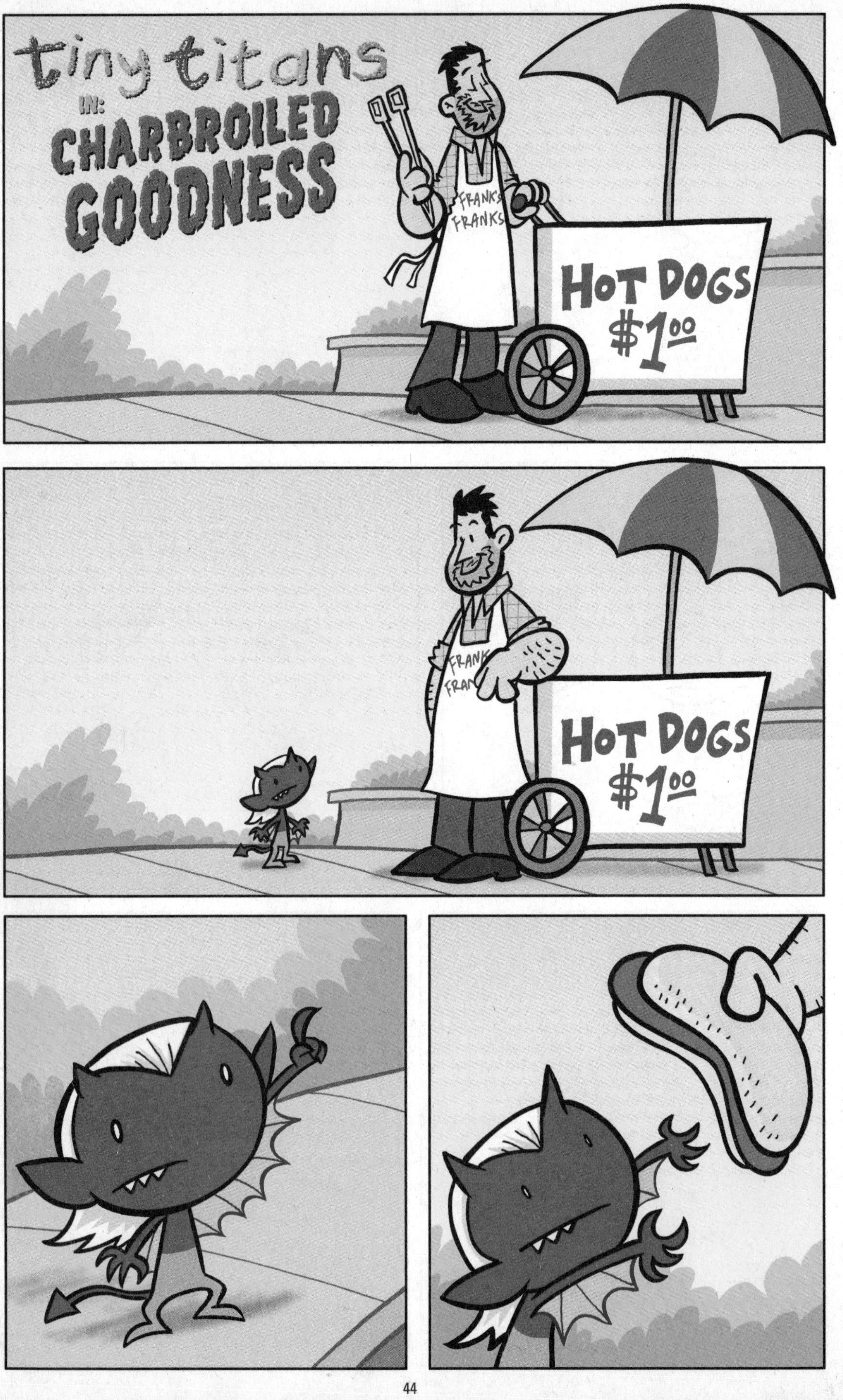
tiny titans
IN: CHARBROILED GOODNESS
FRANK'S FRANKS
HOT DOGS $1.00
HOT DOGS $1.00

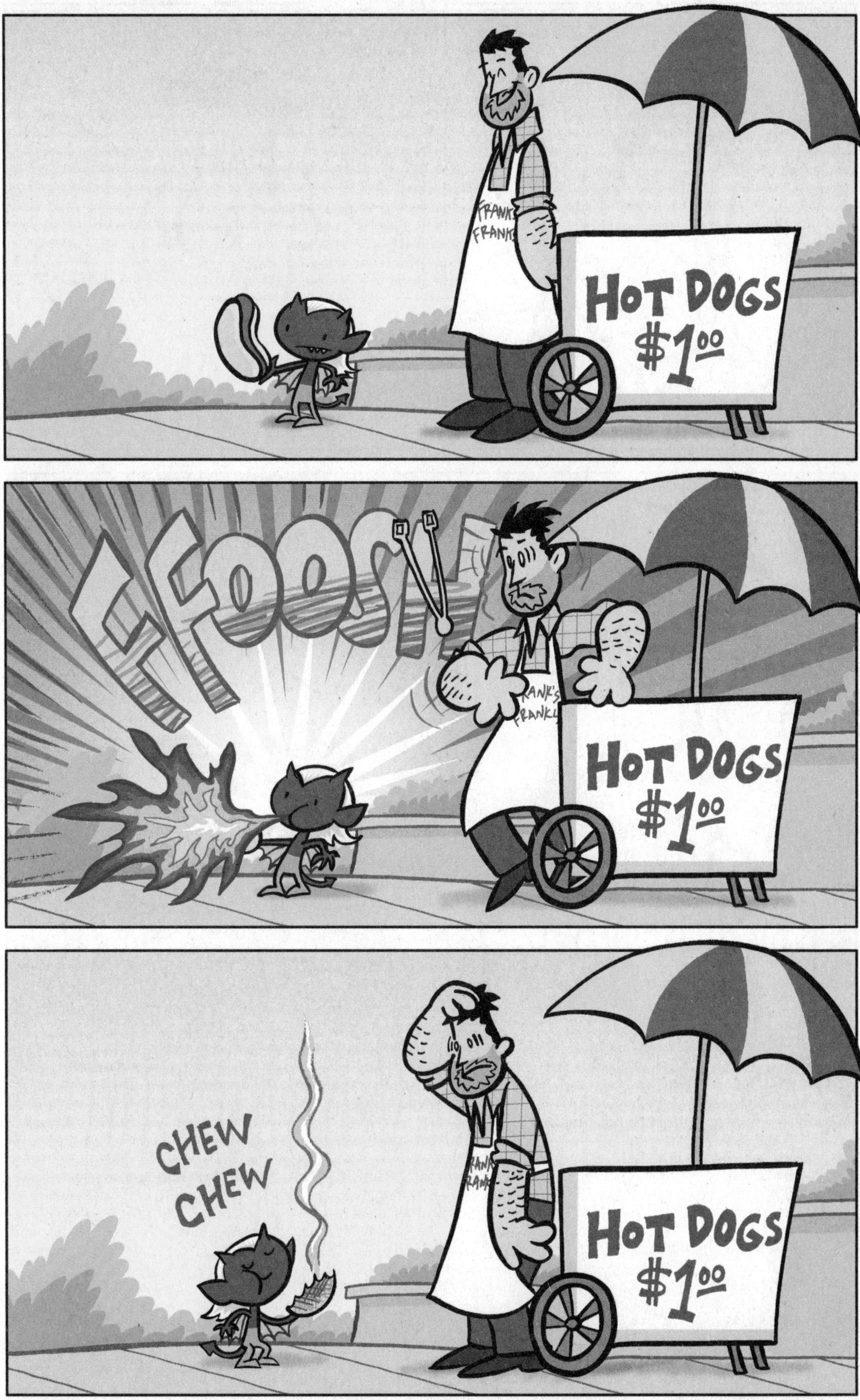
FRANK'S FRANKS
HOT DOGS $1.00
HOT DOGS $1.00
HOT DOGS $1.00
CHEW CHEW

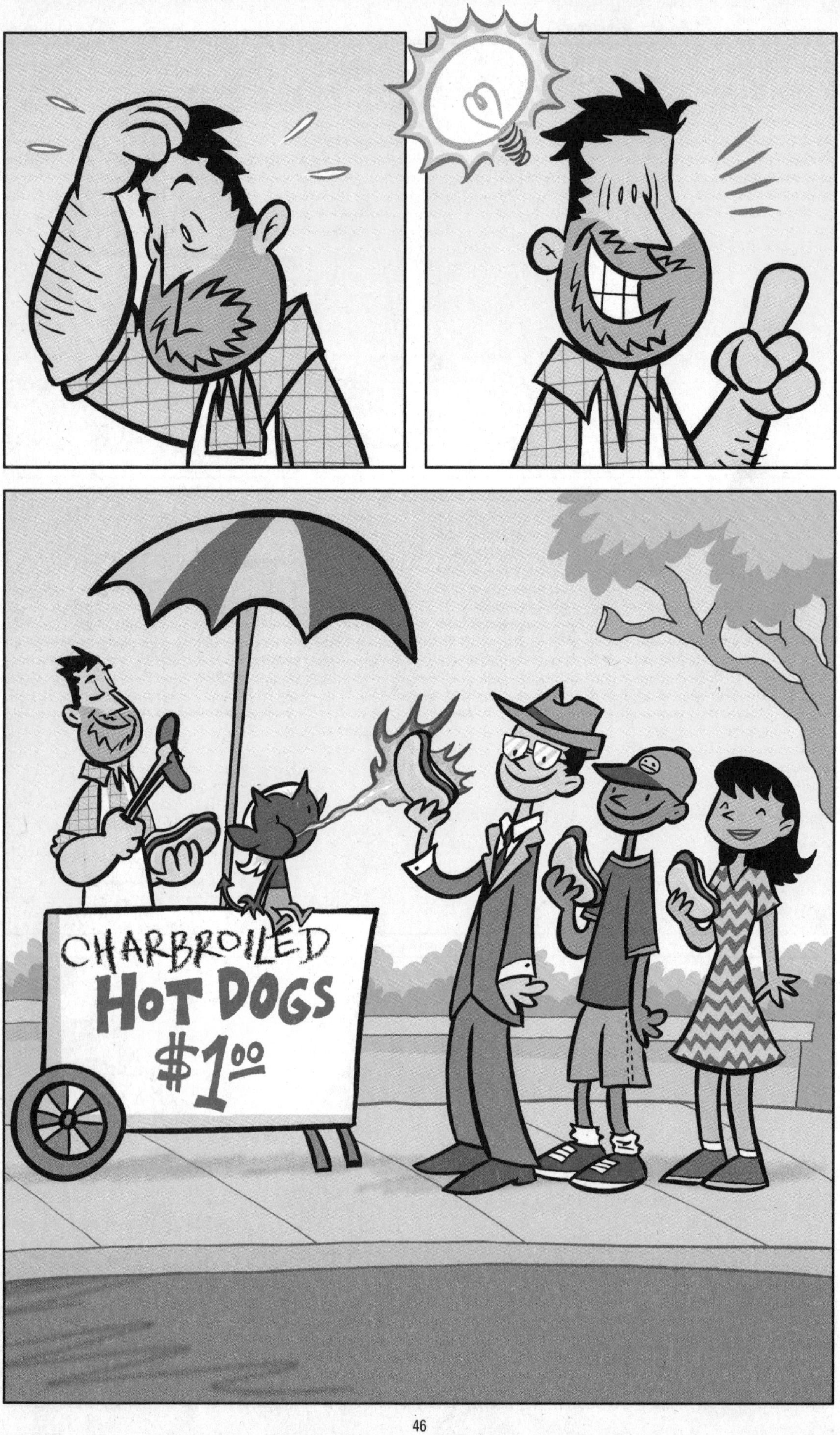
CHARBROILED
HOT DOGS
$1.00

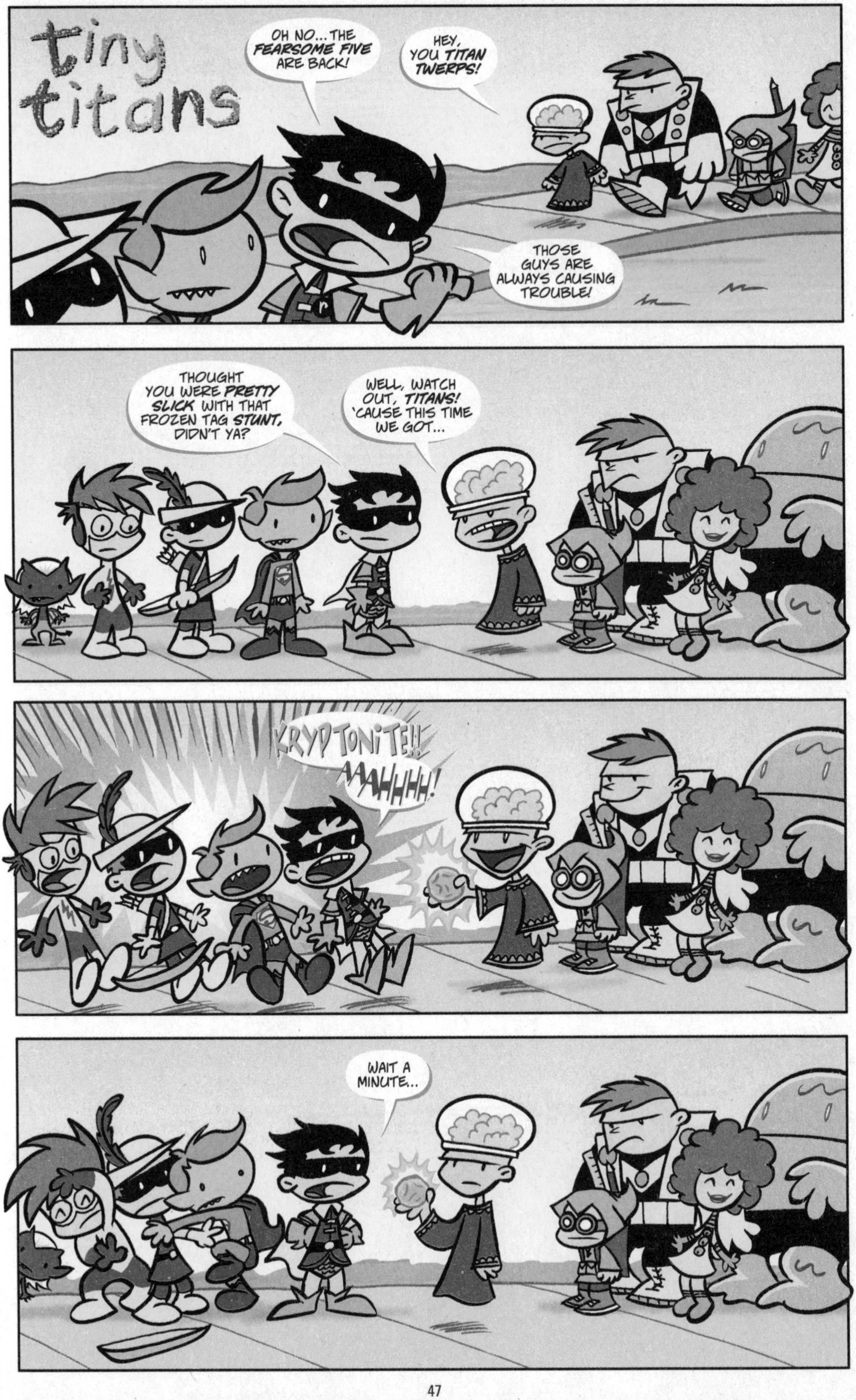
tiny titans
OH NO... THE FEARSOME FIVE ARE BACK!
HEY, YOU TITAN TWERPS!
THOSE GUYS ARE ALWAYS CAUSING TROUBLE!
THOUGHT YOU WERE PRETTY SLICK WITH THAT FROZEN TAG STUNT, DIDN'T YA?
WELL, WATCH OUT, TITANS! 'CAUSE THIS TIME WE GOT...
KRYPTONITE!!
AAAHHHH!
WAIT A MINUTE...

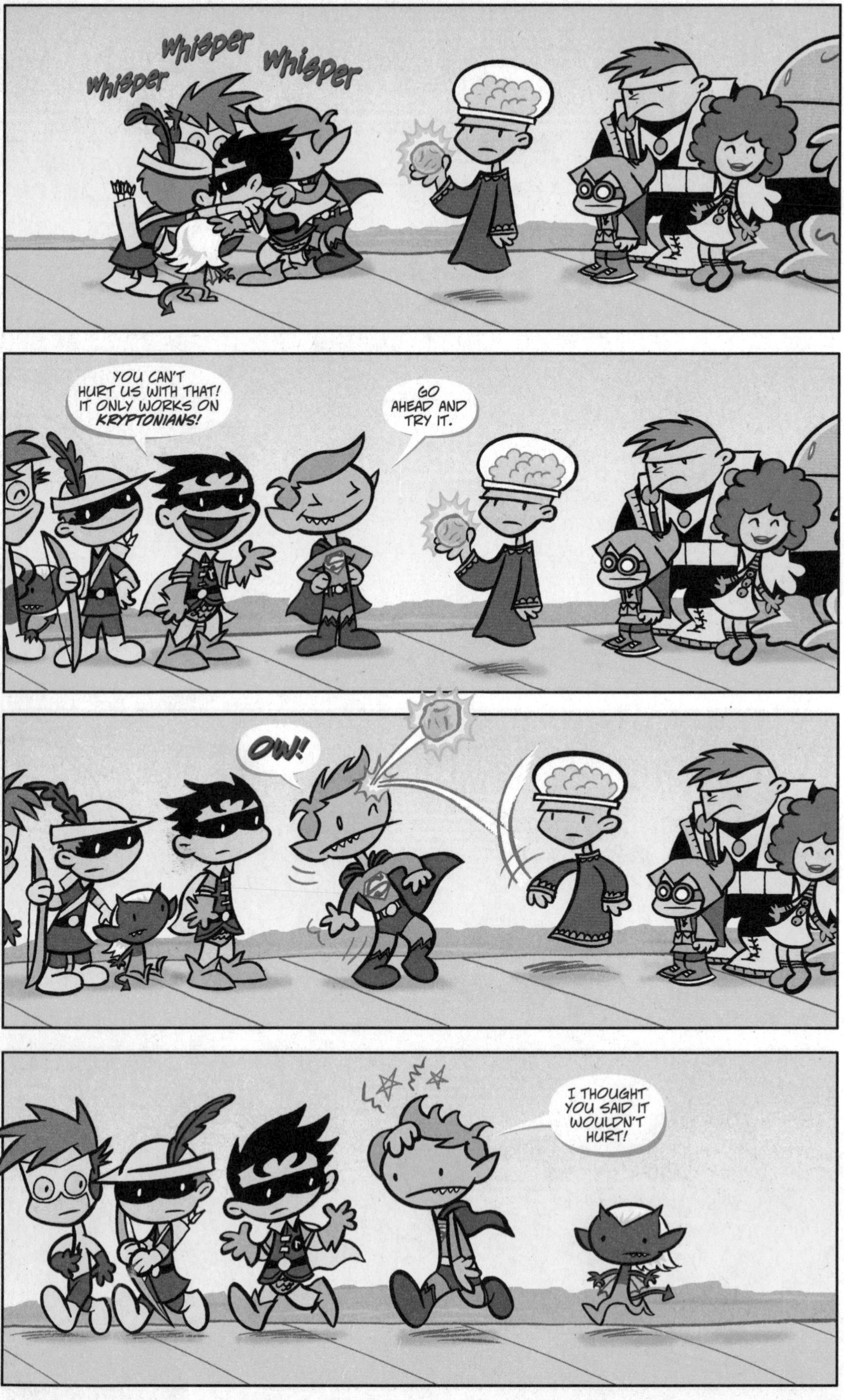
whisper
whisper
whisper
YOU CAN'T HURT US WITH THAT! IT ONLY WORKS ON KRYPTONIANS!
GO AHEAD AND TRY IT.
OW!
I THOUGHT YOU SAID IT WOULDN'T HURT!

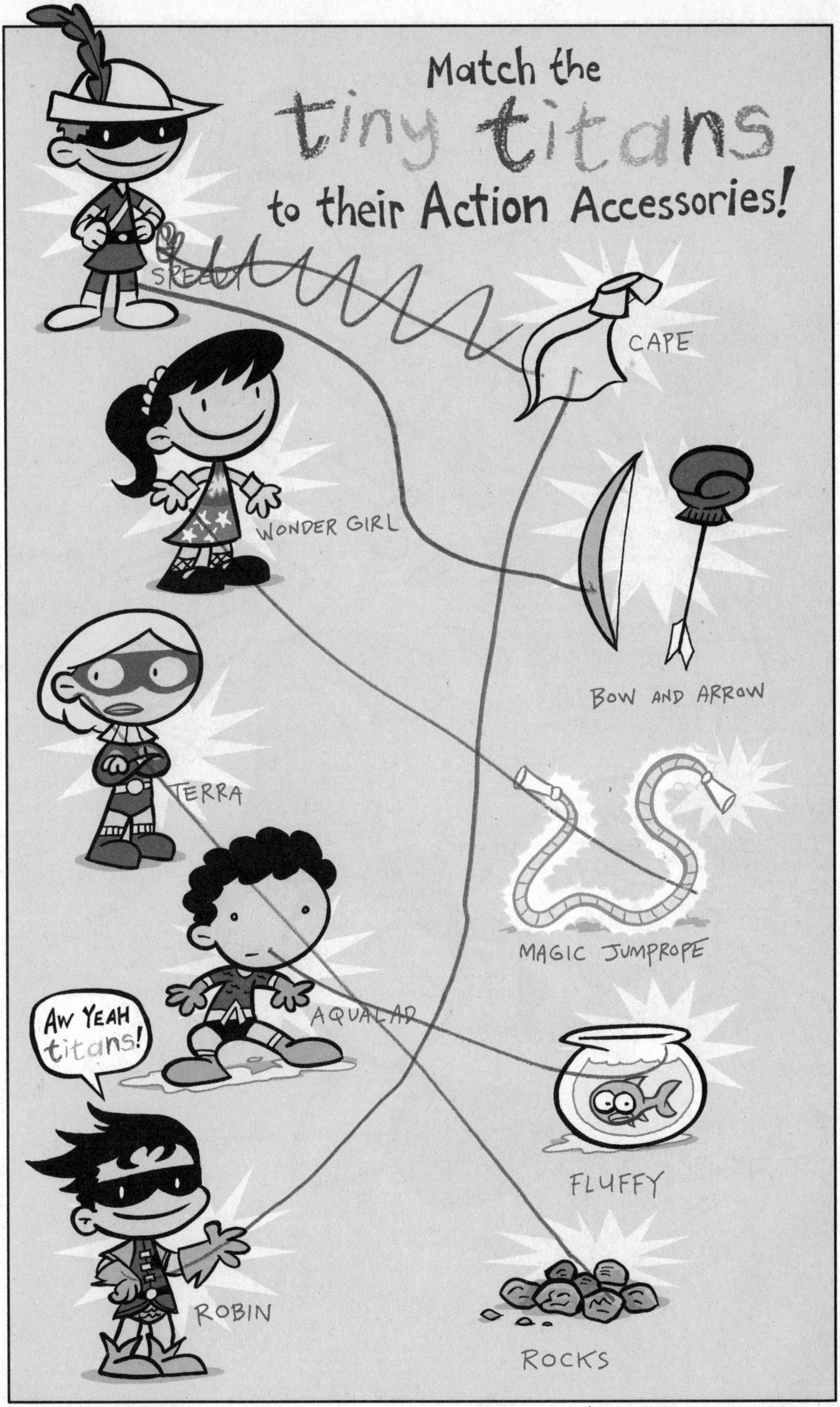
Match the
tiny titans
to their Action Accessories!
SPEEDY
CAPE
WONDER GIRL
BOW AND ARROW
TERRA
MAGIC JUMPROPE
AQUALAD
AW YEAH titans!
FLUFFY
ROBIN
ROCKS

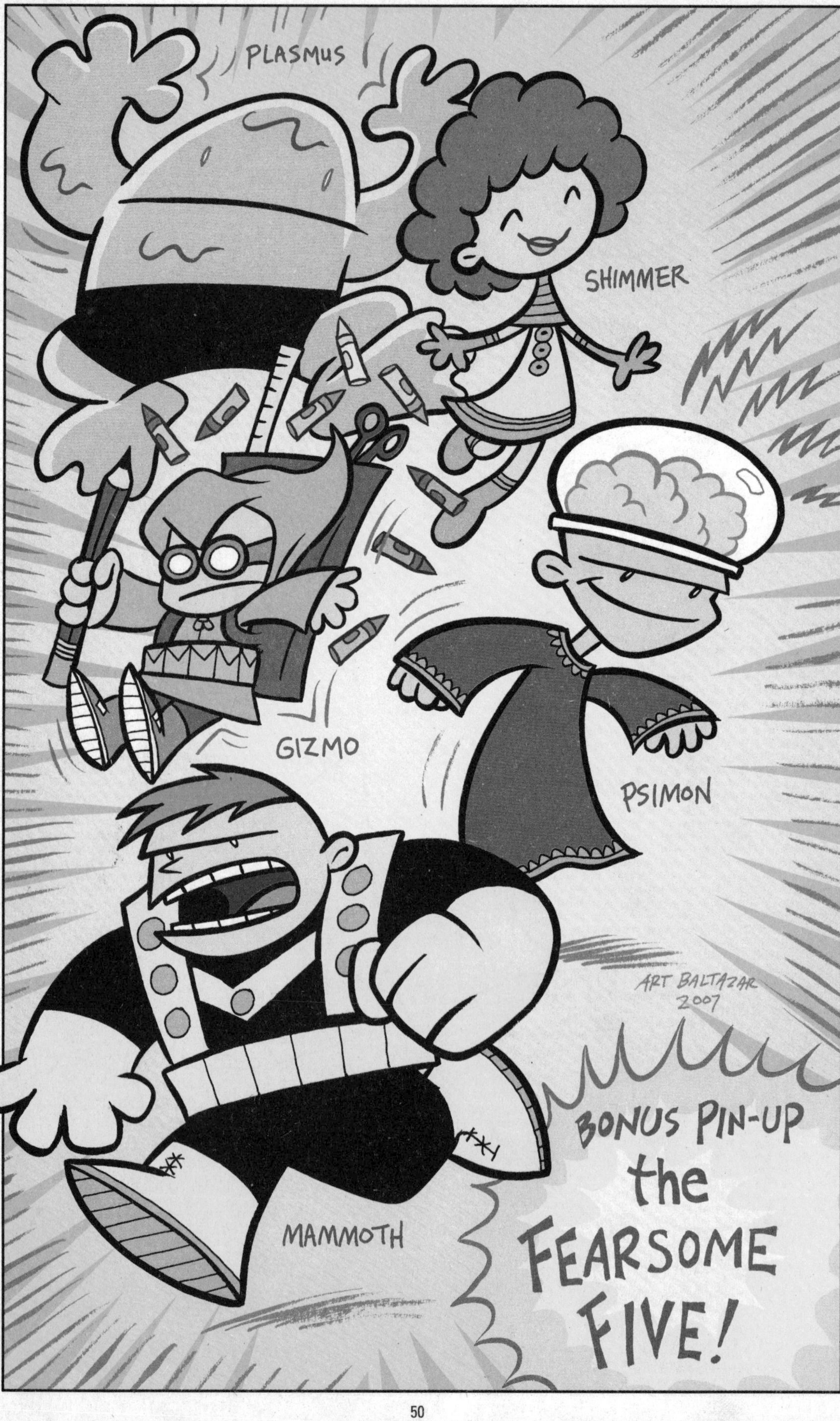
PLASMUS
SHIMMER
GIZMO
PSIMON
MAMMOTH
ART BALTAZAR 2007
BONUS PIN-UP
the FEARSOME FIVE!

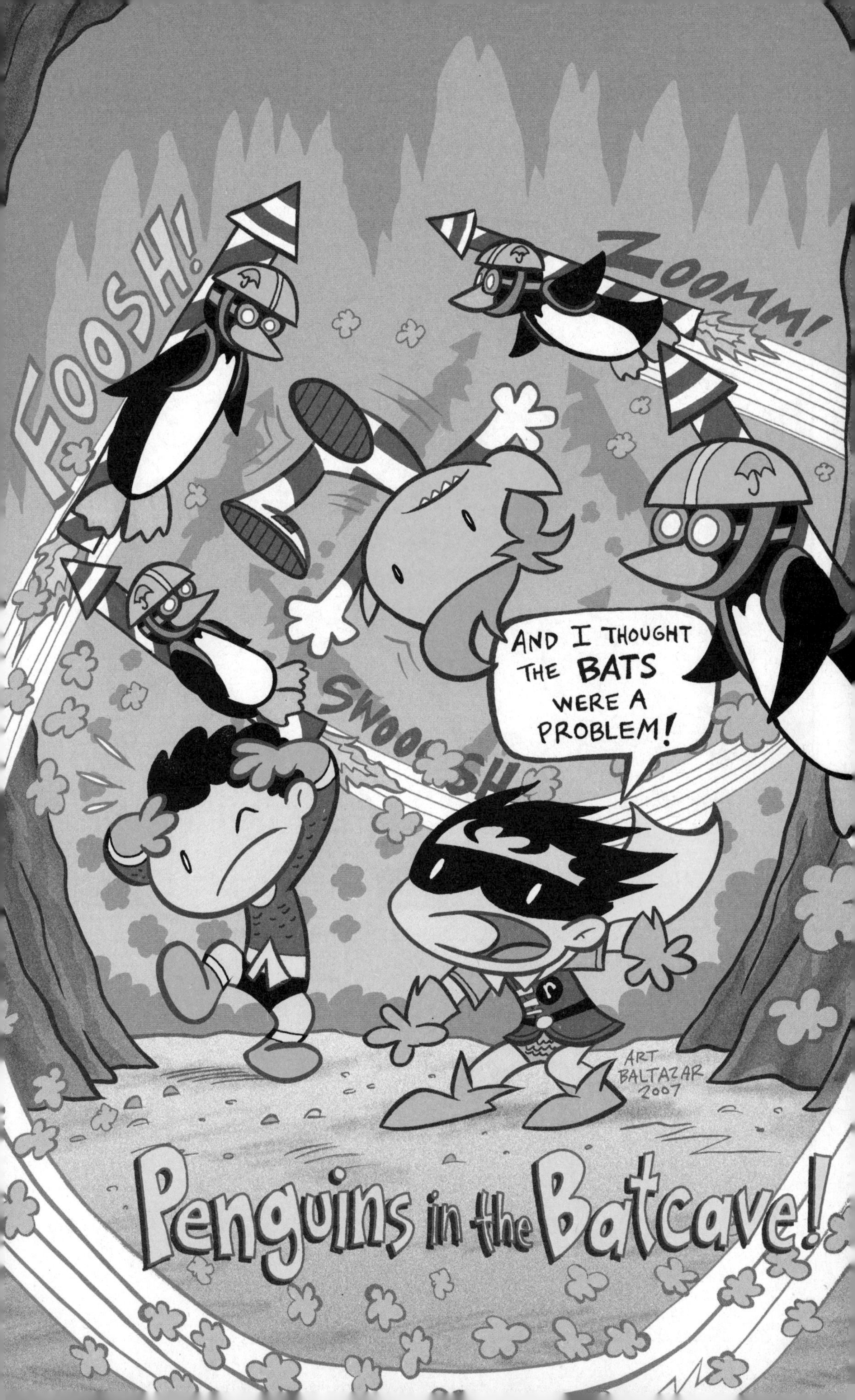
FOOSH!
ZOOMM!
SWOOOSH
AND I THOUGHT THE BATS WERE A PROBLEM!
ART BALTAZAR 2007
Penguins in the Batcave!

tiny titans

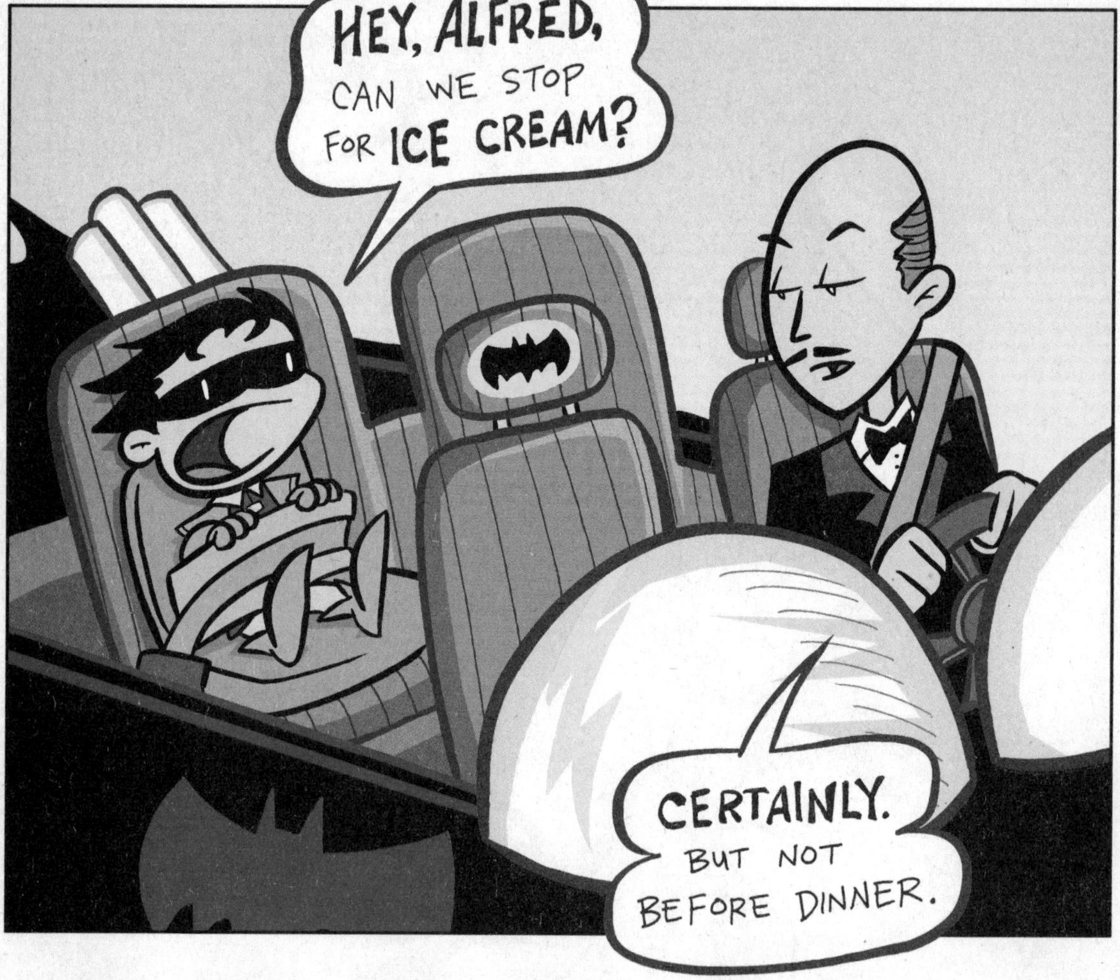
HEY, ALFRED, CAN WE STOP FOR ICE CREAM?
CERTAINLY. BUT NOT BEFORE DINNER.

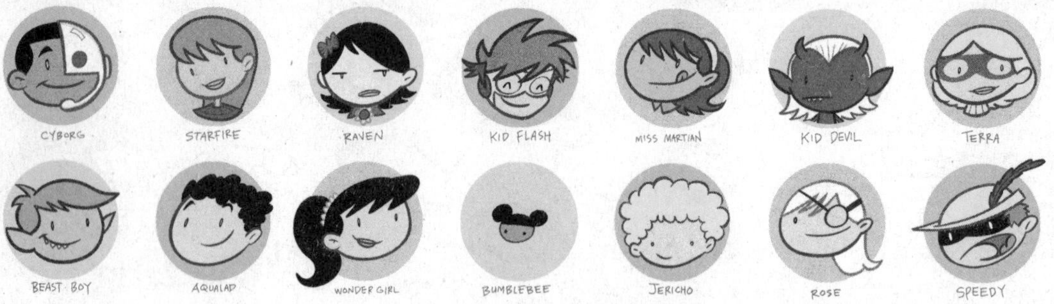
CYBORG
STARFIRE
RAVEN
KID FLASH
MISS MARTIAN
KID DEVIL
TERRA
BEAST BOY
AQUALAD
WONDER GIRL
BUMBLEBEE
JERICHO
ROSE
SPEEDY

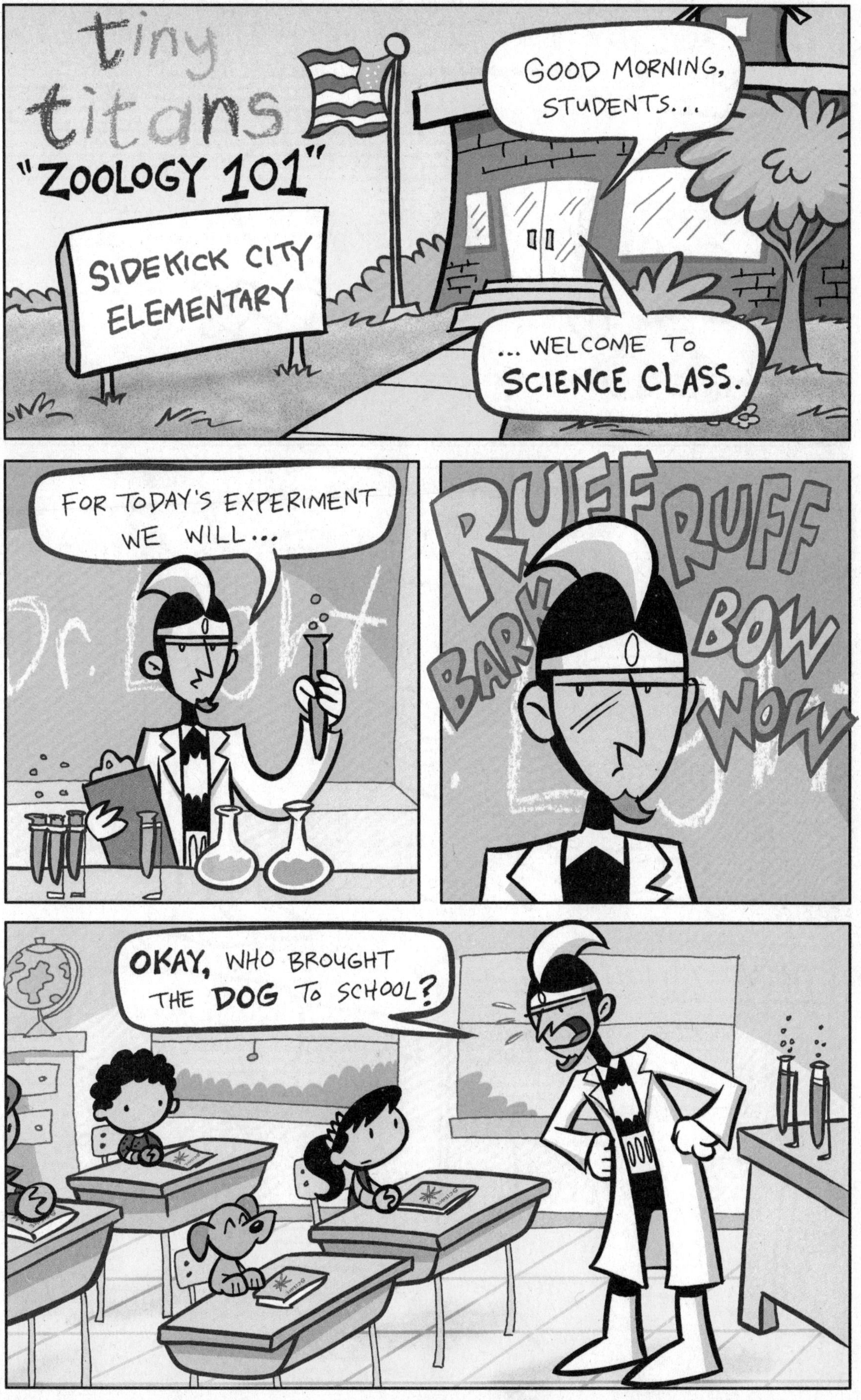
tiny titans
"ZOOLOGY 101"
SIDEKICK CITY ELEMENTARY
GOOD MORNING, STUDENTS...
... WELCOME TO SCIENCE CLASS.
FOR TODAY'S EXPERIMENT WE WILL...
Dr. Light
RUFF RUFF
BARK BOW WOW
OKAY, WHO BROUGHT THE DOG TO SCHOOL?

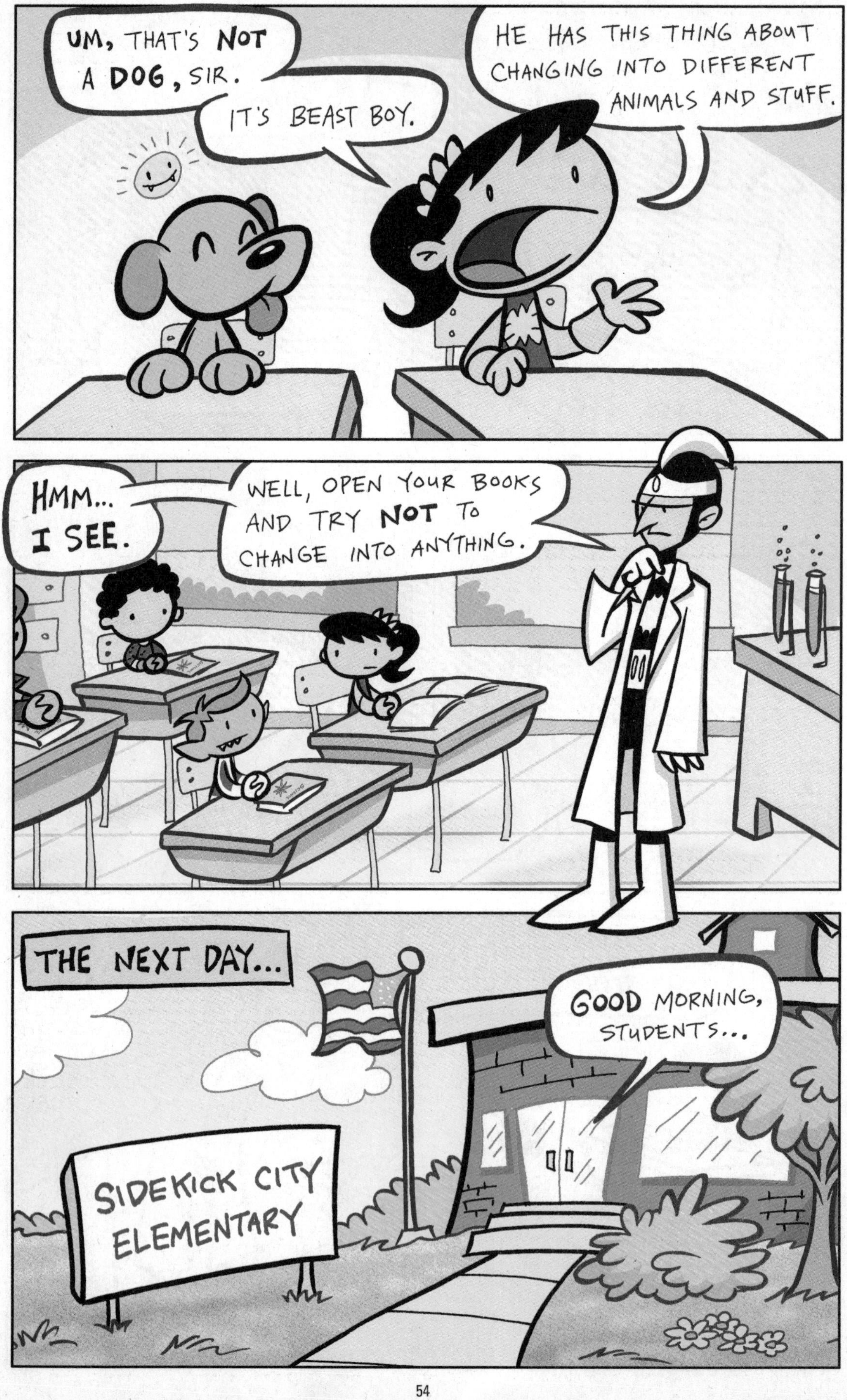
UM, THAT'S NOT A DOG, SIR.
IT'S BEAST BOY.
HE HAS THIS THING ABOUT CHANGING INTO DIFFERENT ANIMALS AND STUFF.
HMM... I SEE.
WELL, OPEN YOUR BOOKS AND TRY NOT TO CHANGE INTO ANYTHING.
THE NEXT DAY...
GOOD MORNING, STUDENTS...
SIDEKICK CITY ELEMENTARY

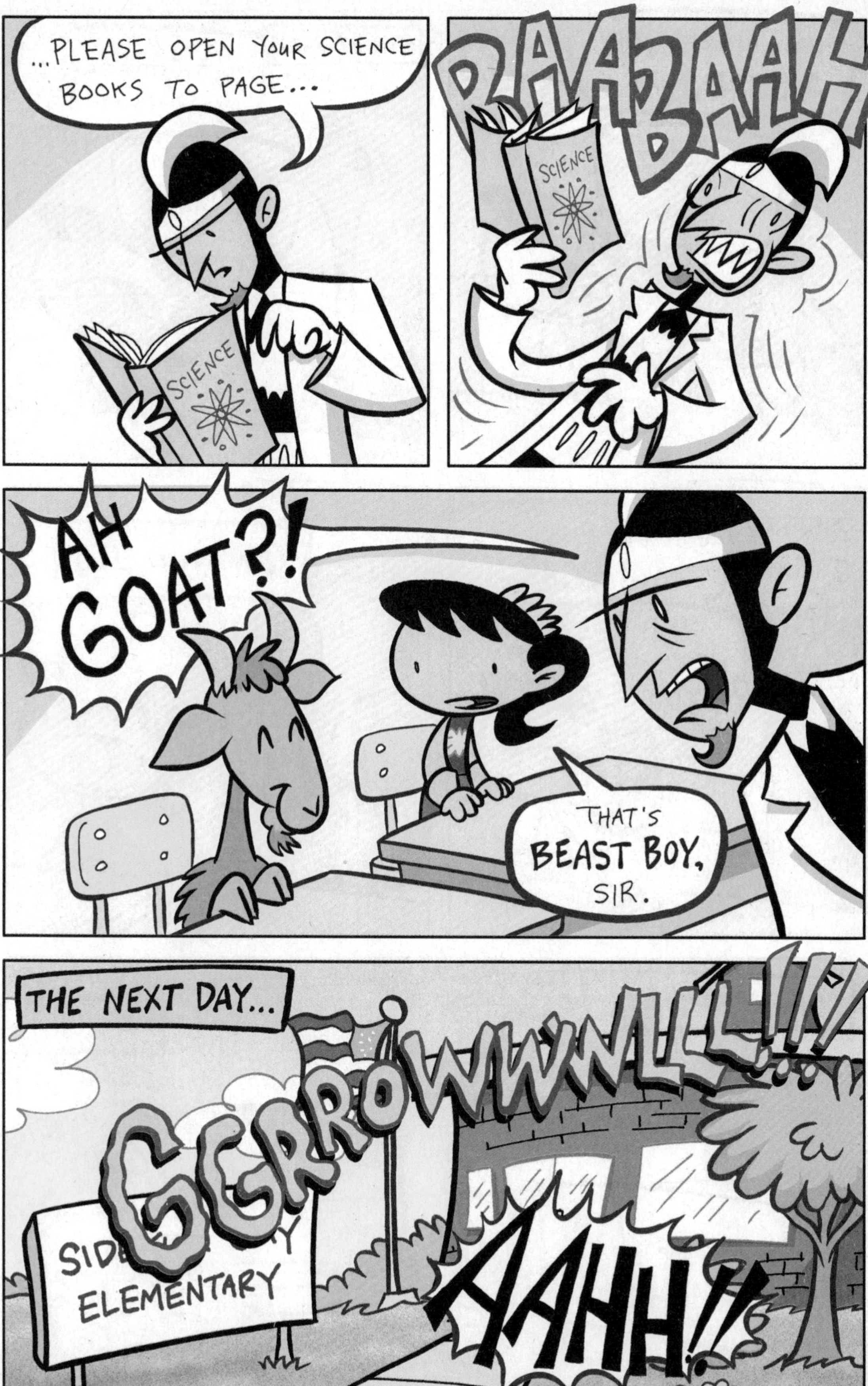
...PLEASE OPEN YOUR SCIENCE BOOKS TO PAGE...
SCIENCE
RAABAAH
SCIENCE
AH GOAT?!
THAT'S BEAST BOY, SIR.
THE NEXT DAY...
GGRROWWNLLL!!!
SIDE ELEMENTARY
AAHH!!

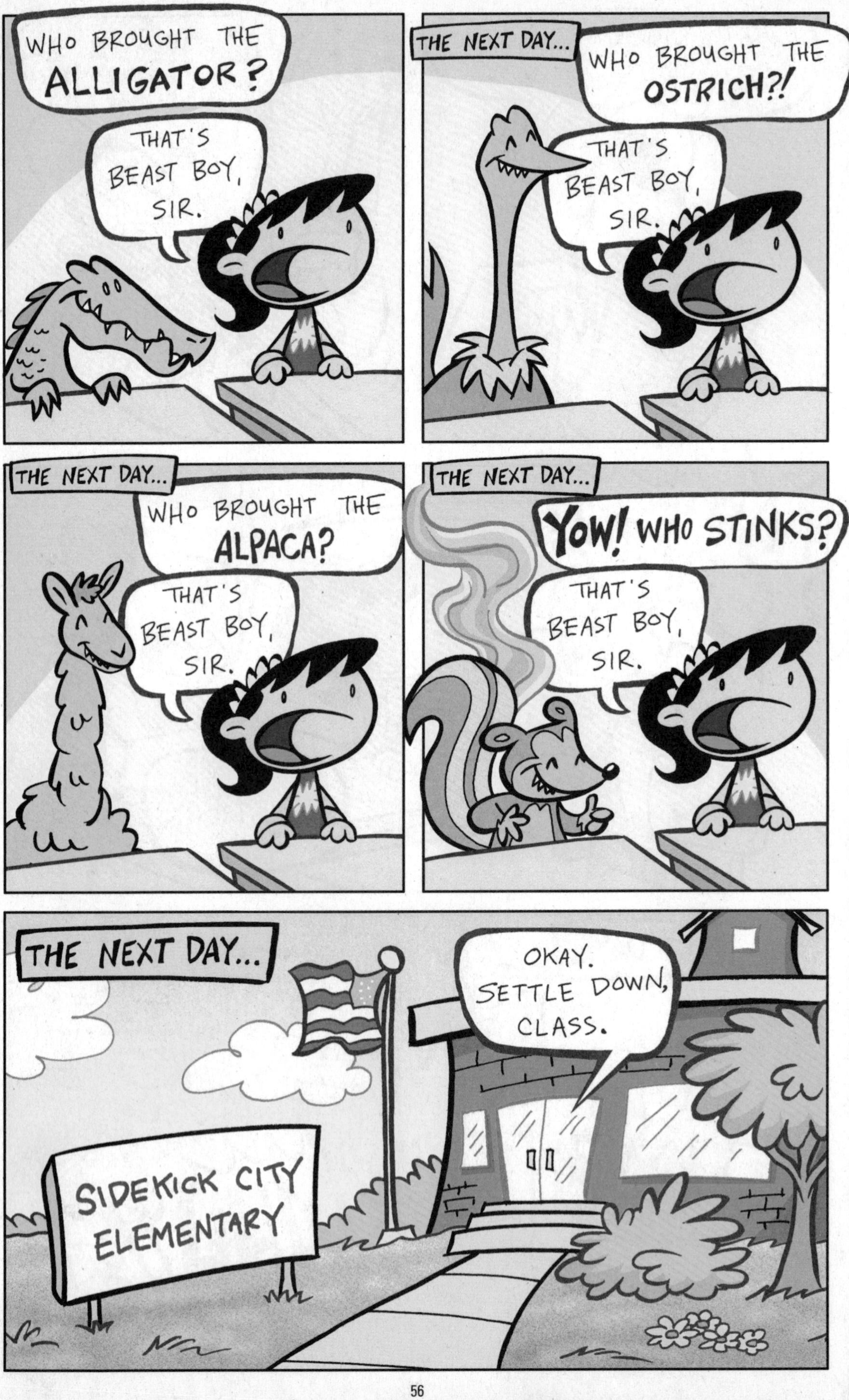
WHO BROUGHT THE ALLIGATOR?
THAT'S BEAST BOY, SIR.
THE NEXT DAY...
WHO BROUGHT THE OSTRICH?!
THAT'S BEAST BOY, SIR.
THE NEXT DAY...
WHO BROUGHT THE ALPACA?
THAT'S BEAST BOY, SIR.
THE NEXT DAY...
YOW! WHO STINKS?
THAT'S BEAST BOY, SIR.
THE NEXT DAY...
OKAY. SETTLE DOWN, CLASS.
SIDEKICK CITY ELEMENTARY

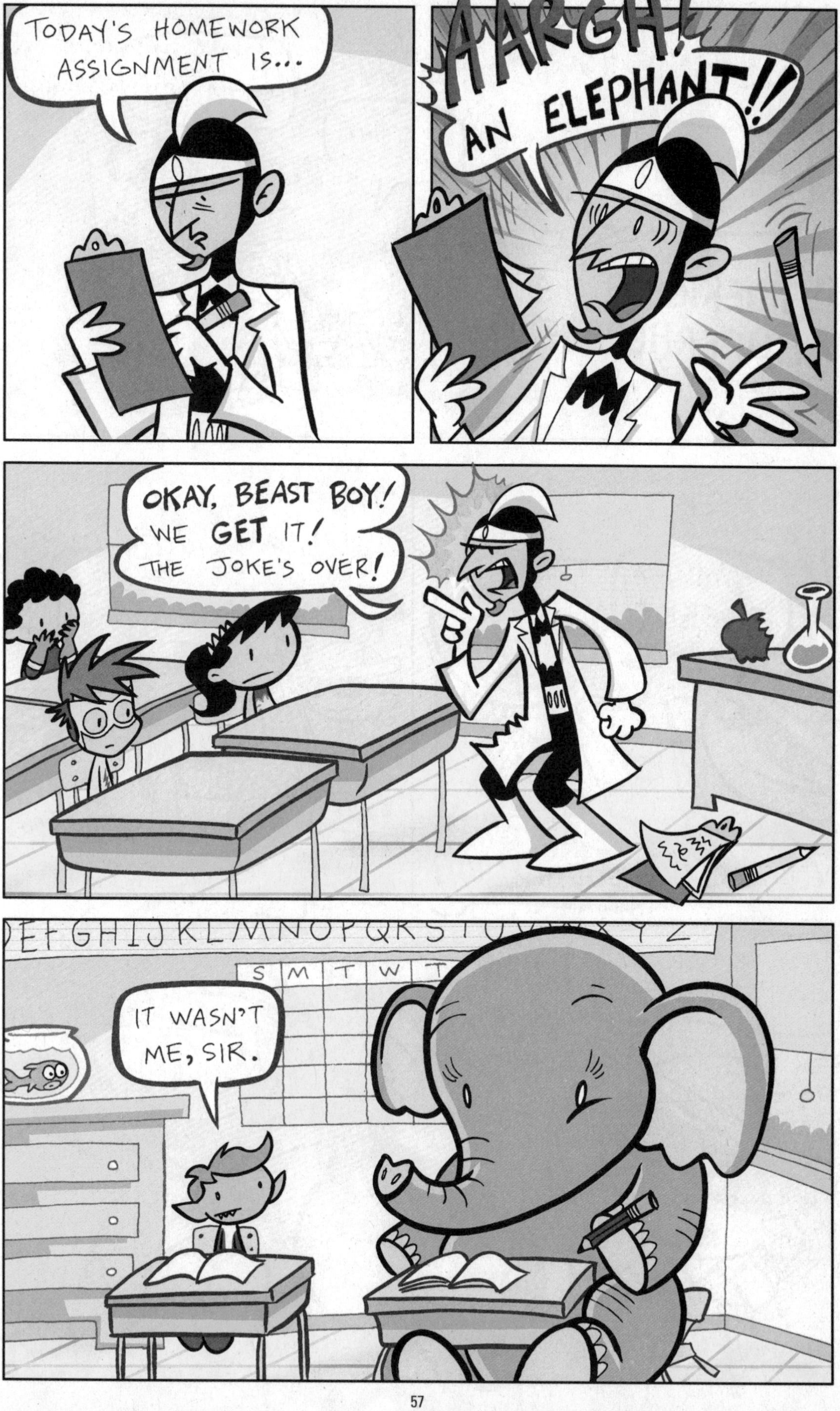
TODAY'S HOMEWORK ASSIGNMENT IS...
AARGH!
AN ELEPHANT!!
OKAY, BEAST BOY! WE GET IT! THE JOKE'S OVER!
IT WASN'T ME, SIR.

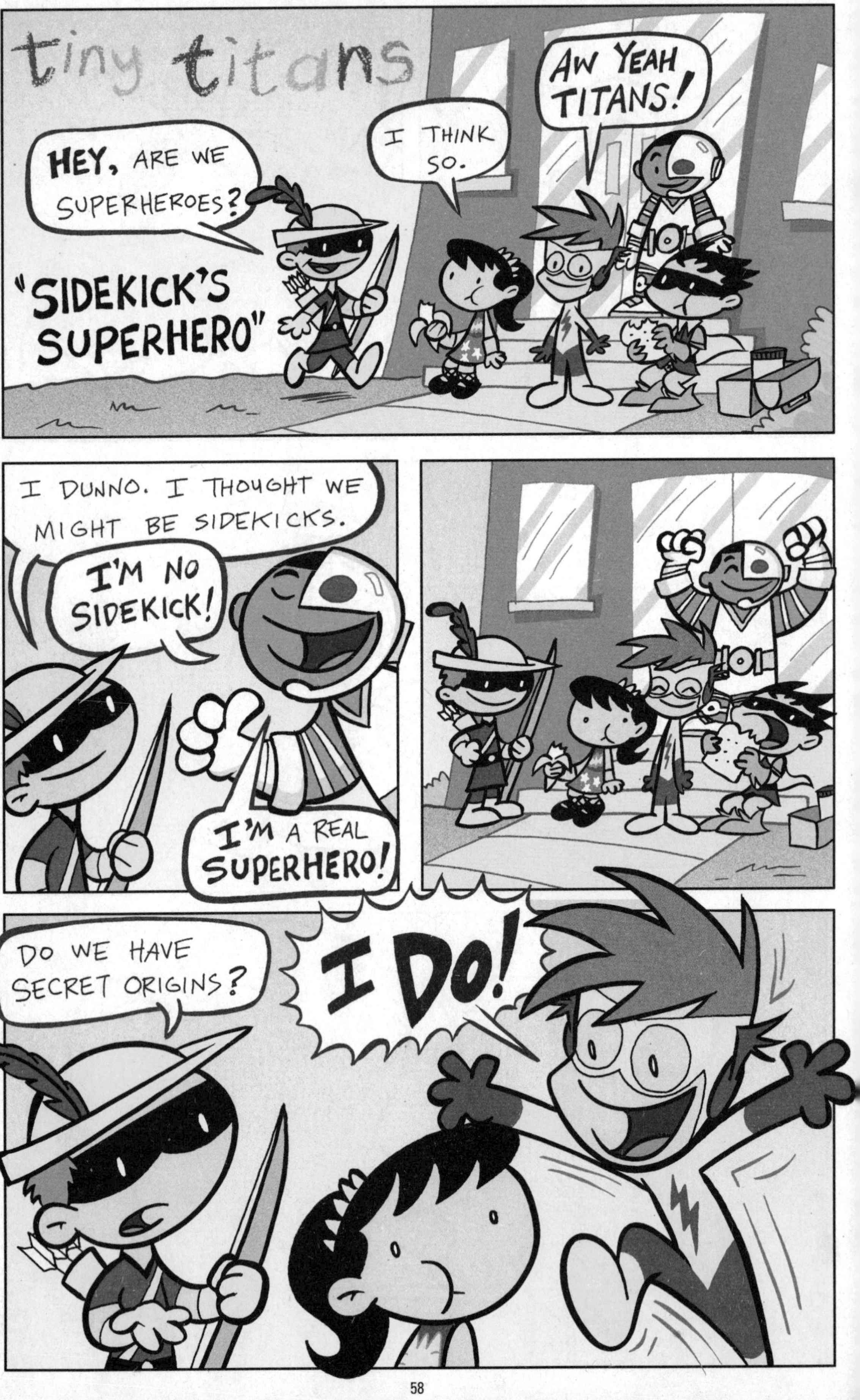
tiny titans
"SIDEKICK'S SUPERHERO"
HEY, ARE WE SUPERHEROES?
I THINK SO.
AW YEAH TITANS!
I DUNNO. I THOUGHT WE MIGHT BE SIDEKICKS.
I'M NO SIDEKICK!
I'M A REAL SUPERHERO!
DO WE HAVE SECRET ORIGINS?
I DO!

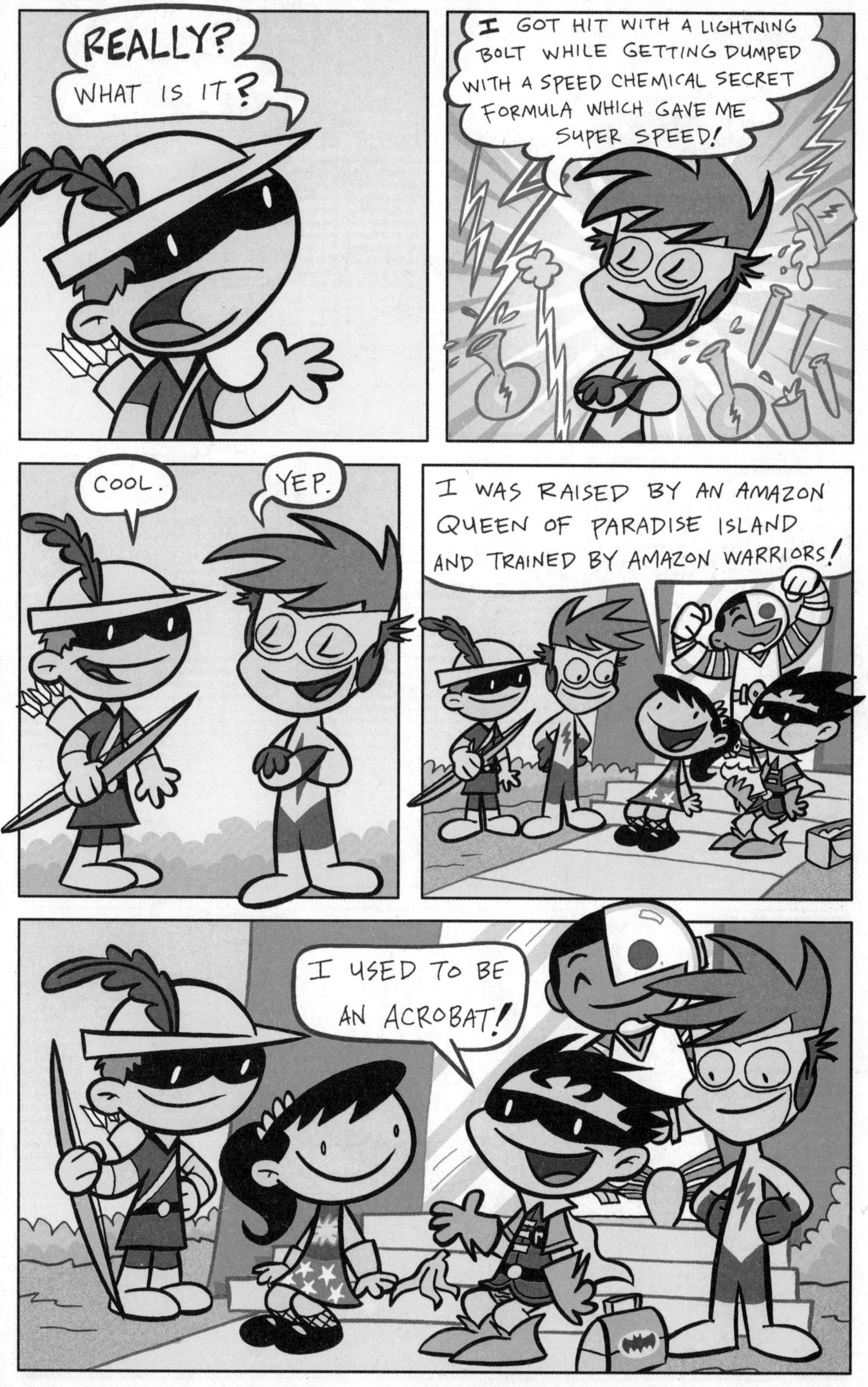
REALLY? WHAT IS IT?
I GOT HIT WITH A LIGHTNING BOLT WHILE GETTING DUMPED WITH A SPEED CHEMICAL SECRET FORMULA WHICH GAVE ME SUPER SPEED!
COOL.
YEP.
I WAS RAISED BY AN AMAZON QUEEN OF PARADISE ISLAND AND TRAINED BY AMAZON WARRIORS!
I USED TO BE AN ACROBAT!

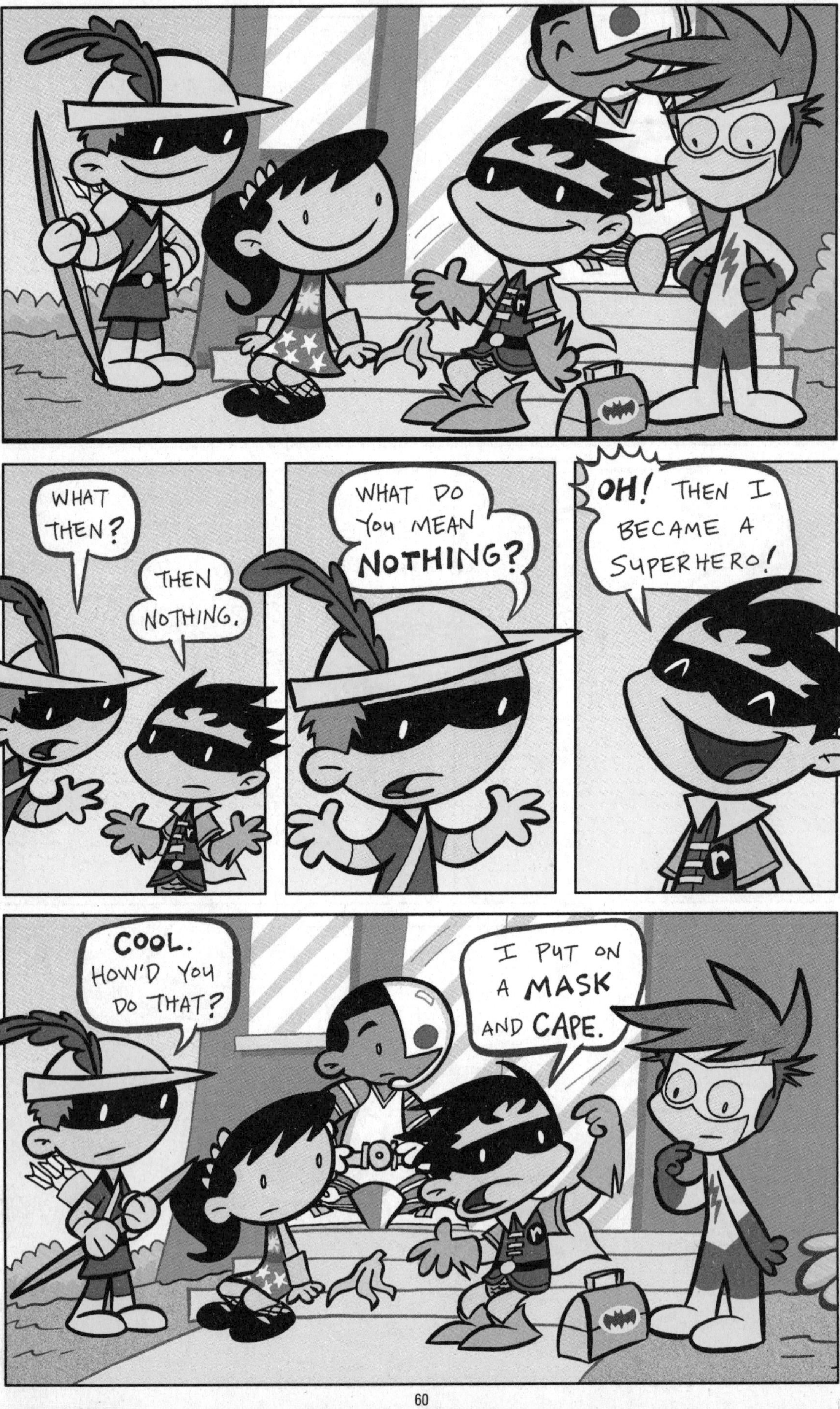
WHAT THEN?
THEN NOTHING.
WHAT DO YOU MEAN NOTHING?
OH! THEN I BECAME A SUPERHERO!
COOL. HOW'D YOU DO THAT?
I PUT ON A MASK AND CAPE.

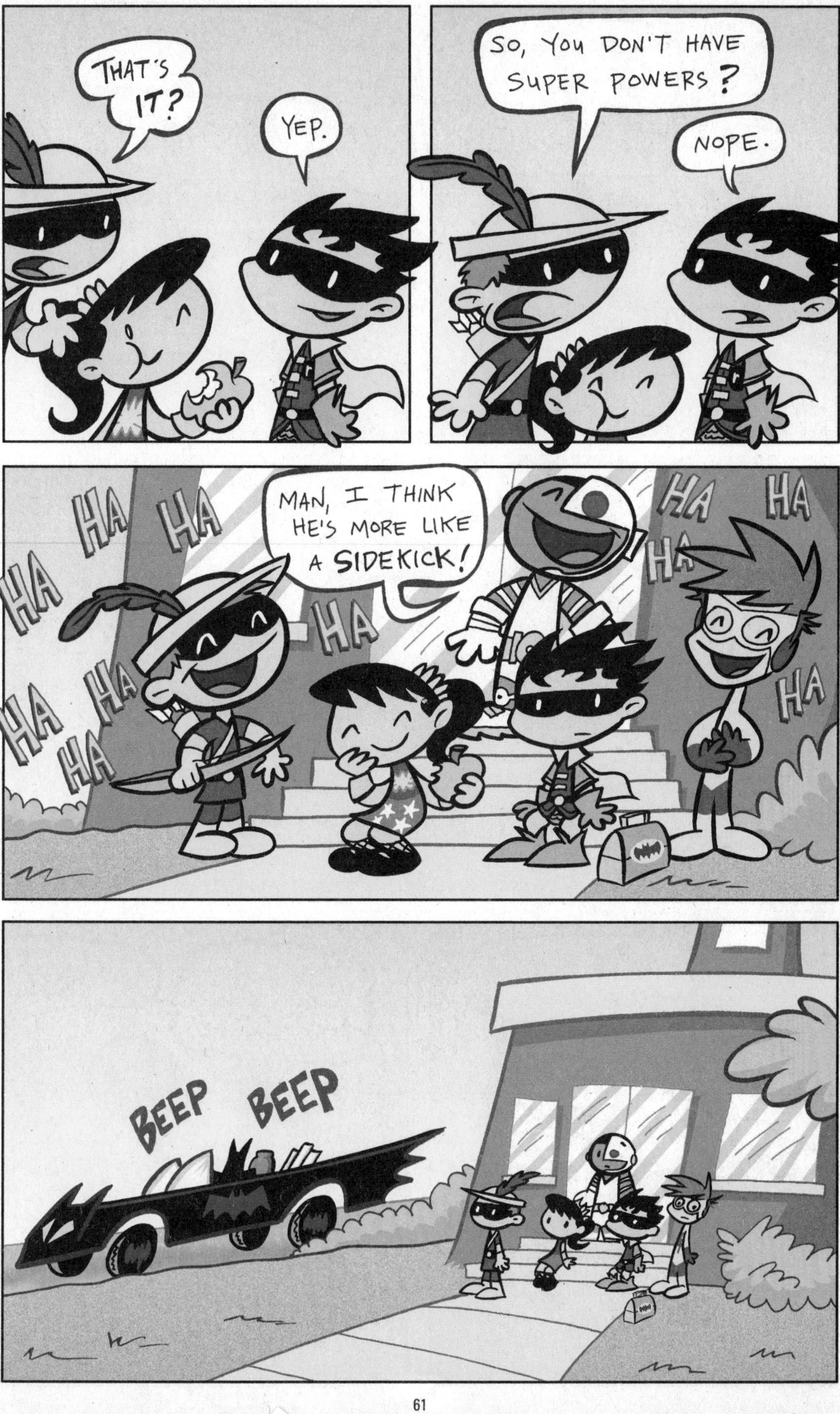
THAT'S IT?
YEP.
SO, YOU DON'T HAVE SUPER POWERS?
NOPE.
HA HA HA
HA
HA HA HA
MAN, I THINK HE'S MORE LIKE A SIDEKICK!
HA
HA HA HA
HA
BEEP BEEP

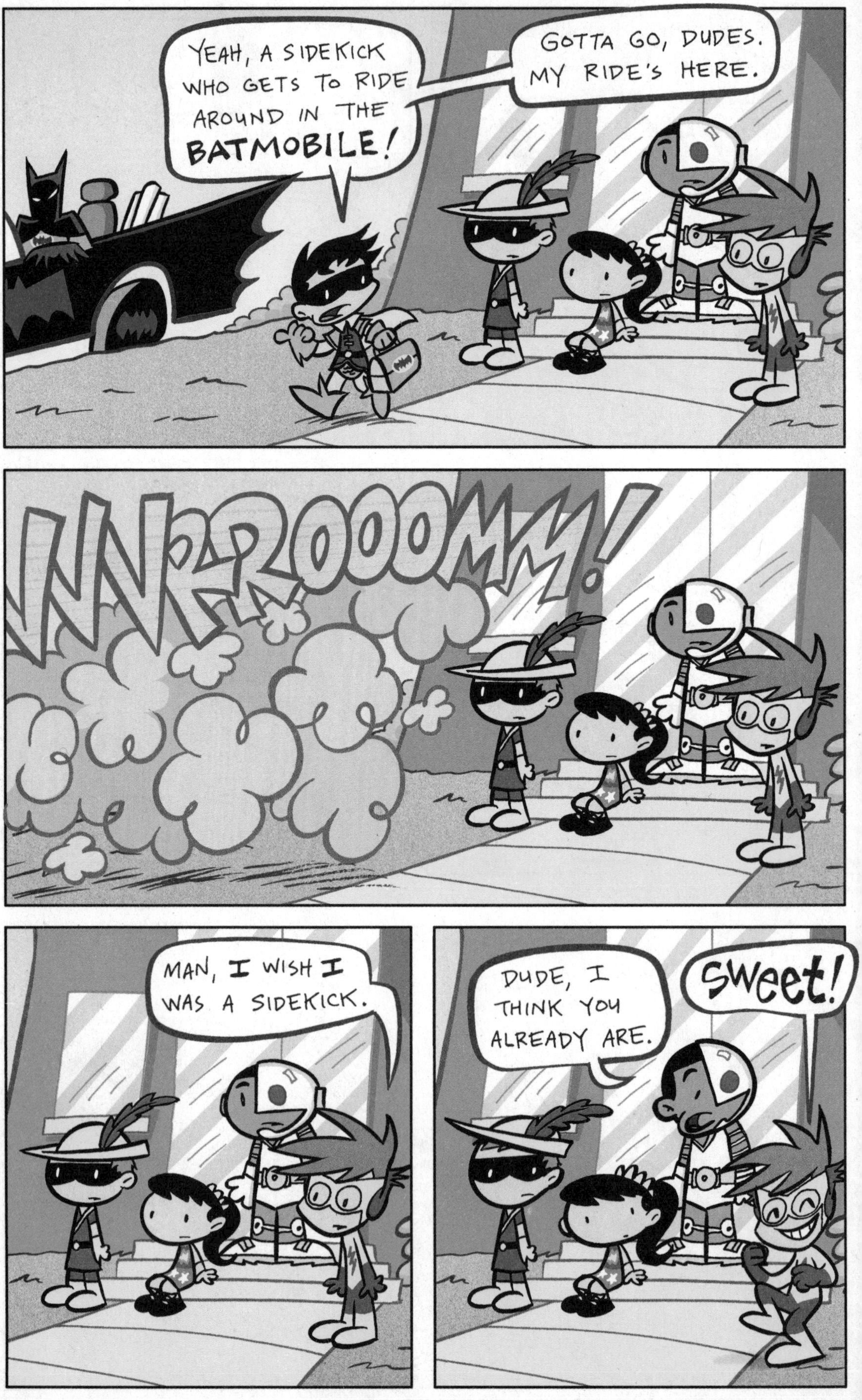
YEAH, A SIDEKICK WHO GETS TO RIDE AROUND IN THE BATMOBILE!
GOTTA GO, DUDES. MY RIDE'S HERE.
WWROOOMM!
MAN, I WISH I WAS A SIDEKICK.
DUDE, I THINK YOU ALREADY ARE.
Sweet!

THANK YOU, AQUALAD.

tiny titans
"LI'L BRO JERICHO"

YOUR FLUFFY THE GOLDFISH DEMONSTRATION WAS... INTERESTING.

NEXT UP FOR **SHOW 'N' TELL** IS...

AQUALAD
ROSE
SPEEDY
CASSIE
ID FLASH

...ROSE WILSON!

OOOHH! THAT'S US!

WELL, ROSE, WHAT DID YOU BRING TO SHOW THE CLASS?

MY LITTLE BROTHER!

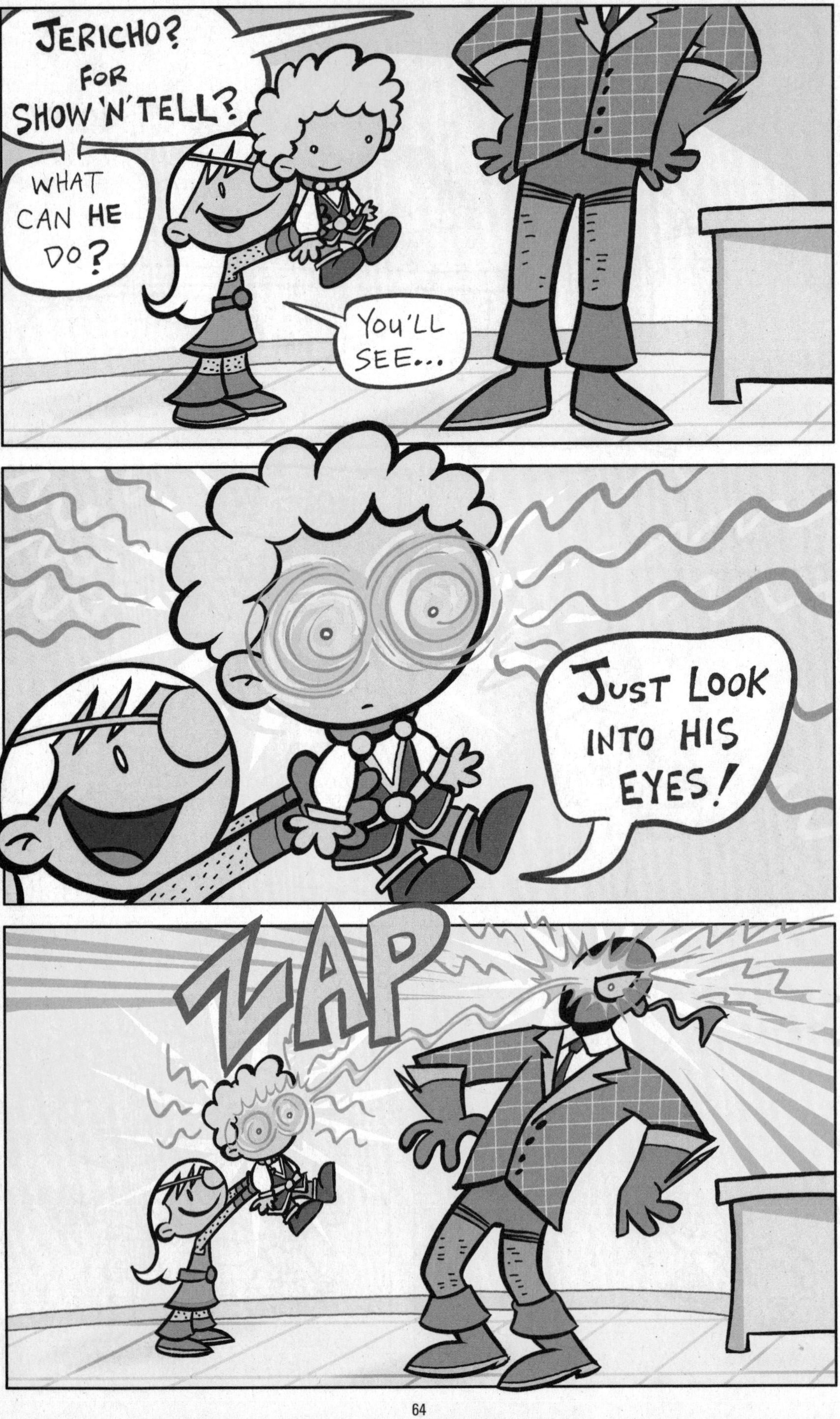
JERICHO? FOR SHOW 'N' TELL?
WHAT CAN HE DO?
YOU'LL SEE...
JUST LOOK INTO HIS EYES!
ZAP

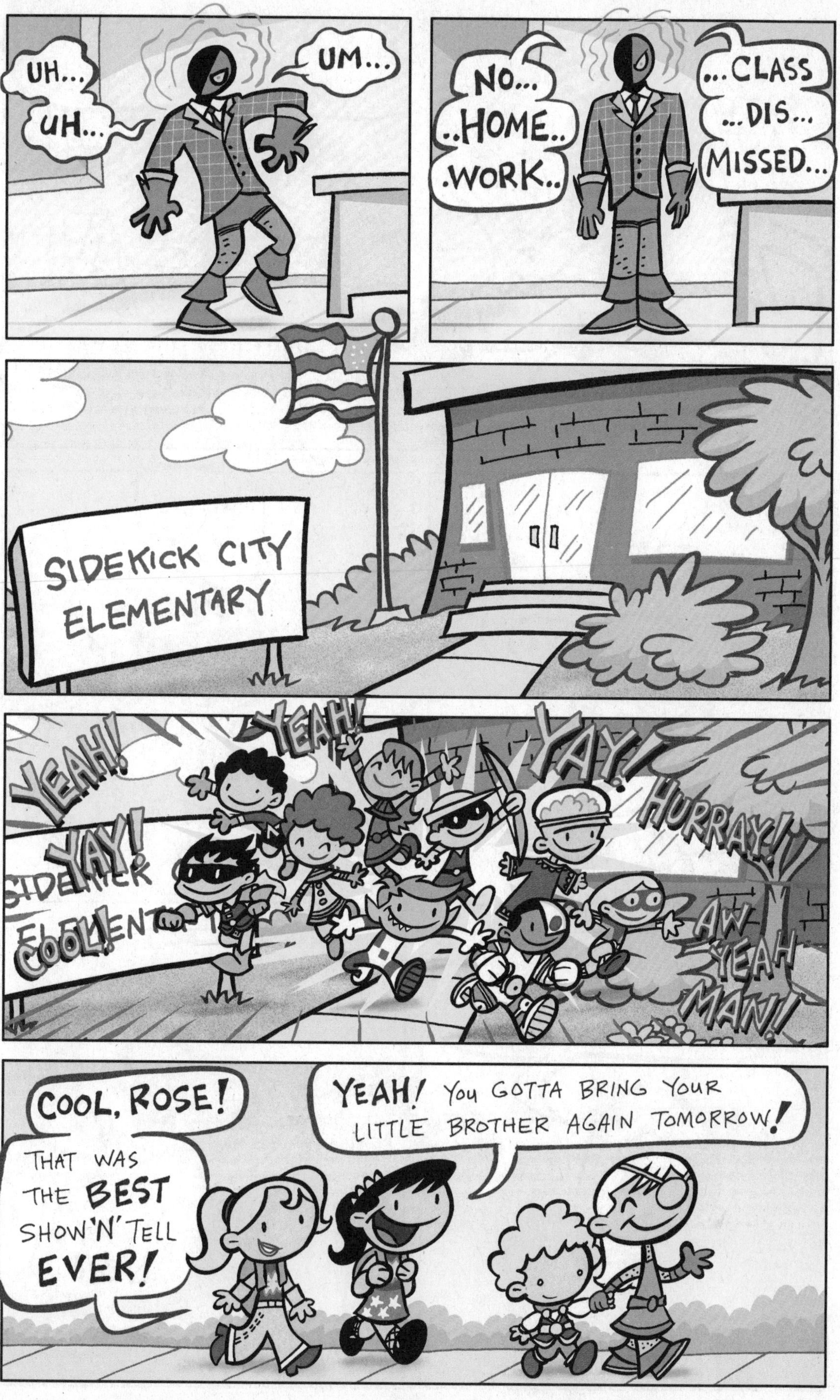
UH...
UH...
UM...
NO... ..HOME.. .WORK..
...CLASS ...DIS... MISSED...
SIDEKICK CITY ELEMENTARY
YEAH!
YEAH!
YAY!
YAY!
HURRAY!
COOL!
AW YEAH MAN!
COOL, ROSE!
THAT WAS THE BEST SHOW'N'TELL EVER!
YEAH! YOU GOTTA BRING YOUR LITTLE BROTHER AGAIN TOMORROW!

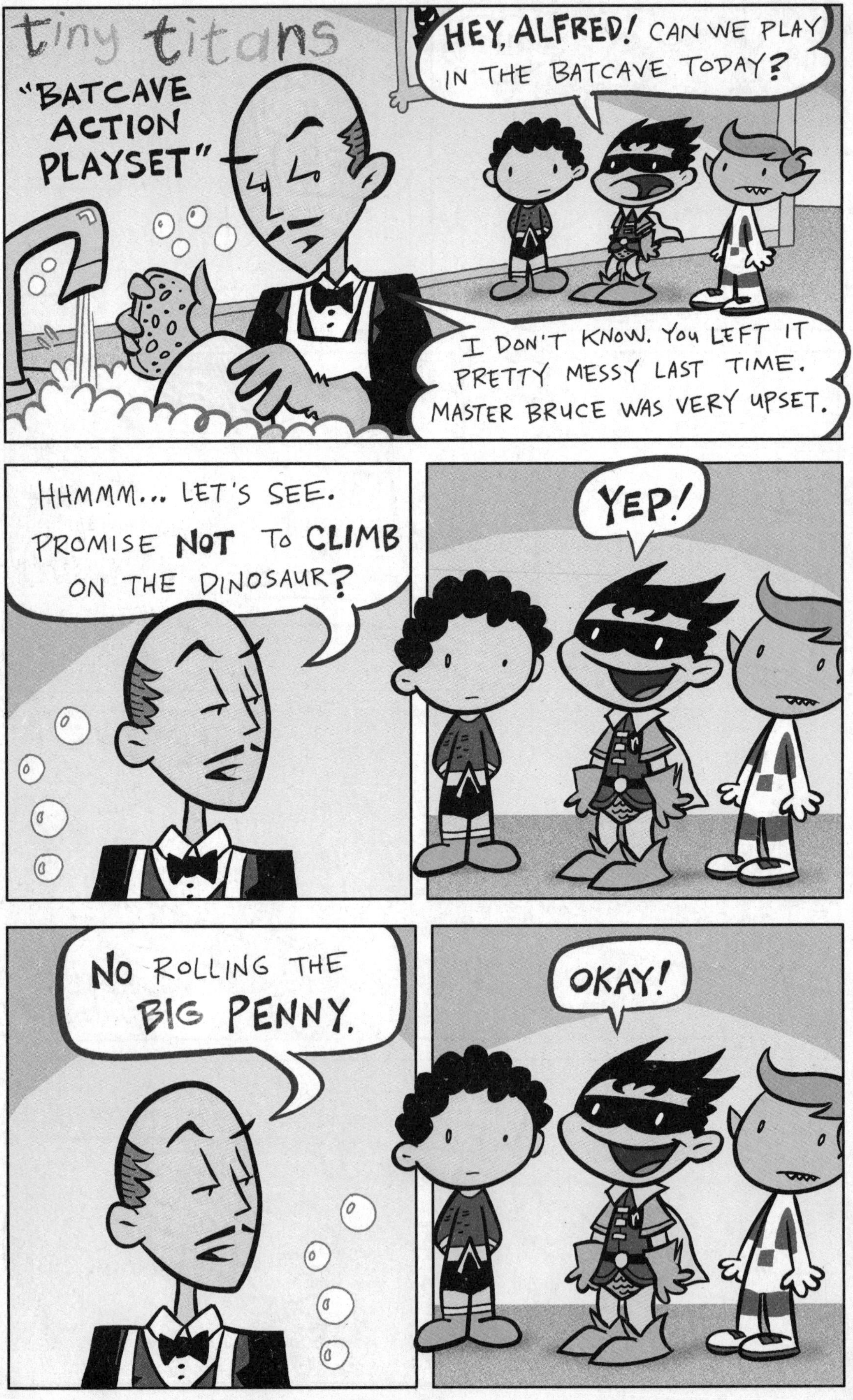
tiny titans
"BATCAVE ACTION PLAYSET"
HEY, ALFRED! CAN WE PLAY IN THE BATCAVE TODAY?
I DON'T KNOW. YOU LEFT IT PRETTY MESSY LAST TIME. MASTER BRUCE WAS VERY UPSET.
HHMMM... LET'S SEE. PROMISE NOT TO CLIMB ON THE DINOSAUR?
YEP!
NO ROLLING THE BIG PENNY.
OKAY!

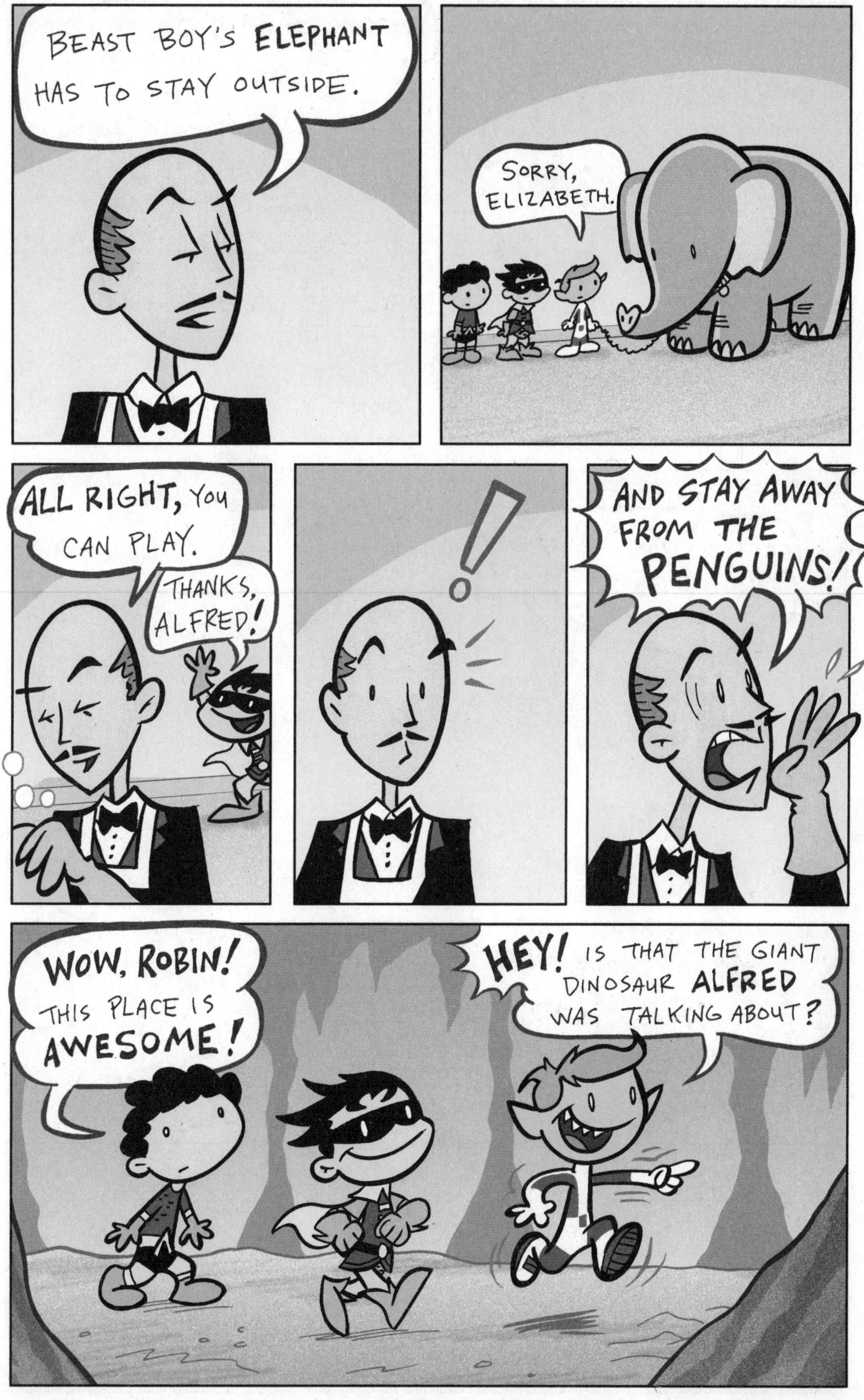
BEAST BOY'S ELEPHANT HAS TO STAY OUTSIDE.
SORRY, ELIZABETH.
ALL RIGHT, YOU CAN PLAY.
THANKS, ALFRED!
!
AND STAY AWAY FROM THE PENGUINS!
WOW, ROBIN! THIS PLACE IS AWESOME!
HEY! IS THAT THE GIANT DINOSAUR ALFRED WAS TALKING ABOUT?

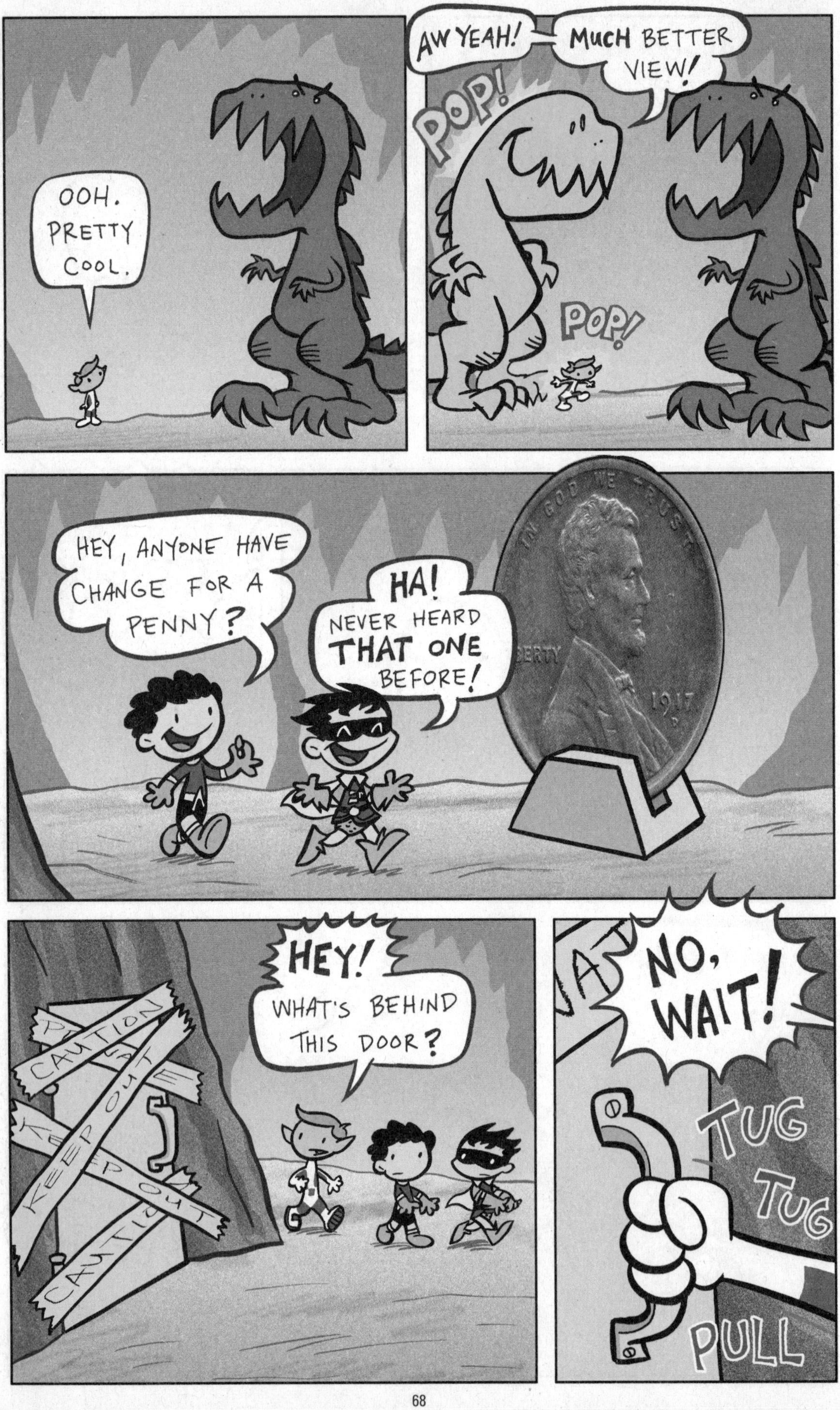
OOH. PRETTY COOL.
AW YEAH!
MUCH BETTER VIEW!
POP!
POP!
HEY, ANYONE HAVE CHANGE FOR A PENNY?
HA! NEVER HEARD THAT ONE BEFORE!
IN GOD WE TRUST
1917
CAUTION
KEEP OUT
CAUTION
HEY! WHAT'S BEHIND THIS DOOR?
NO, WAIT!
TUG
TUG
PULL

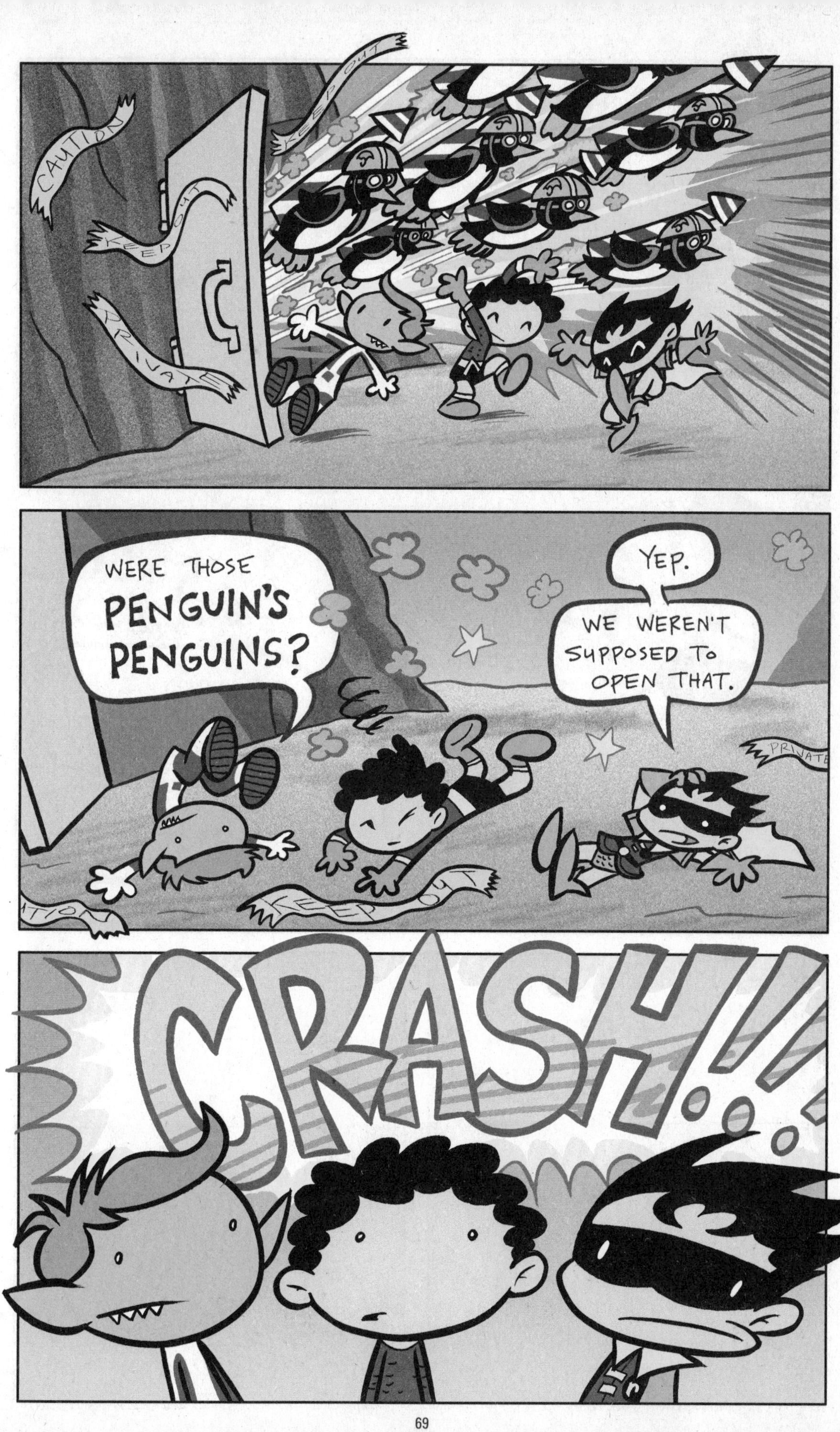
CAUTION
KEEP OUT
KEEP OUT
PRIVATE
WERE THOSE PENGUIN'S PENGUINS?
YEP.
WE WEREN'T SUPPOSED TO OPEN THAT.
CRASH!!

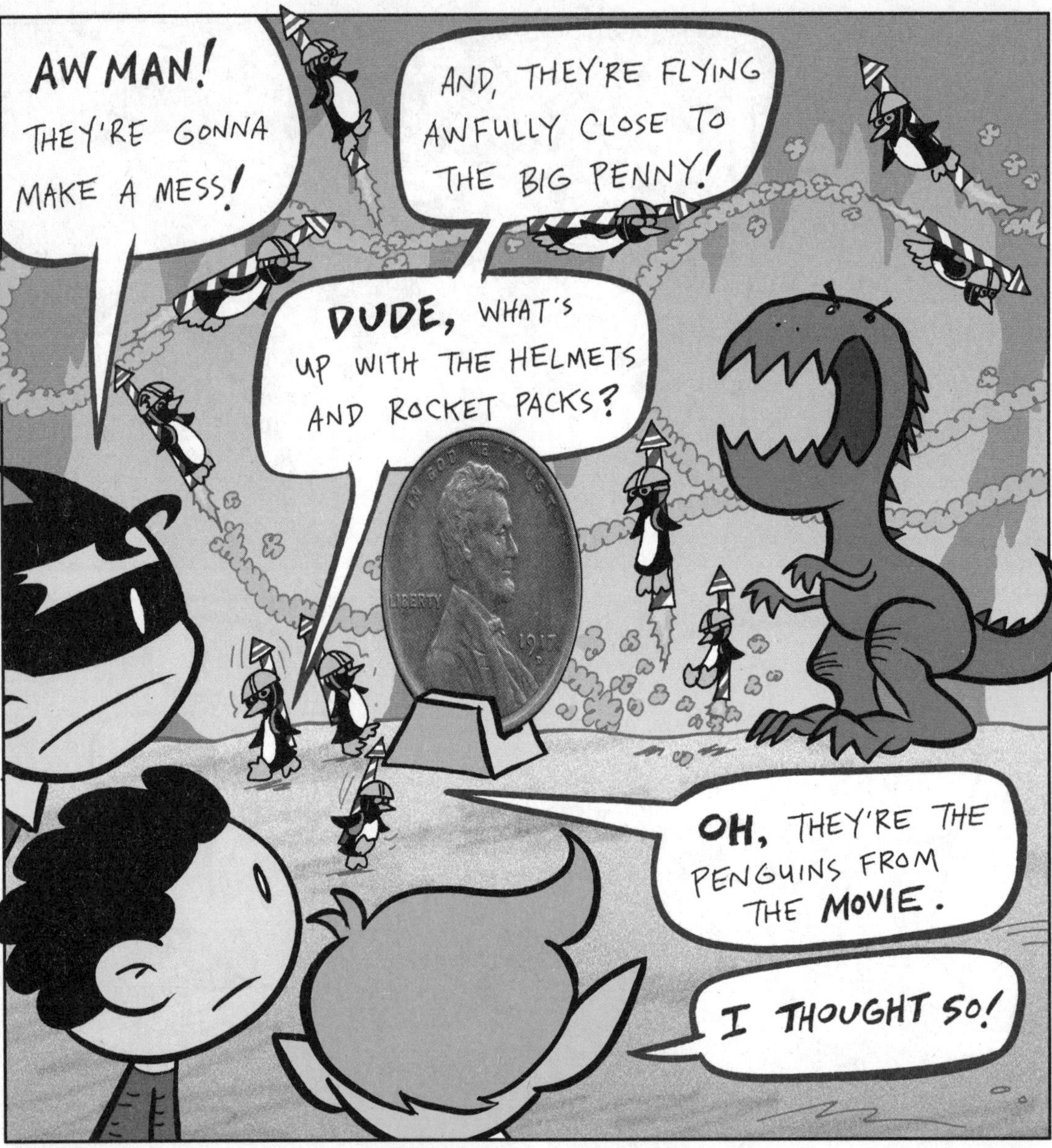
AW MAN! THEY'RE GONNA MAKE A MESS!
AND, THEY'RE FLYING AWFULLY CLOSE TO THE BIG PENNY!
DUDE, WHAT'S UP WITH THE HELMETS AND ROCKET PACKS?
OH, THEY'RE THE PENGUINS FROM THE MOVIE.
I THOUGHT SO!

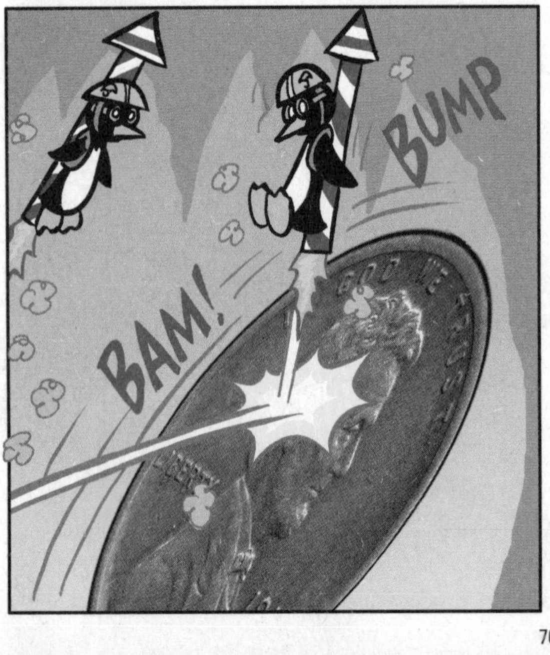
BUMP
BAM!

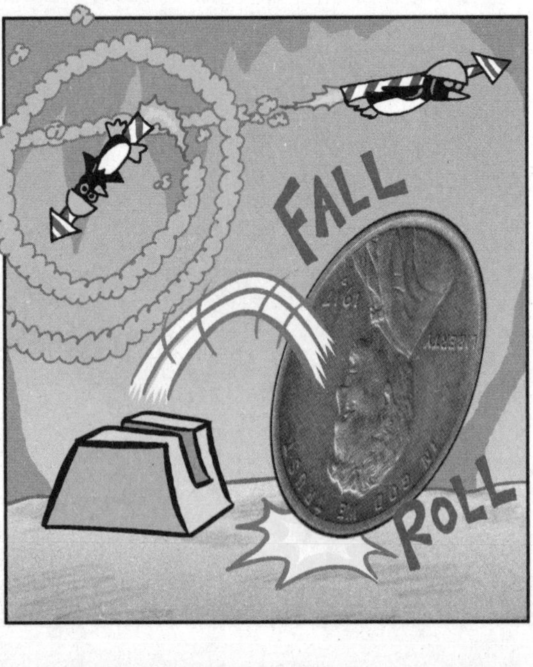
FALL
ROLL

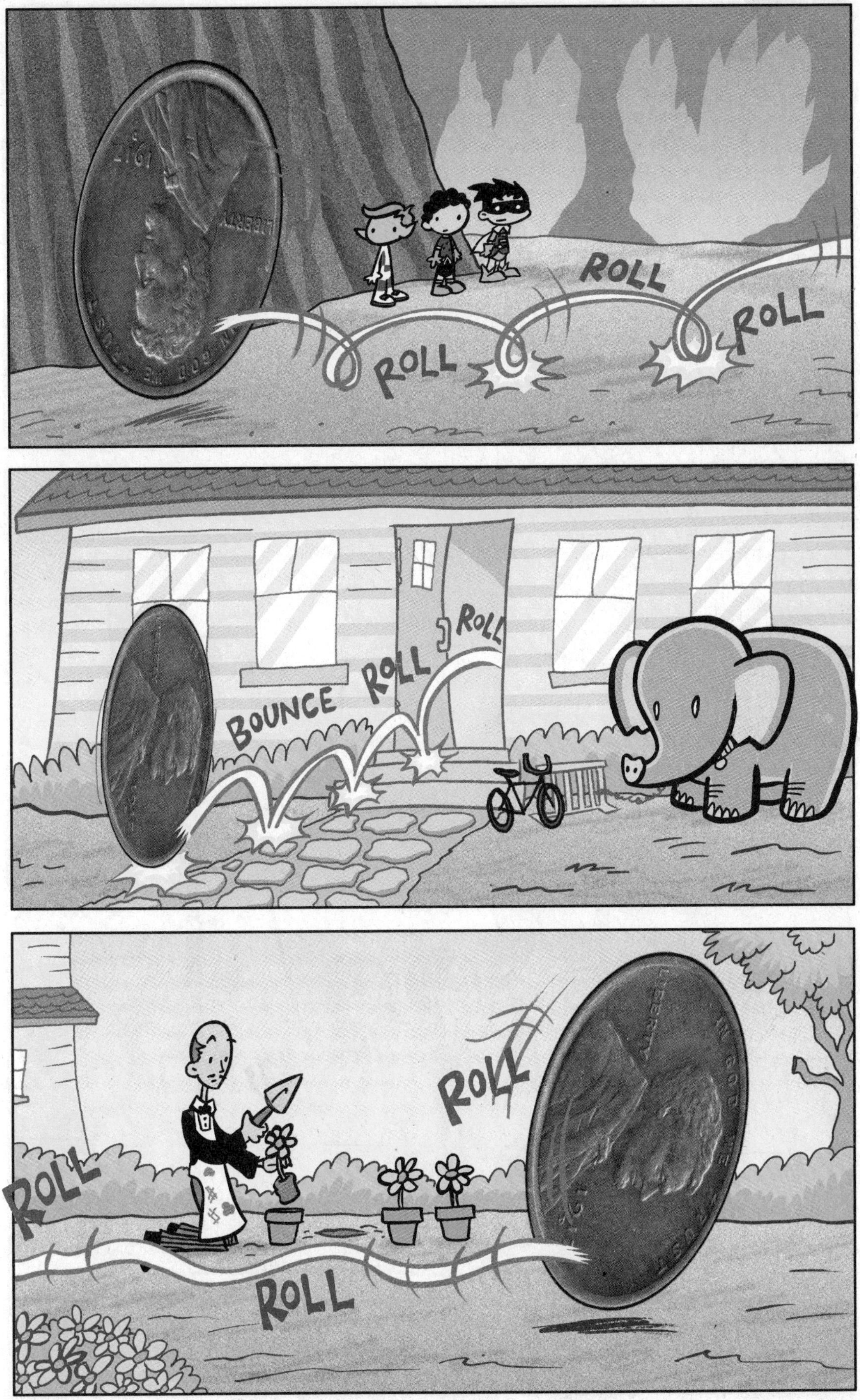

ROLL
ROLL
ROLL
BOUNCE
ROLL
ROLL
ROLL
ROLL
ROLL

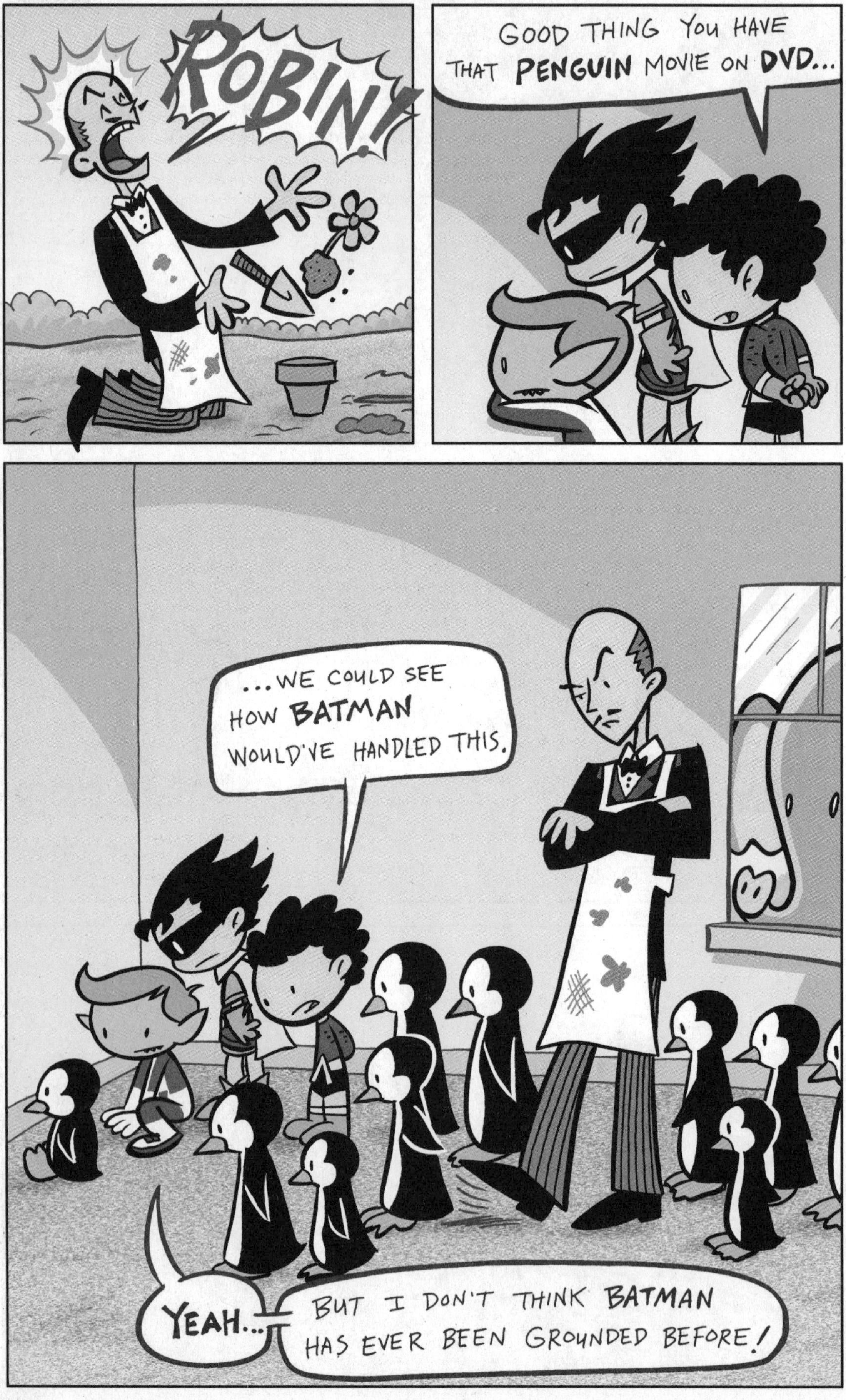

ROBIN!
GOOD THING YOU HAVE THAT PENGUIN MOVIE ON DVD...
...WE COULD SEE HOW BATMAN WOULD'VE HANDLED THIS.
YEAH...
BUT I DON'T THINK BATMAN HAS EVER BEEN GROUNDED BEFORE!

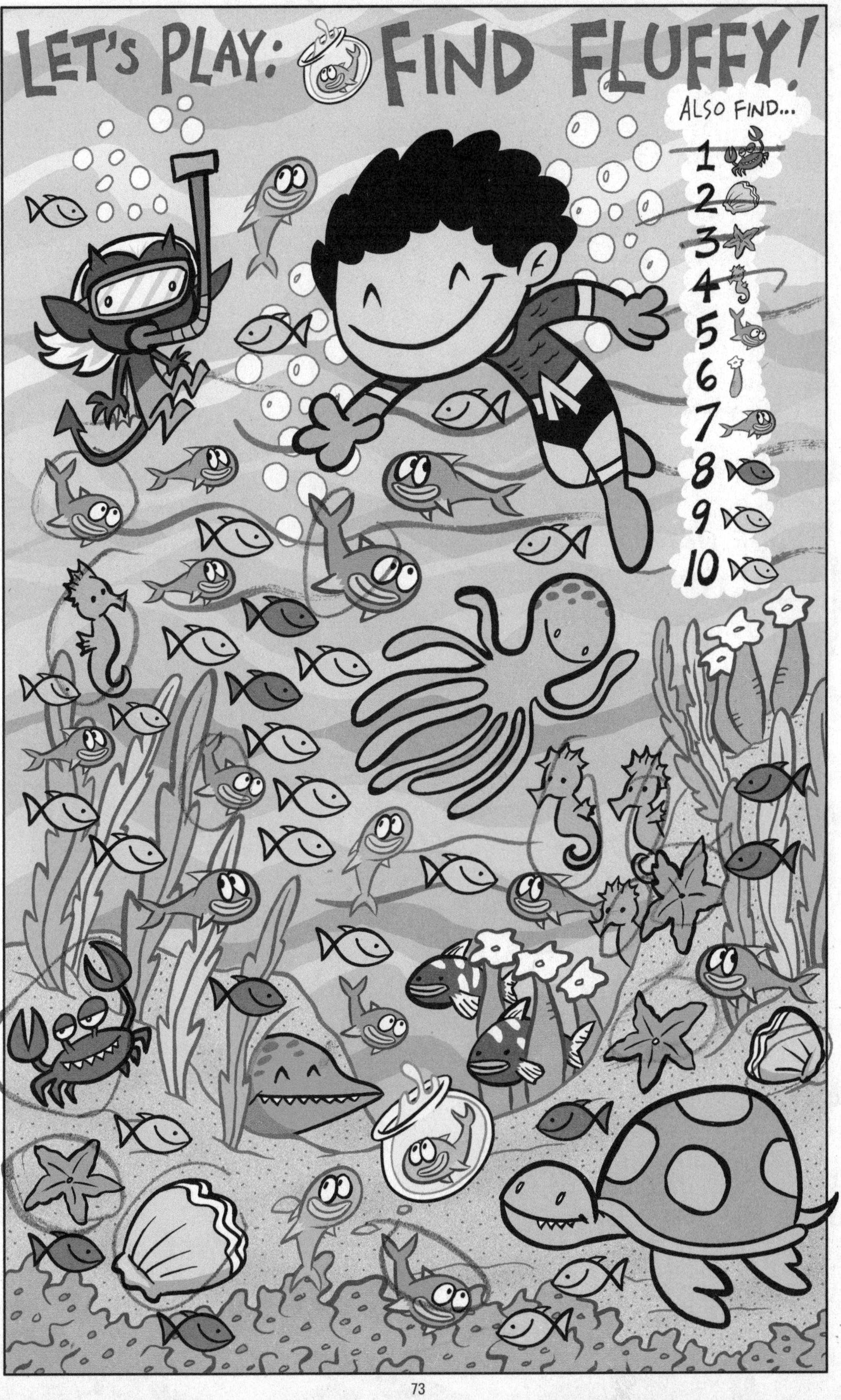
LET'S PLAY: FIND FLUFFY!
ALSO FIND...
1
2
3
4
5
6
7
8
9
10

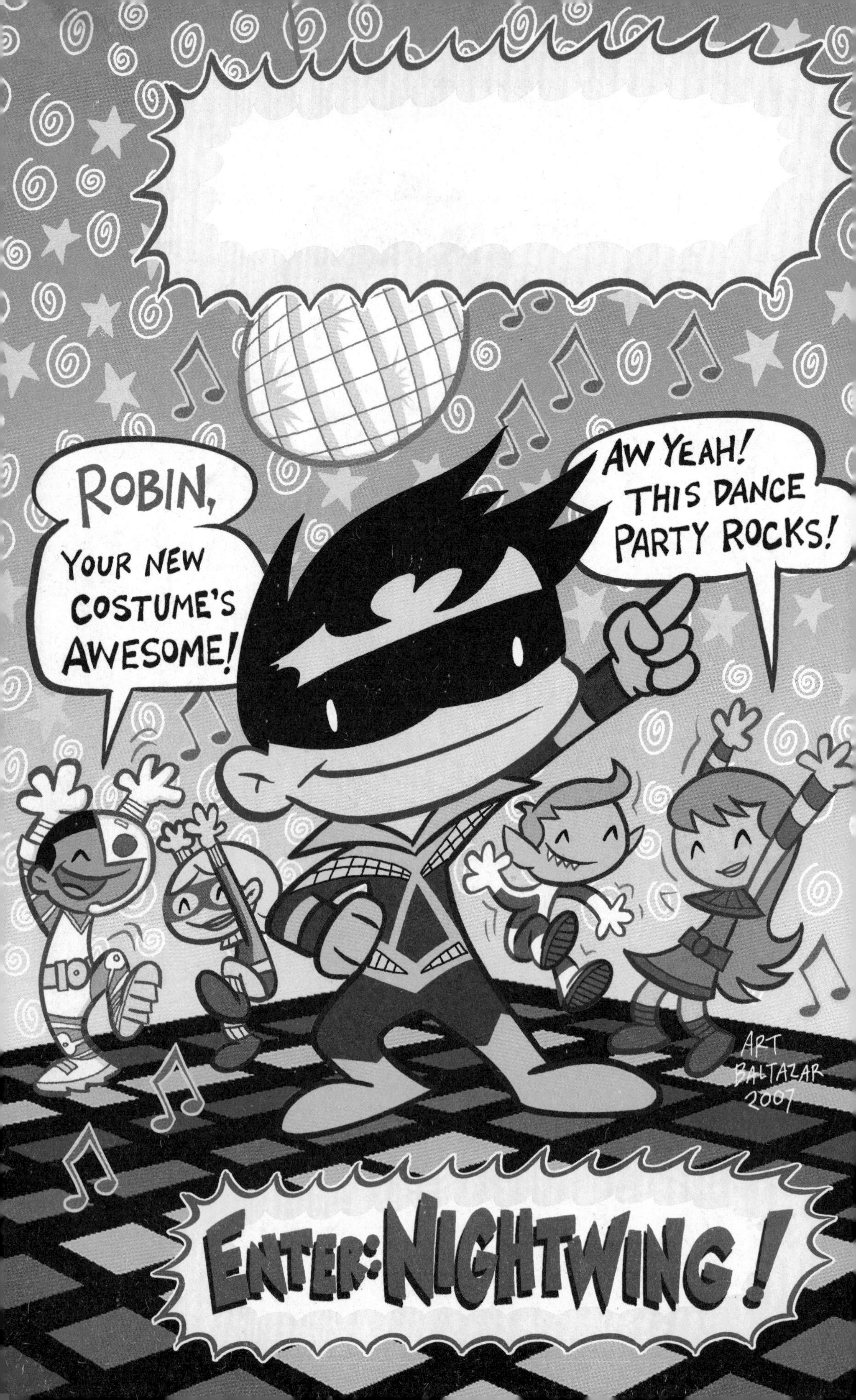
ROBIN, YOUR NEW COSTUME'S AWESOME!
AW YEAH! THIS DANCE PARTY ROCKS!
ART BALTAZAR 2007
ENTER: NIGHTWING!

tiny titans

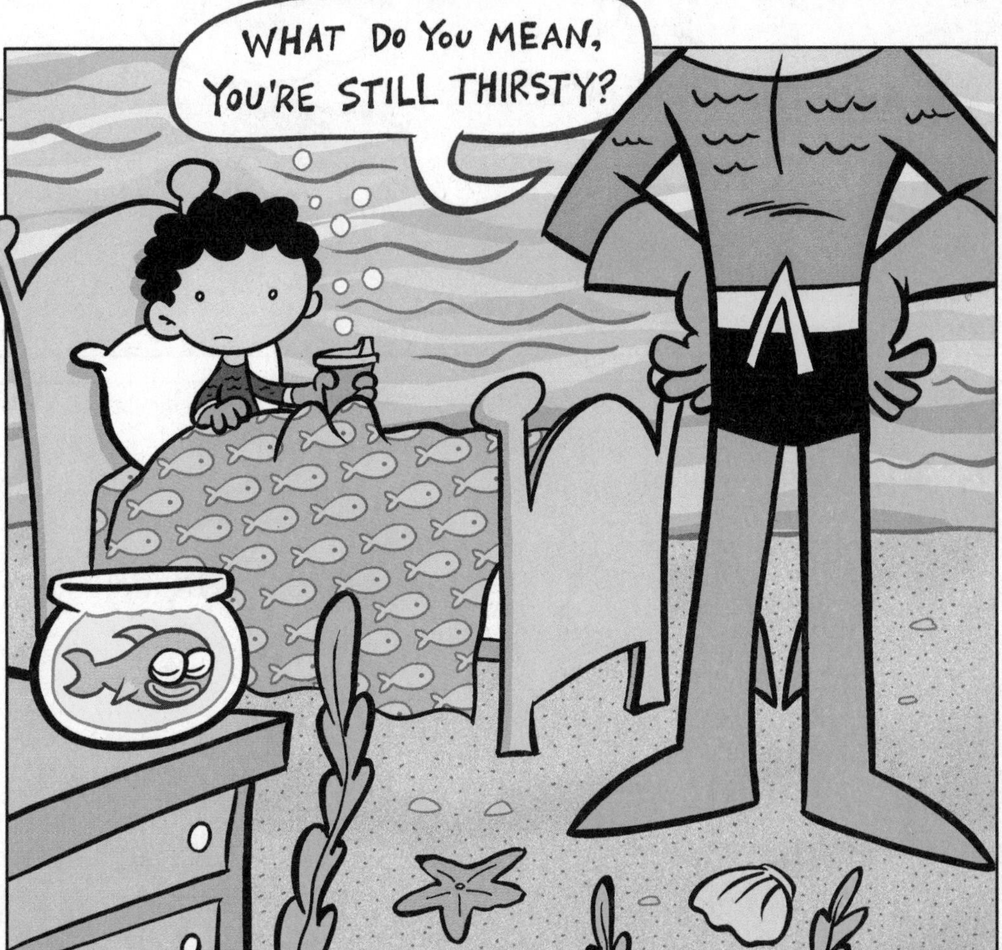
WHAT Do You MEAN, YOU'RE STILL THIRSTY?

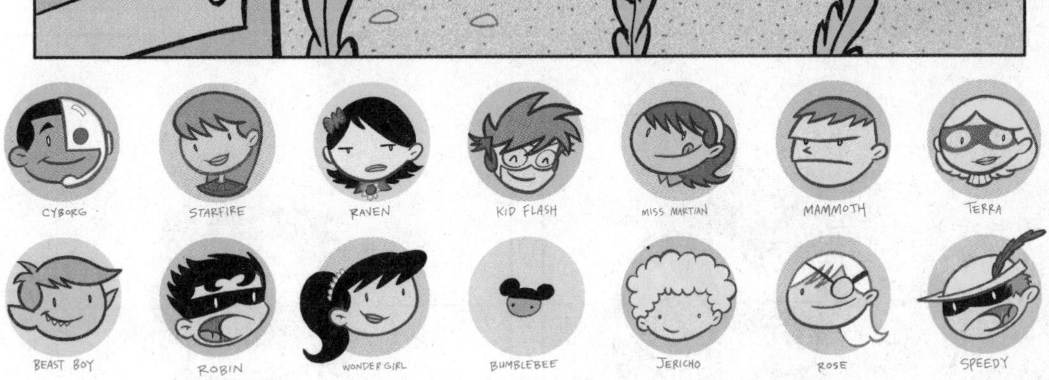
CYBORG
STARFIRE
RAVEN
KID FLASH
MISS MARTIAN
MAMMOTH
TERRA
BEAST BOY
ROBIN
WONDER GIRL
BUMBLEBEE
JERICHO
ROSE
SPEEDY

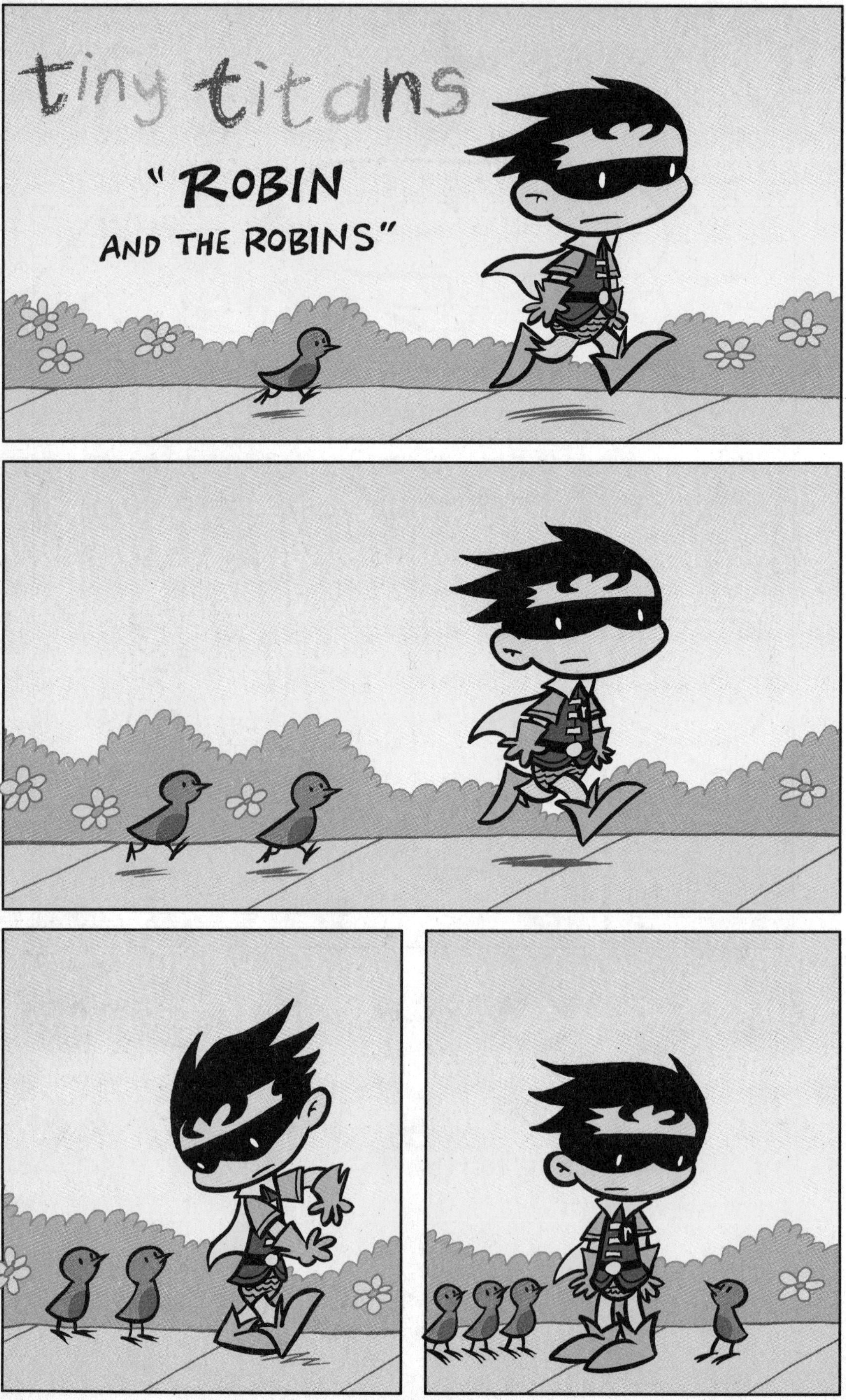
tiny titans
"ROBIN AND THE ROBINS"

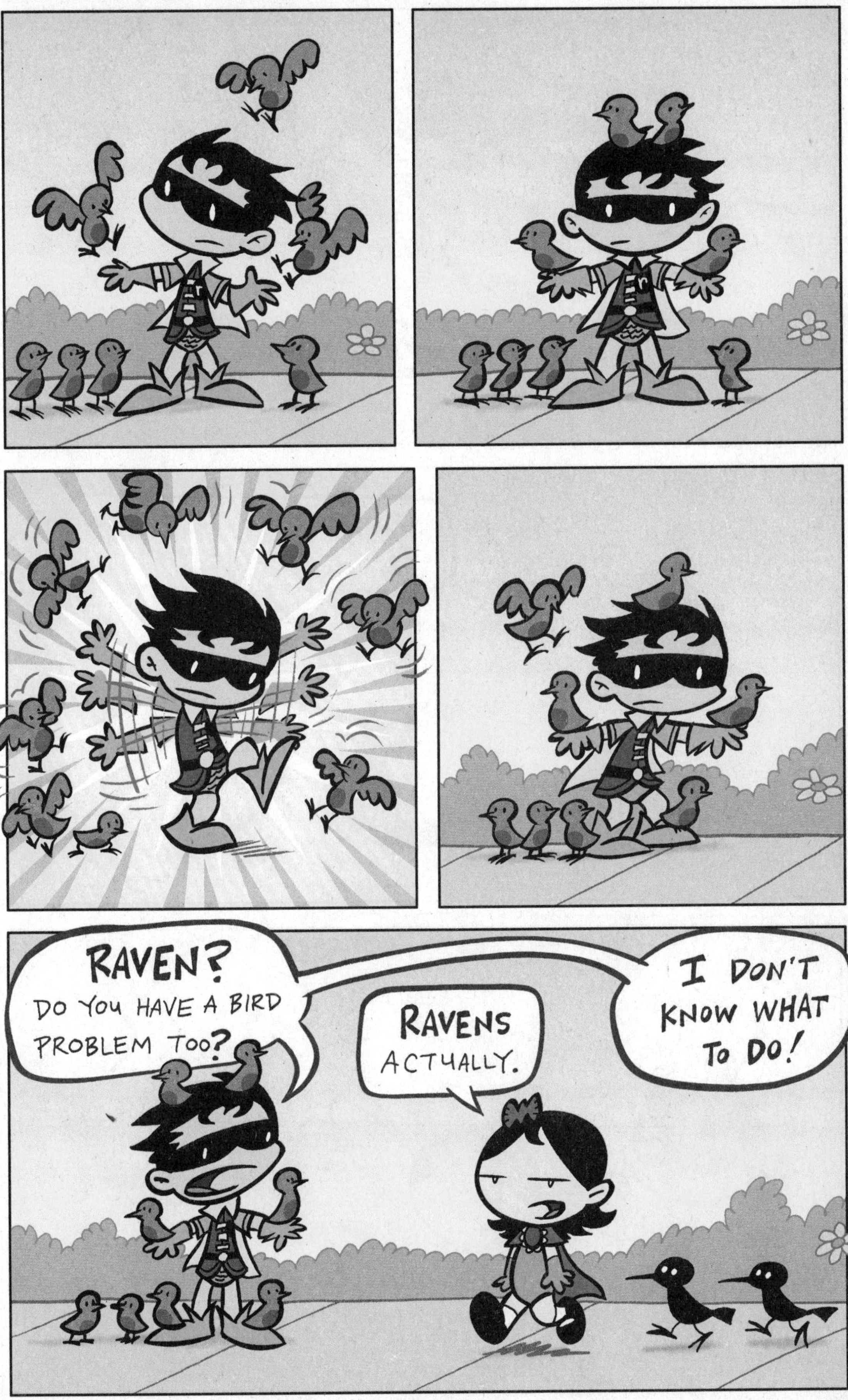
RAVEN? DO YOU HAVE A BIRD PROBLEM TOO?
RAVENS ACTUALLY.
I DON'T KNOW WHAT TO DO!

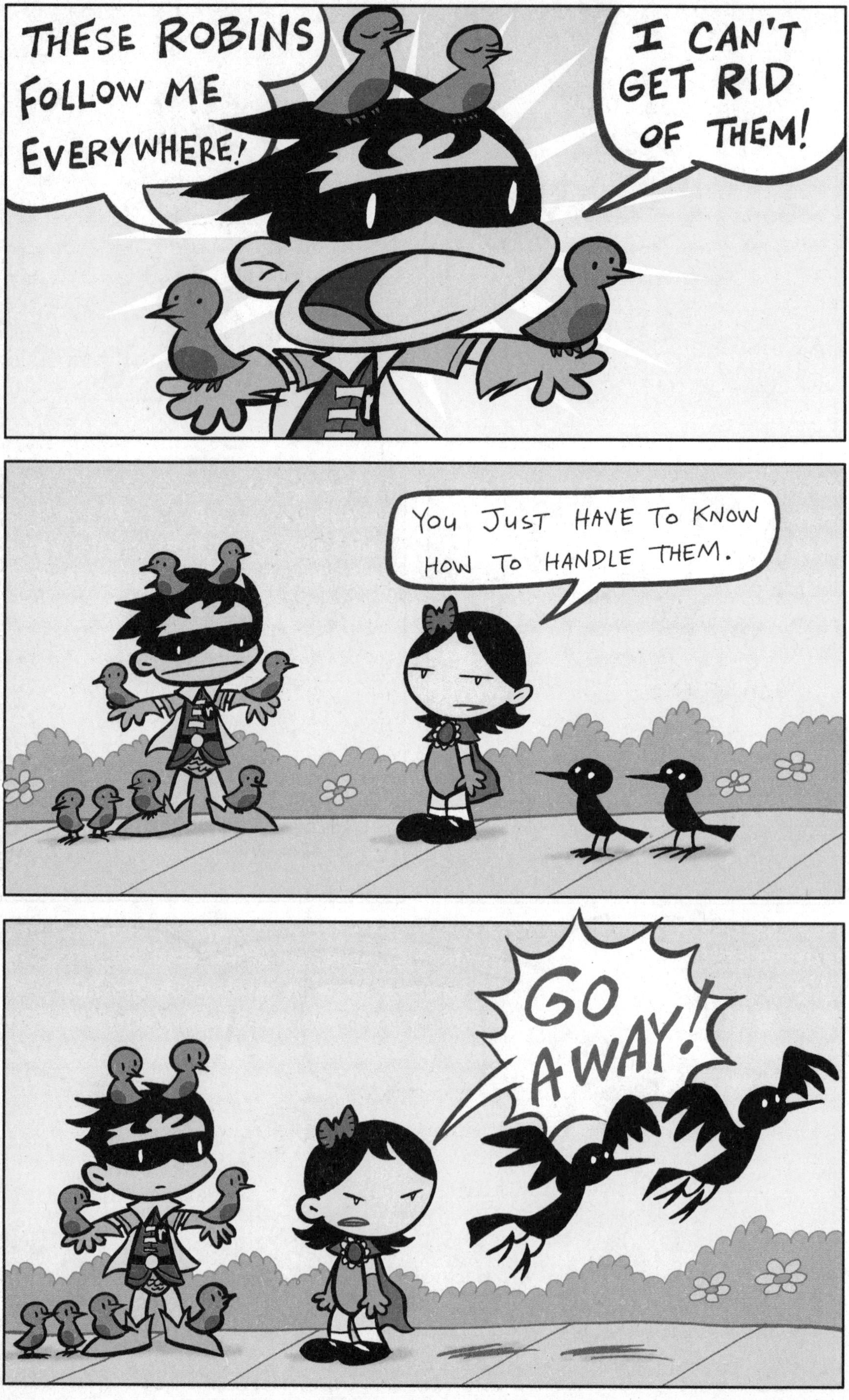
THESE ROBINS FOLLOW ME EVERYWHERE!
I CAN'T GET RID OF THEM!
YOU JUST HAVE TO KNOW HOW TO HANDLE THEM.
GO AWAY!

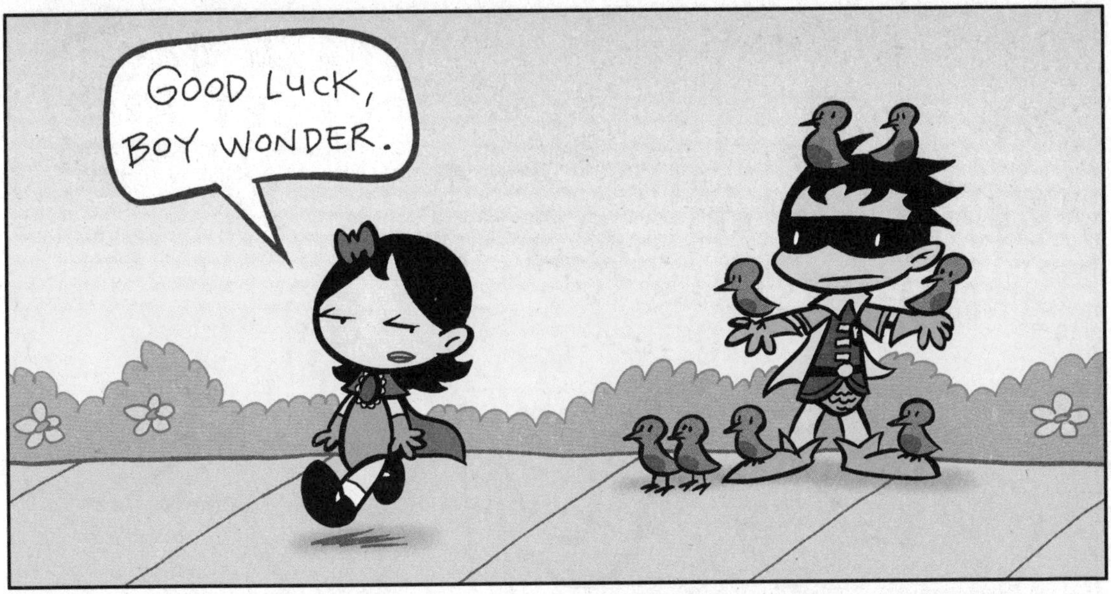
GOOD LUCK, BOY WONDER.

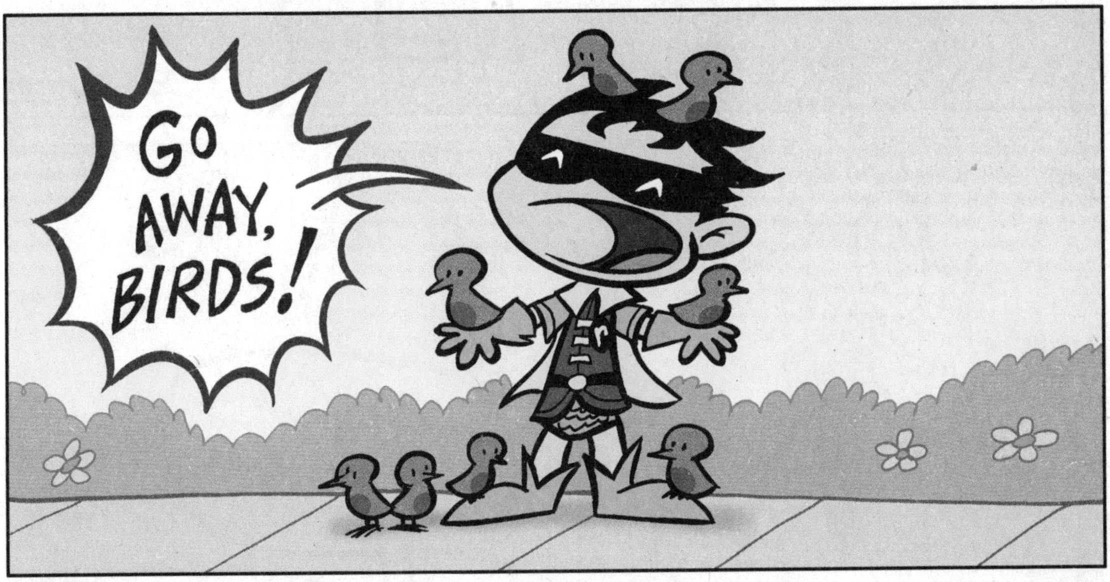
GO AWAY, BIRDS!

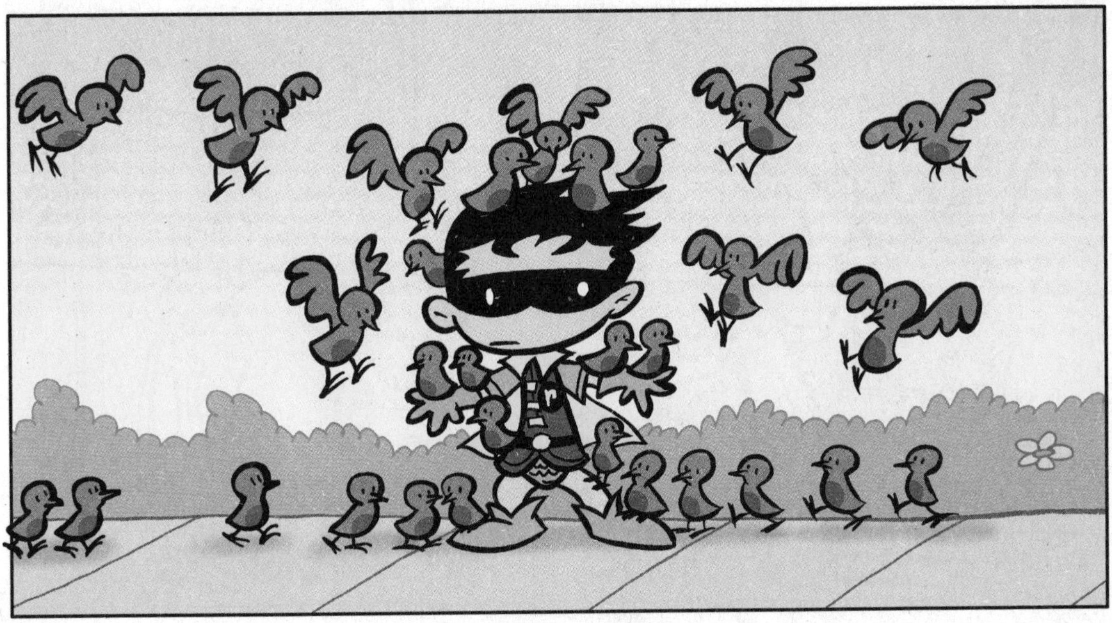

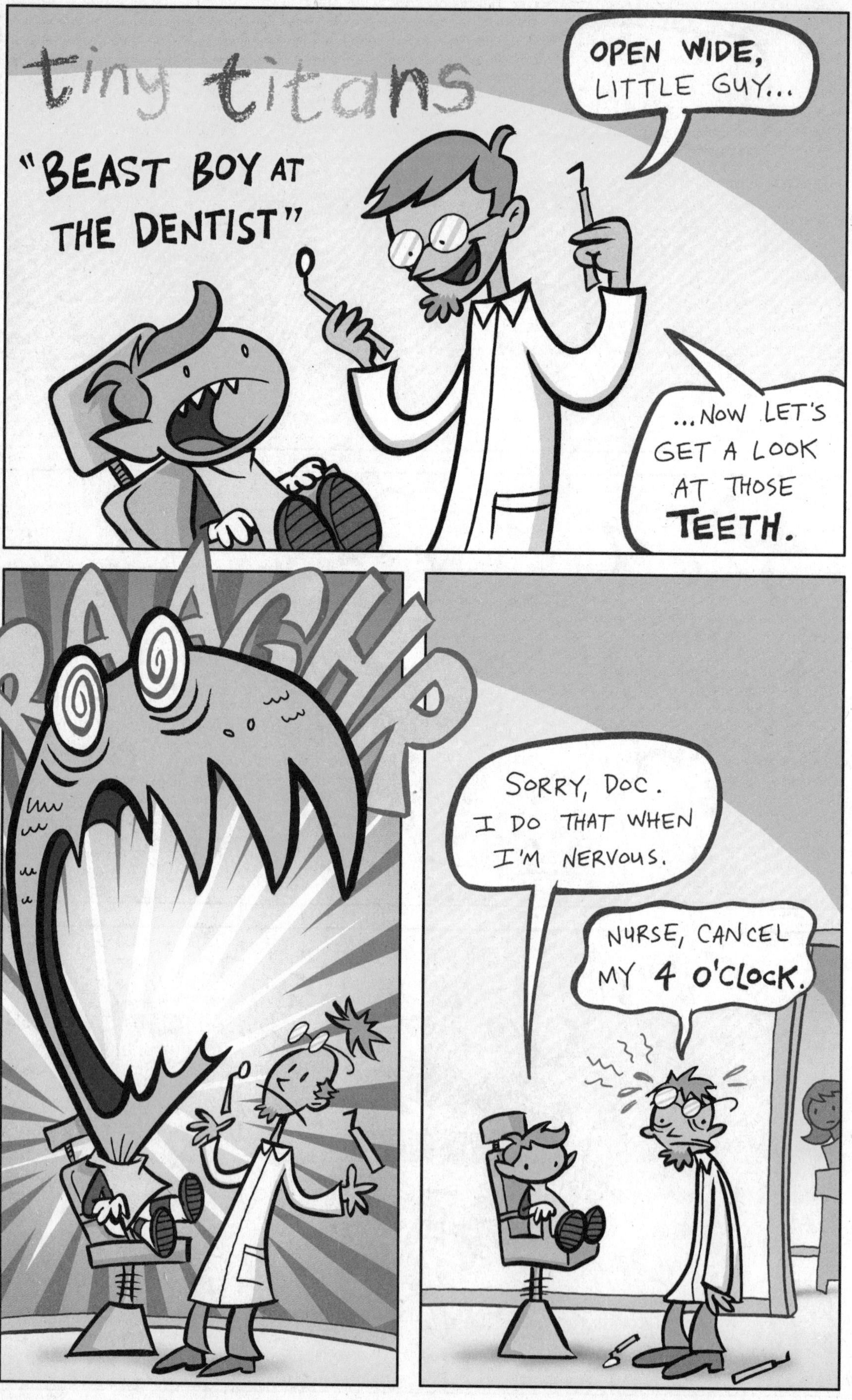
tiny titans
"BEAST BOY AT THE DENTIST"
OPEN WIDE, LITTLE GUY...
...NOW LET'S GET A LOOK AT THOSE TEETH.
RAAGHR
SORRY, DOC. I DO THAT WHEN I'M NERVOUS.
NURSE, CANCEL MY 4 O'CLOCK.

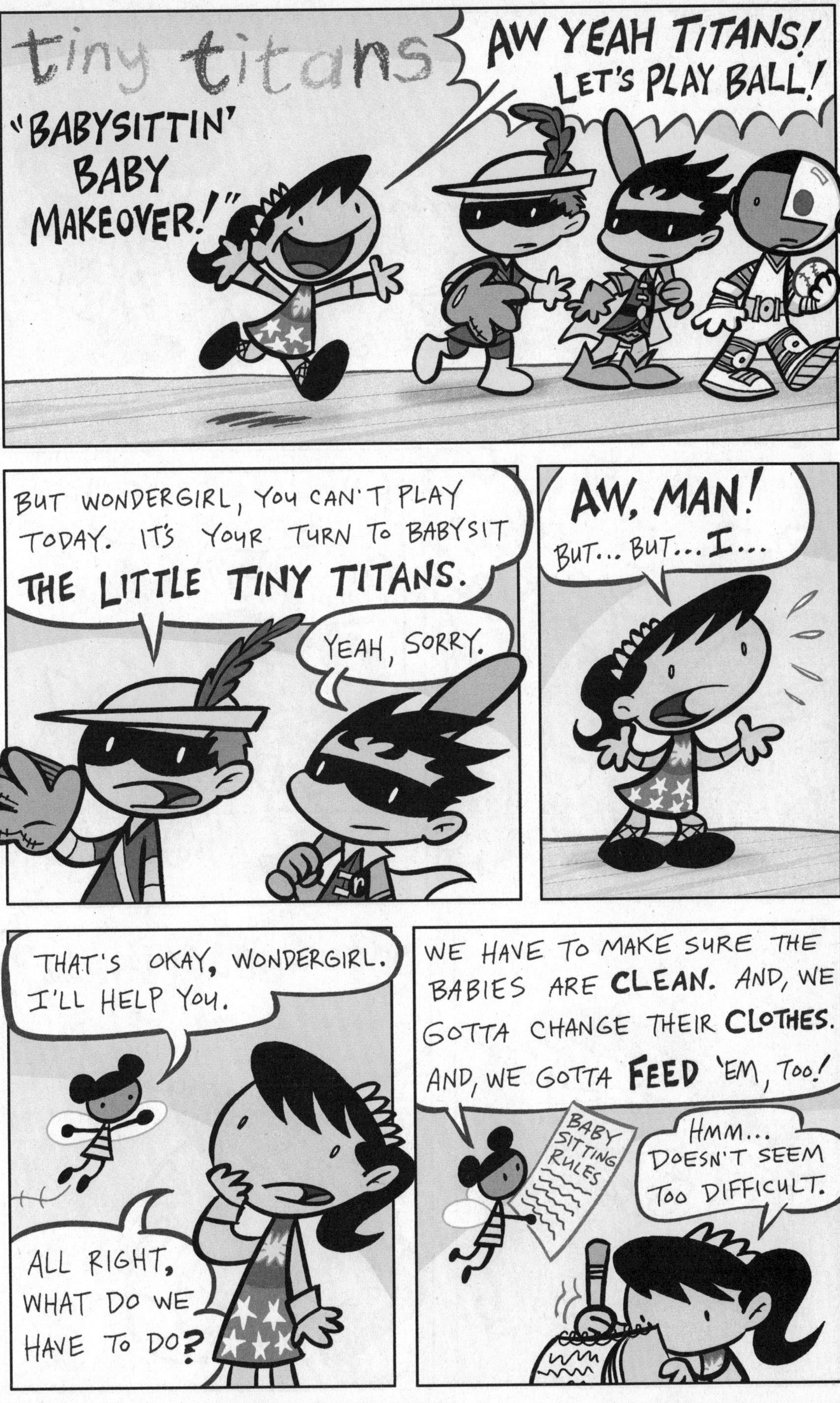
tiny titans
"BABYSITTIN' BABY MAKEOVER!"
AW YEAH TITANS! LET'S PLAY BALL!
BUT WONDERGIRL, YOU CAN'T PLAY TODAY. IT'S YOUR TURN TO BABYSIT THE LITTLE TINY TITANS.
YEAH, SORRY.
AW, MAN! BUT... BUT... I...
THAT'S OKAY, WONDERGIRL. I'LL HELP YOU.
ALL RIGHT, WHAT DO WE HAVE TO DO?
WE HAVE TO MAKE SURE THE BABIES ARE CLEAN. AND, WE GOTTA CHANGE THEIR CLOTHES. AND, WE GOTTA FEED 'EM, TOO!
BABY SITTING RULES
HMM... DOESN'T SEEM TOO DIFFICULT.

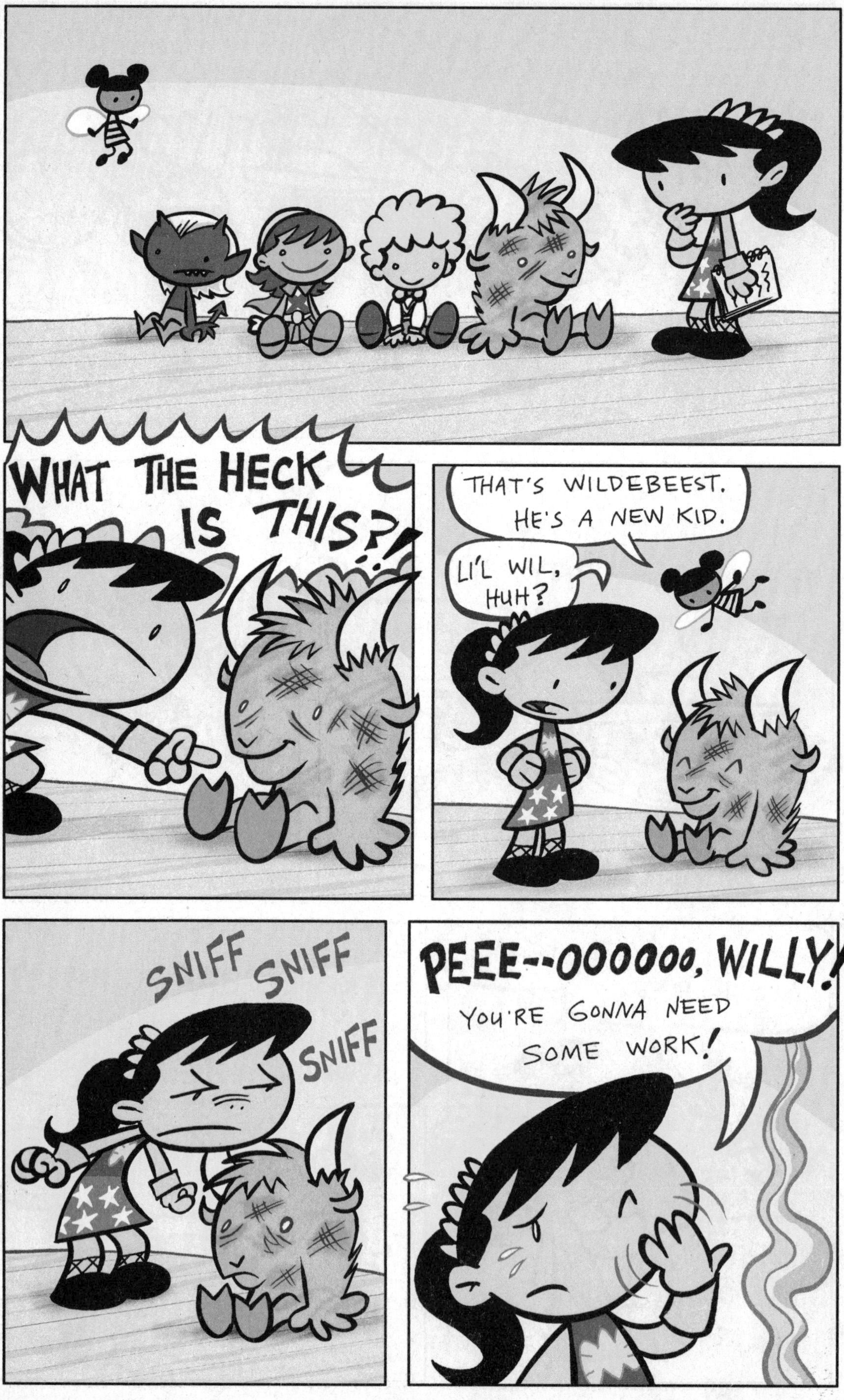
WHAT THE HECK IS THIS?!
THAT'S WILDEBEEST. HE'S A NEW KID.
LI'L WIL, HUH?
SNIFF SNIFF
SNIFF
PEEE--OOOOOO, WILLY!
YOU'RE GONNA NEED SOME WORK!

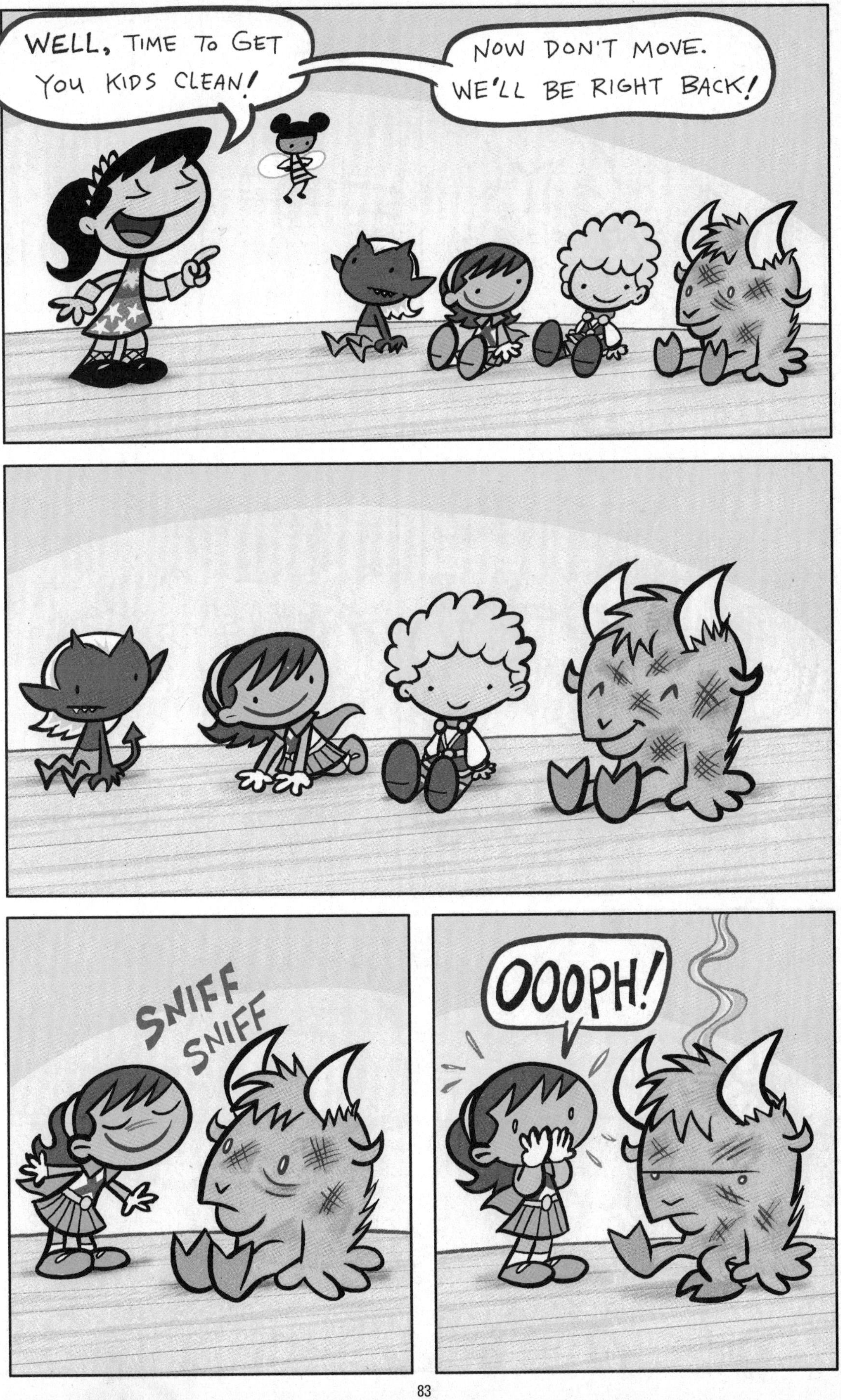
WELL, TIME TO GET YOU KIDS CLEAN!
NOW DON'T MOVE. WE'LL BE RIGHT BACK!
SNIFF SNIFF
OOOPH!

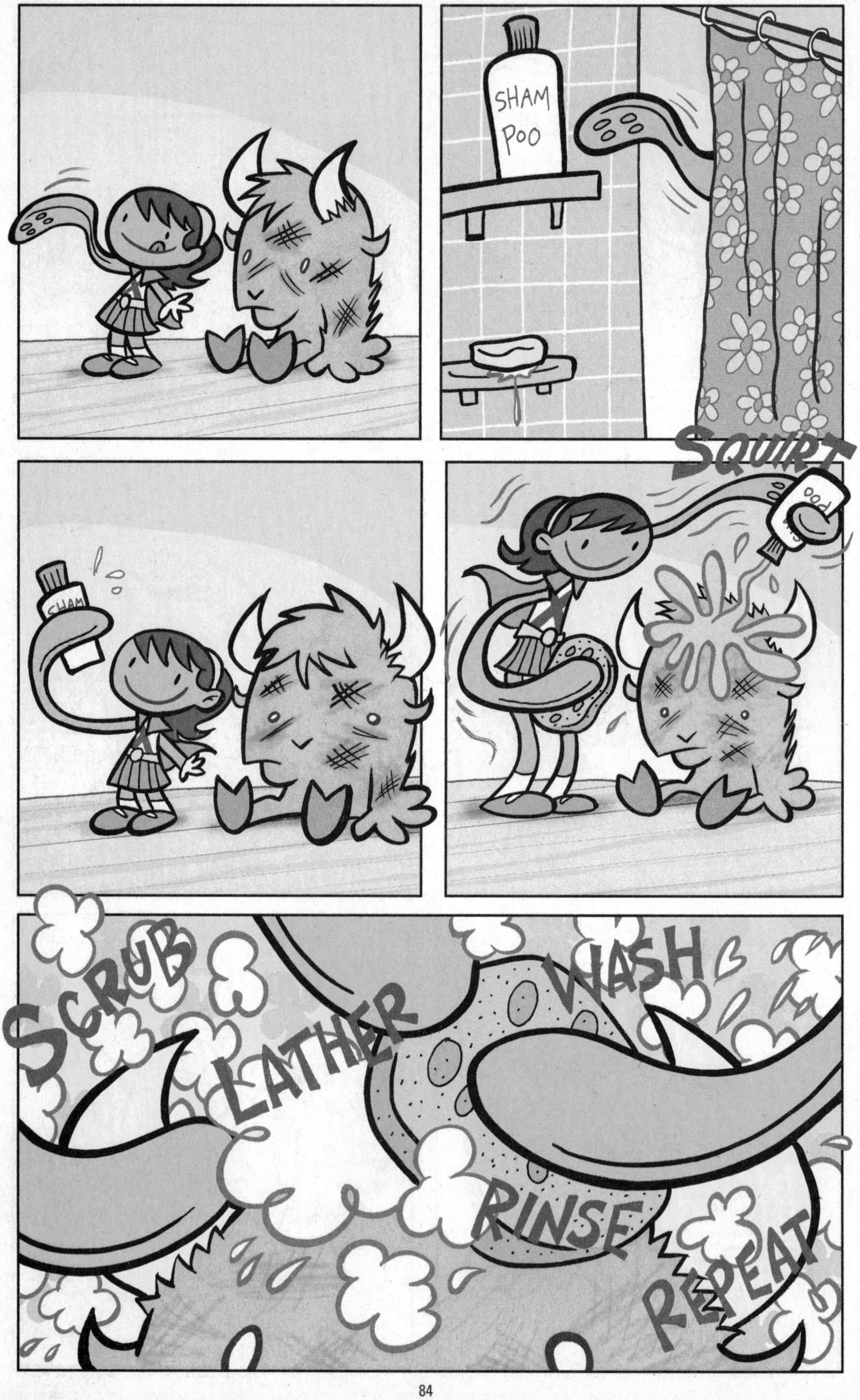
SHAM
POO
SHAM
SQUIRT
POO
SCRUB
LATHER
WASH
RINSE
REPEAT

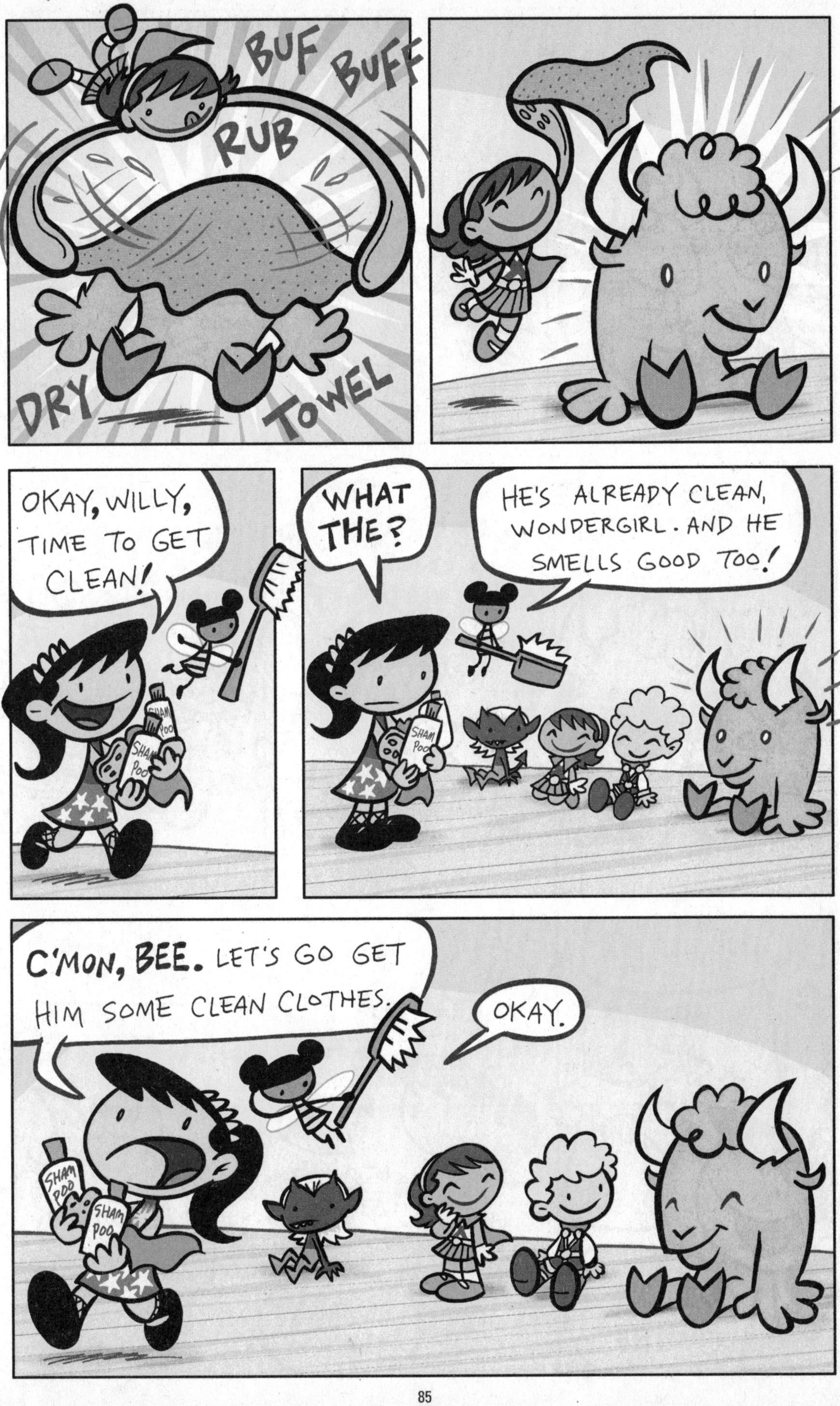
BUF
BUFF
RUB
DRY
TOWEL
OKAY, WILLY, TIME TO GET CLEAN!
SHAMPOO
SHAMPOO
WHAT THE?
HE'S ALREADY CLEAN, WONDERGIRL. AND HE SMELLS GOOD TOO!
SHAMPOO
C'MON, BEE. LET'S GO GET HIM SOME CLEAN CLOTHES.
OKAY.
SHAMPOO
SHAMPOO

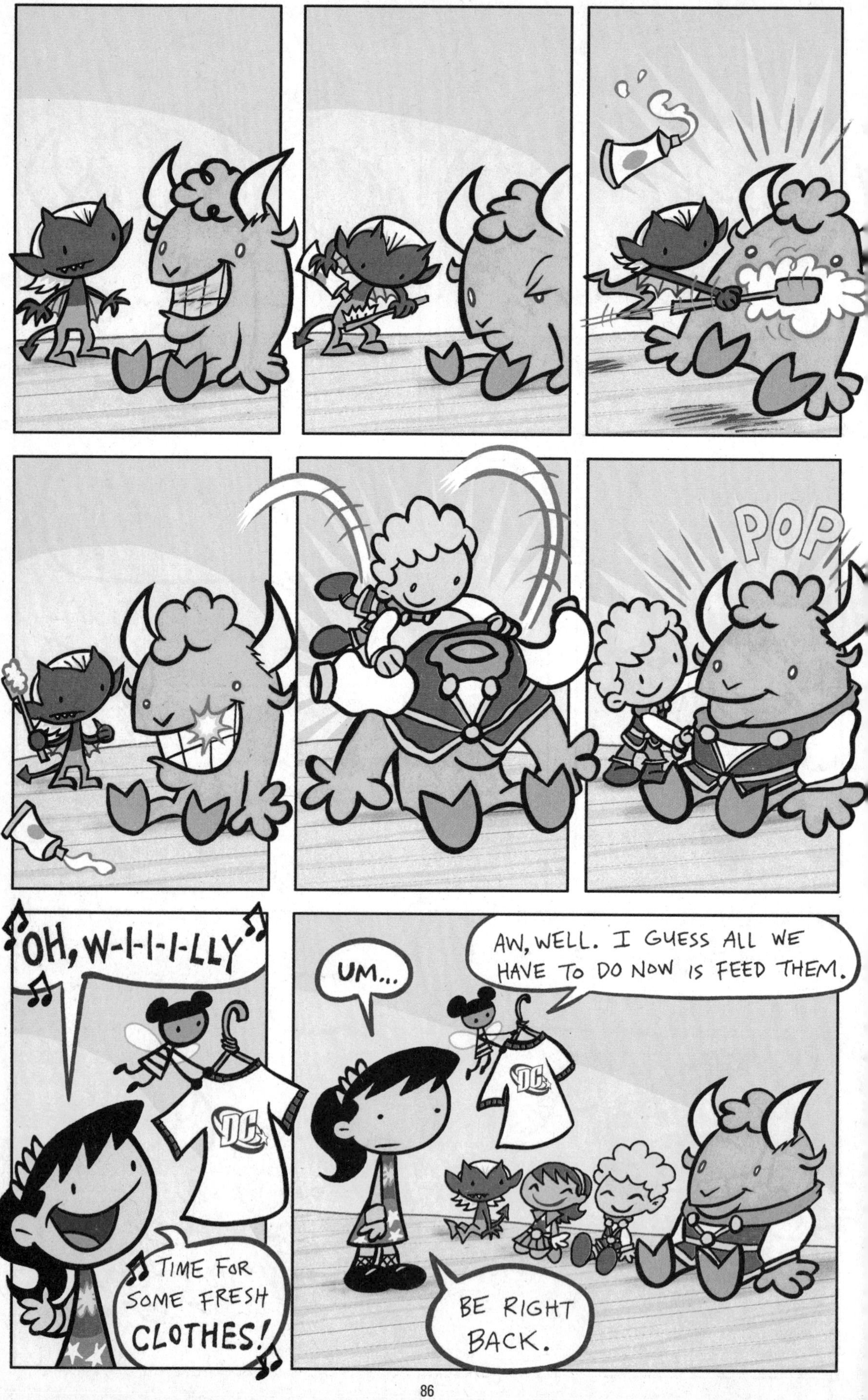
POP
OH, W-I-I-I-LLY
TIME FOR SOME FRESH CLOTHES!
UM...
AW, WELL. I GUESS ALL WE HAVE TO DO NOW IS FEED THEM.
BE RIGHT BACK.

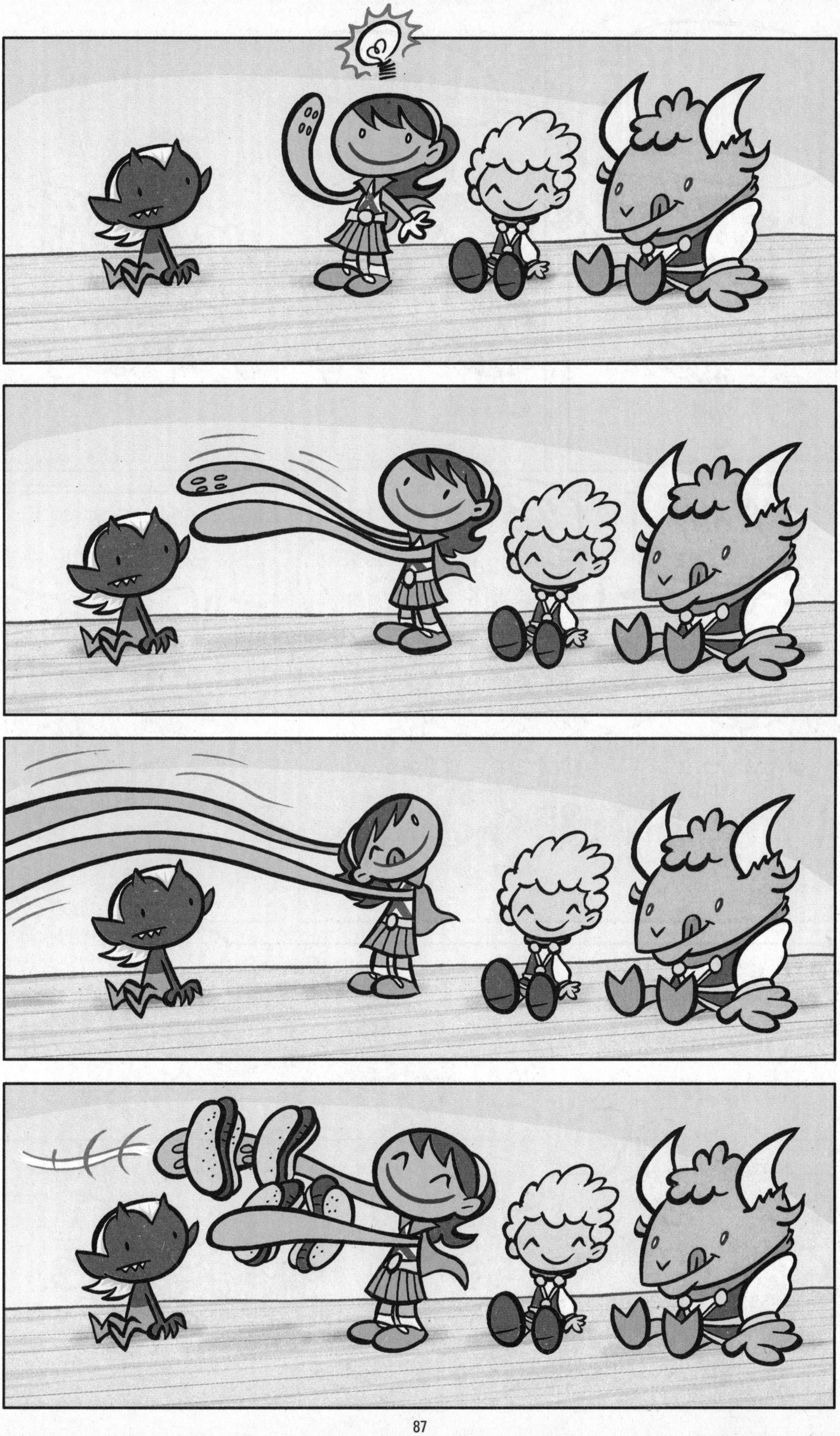

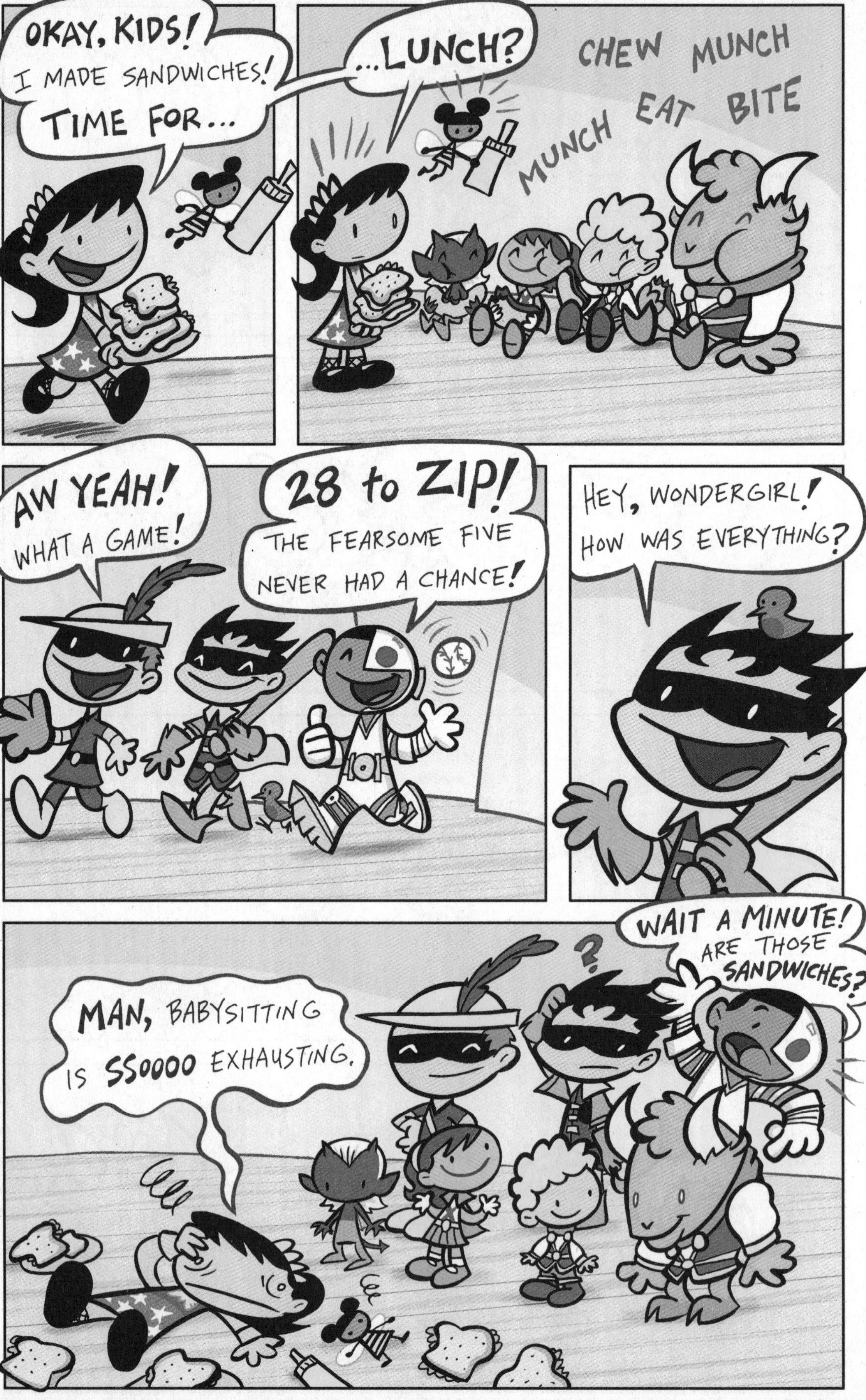
OKAY, KIDS! I MADE SANDWICHES! TIME FOR...
...LUNCH?
CHEW MUNCH
MUNCH EAT BITE
AW YEAH! WHAT A GAME!
28 to ZIP! THE FEARSOME FIVE NEVER HAD A CHANCE!
HEY, WONDERGIRL! HOW WAS EVERYTHING?
MAN, BABYSITTING IS SSOOOO EXHAUSTING.
?
WAIT A MINUTE! ARE THOSE SANDWICHES?

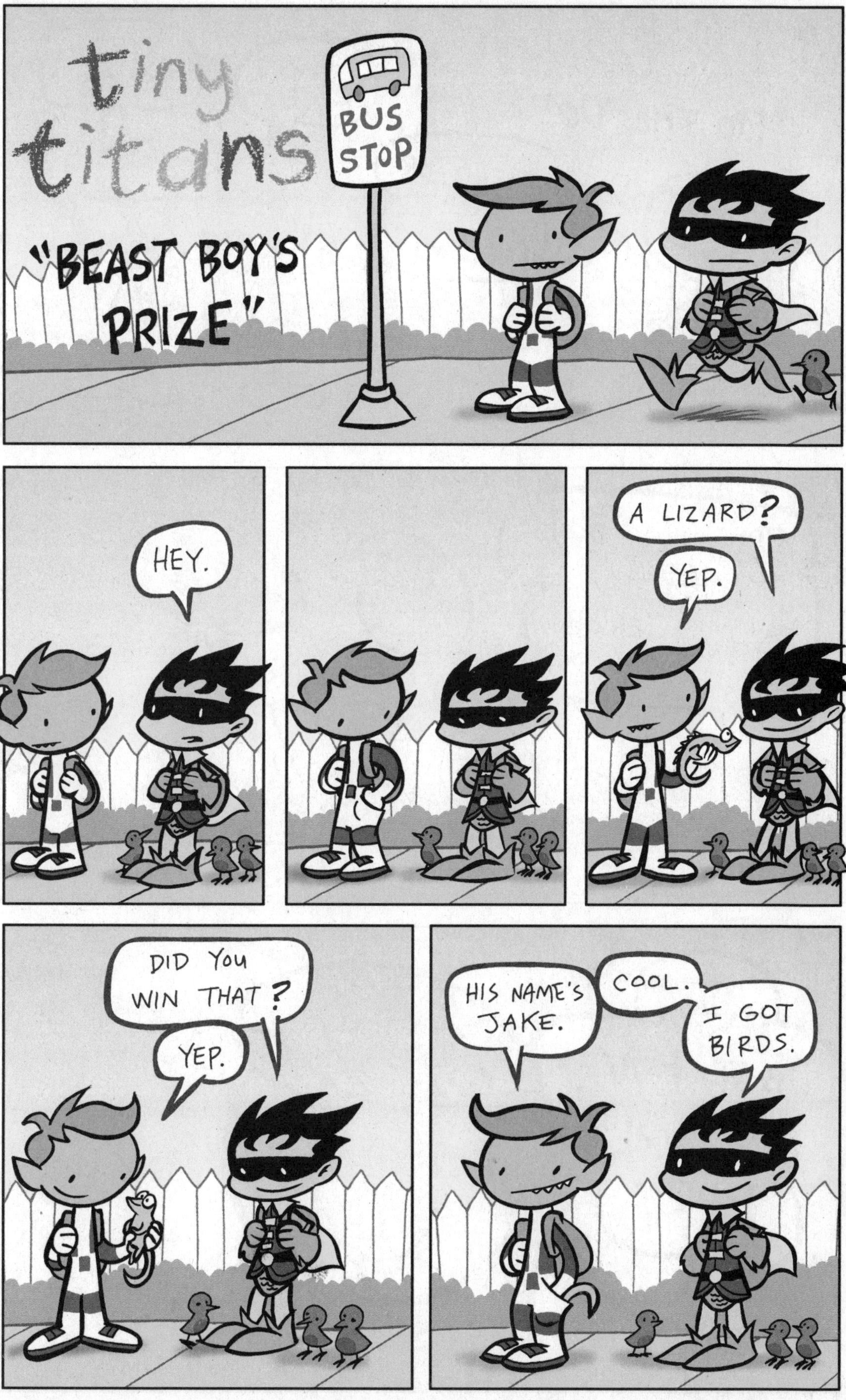
tiny titans
BUS STOP
"BEAST BOY'S PRIZE"
HEY.
A LIZARD?
YEP.
DID YOU WIN THAT?
YEP.
HIS NAME'S JAKE.
COOL.
I GOT BIRDS.

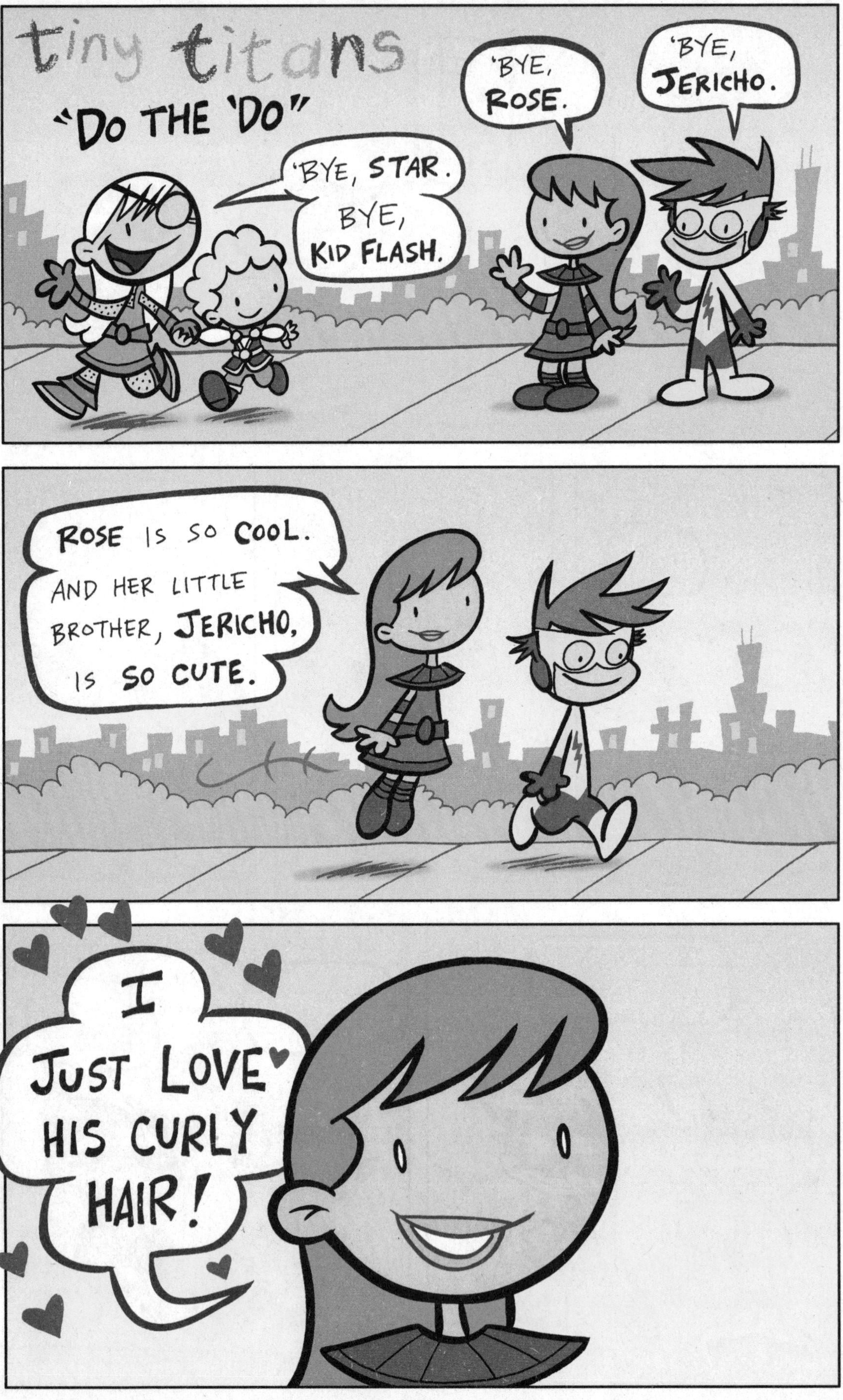
tiny titans
"DO THE 'DO"
'BYE, STAR. BYE, KID FLASH.
'BYE, ROSE.
'BYE, JERICHO.
ROSE IS SO COOL. AND HER LITTLE BROTHER, JERICHO, IS SO CUTE.
I JUST LOVE HIS CURLY HAIR!

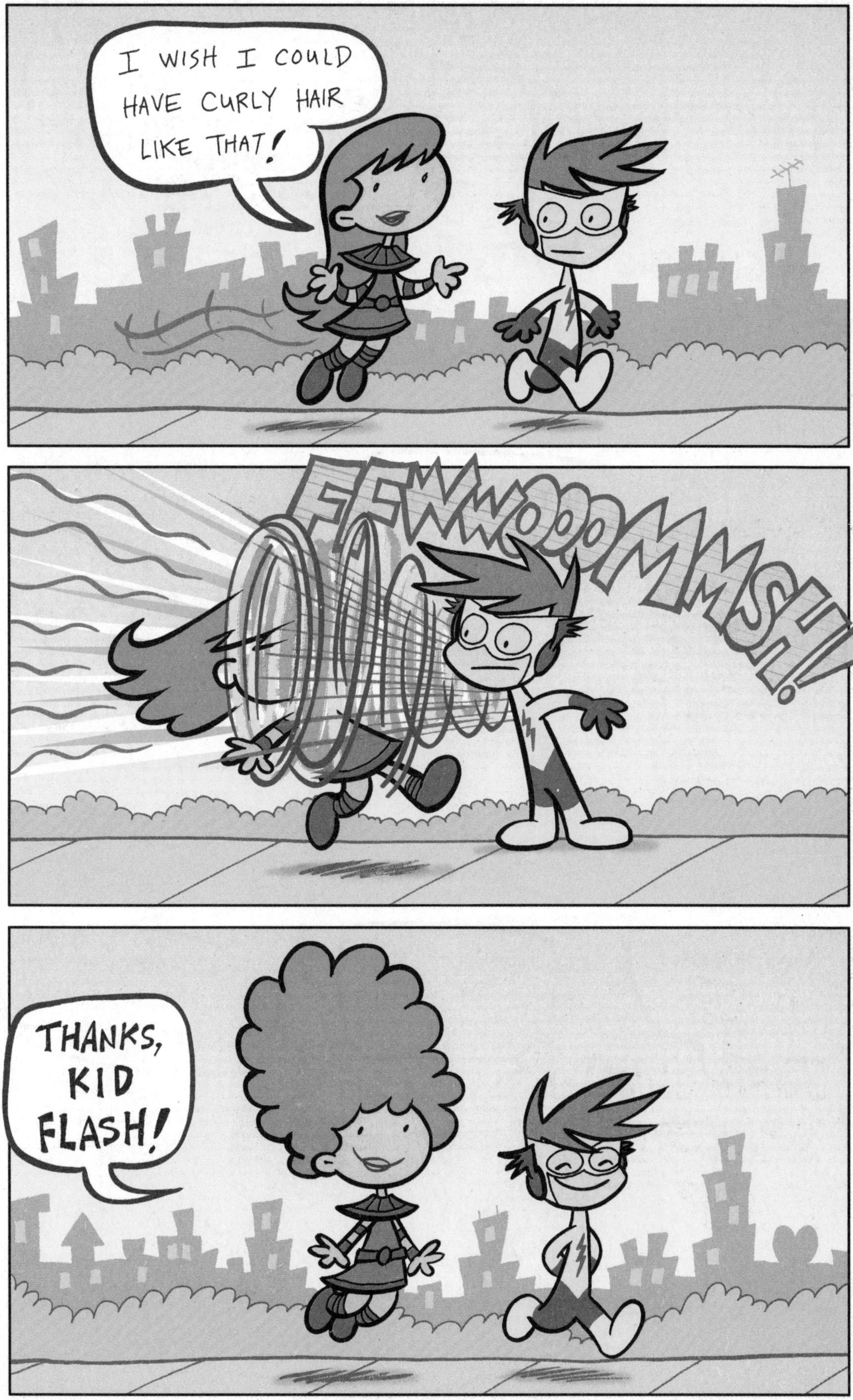
I WISH I COULD HAVE CURLY HAIR LIKE THAT!
FFWWOOOMMMSH!!
THANKS, KID FLASH!

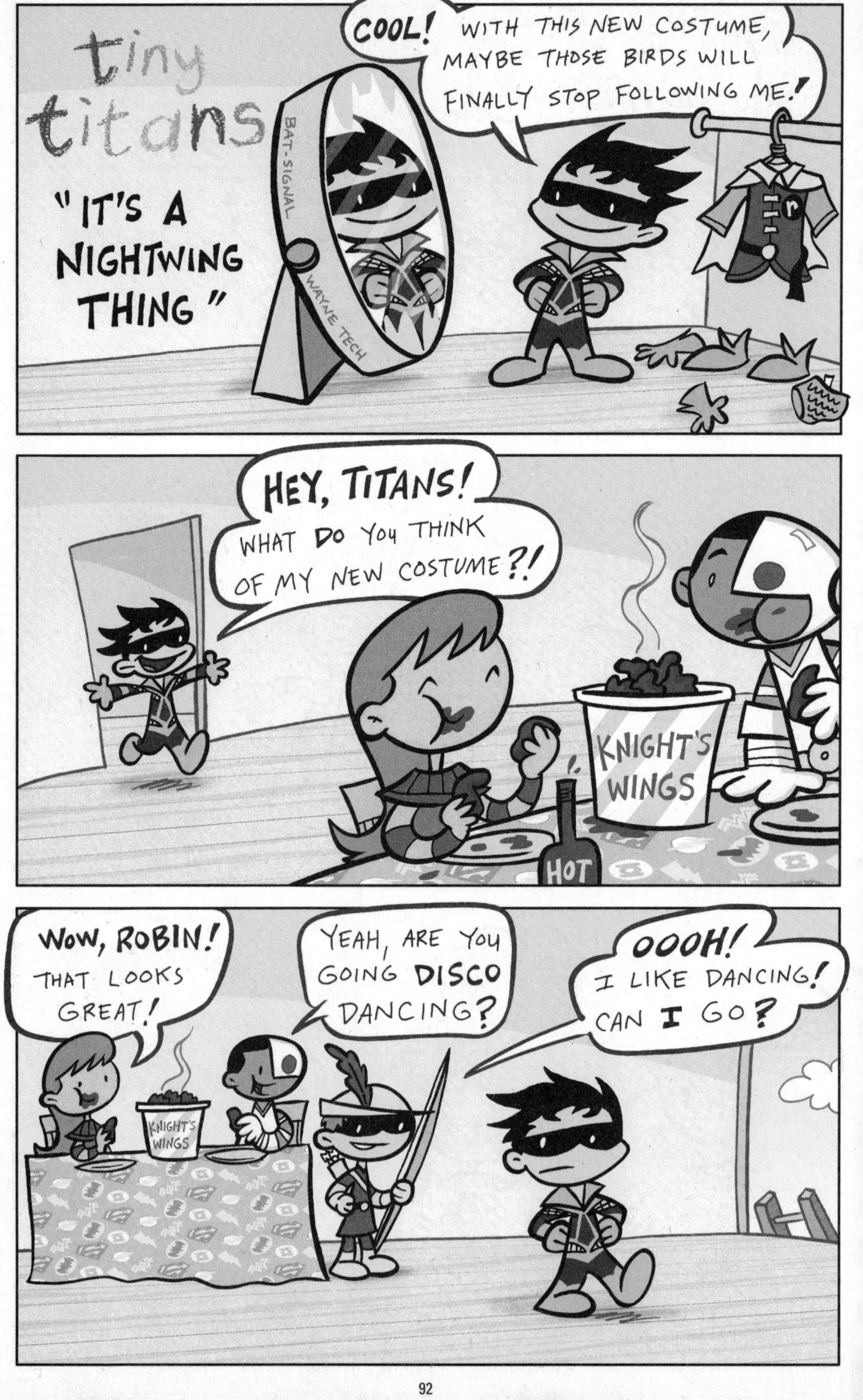
tiny titans
"IT'S A NIGHTWING THING"
BAT-SIGNAL
WAYNE TECH
COOL! WITH THIS NEW COSTUME, MAYBE THOSE BIRDS WILL FINALLY STOP FOLLOWING ME!
HEY, TITANS! WHAT DO YOU THINK OF MY NEW COSTUME?!
KNIGHT'S WINGS
HOT
WOW, ROBIN! THAT LOOKS GREAT!
YEAH, ARE YOU GOING DISCO DANCING?
OOOH! I LIKE DANCING! CAN I GO?
KNIGHT'S WINGS

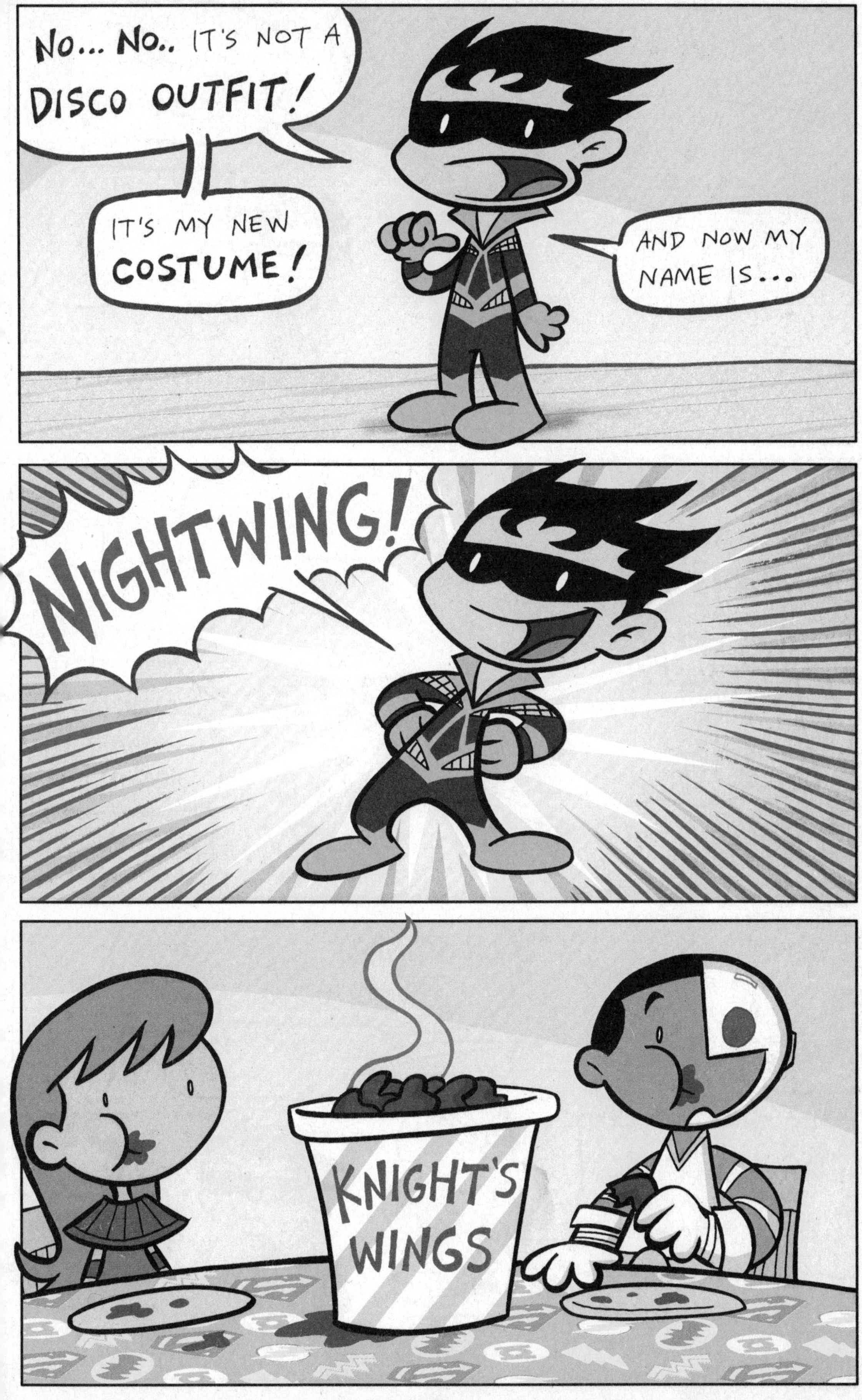
No... No.. IT'S NOT A DISCO OUTFIT!
IT'S MY NEW COSTUME!
AND NOW MY NAME IS...
NIGHTWING!
KNIGHT'S WINGS

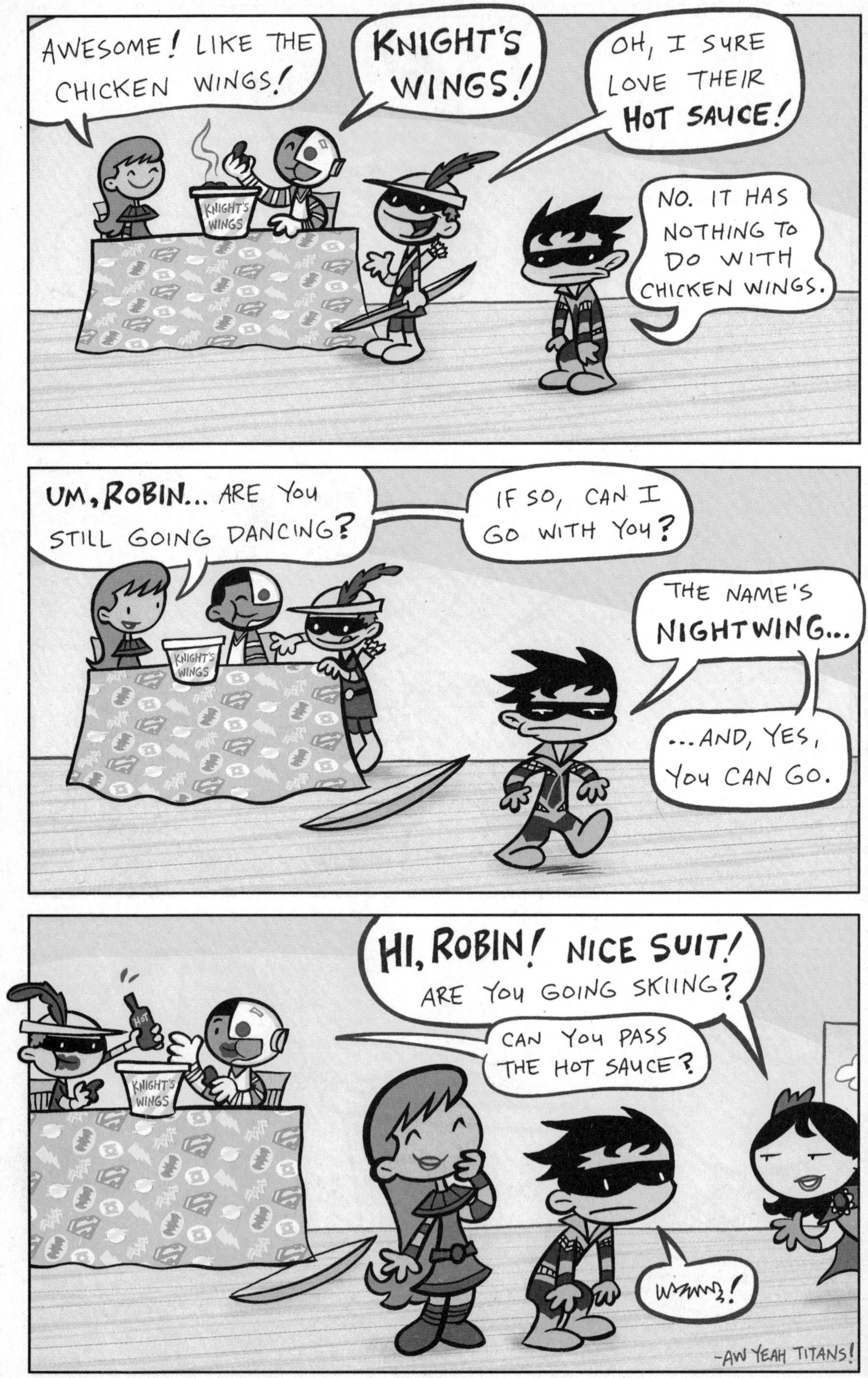
AWESOME! LIKE THE CHICKEN WINGS!
KNIGHT'S WINGS!
KNIGHT'S WINGS
OH, I SURE LOVE THEIR HOT SAUCE!
NO. IT HAS NOTHING TO DO WITH CHICKEN WINGS.
UM, ROBIN... ARE YOU STILL GOING DANCING?
IF SO, CAN I GO WITH YOU?
KNIGHT'S WINGS
THE NAME'S NIGHTWING...
...AND, YES, YOU CAN GO.
HOT
KNIGHT'S WINGS
HI, ROBIN! NICE SUIT! ARE YOU GOING SKIING?
CAN YOU PASS THE HOT SAUCE?
-AW YEAH TITANS!

tiny titans
MATCH GAME!

WHICH TWO TINY TITANS ARE THE SAME?

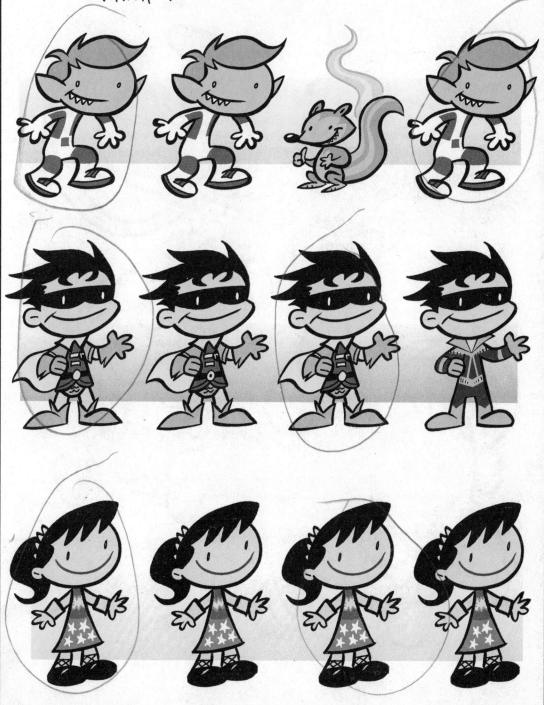

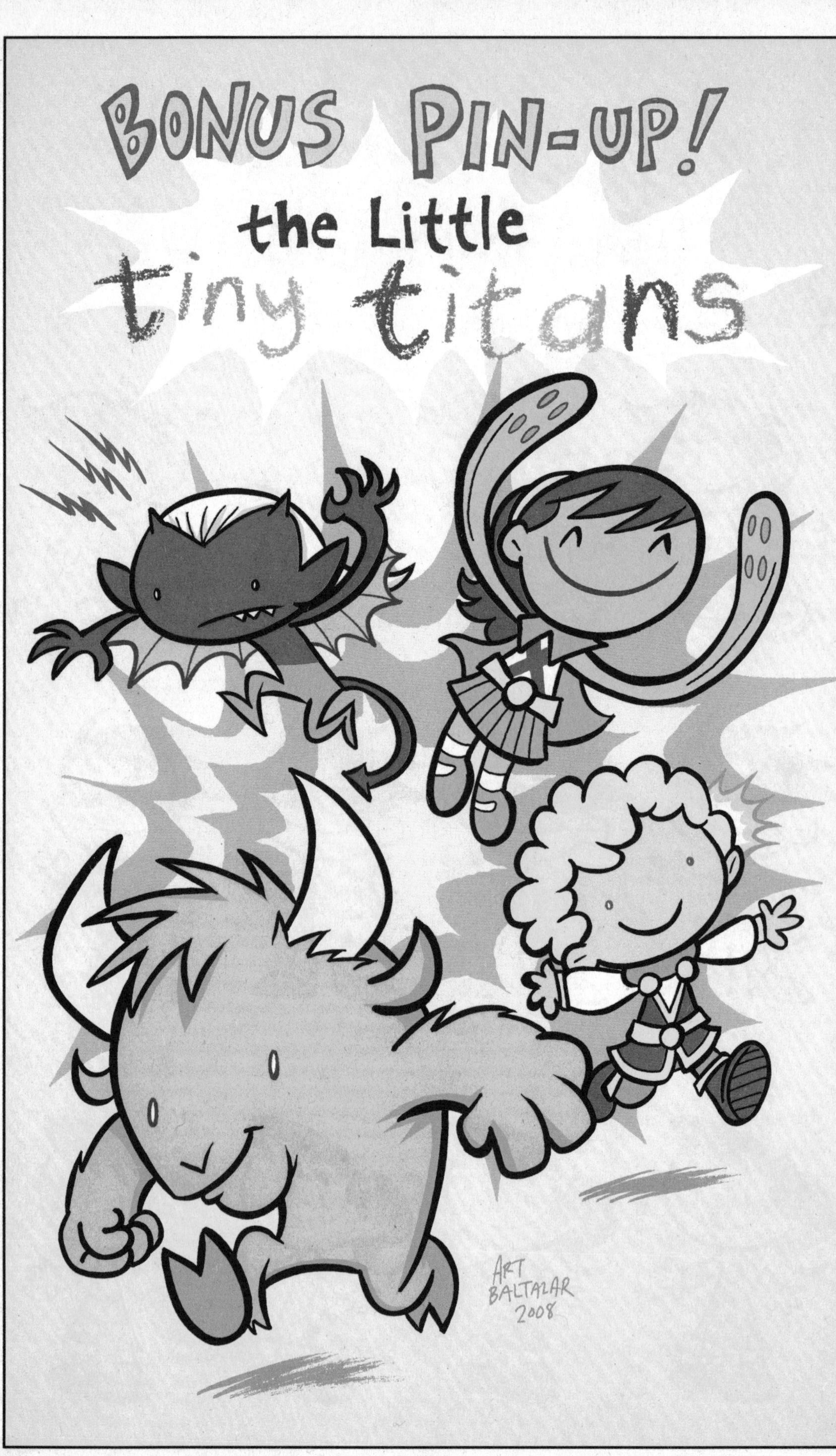
BONUS PIN-UP!
the Little
tiny titans
ART BALTAZAR 2008

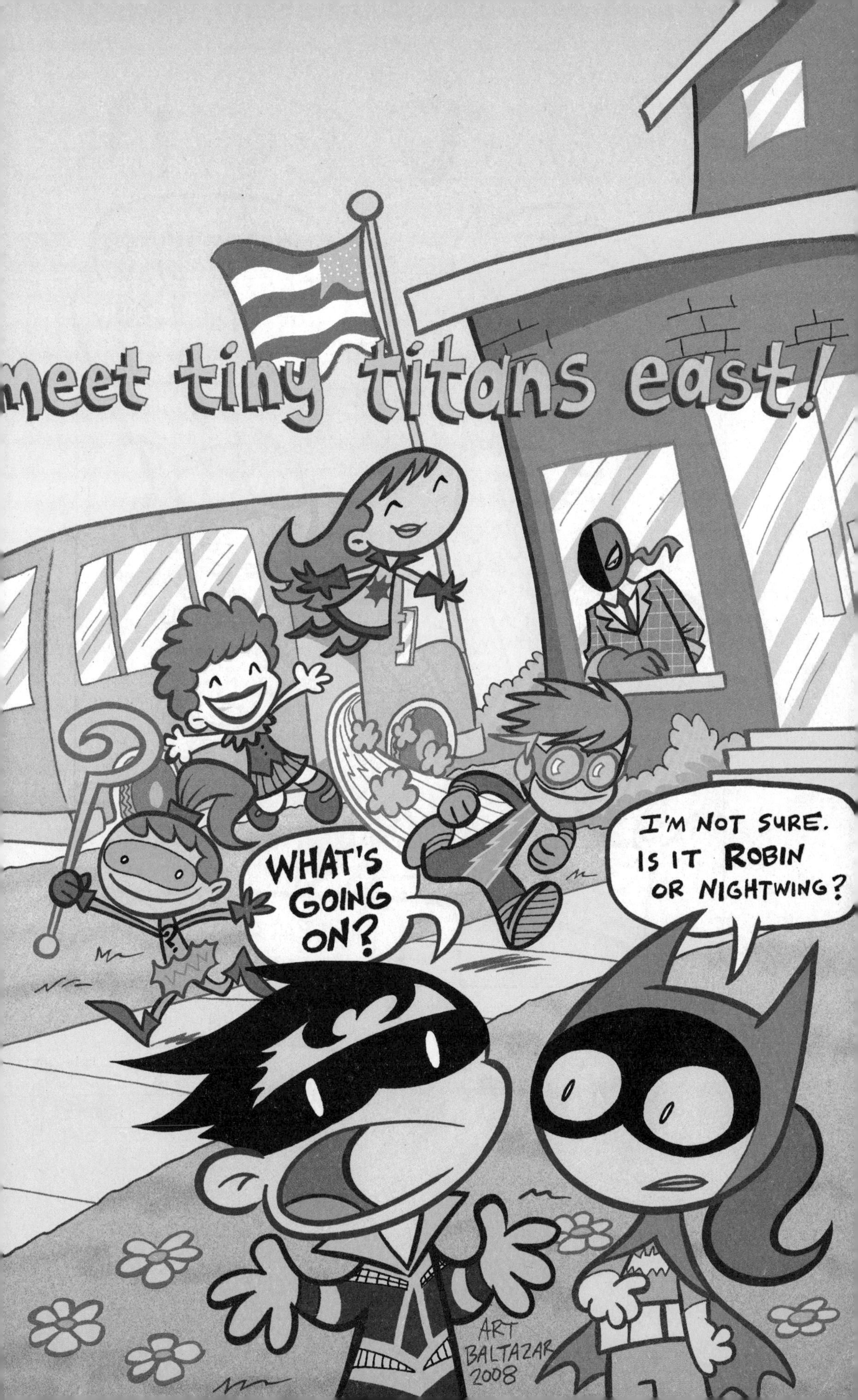
meet tiny titans east!
WHAT'S GOING ON?
I'M NOT SURE. IS IT ROBIN OR NIGHTWING?
ART BALTAZAR 2008

tiny titans

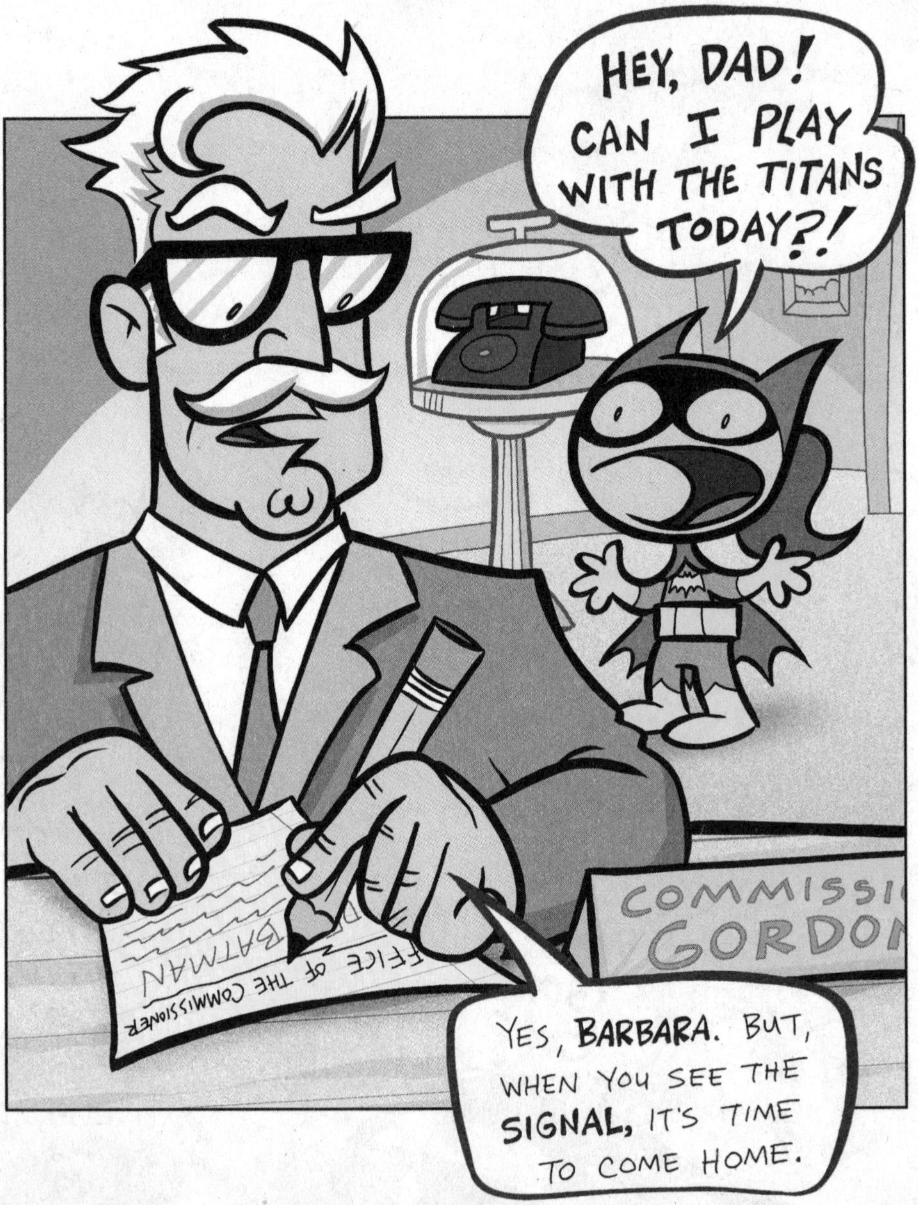
HEY, DAD! CAN I PLAY WITH THE TITANS TODAY?!
YES, BARBARA. BUT, WHEN YOU SEE THE SIGNAL, IT'S TIME TO COME HOME.

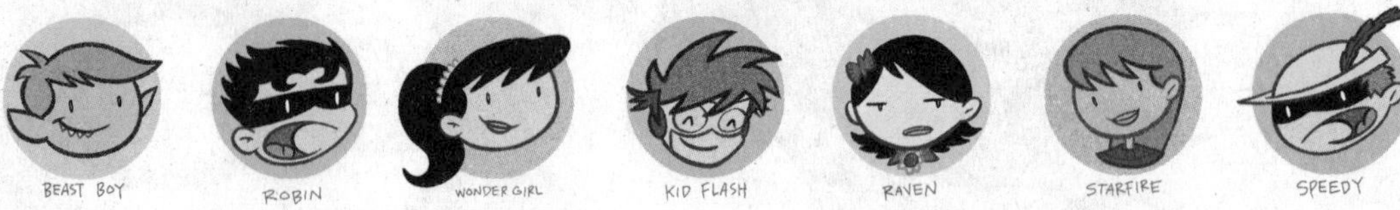
BEAST BOY
ROBIN
WONDER GIRL
KID FLASH
RAVEN
STARFIRE
SPEEDY

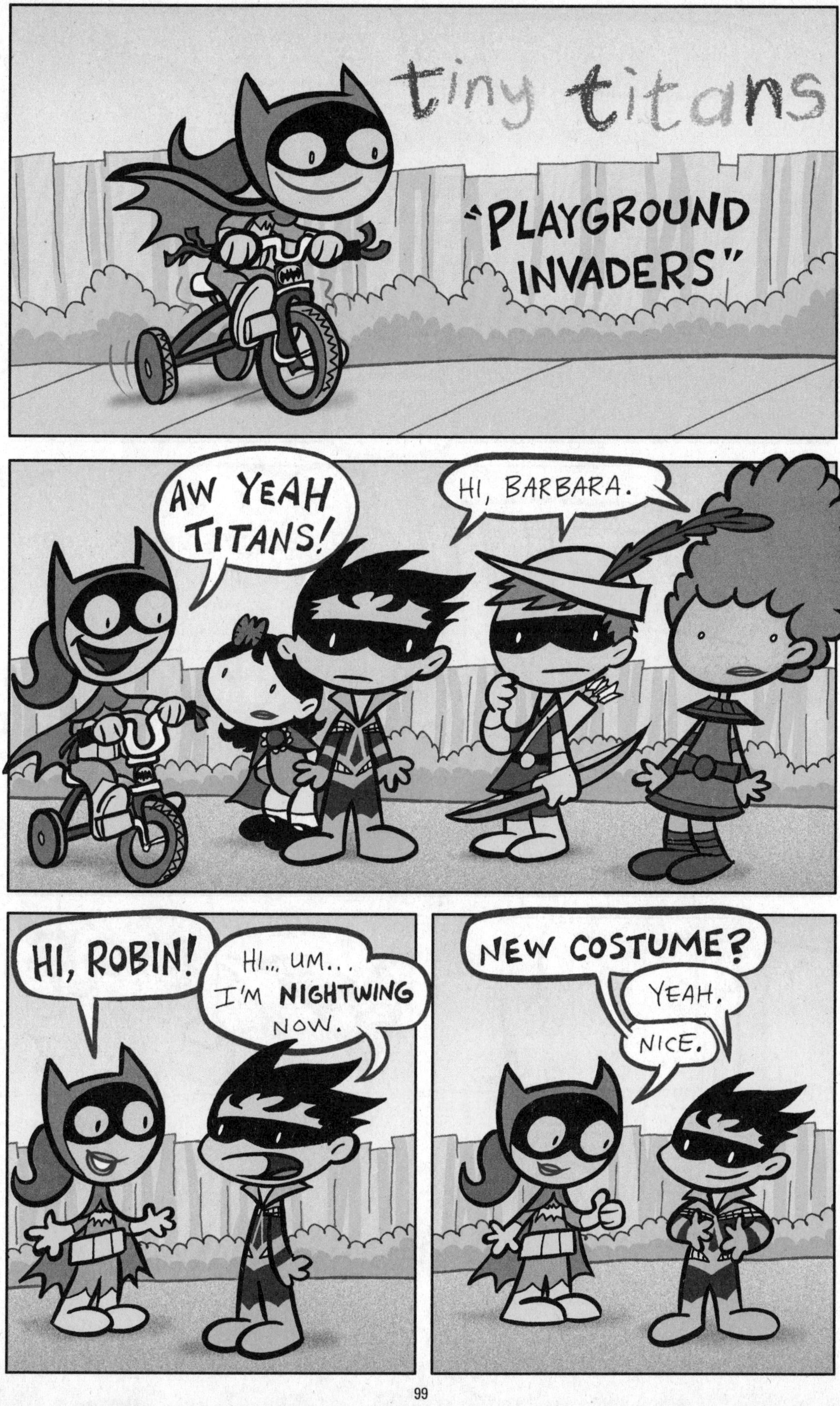
tiny titans
"PLAYGROUND INVADERS"
AW YEAH TITANS!
HI, BARBARA.
HI, ROBIN!
HI... UM... I'M NIGHTWING NOW.
NEW COSTUME?
YEAH.
NICE.

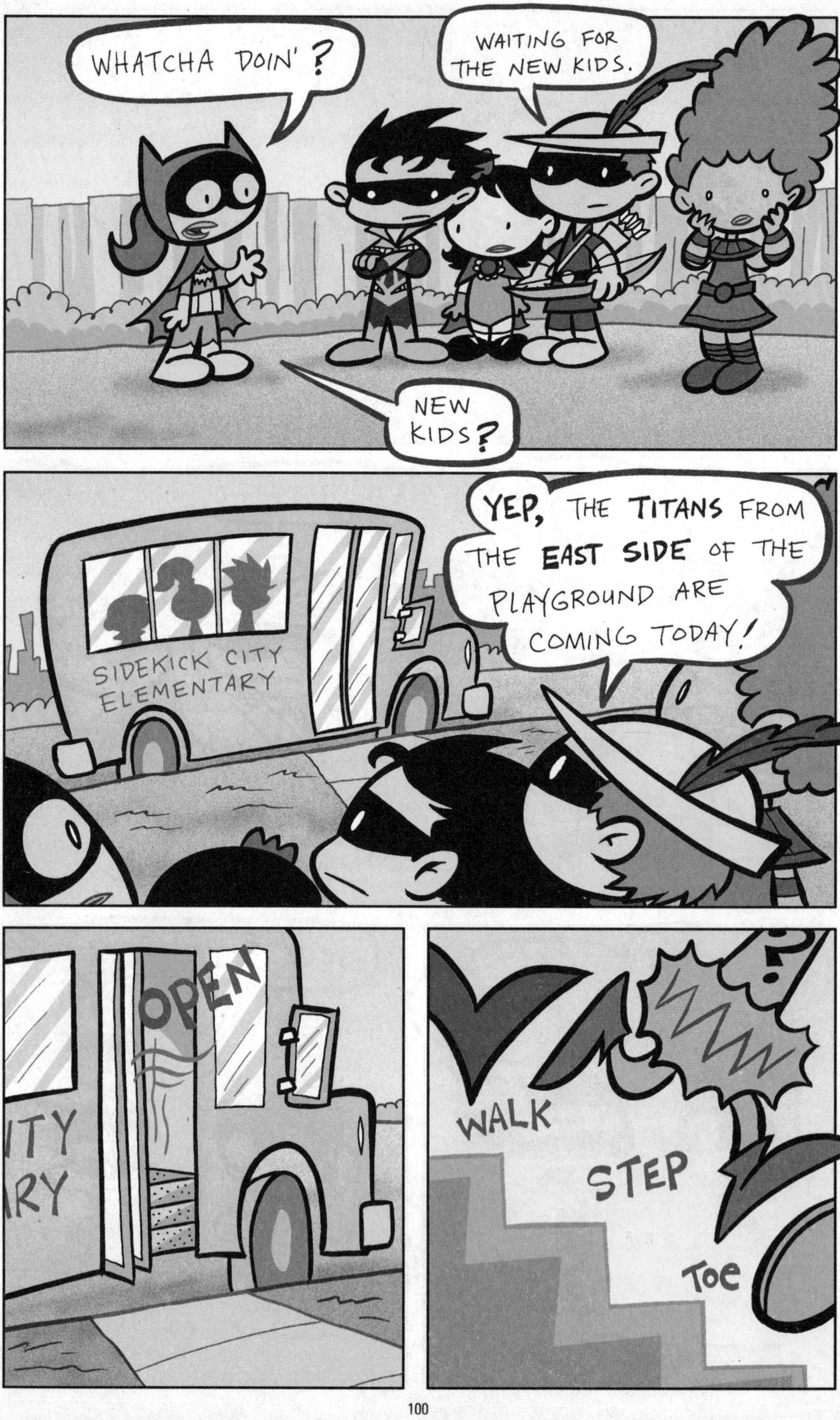
WHATCHA DOIN'?
WAITING FOR THE NEW KIDS.
NEW KIDS?
YEP, THE TITANS FROM THE EAST SIDE OF THE PLAYGROUND ARE COMING TODAY!
SIDEKICK CITY ELEMENTARY
OPEN
WALK
STEP
TOE

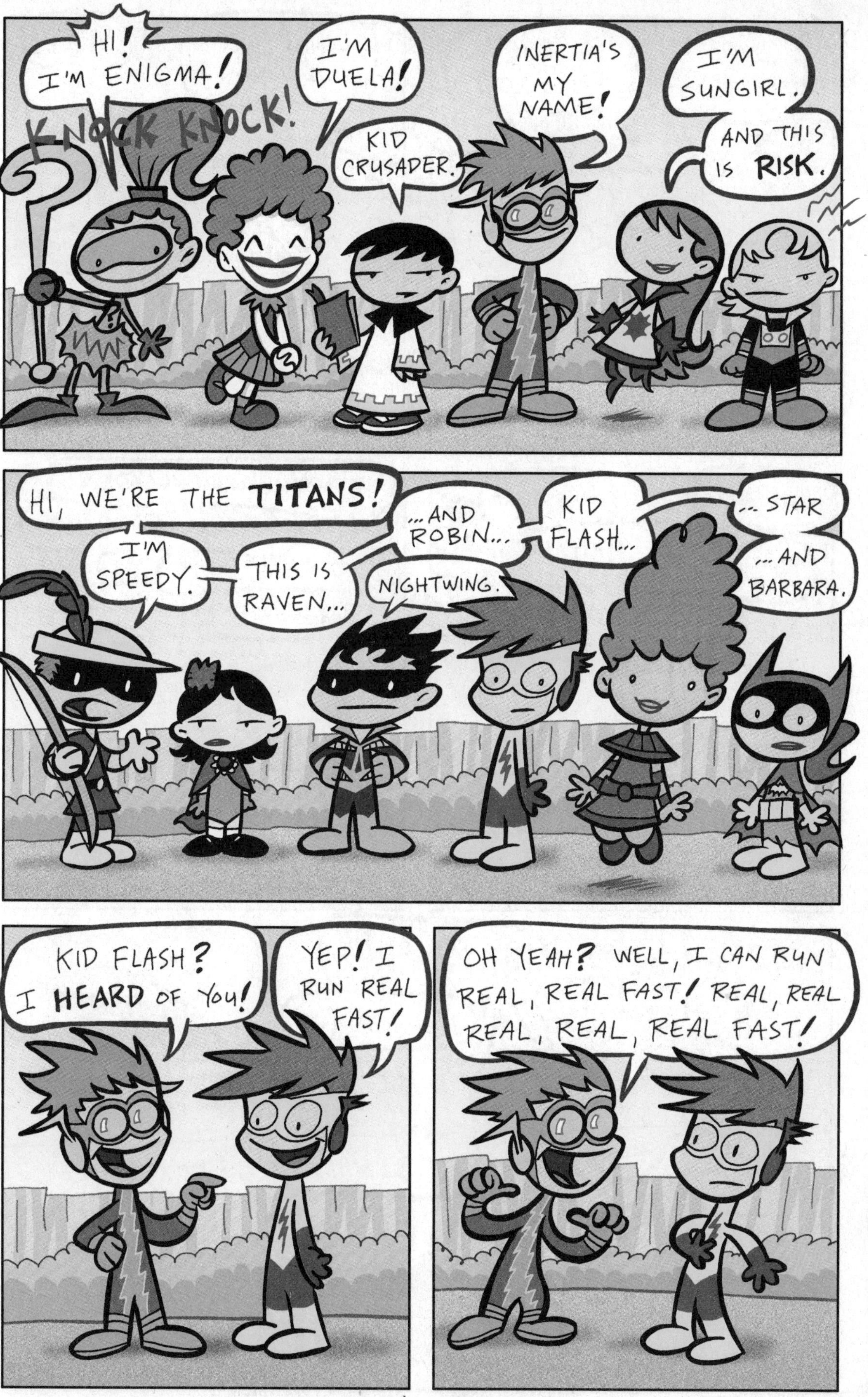
HI! I'M ENIGMA!
KNOCK KNOCK!
I'M DUELA!
KID CRUSADER.
INERTIA'S MY NAME!
I'M SUNGIRL.
AND THIS IS RISK.
HI, WE'RE THE TITANS!
I'M SPEEDY.
THIS IS RAVEN...
...AND ROBIN...
NIGHTWING.
KID FLASH...
...STAR
...AND BARBARA.
KID FLASH? I HEARD OF YOU!
YEP! I RUN REAL FAST!
OH YEAH? WELL, I CAN RUN REAL, REAL FAST! REAL, REAL REAL, REAL, REAL FAST!

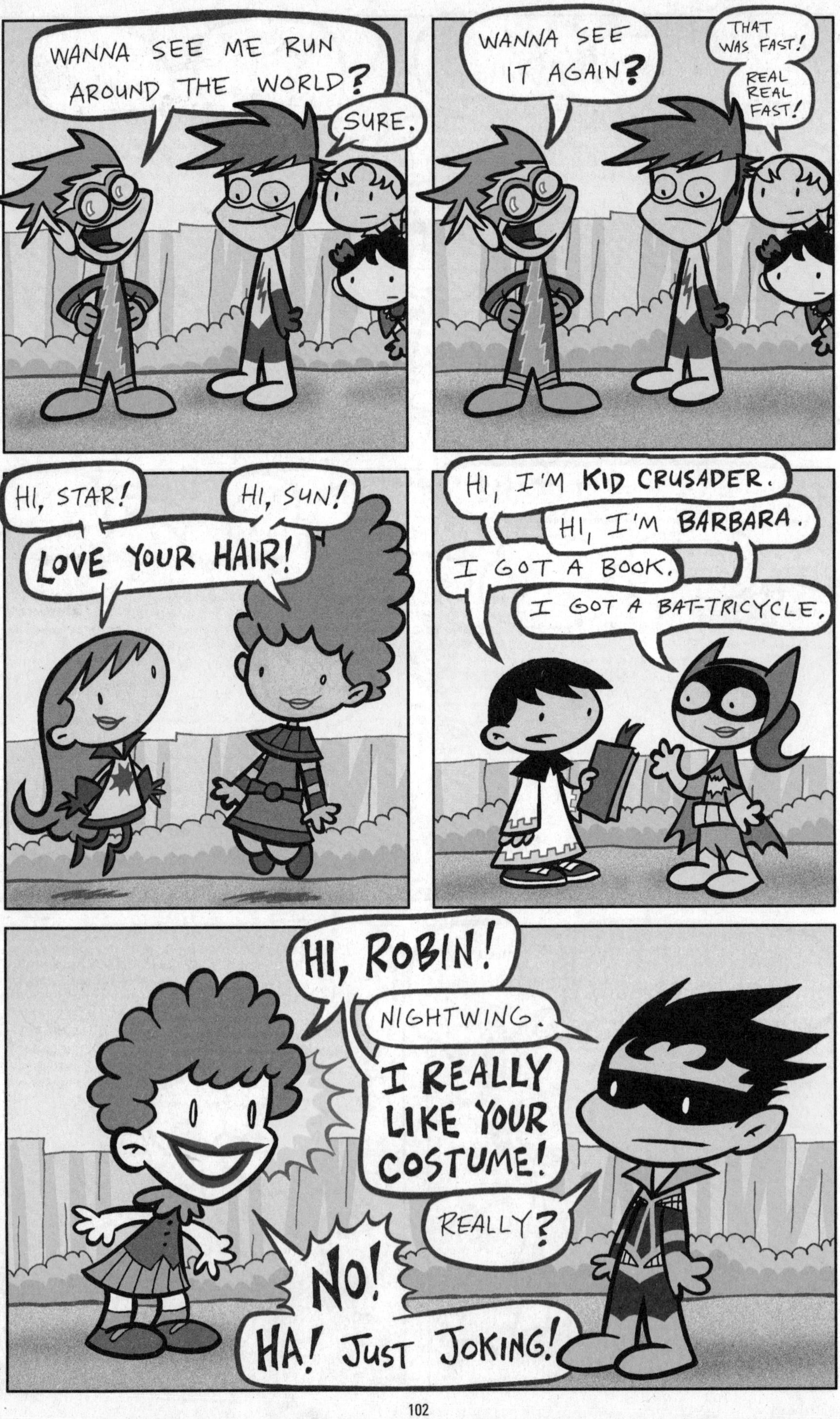
WANNA SEE ME RUN AROUND THE WORLD?
SURE.
WANNA SEE IT AGAIN?
THAT WAS FAST!
REAL REAL FAST!
HI, STAR!
HI, SUN!
LOVE YOUR HAIR!
HI, I'M KID CRUSADER.
HI, I'M BARBARA.
I GOT A BOOK.
I GOT A BAT-TRICYCLE.
HI, ROBIN!
NIGHTWING.
I REALLY LIKE YOUR COSTUME!
REALLY?
NO!
HA! JUST JOKING!

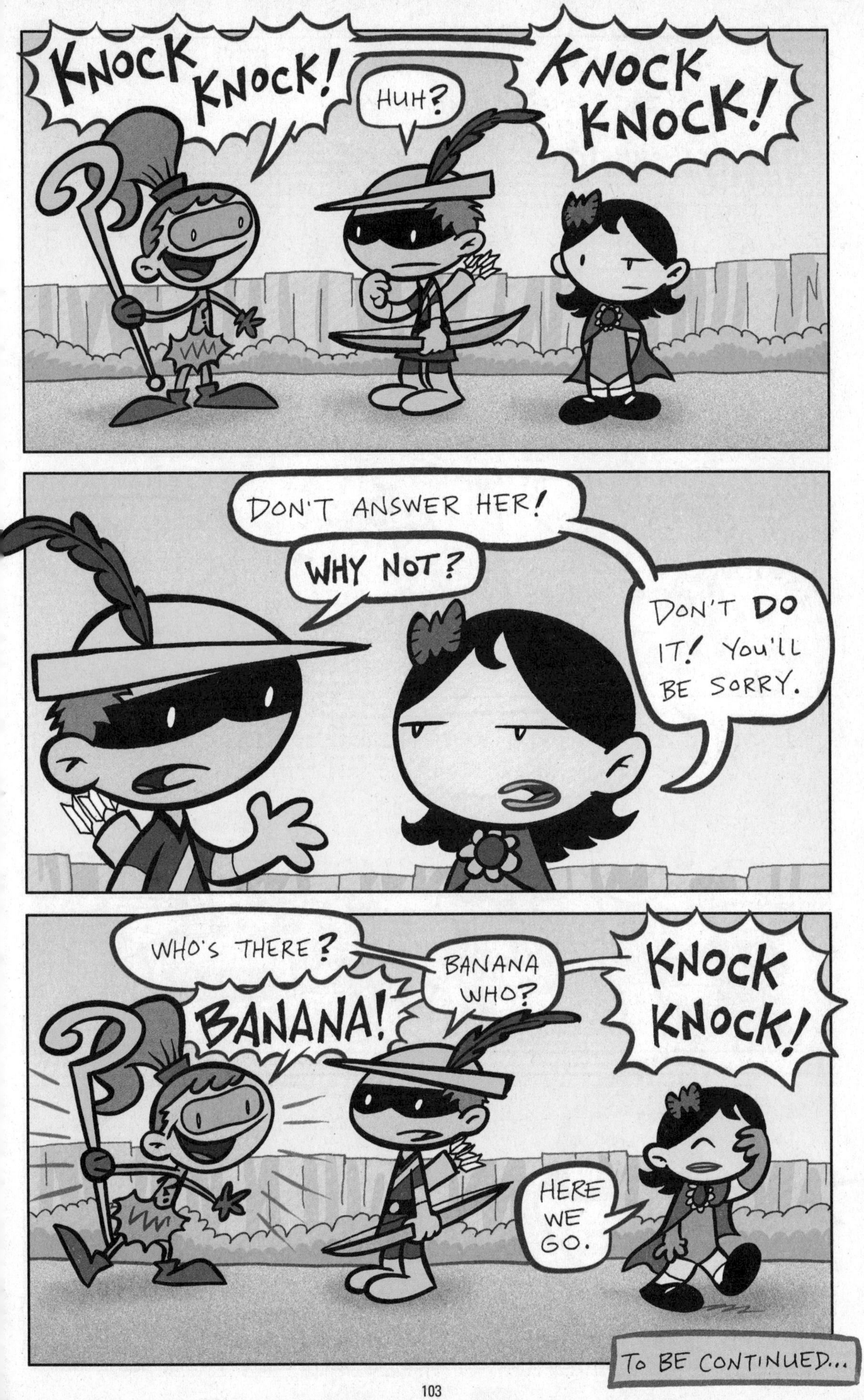
KNOCK KNOCK!
HUH?
KNOCK KNOCK!
DON'T ANSWER HER!
WHY NOT?
DON'T DO IT! YOU'LL BE SORRY.
WHO'S THERE?
BANANA!
BANANA WHO?
KNOCK KNOCK!
HERE WE GO.
TO BE CONTINUED...

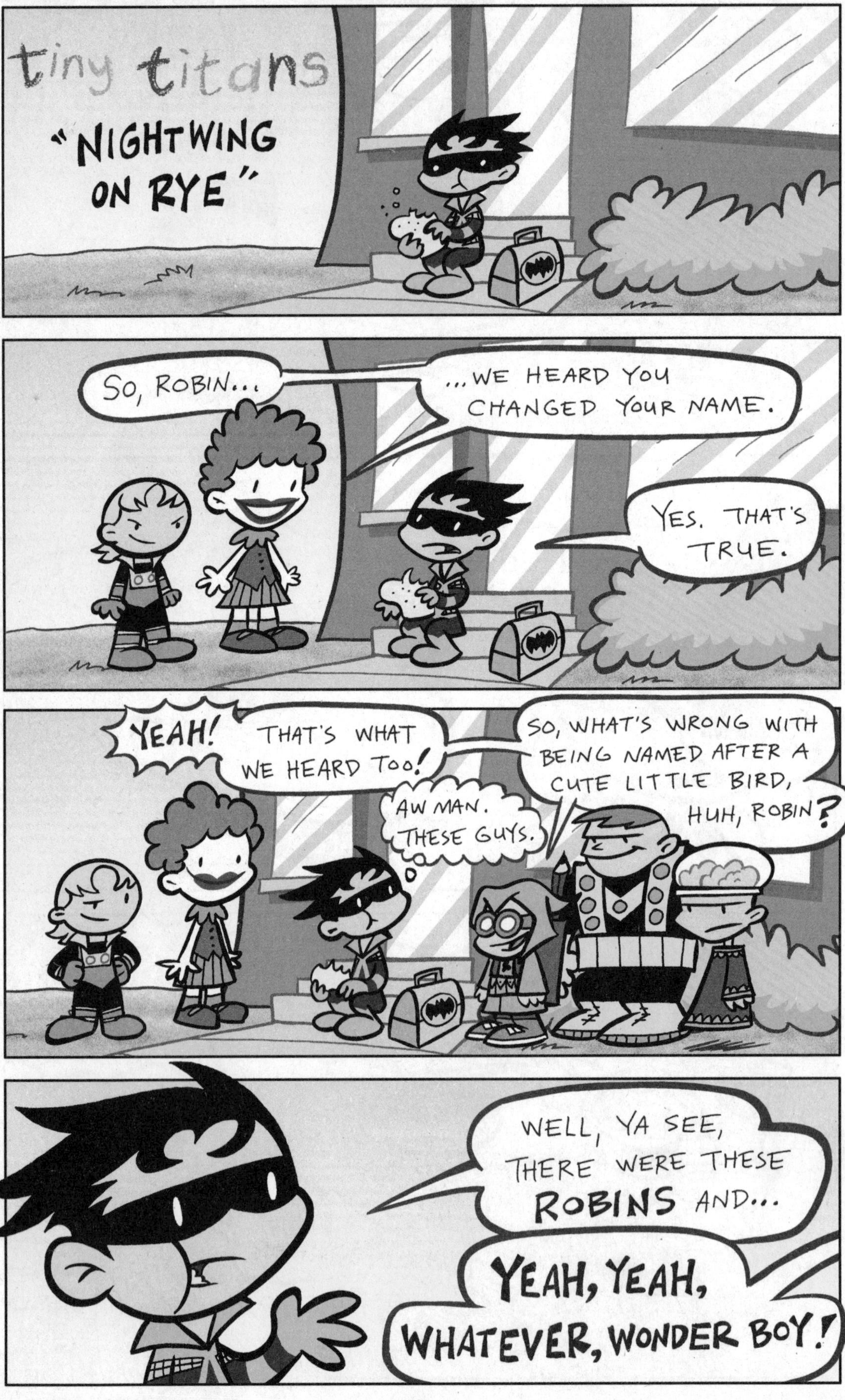
tiny titans
"NIGHTWING ON RYE"
SO, ROBIN...
...WE HEARD YOU CHANGED YOUR NAME.
YES. THAT'S TRUE.
YEAH! THAT'S WHAT WE HEARD TOO!
SO, WHAT'S WRONG WITH BEING NAMED AFTER A CUTE LITTLE BIRD, HUH, ROBIN?
AW MAN. THESE GUYS.
WELL, YA SEE, THERE WERE THESE ROBINS AND...
YEAH, YEAH, WHATEVER, WONDER BOY!

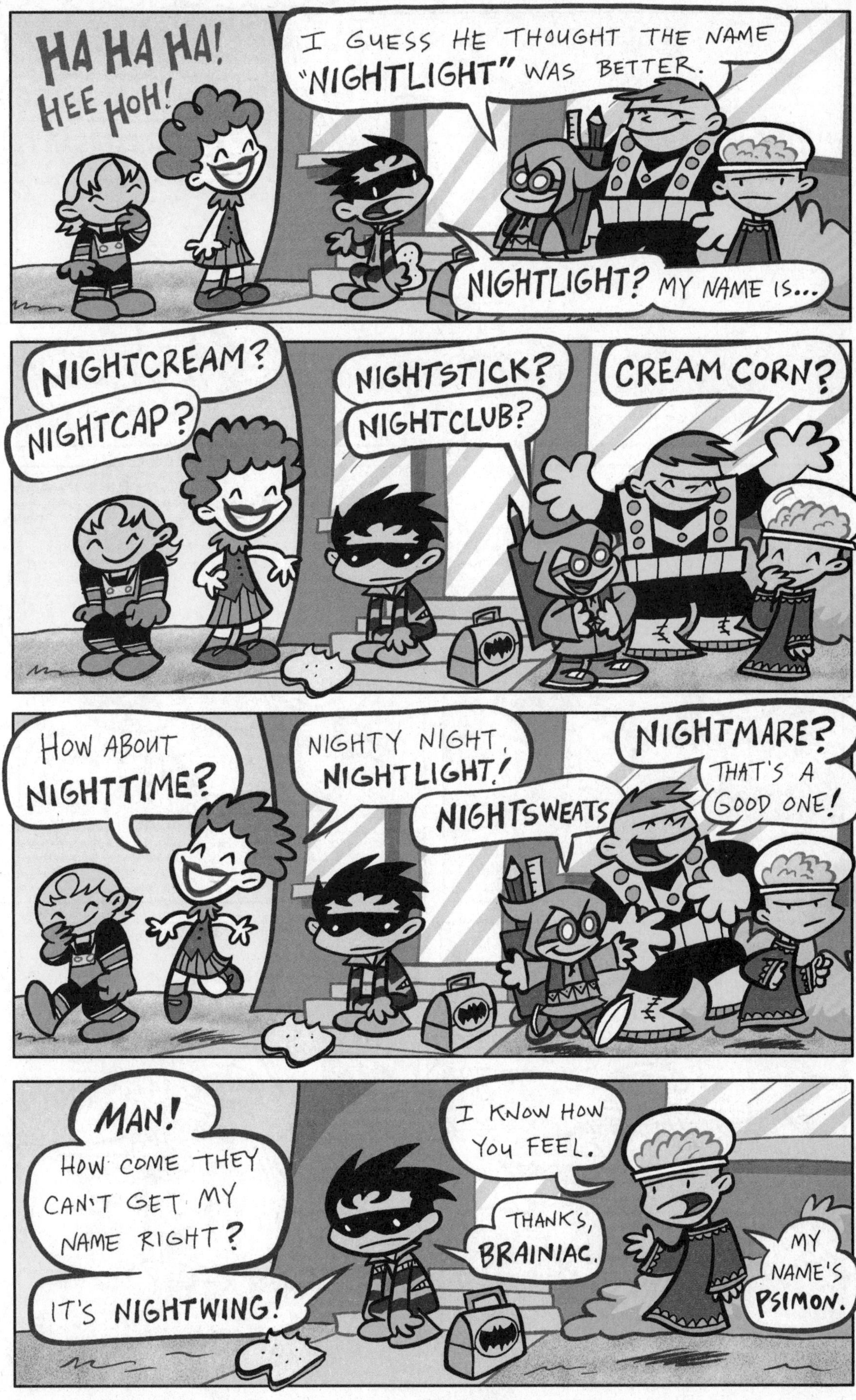
HA HA HA! HEE HOH!
I GUESS HE THOUGHT THE NAME "NIGHTLIGHT" WAS BETTER.
NIGHTLIGHT? MY NAME IS...
NIGHTCREAM?
NIGHTCAP?
NIGHTSTICK?
NIGHTCLUB?
CREAM CORN?
HOW ABOUT NIGHTTIME?
NIGHTY NIGHT, NIGHTLIGHT!
NIGHTSWEATS
NIGHTMARE? THAT'S A GOOD ONE!
MAN! HOW COME THEY CAN'T GET MY NAME RIGHT?
IT'S NIGHTWING!
I KNOW HOW YOU FEEL.
THANKS, BRAINIAC.
MY NAME'S PSIMON.

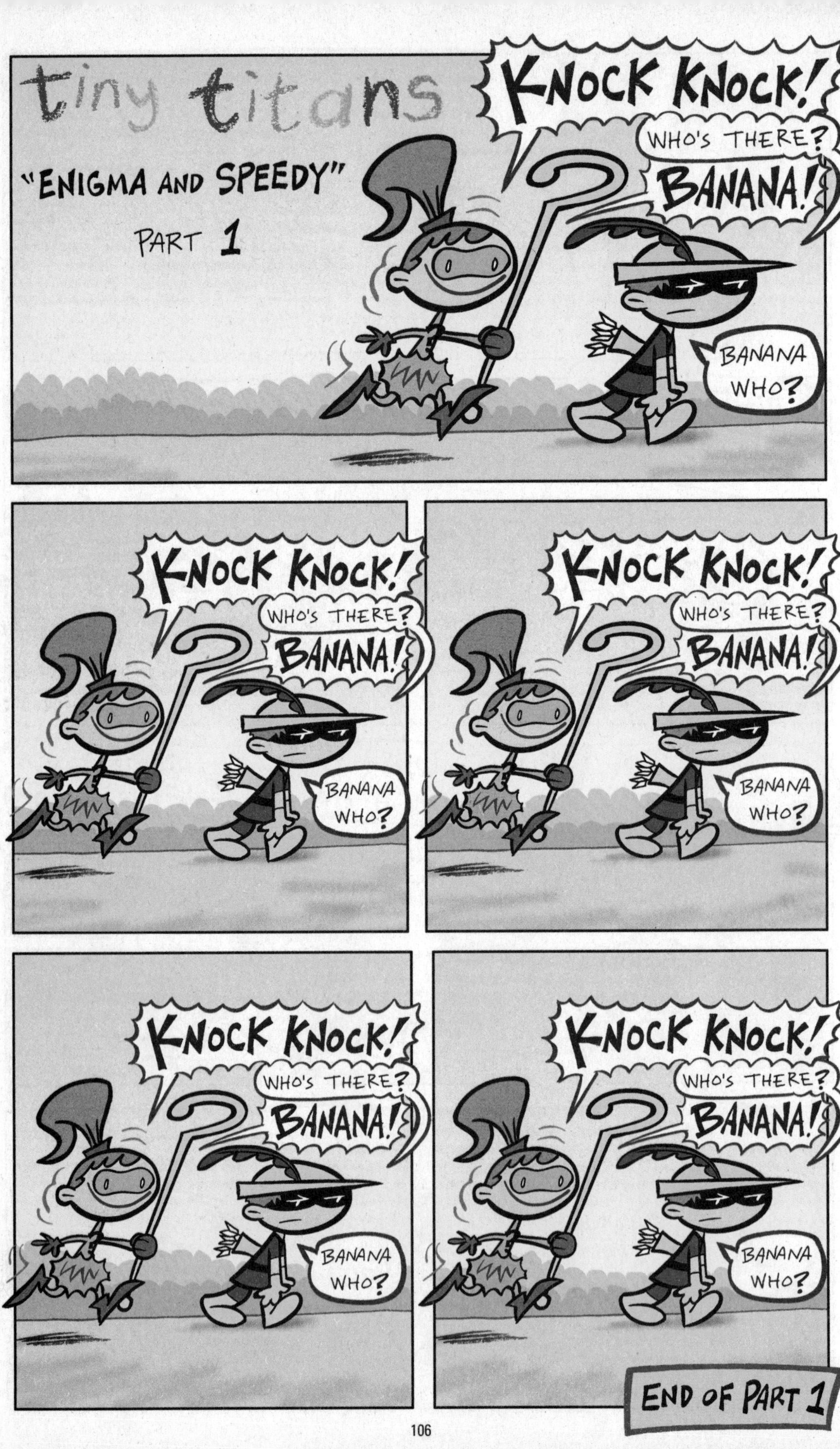

tiny titans
"ENIGMA AND SPEEDY"
PART 1
KNOCK KNOCK!
WHO'S THERE?
BANANA!
BANANA WHO?
KNOCK KNOCK!
WHO'S THERE?
BANANA!
BANANA WHO?
KNOCK KNOCK!
WHO'S THERE?
BANANA!
BANANA WHO?
KNOCK KNOCK!
WHO'S THERE?
BANANA!
BANANA WHO?
KNOCK KNOCK!
WHO'S THERE?
BANANA!
BANANA WHO?
END OF PART 1

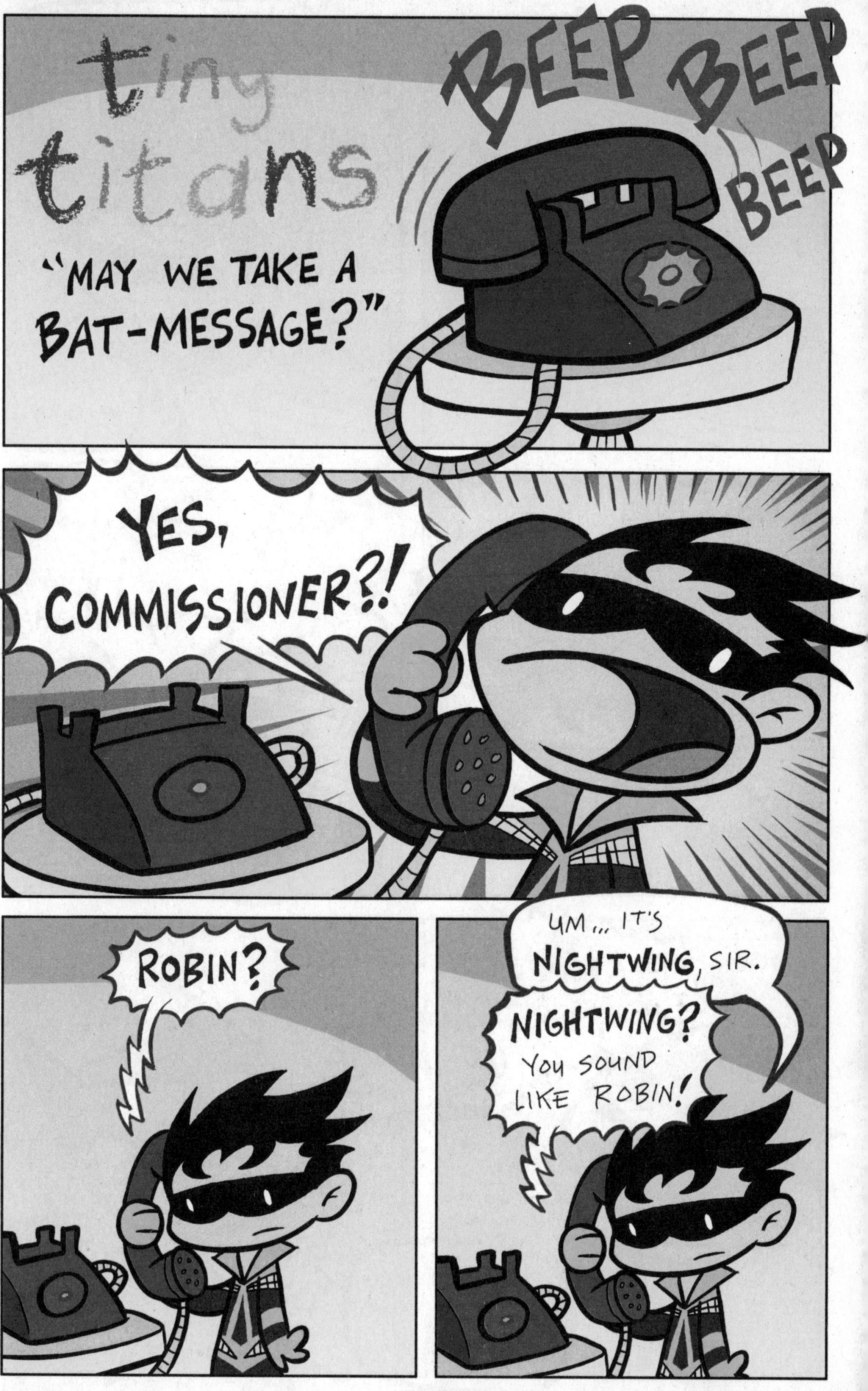

tiny titans
BEEP BEEP BEEP
"MAY WE TAKE A BAT-MESSAGE?"
YES, COMMISSIONER?!
ROBIN?
UM... IT'S NIGHTWING, SIR.
NIGHTWING? YOU SOUND LIKE ROBIN!

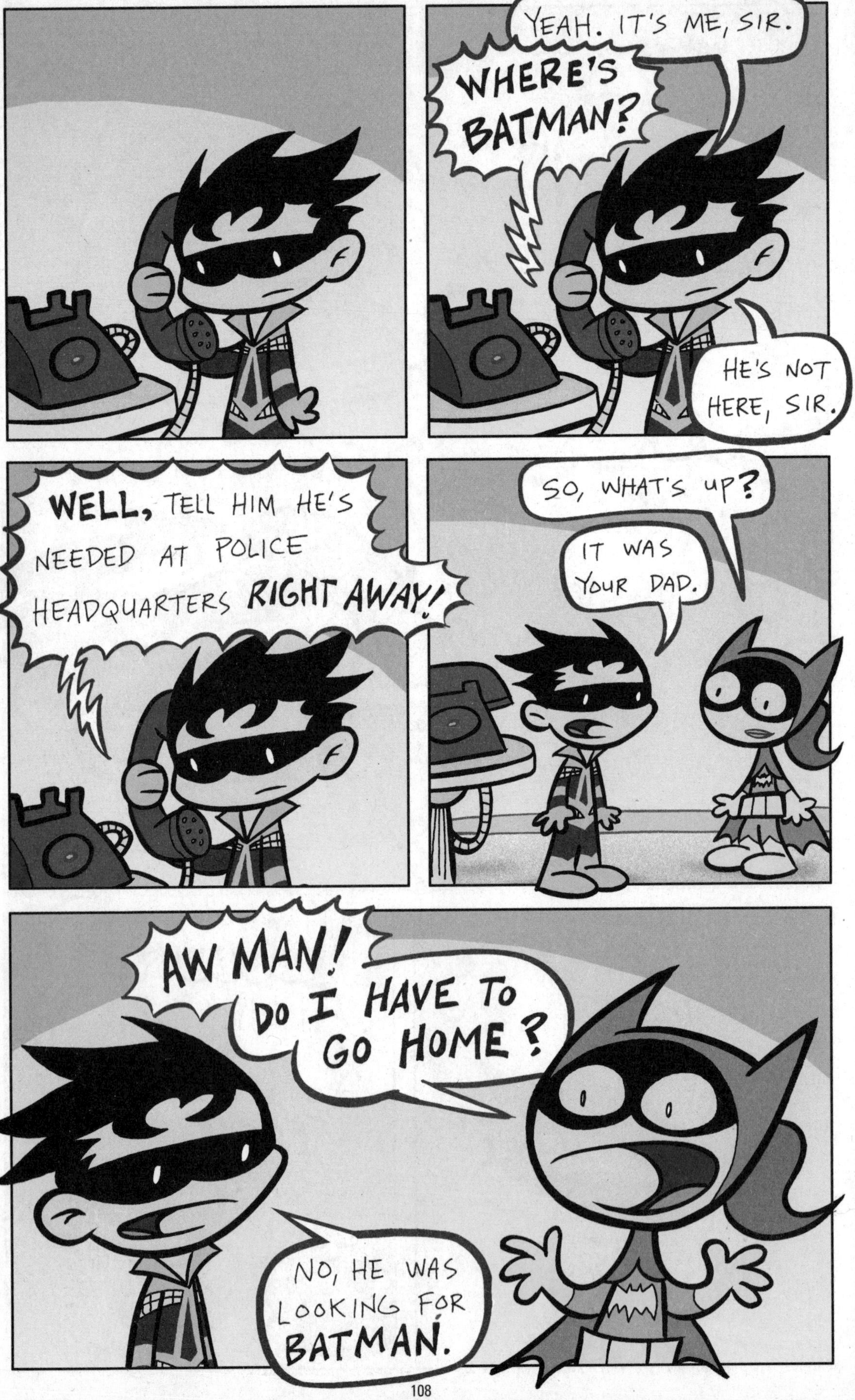
YEAH. IT'S ME, SIR.
WHERE'S BATMAN?
HE'S NOT HERE, SIR.
WELL, TELL HIM HE'S NEEDED AT POLICE HEADQUARTERS RIGHT AWAY!
SO, WHAT'S UP?
IT WAS YOUR DAD.
AW MAN! DO I HAVE TO GO HOME?
NO, HE WAS LOOKING FOR BATMAN.

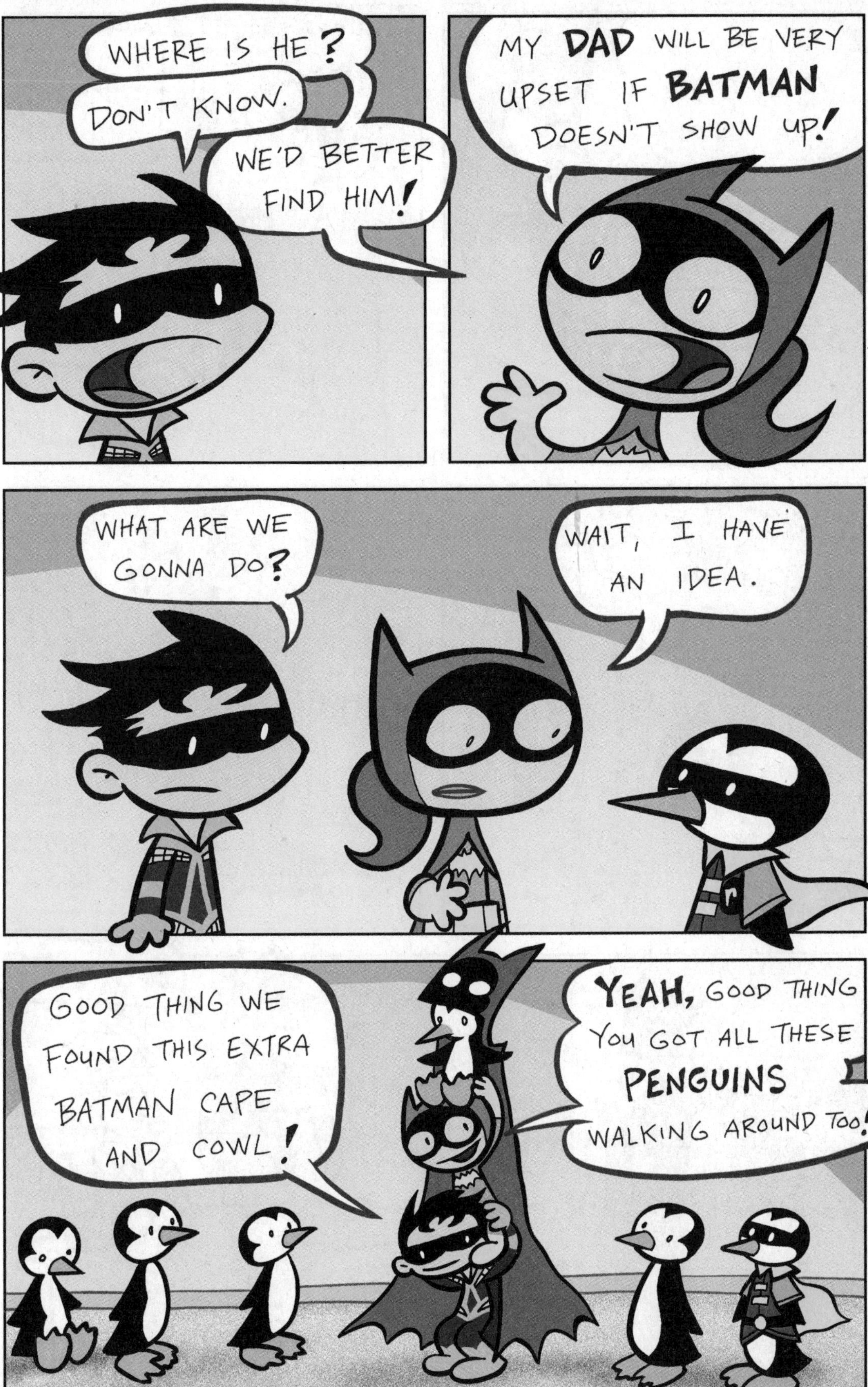
WHERE IS HE?
DON'T KNOW.
WE'D BETTER FIND HIM!
MY DAD WILL BE VERY UPSET IF BATMAN DOESN'T SHOW UP!
WHAT ARE WE GONNA DO?
WAIT, I HAVE AN IDEA.
GOOD THING WE FOUND THIS EXTRA BATMAN CAPE AND COWL!
YEAH, GOOD THING YOU GOT ALL THESE PENGUINS WALKING AROUND TOO!

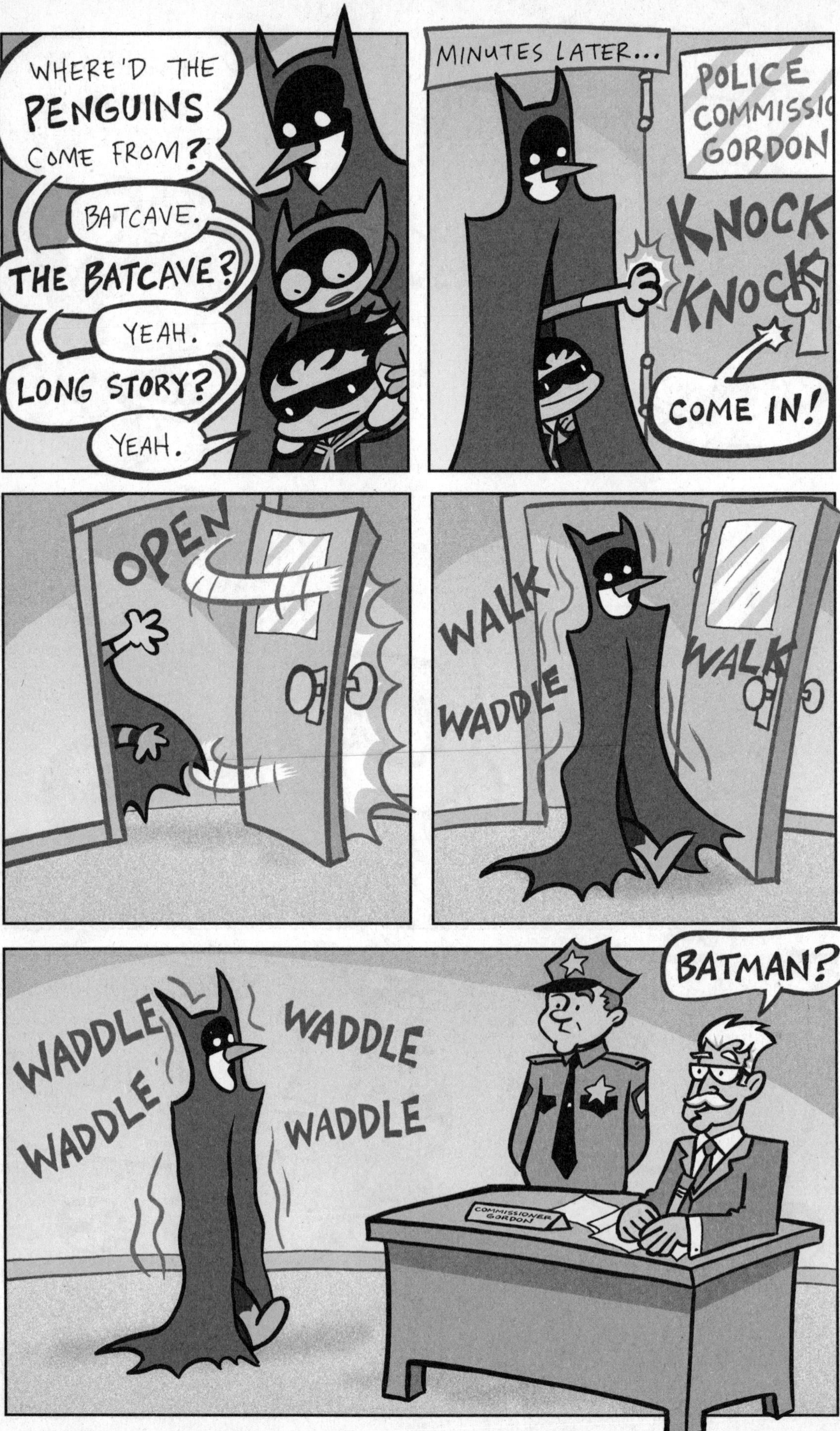
WHERE'D THE PENGUINS COME FROM?
BATCAVE.
THE BATCAVE?
YEAH.
LONG STORY?
YEAH.
MINUTES LATER...
POLICE COMMISSIO GORDON
KNOCK KNOCK
COME IN!
OPEN
WALK
WADDLE
WALK
WADDLE
WADDLE
WADDLE
WADDLE
COMMISSIONER GORDON
BATMAN?

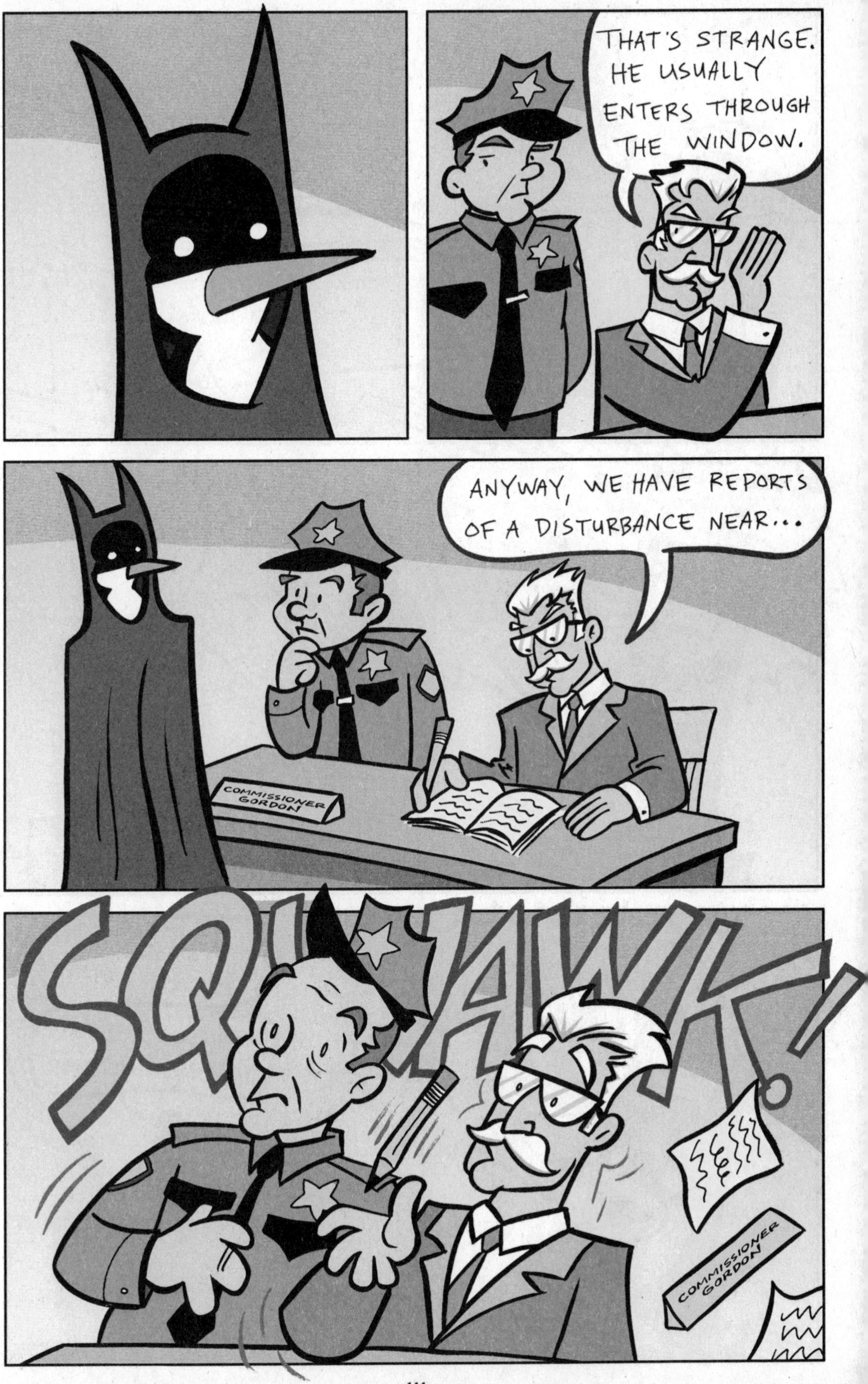
THAT'S STRANGE. HE USUALLY ENTERS THROUGH THE WINDOW.
ANYWAY, WE HAVE REPORTS OF A DISTURBANCE NEAR...
COMMISSIONER GORDON
SQUAWK!
COMMISSIONER GORDON

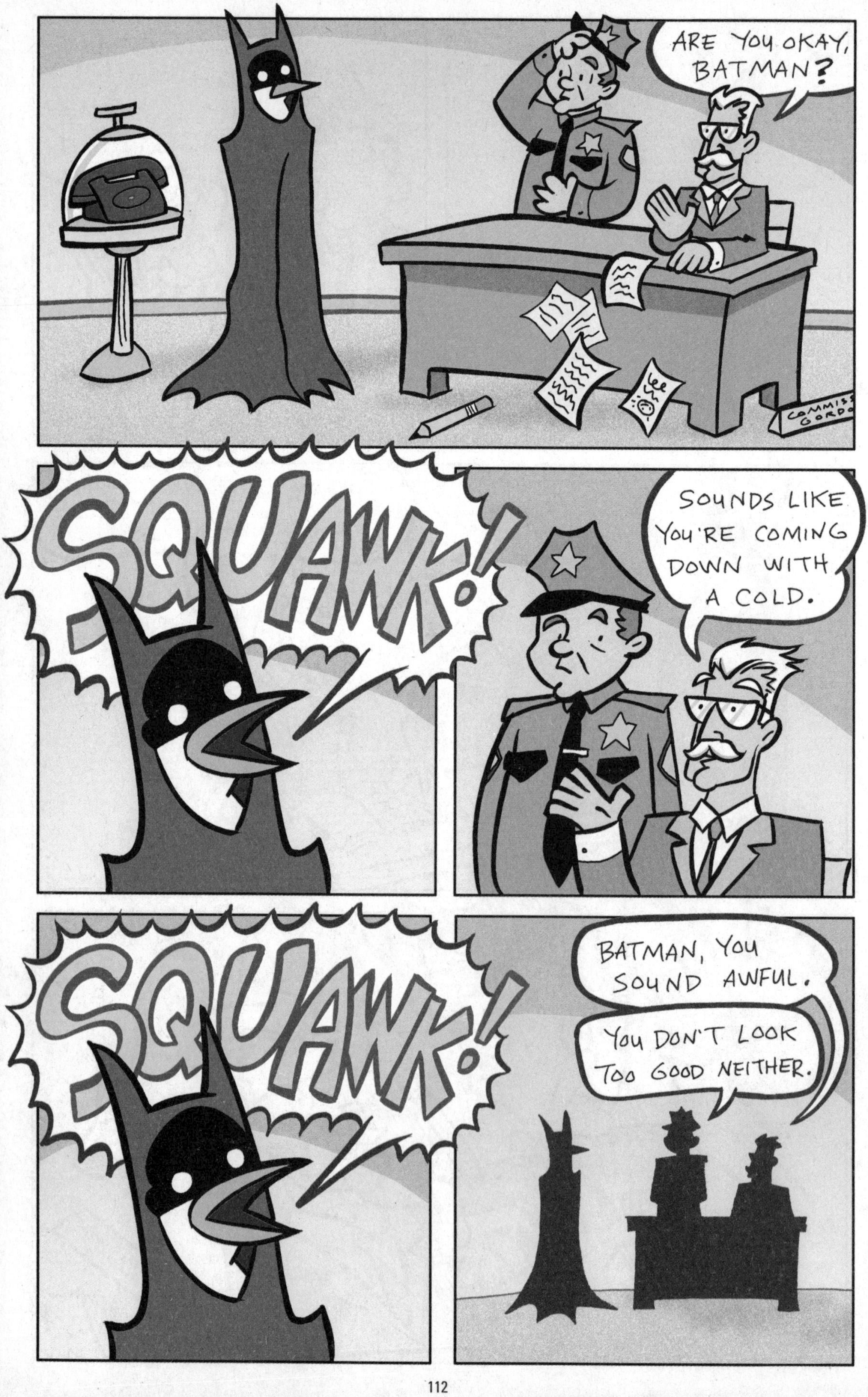
ARE YOU OKAY, BATMAN?
SQUAWK!
SOUNDS LIKE YOU'RE COMING DOWN WITH A COLD.
SQUAWK!
BATMAN, YOU SOUND AWFUL.
YOU DON'T LOOK TOO GOOD NEITHER.

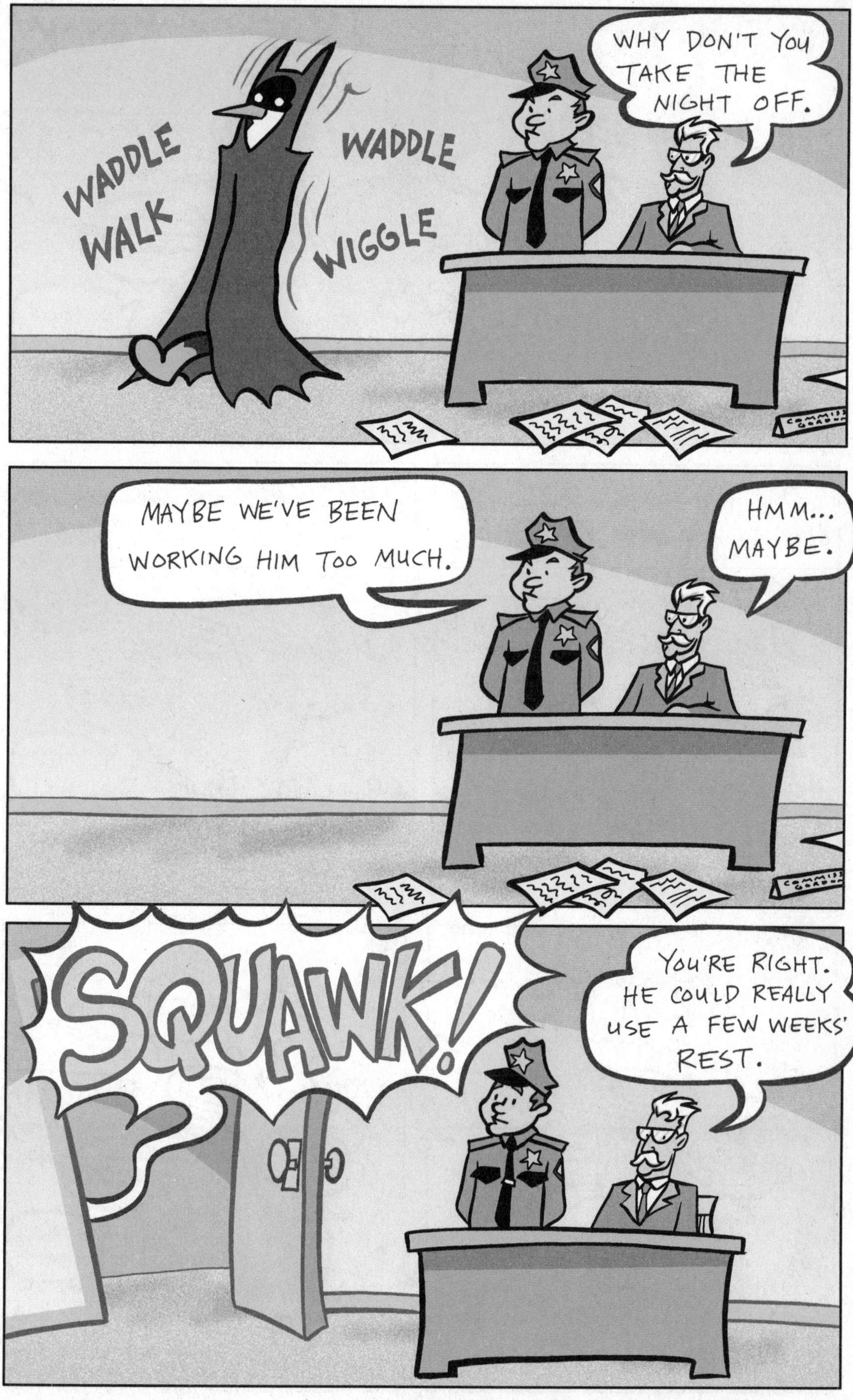
WADDLE
WALK
WADDLE
WIGGLE
WHY DON'T YOU TAKE THE NIGHT OFF.
MAYBE WE'VE BEEN WORKING HIM TOO MUCH.
HMM... MAYBE.
SQUAWK!
YOU'RE RIGHT. HE COULD REALLY USE A FEW WEEKS' REST.

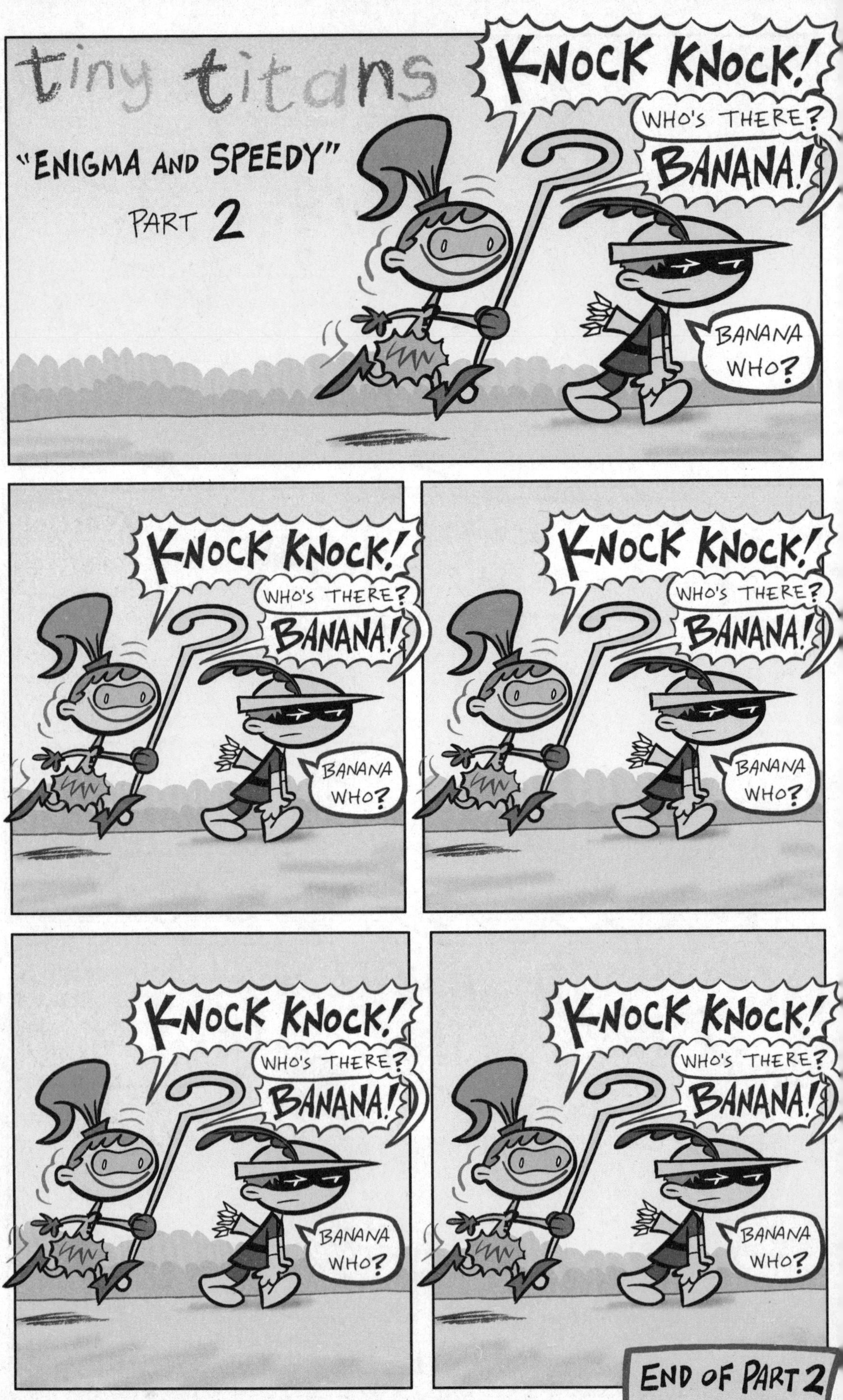
tiny titans
"ENIGMA AND SPEEDY"
PART 2
KNOCK KNOCK!
WHO'S THERE?
BANANA!
BANANA WHO?
KNOCK KNOCK!
WHO'S THERE?
BANANA!
BANANA WHO?
KNOCK KNOCK!
WHO'S THERE?
BANANA!
BANANA WHO?
KNOCK KNOCK!
WHO'S THERE?
BANANA!
BANANA WHO?
KNOCK KNOCK!
WHO'S THERE?
BANANA!
BANANA WHO?
END OF PART 2

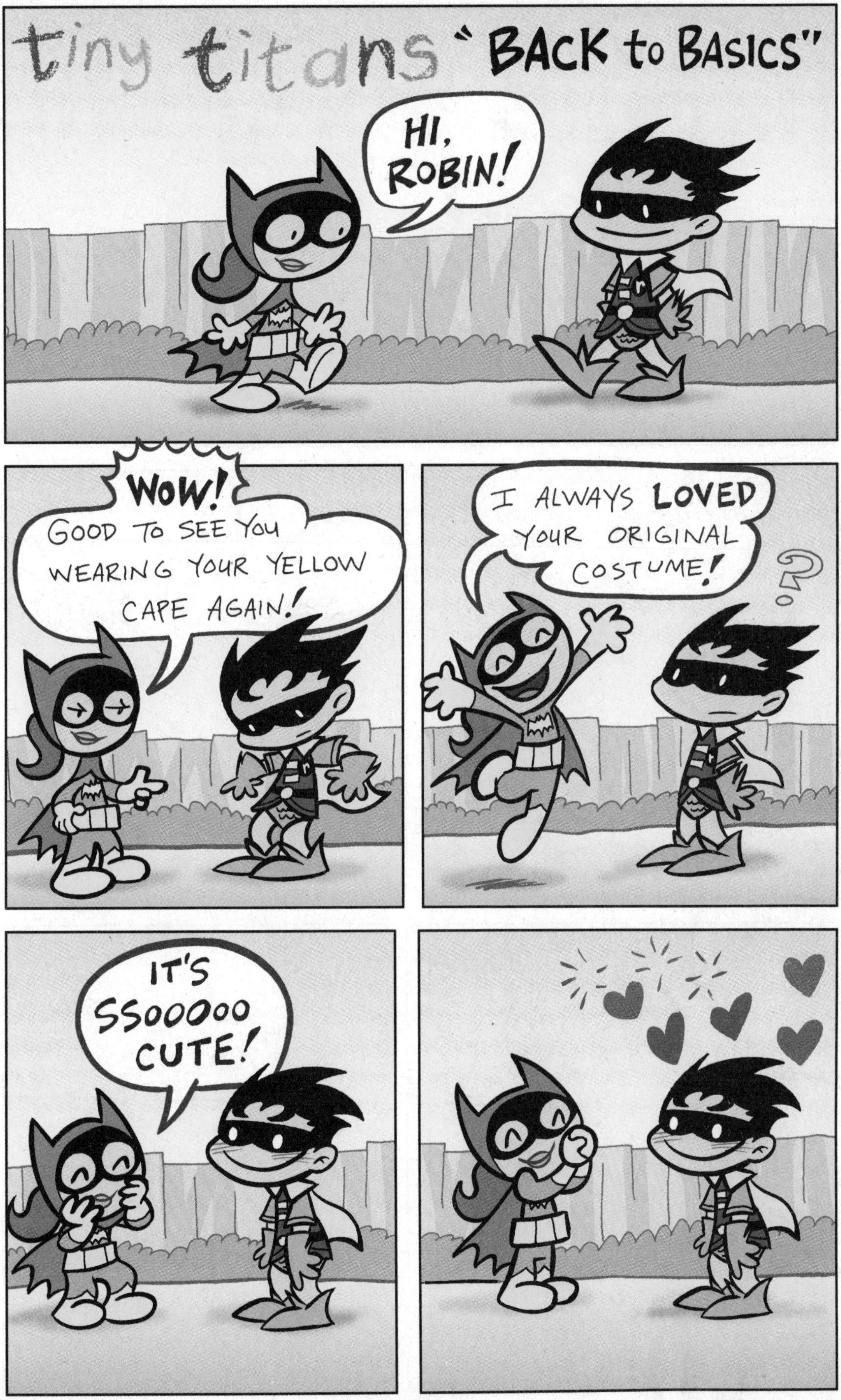
tiny titans "BACK to BASICS"
HI, ROBIN!
WOW! GOOD TO SEE YOU WEARING YOUR YELLOW CAPE AGAIN!
I ALWAYS LOVED YOUR ORIGINAL COSTUME!
?
IT'S SSOOOOO CUTE!

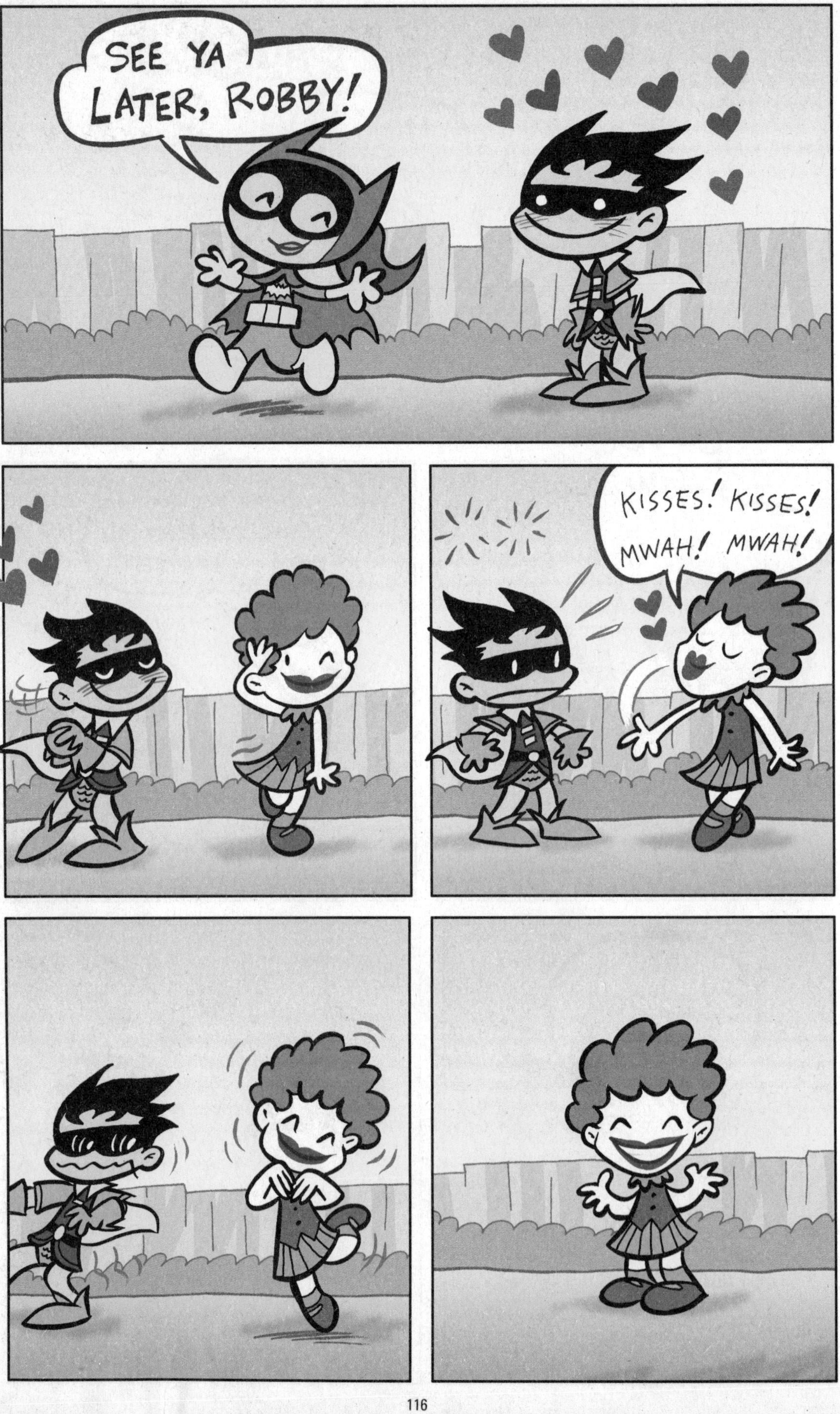
SEE YA LATER, ROBBY!
KISSES! KISSES! MWAH! MWAH!

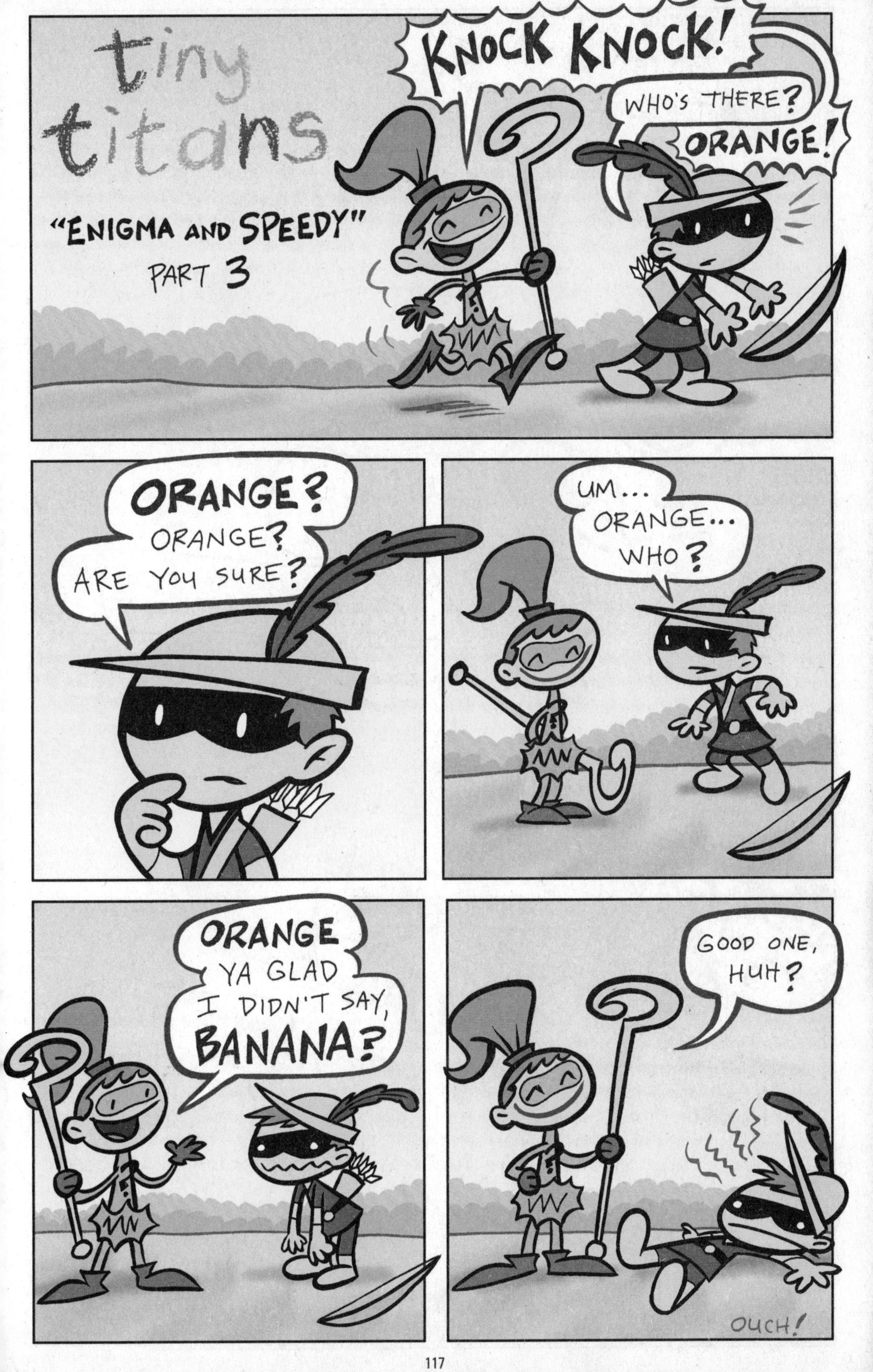
tiny titans
"ENIGMA AND SPEEDY"
PART 3
KNOCK KNOCK!
WHO'S THERE?
ORANGE!
ORANGE? ORANGE? ARE YOU SURE?
UM... ORANGE... WHO?
ORANGE YA GLAD I DIDN'T SAY, BANANA?
GOOD ONE, HUH?
OUCH!

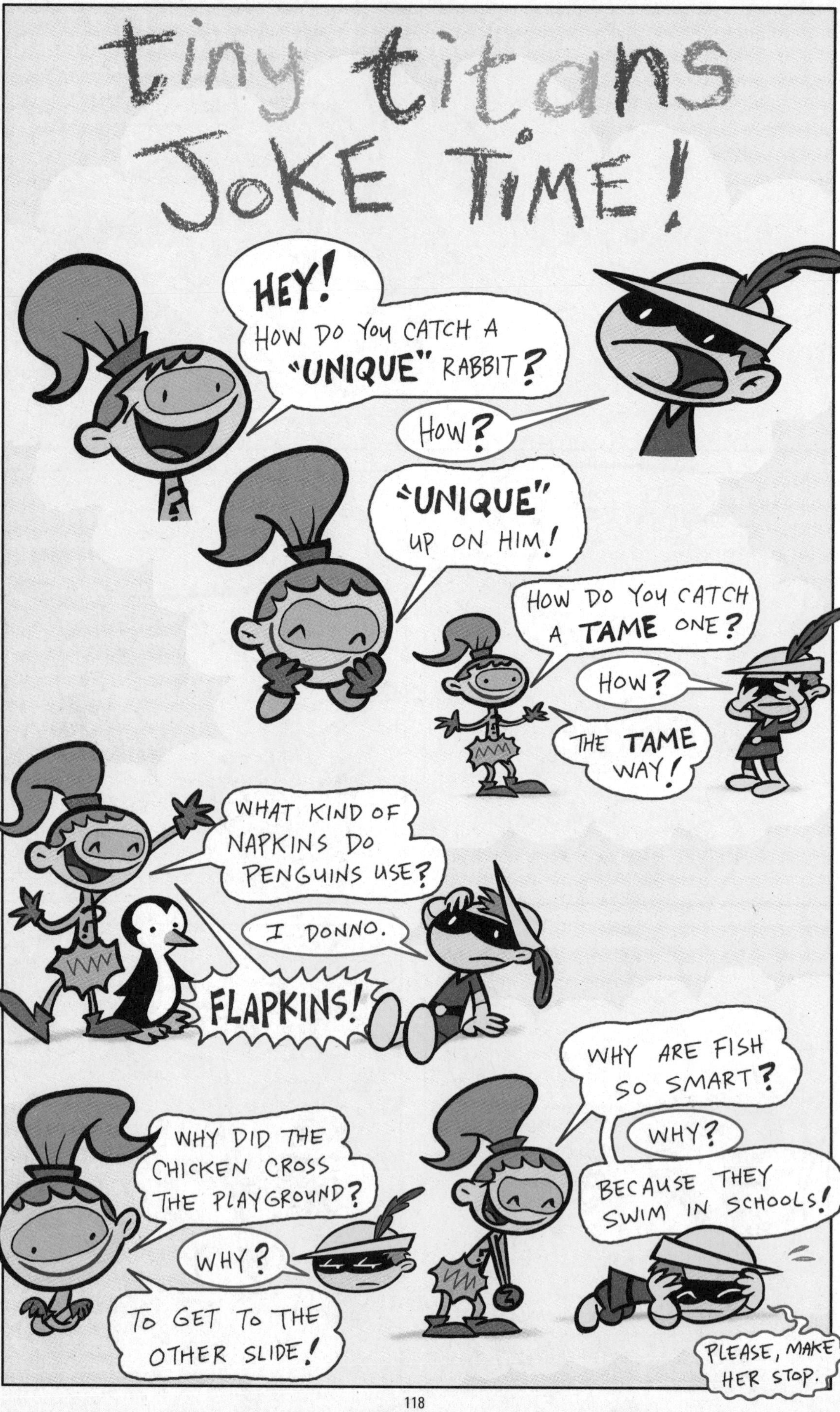
tiny titans JOKE TIME!
HEY! HOW DO YOU CATCH A "UNIQUE" RABBIT?
HOW?
"UNIQUE" UP ON HIM!
HOW DO YOU CATCH A TAME ONE?
HOW?
THE TAME WAY!
WHAT KIND OF NAPKINS DO PENGUINS USE?
I DONNO.
FLAPKINS!
WHY DID THE CHICKEN CROSS THE PLAYGROUND?
WHY?
TO GET TO THE OTHER SLIDE!
WHY ARE FISH SO SMART?
WHY?
BECAUSE THEY SWIM IN SCHOOLS!
PLEASE, MAKE HER STOP.

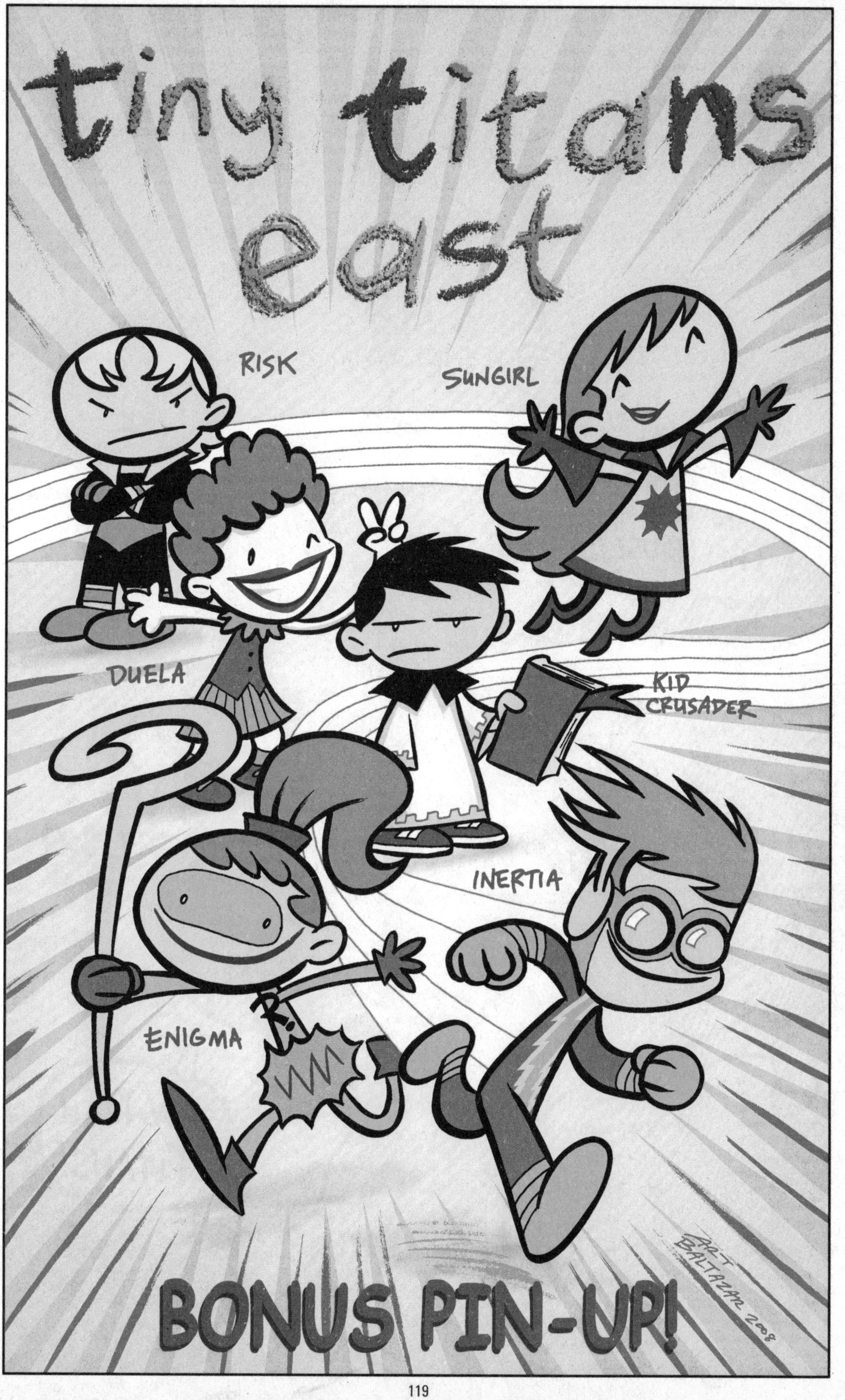
tiny titans east
RISK
SUNGIRL
DUELA
KID CRUSADER
INERTIA
ENIGMA
ART BALTAZAR 2008
BONUS PIN-UP!

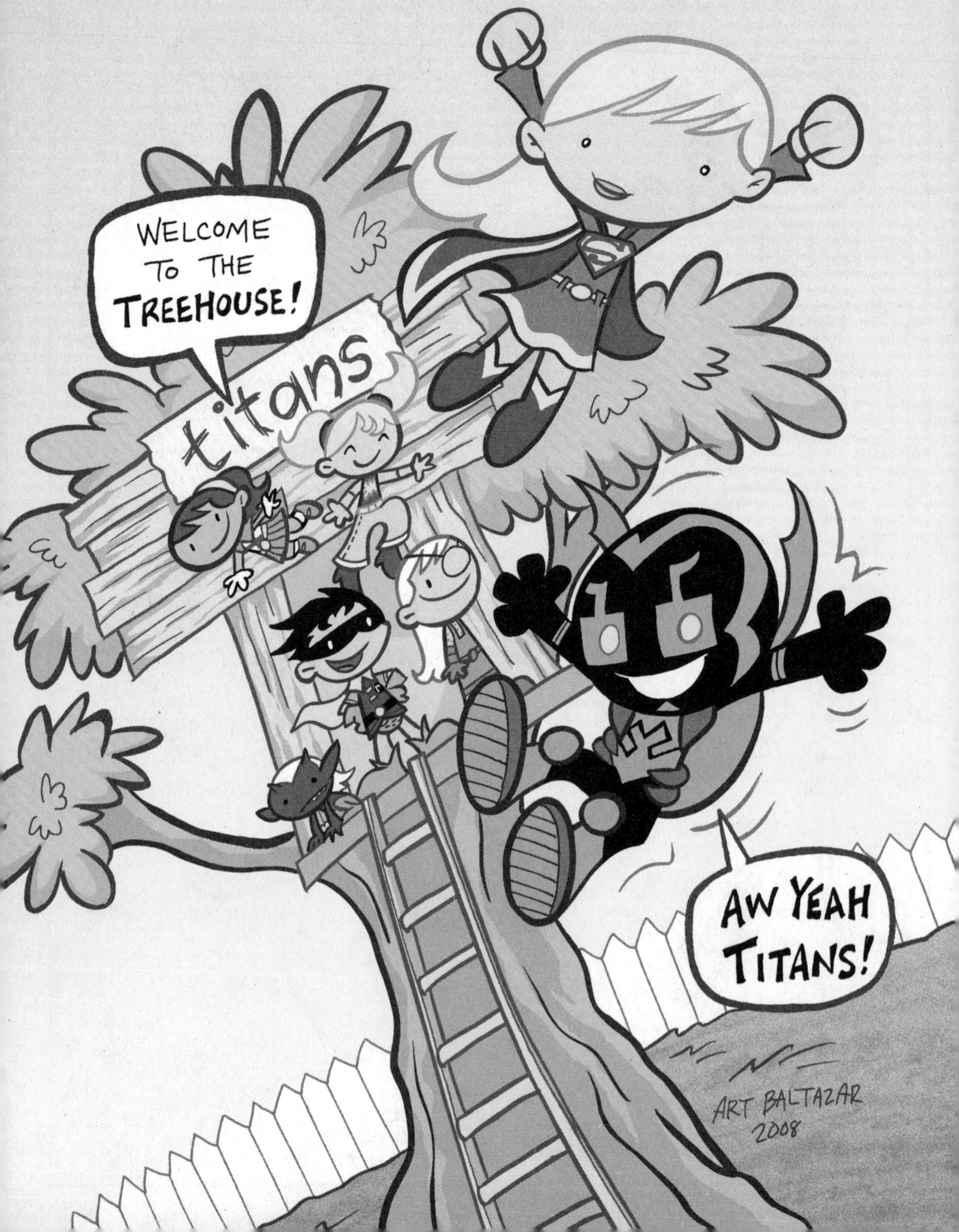
WELCOME TO THE TREEHOUSE!
titans
AW YEAH TITANS!
ART BALTAZAR 2008

tiny titans

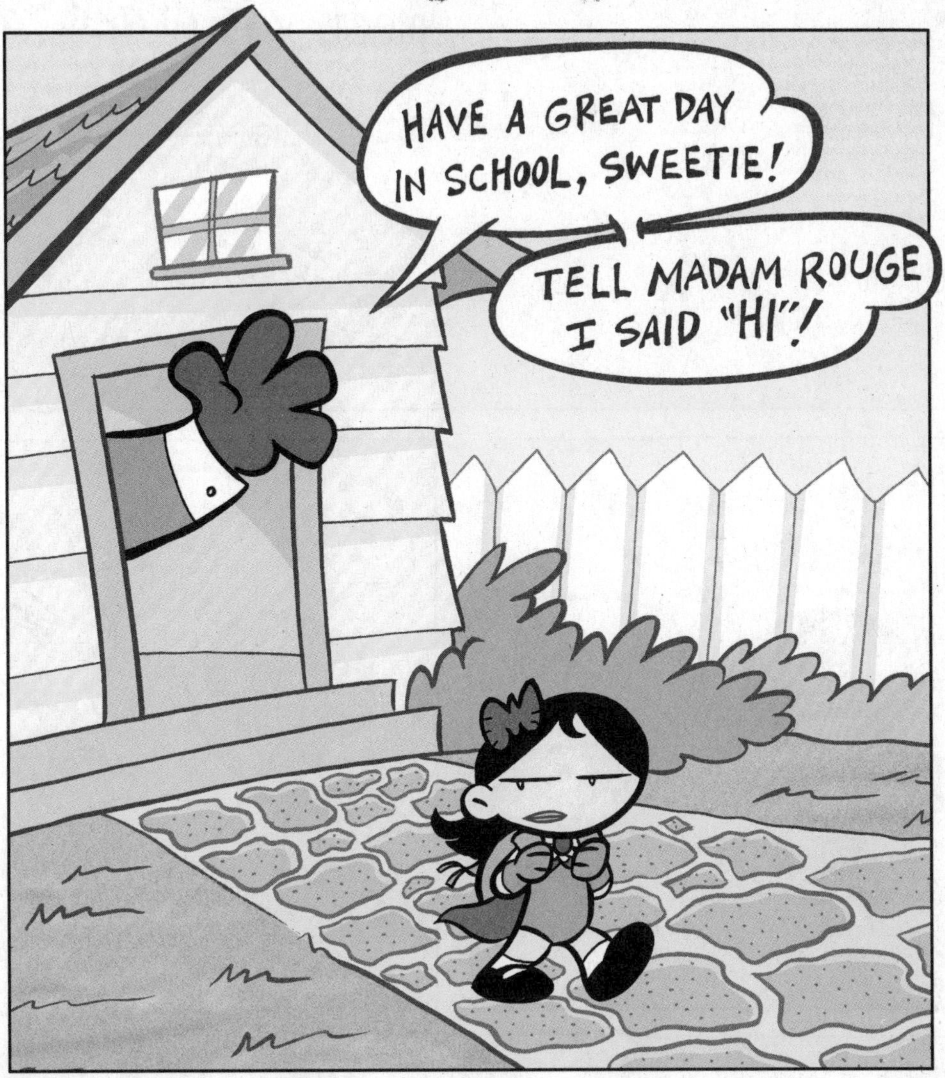
HAVE A GREAT DAY IN SCHOOL, SWEETIE!
TELL MADAM ROUGE I SAID "HI"!

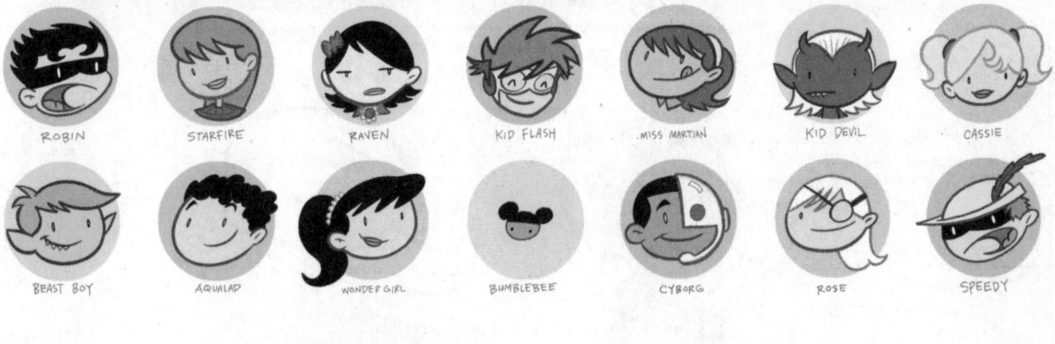
ROBIN
STARFIRE
RAVEN
KID FLASH
MISS MARTIAN
KID DEVIL
CASSIE
BEAST BOY
AQUALAD
WONDER GIRL
BUMBLEBEE
CYBORG
ROSE
SPEEDY

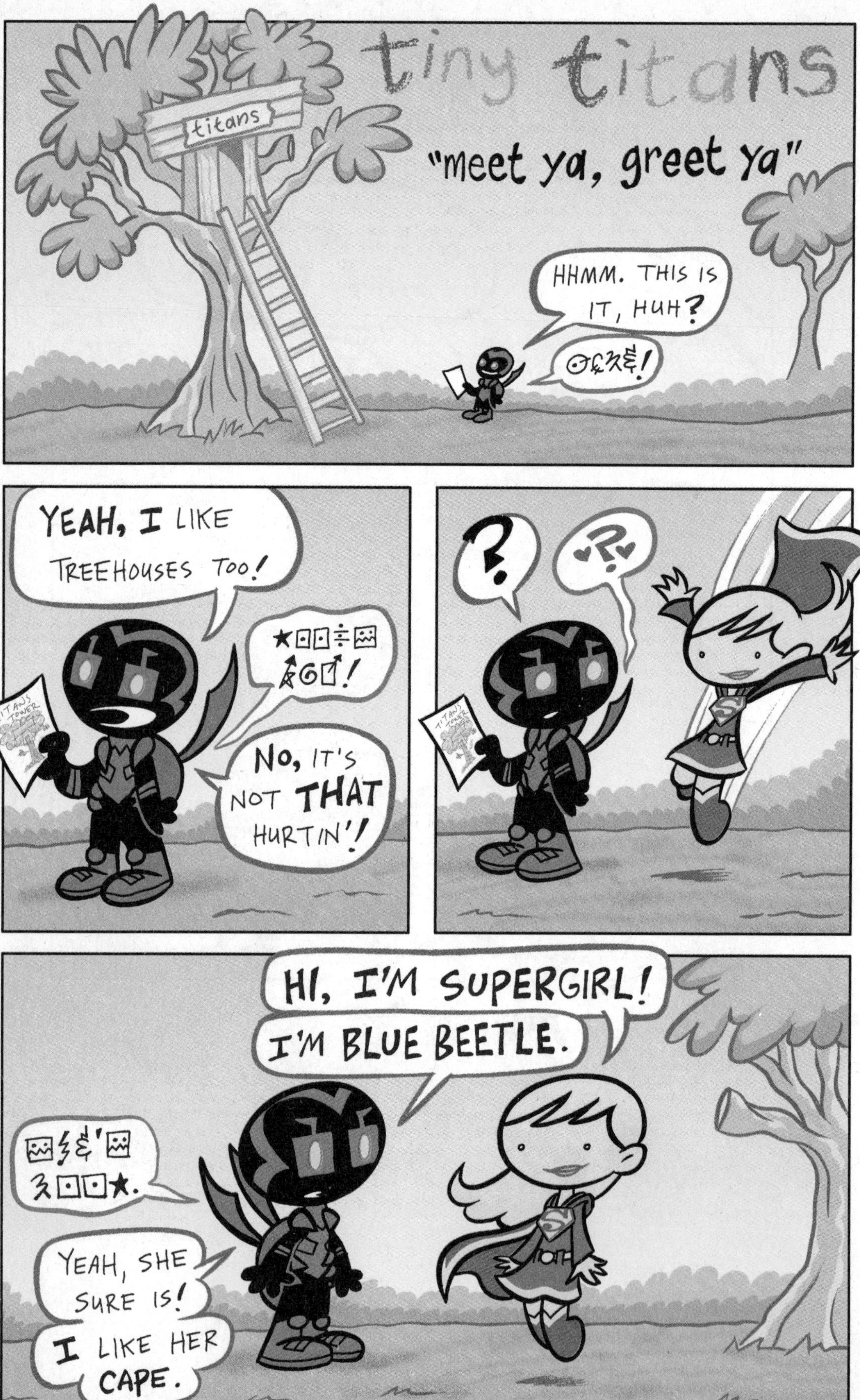
tiny titans
titans
"meet ya, greet ya"
HHMM. THIS IS IT, HUH?
YEAH, I LIKE TREEHOUSES TOO!
NO, IT'S NOT THAT HURTIN'!
?
HI, I'M SUPERGIRL!
I'M BLUE BEETLE.
YEAH, SHE SURE IS! I LIKE HER CAPE.

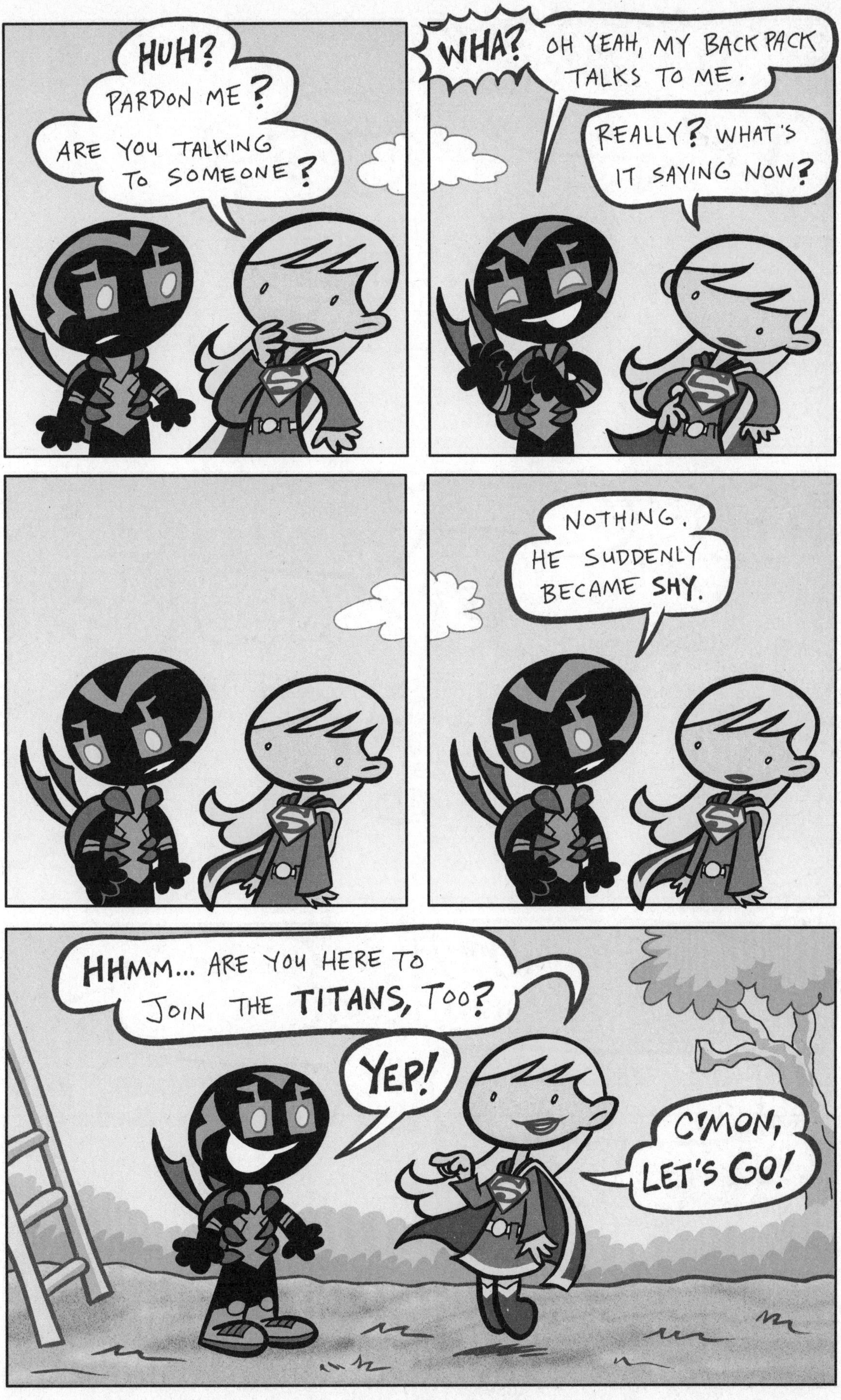
HUH?
PARDON ME?
ARE YOU TALKING TO SOMEONE?
WHA?
OH YEAH, MY BACKPACK TALKS TO ME.
REALLY? WHAT'S IT SAYING NOW?
NOTHING.
HE SUDDENLY BECAME SHY.
HHMM... ARE YOU HERE TO JOIN THE TITANS, TOO?
YEP!
C'MON, LET'S GO!

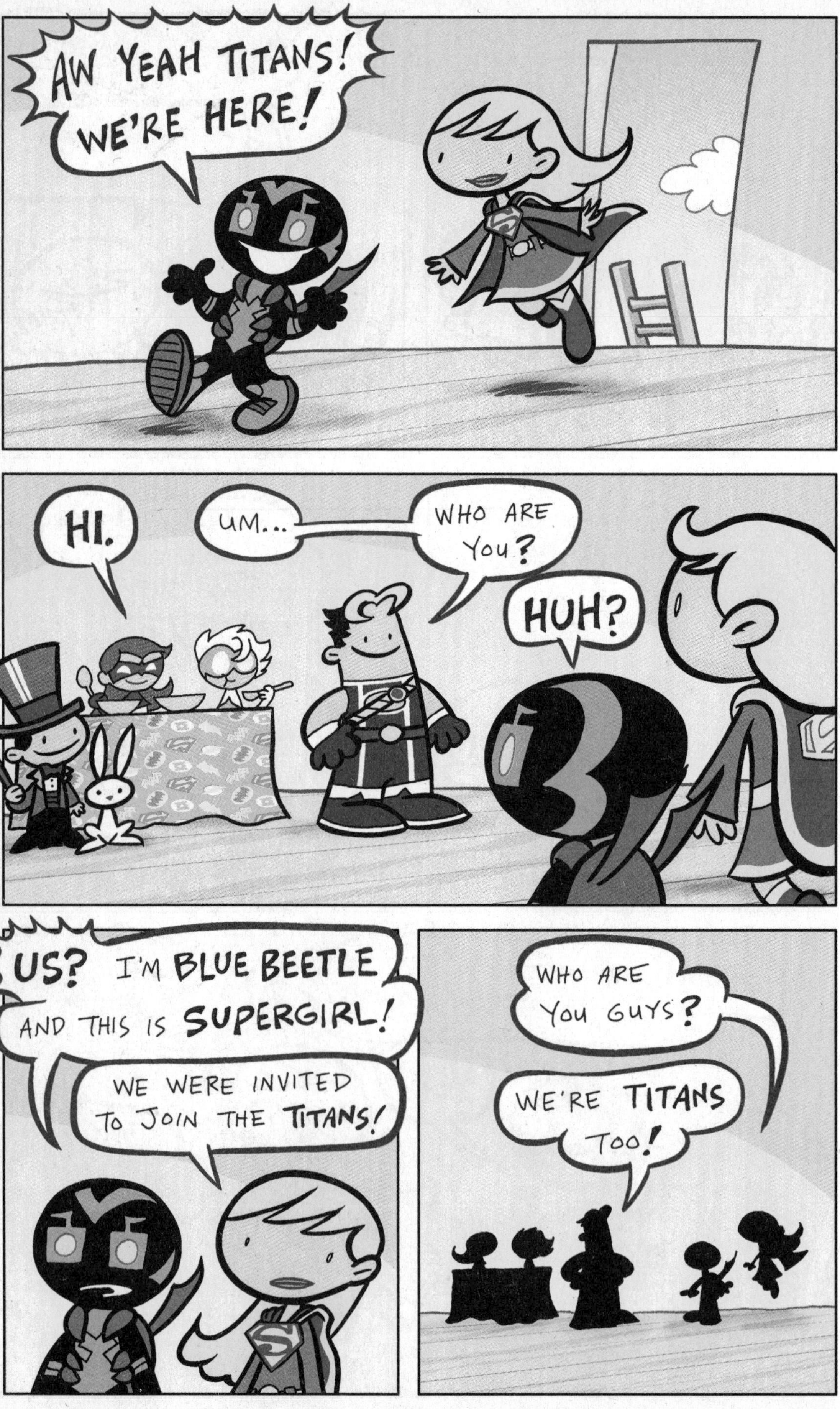
AW YEAH TITANS! WE'RE HERE!
HI.
UM...
WHO ARE YOU?
HUH?
US? I'M BLUE BEETLE AND THIS IS SUPERGIRL!
WE WERE INVITED TO JOIN THE TITANS!
WHO ARE YOU GUYS?
WE'RE TITANS TOO!

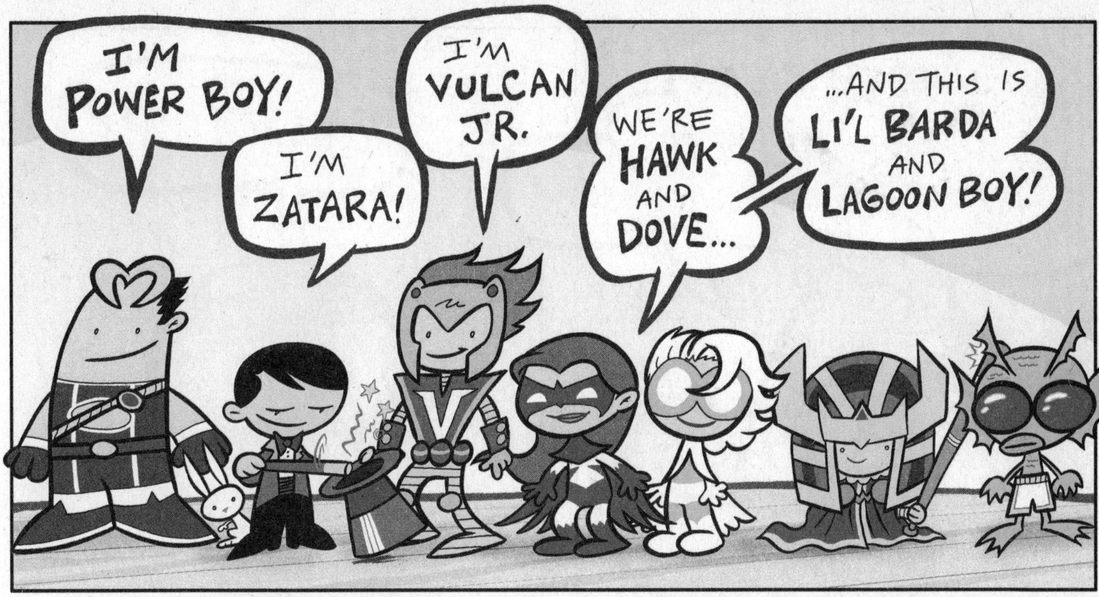
I'M POWER BOY!
I'M ZATARA!
I'M VULCAN JR.
WE'RE HAWK AND DOVE...
...AND THIS IS LI'L BARDA AND LAGOON BOY!

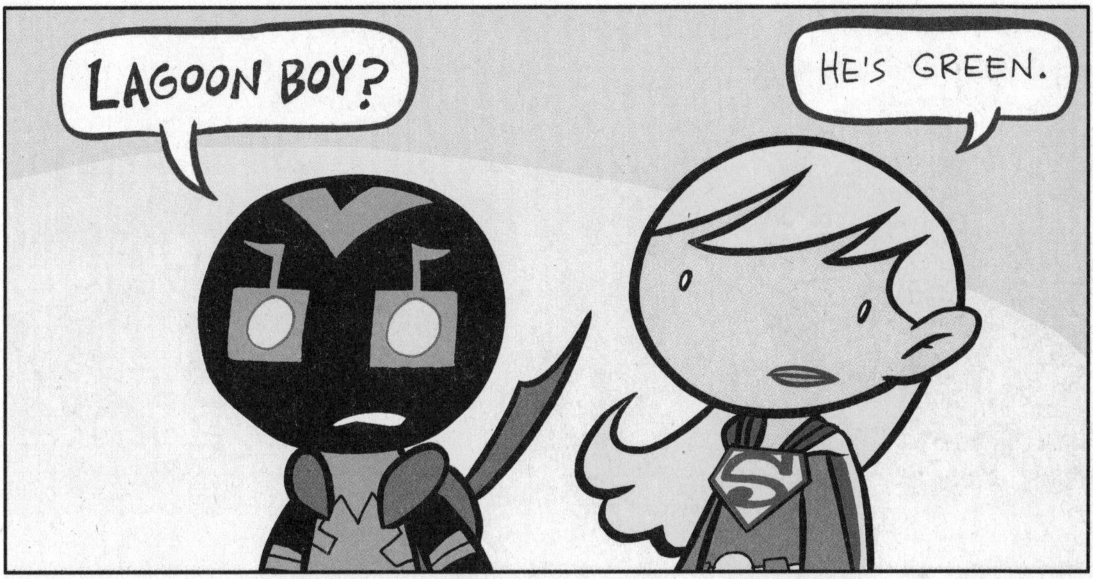
LAGOON BOY?
HE'S GREEN.

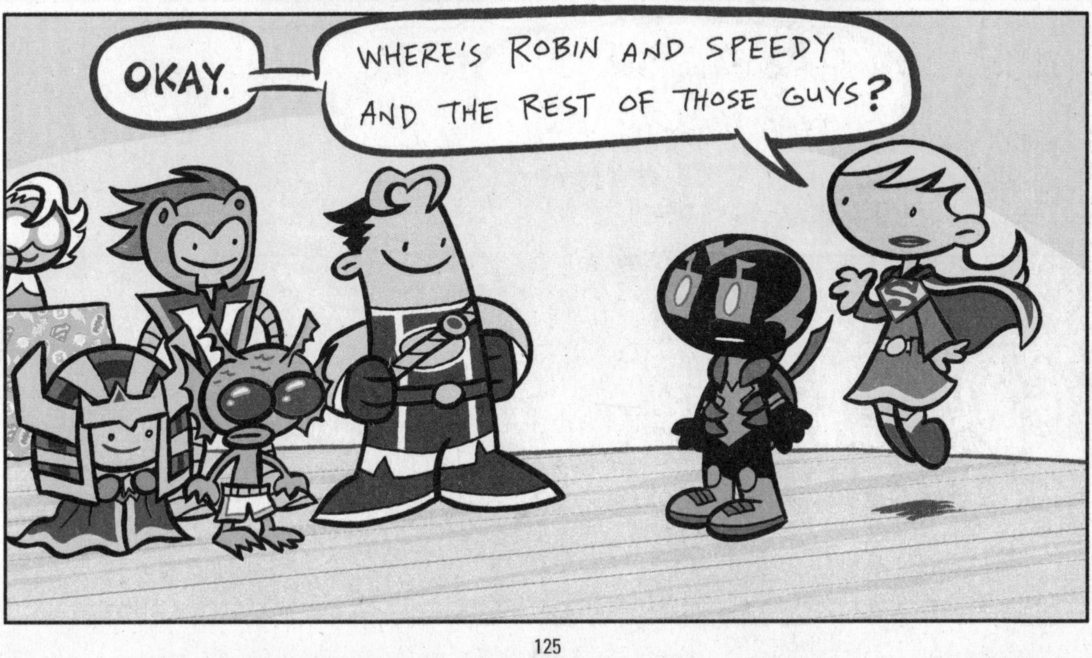
OKAY.
WHERE'S ROBIN AND SPEEDY AND THE REST OF THOSE GUYS?

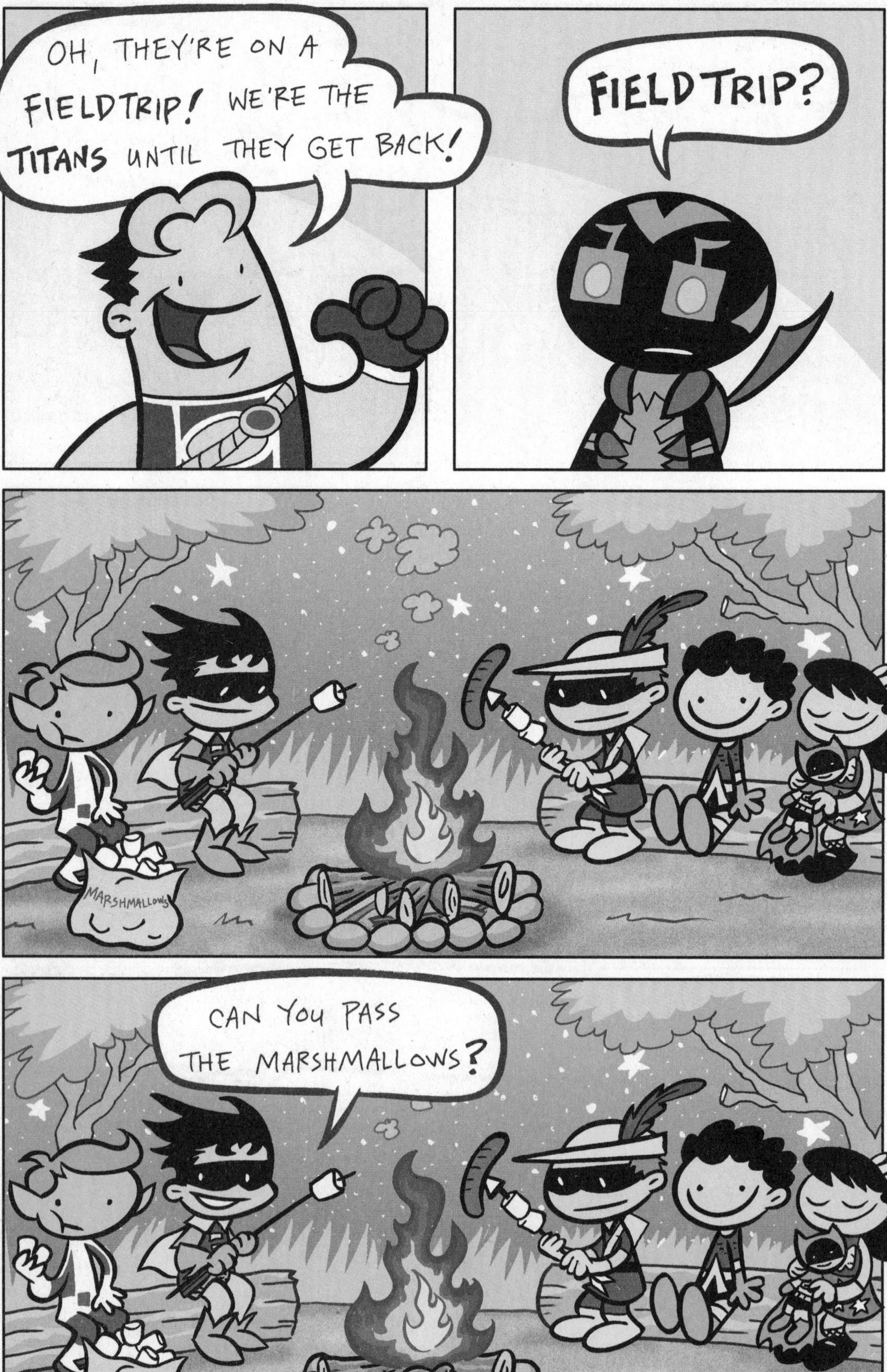
OH, THEY'RE ON A FIELDTRIP! WE'RE THE TITANS UNTIL THEY GET BACK!
FIELD TRIP?
MARSHMALLOWS
CAN YOU PASS THE MARSHMALLOWS?
MARSHMALLOWS

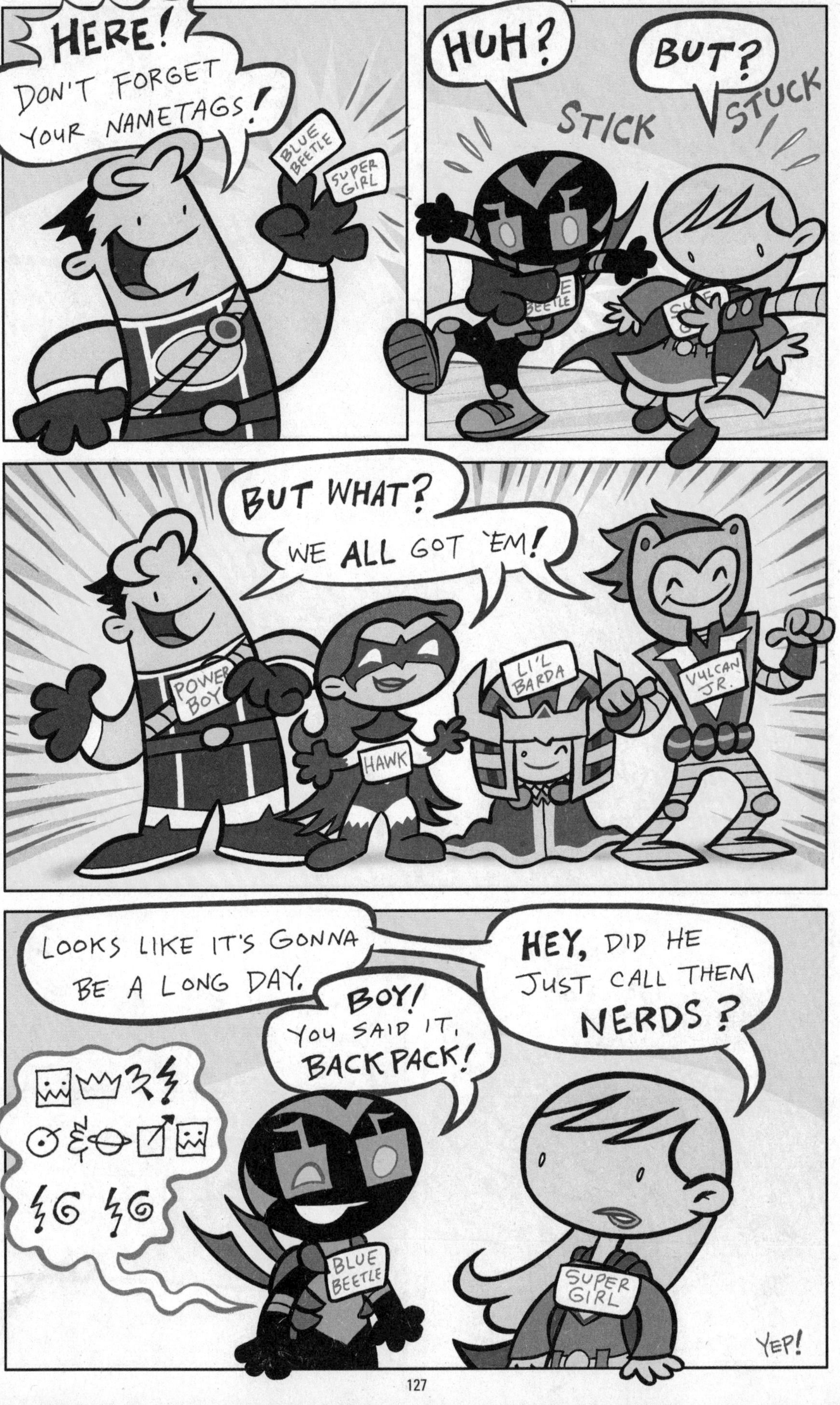
HERE!
DON'T FORGET YOUR NAMETAGS!
BLUE BEETLE
SUPER GIRL
HUH?
BUT?
STICK
STUCK
BUT WHAT?
WE ALL GOT 'EM!
POWER BOY
HAWK
LI'L BARDA
VULCAN JR.
LOOKS LIKE IT'S GONNA BE A LONG DAY.
BOY! YOU SAID IT, BACKPACK!
HEY, DID HE JUST CALL THEM NERDS?
BLUE BEETLE
SUPER GIRL
YEP!

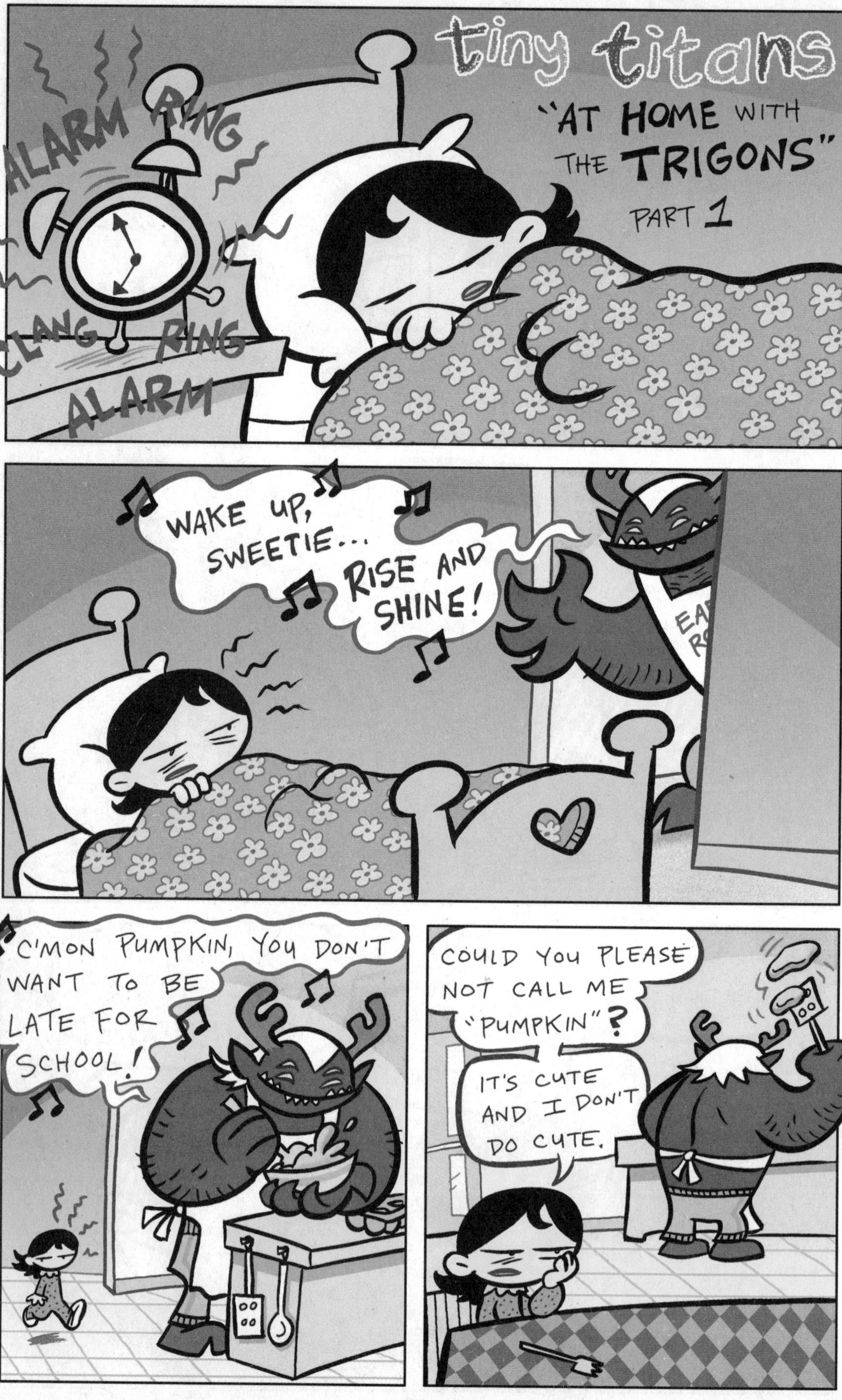
tiny titans
"AT HOME WITH THE TRIGONS"
PART 1
ALARM RING
CLANG RING
ALARM
WAKE UP, SWEETIE... RISE AND SHINE!
C'MON PUMPKIN, YOU DON'T WANT TO BE LATE FOR SCHOOL!
COULD YOU PLEASE NOT CALL ME "PUMPKIN"?
IT'S CUTE AND I DON'T DO CUTE.

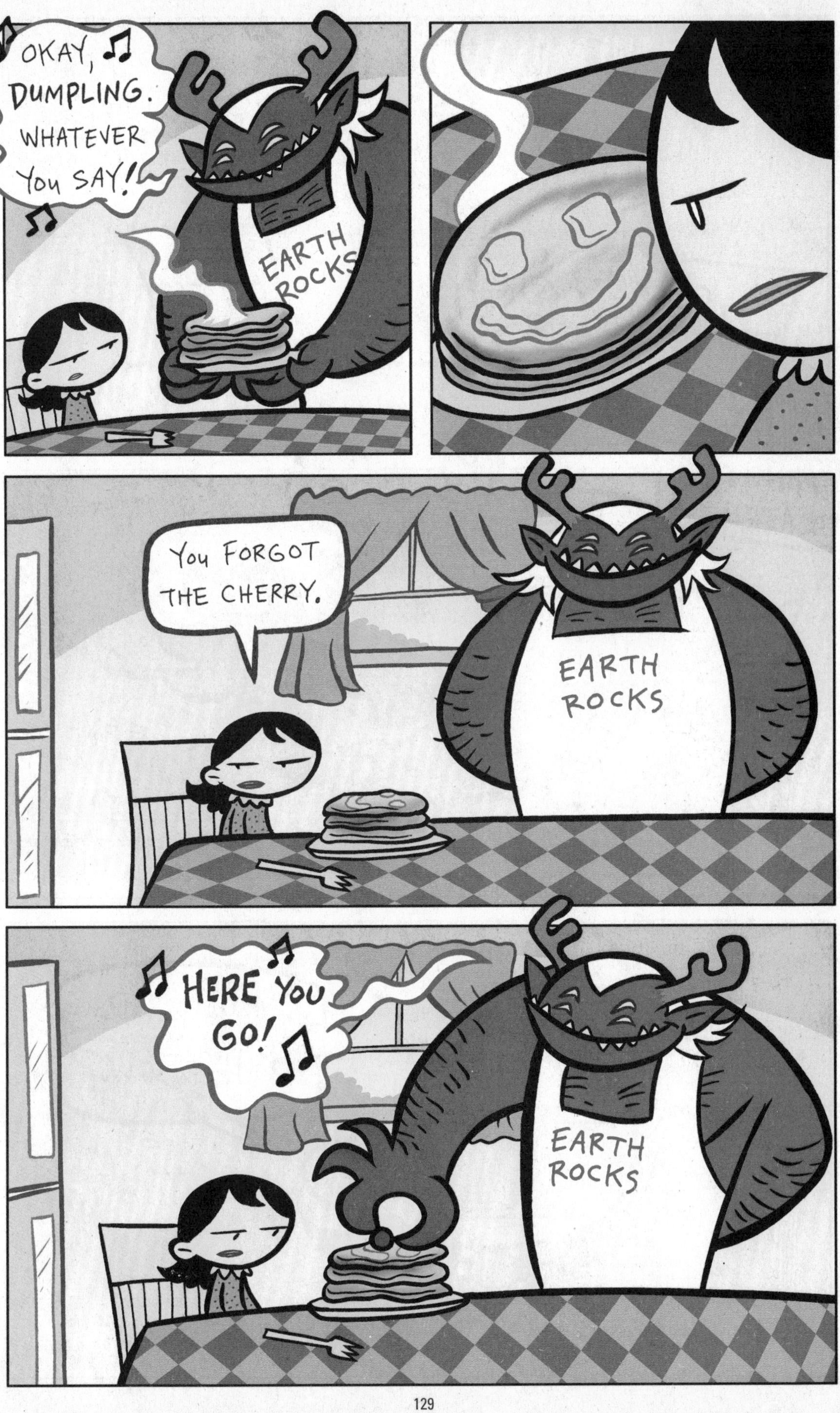
OKAY, DUMPLING. WHATEVER YOU SAY!
EARTH ROCKS
YOU FORGOT THE CHERRY.
EARTH ROCKS
HERE YOU GO!
EARTH ROCKS

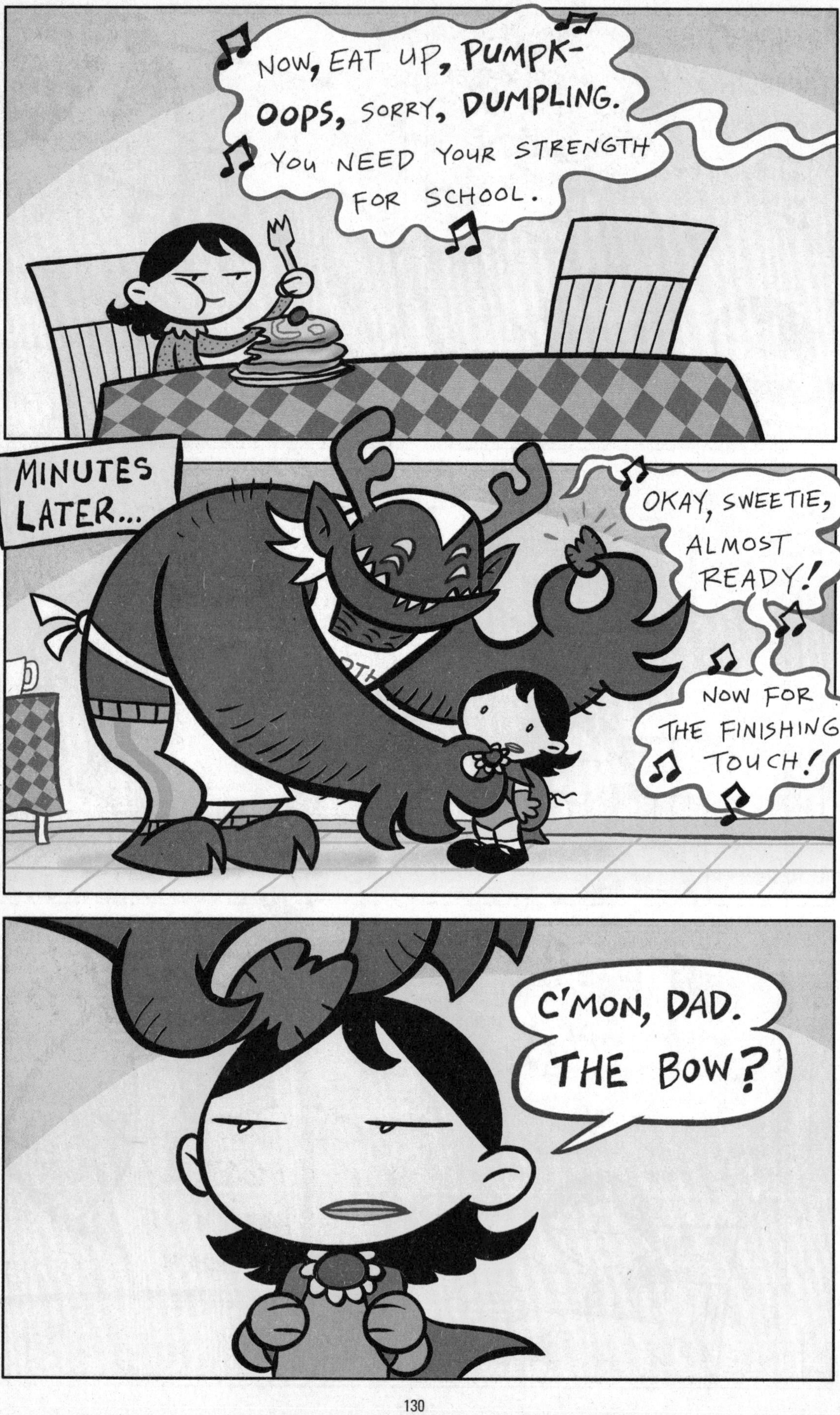
NOW, EAT UP, PUMPK- OOPS, SORRY, DUMPLING. YOU NEED YOUR STRENGTH FOR SCHOOL.
MINUTES LATER...
OKAY, SWEETIE, ALMOST READY!
NOW FOR THE FINISHING TOUCH!
C'MON, DAD. THE BOW?

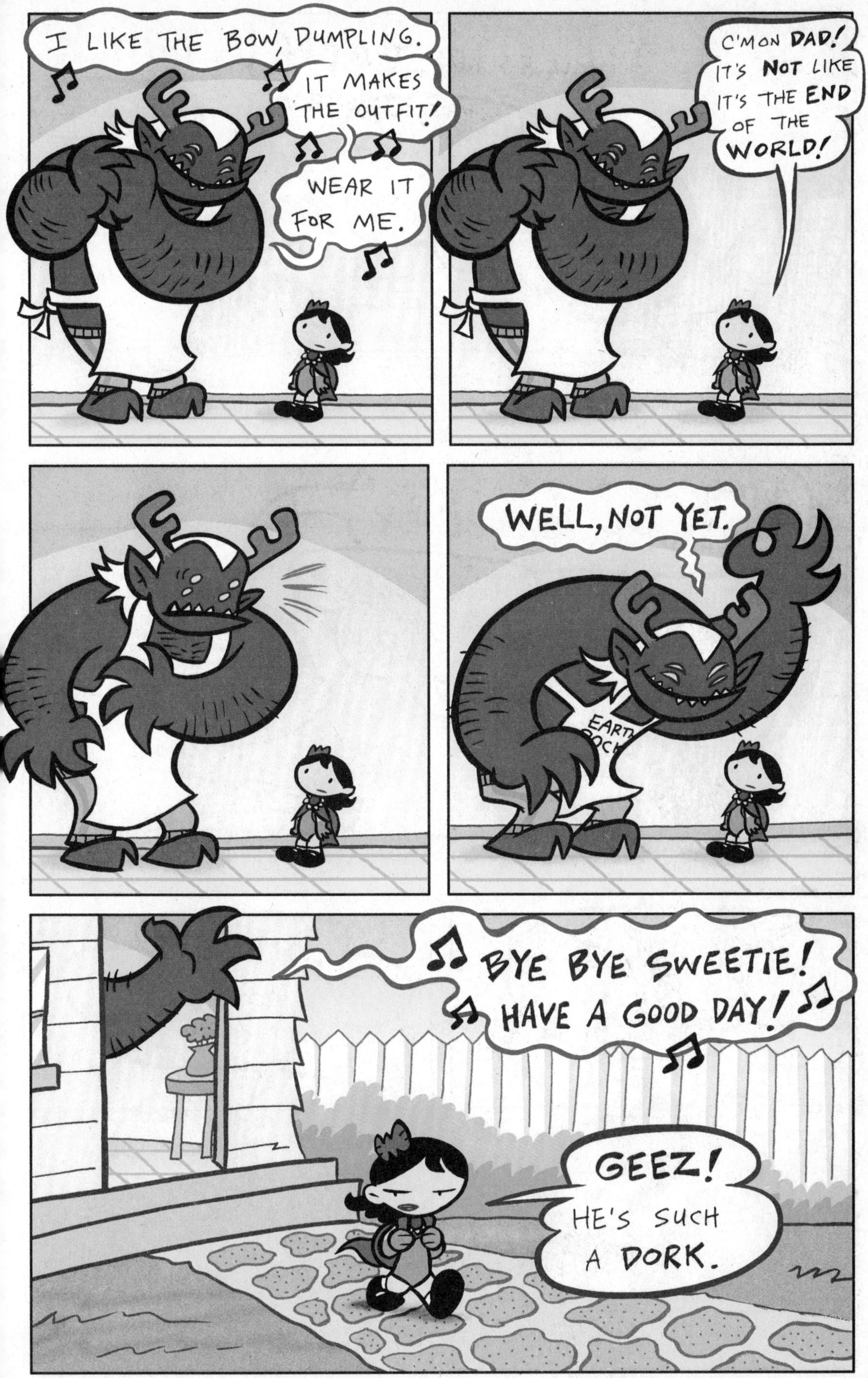
I LIKE THE BOW, DUMPLING.
IT MAKES THE OUTFIT!
WEAR IT FOR ME.
C'MON DAD! IT'S NOT LIKE IT'S THE END OF THE WORLD!
WELL, NOT YET.
BYE BYE SWEETIE! HAVE A GOOD DAY!
GEEZ! HE'S SUCH A DORK.

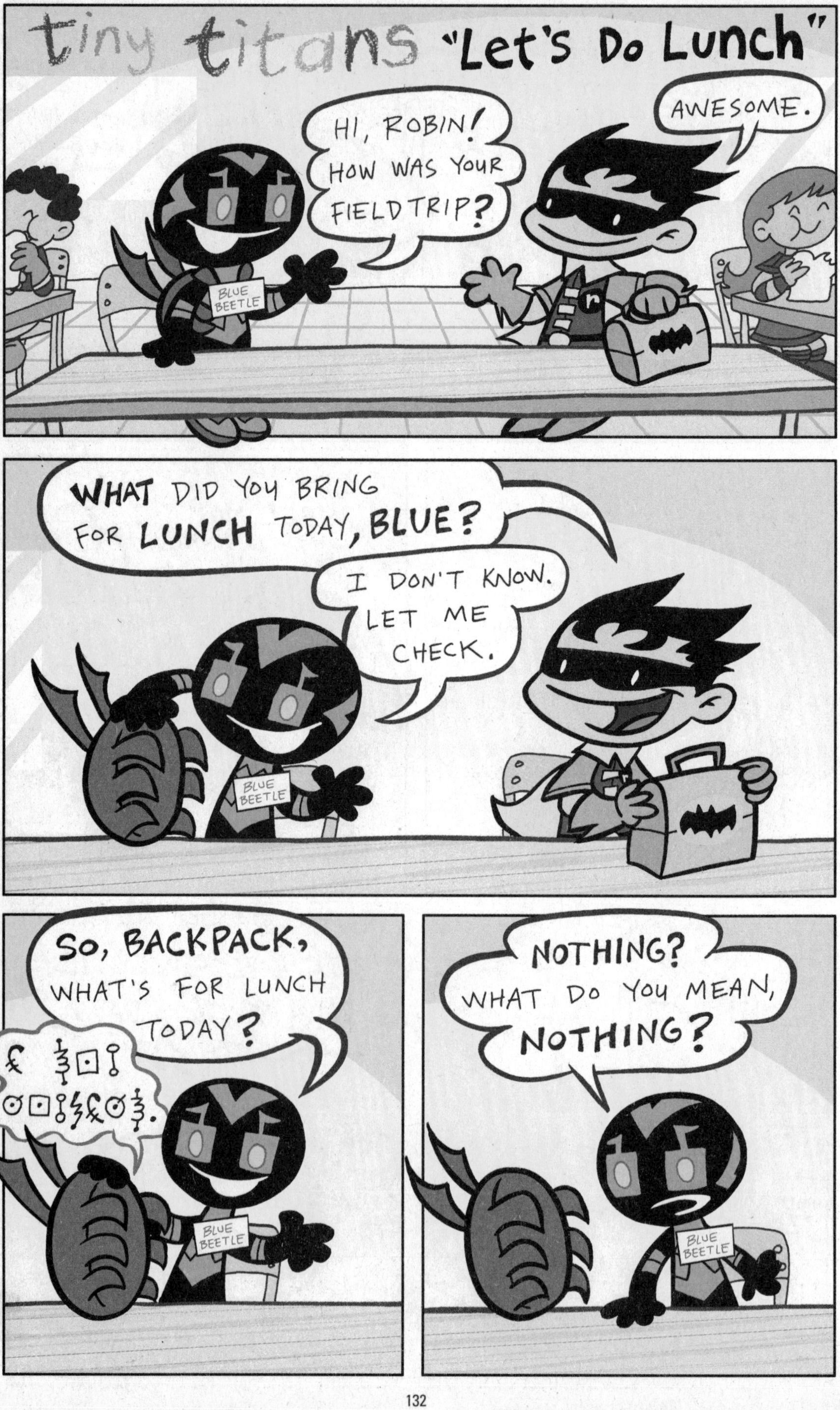
tiny titans "Let's Do Lunch"
HI, ROBIN! HOW WAS YOUR FIELDTRIP?
AWESOME.
BLUE BEETLE
WHAT DID YOU BRING FOR LUNCH TODAY, BLUE?
I DON'T KNOW. LET ME CHECK.
BLUE BEETLE
SO, BACKPACK, WHAT'S FOR LUNCH TODAY?
BLUE BEETLE
NOTHING? WHAT DO YOU MEAN, NOTHING?
BLUE BEETLE

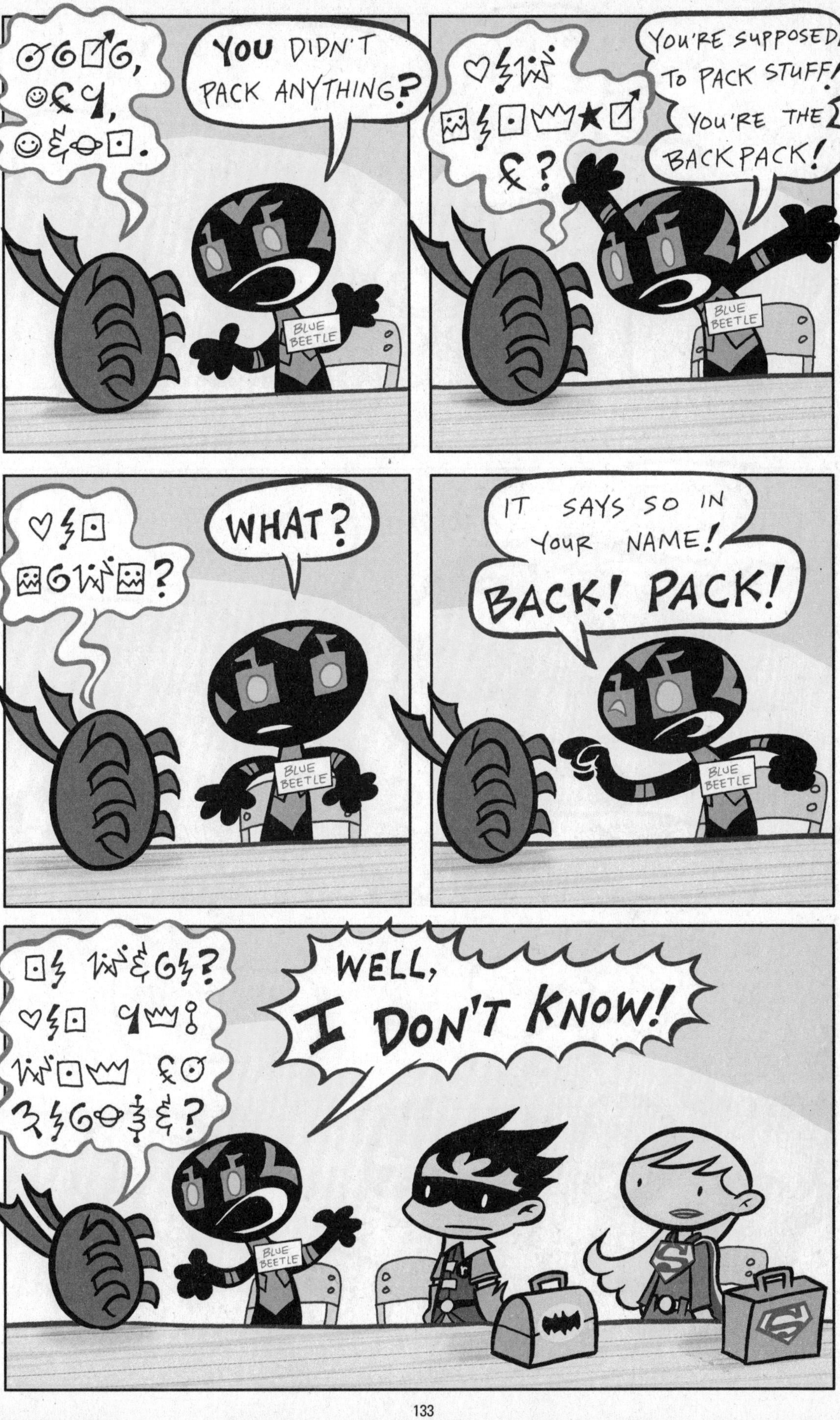
YOU DIDN'T PACK ANYTHING?
BLUE BEETLE
YOU'RE SUPPOSED TO PACK STUFF!
YOU'RE THE BACKPACK!
WHAT?
IT SAYS SO IN YOUR NAME!
BACK! PACK!
WELL, I DON'T KNOW!

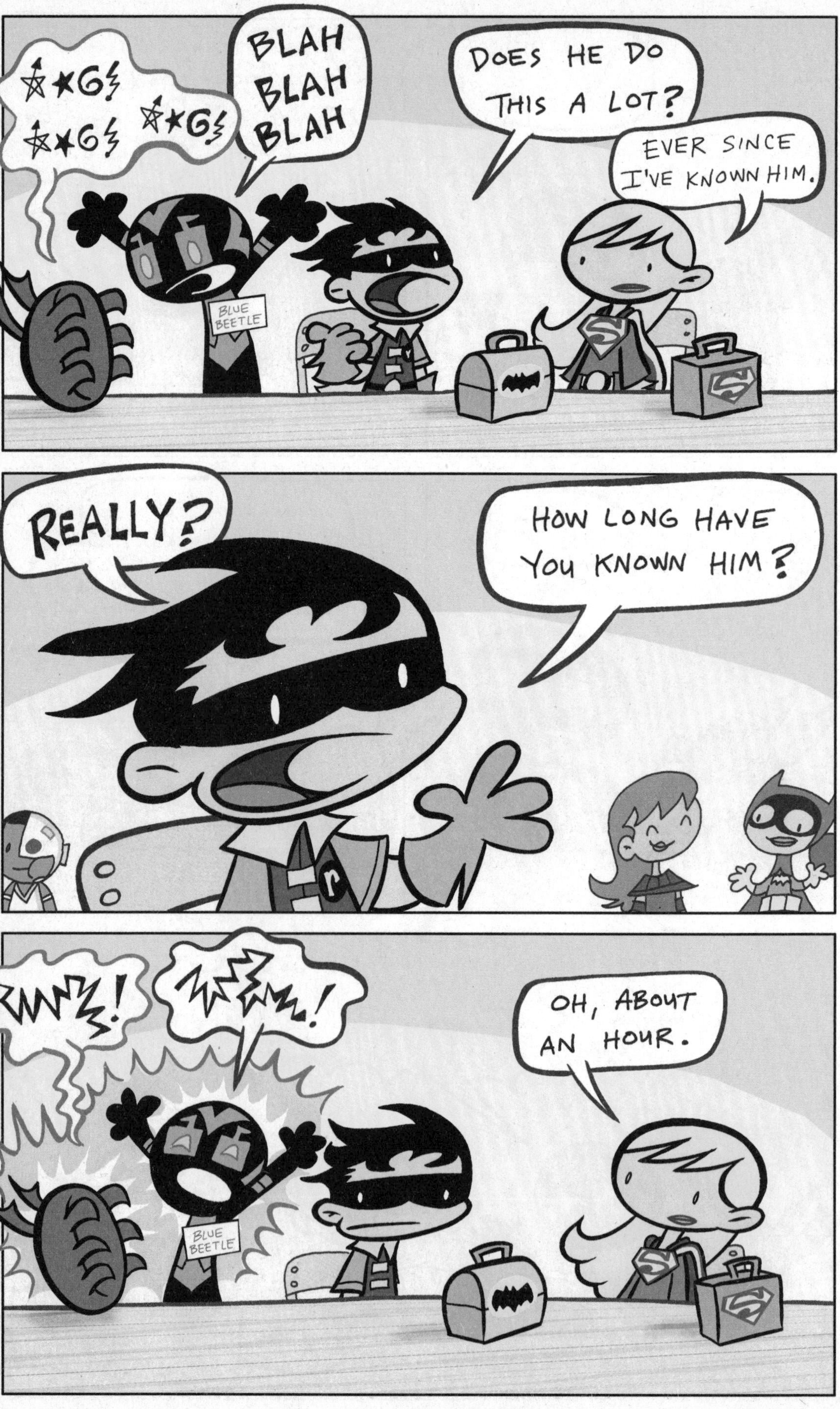
BLAH BLAH BLAH
DOES HE DO THIS A LOT?
EVER SINCE I'VE KNOWN HIM.
BLUE BEETLE
REALLY?
HOW LONG HAVE YOU KNOWN HIM?
OH, ABOUT AN HOUR.
BLUE BEETLE

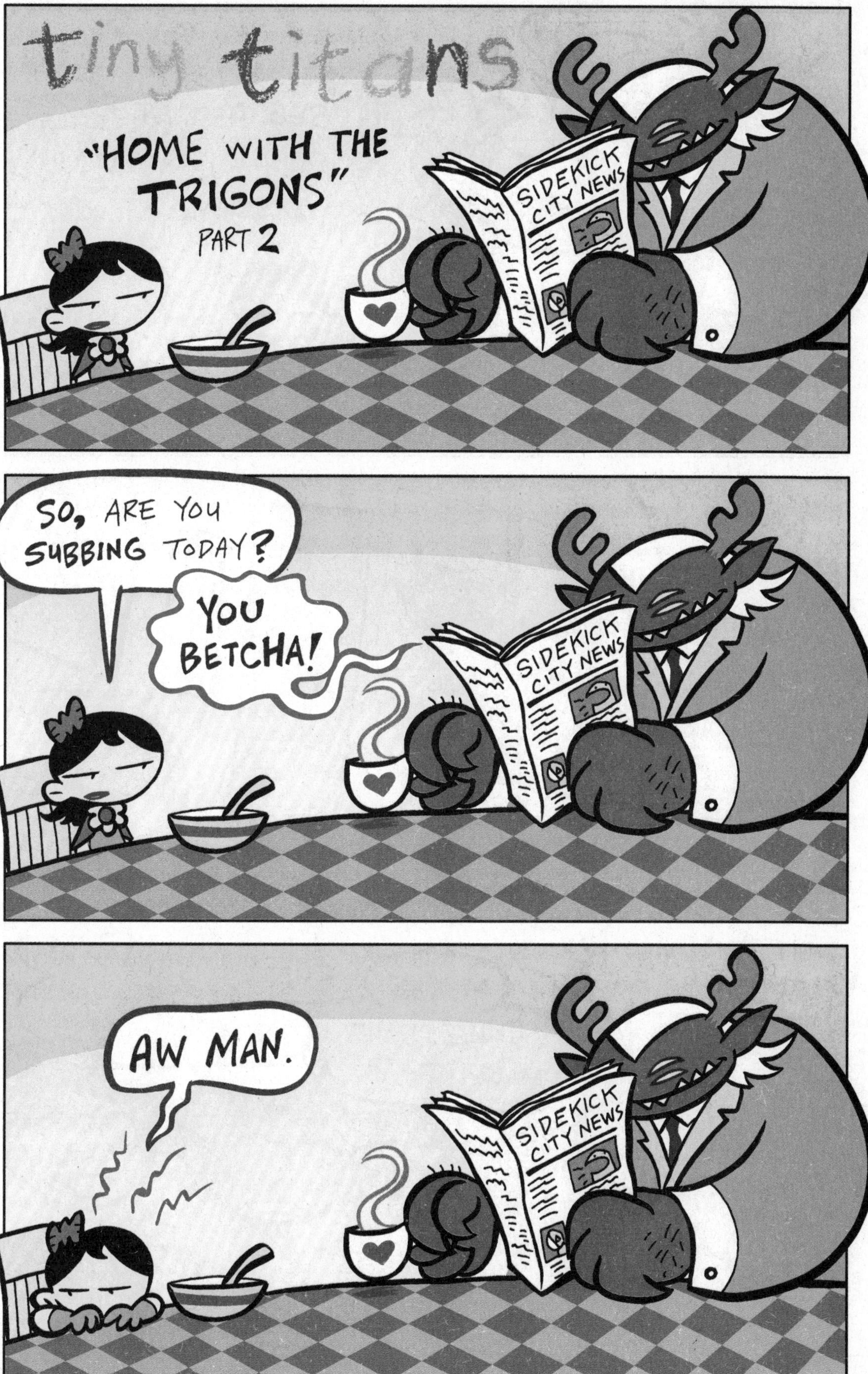
tiny titans
"HOME WITH THE TRIGONS"
PART 2
SIDEKICK CITY NEWS
SO, ARE YOU SUBBING TODAY?
YOU BETCHA!
SIDEKICK CITY NEWS
AW MAN.
SIDEKICK CITY NEWS

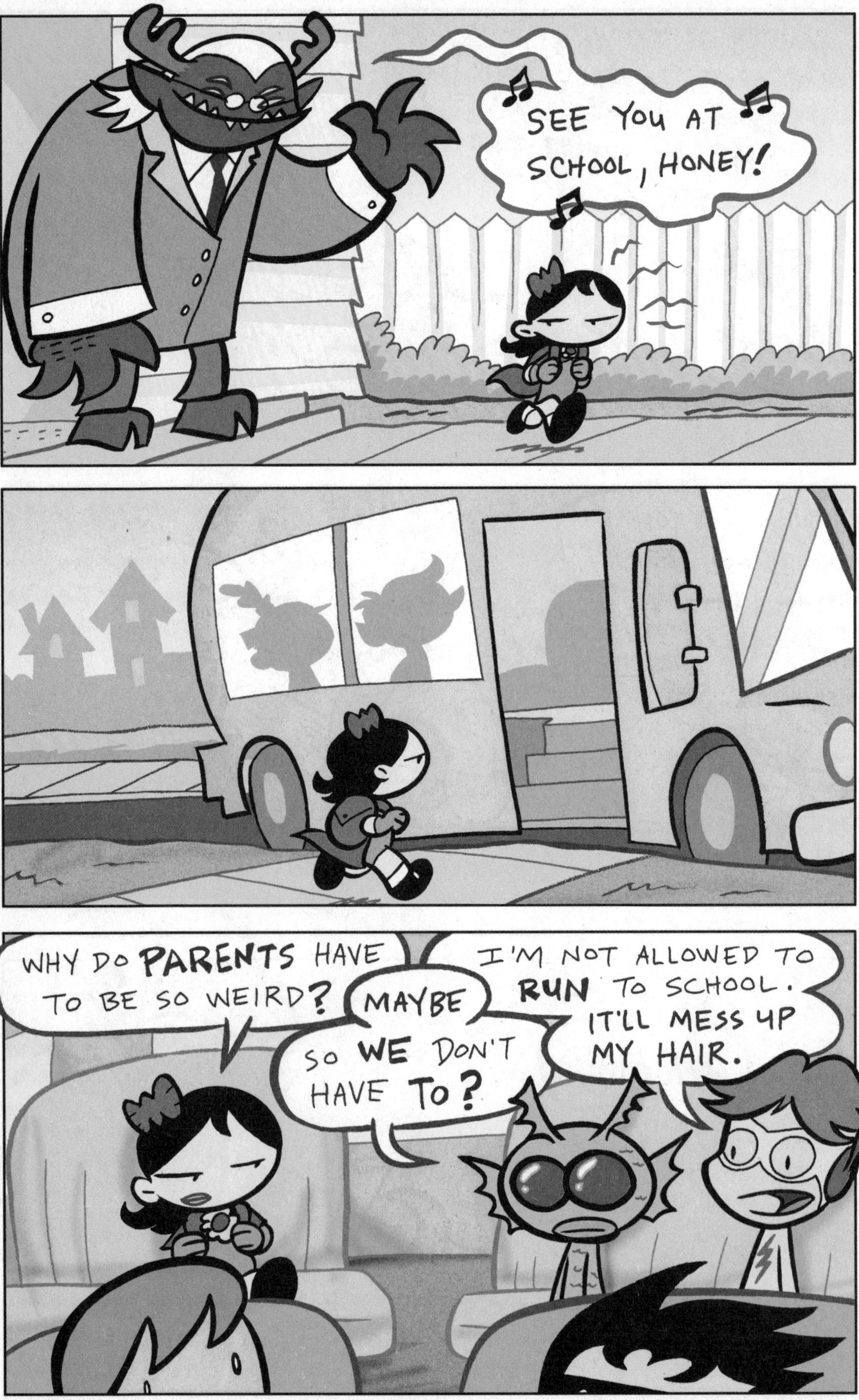
SEE YOU AT SCHOOL, HONEY!
WHY DO PARENTS HAVE TO BE SO WEIRD?
I'M NOT ALLOWED TO RUN TO SCHOOL. IT'LL MESS UP MY HAIR.
MAYBE SO WE DON'T HAVE TO?

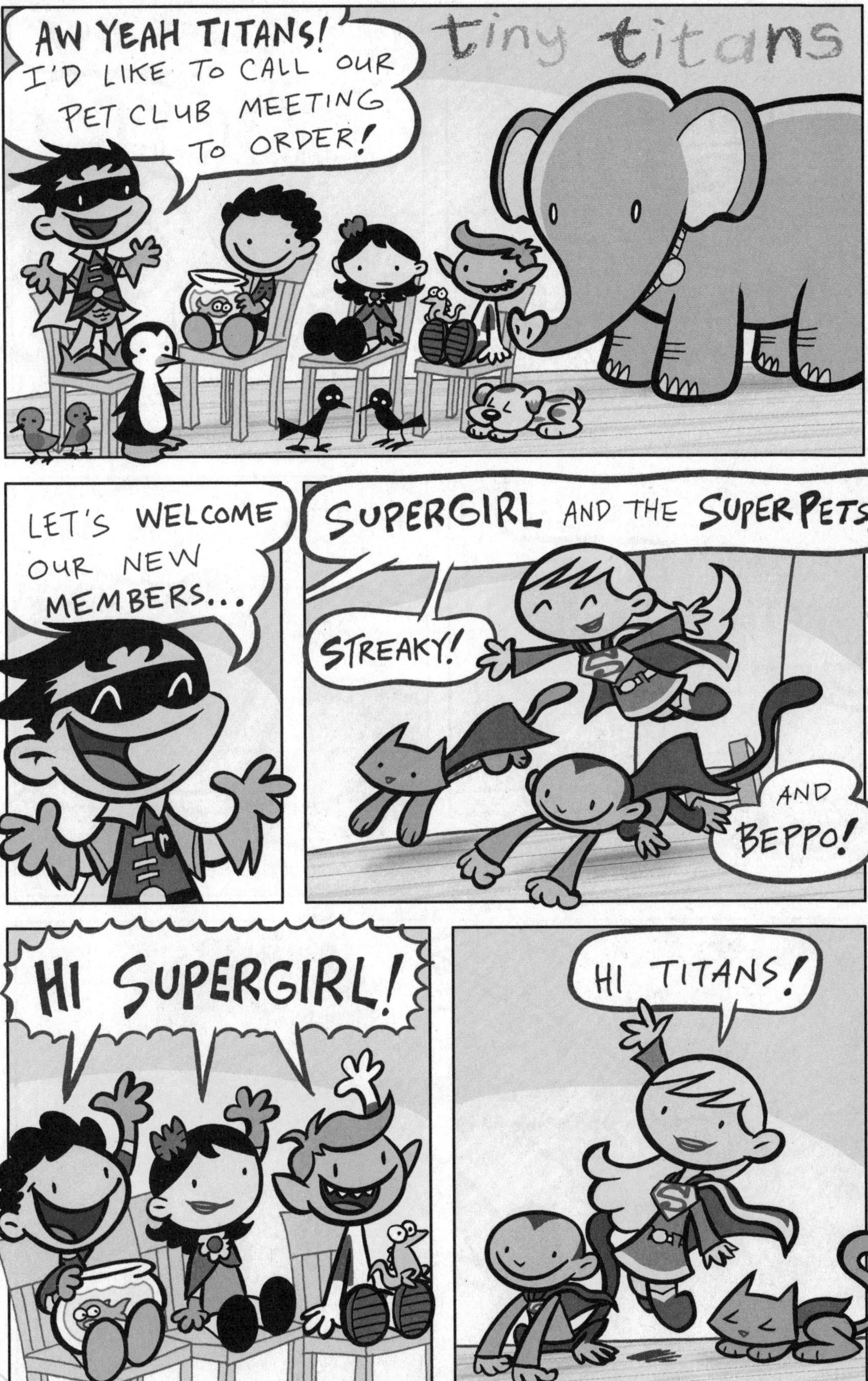
AW YEAH TITANS! I'D LIKE TO CALL OUR PET CLUB MEETING TO ORDER!
tiny titans
LET'S WELCOME OUR NEW MEMBERS...
SUPERGIRL AND THE SUPERPETS!
STREAKY!
AND BEPPO!
HI SUPERGIRL!
HI TITANS!

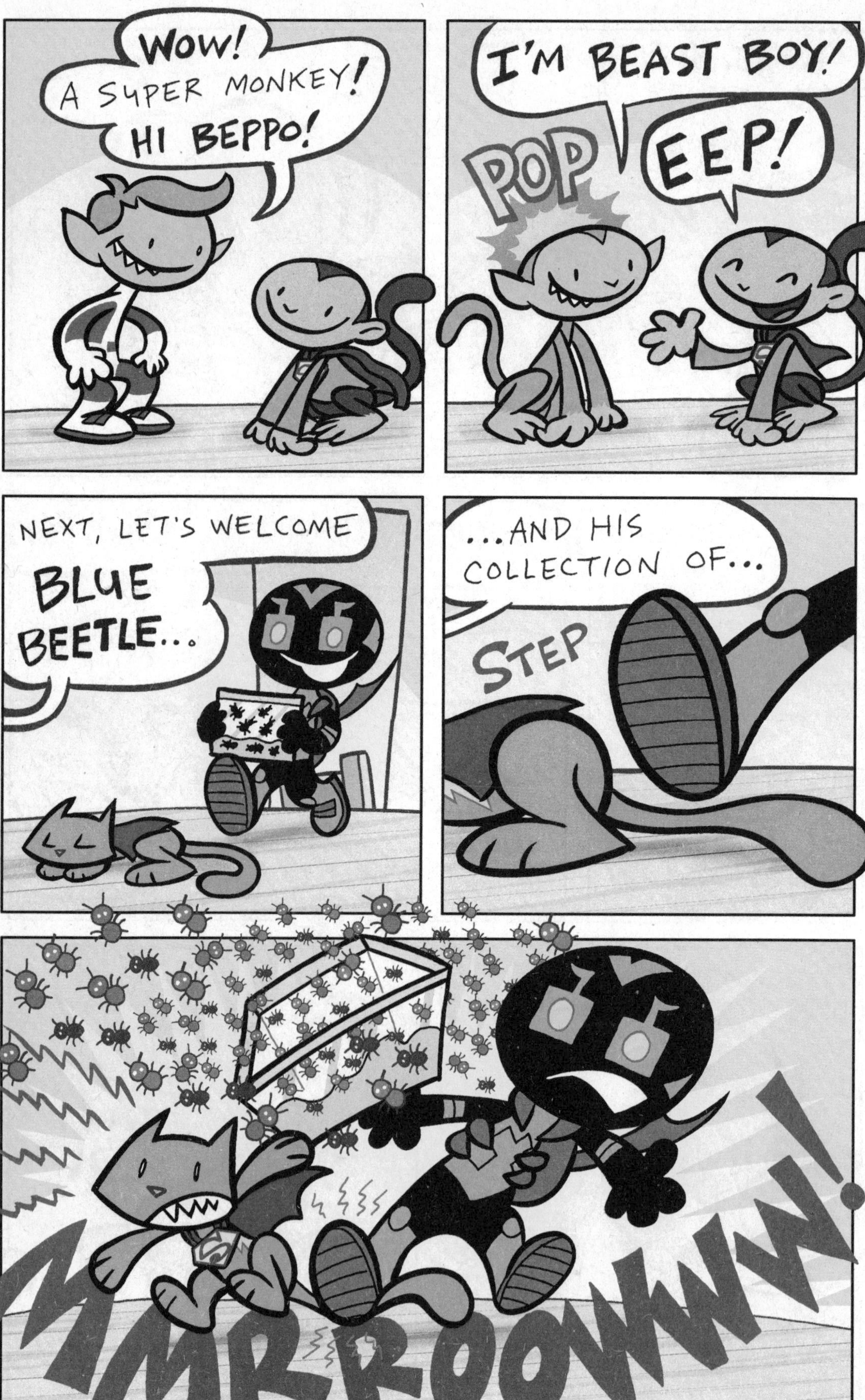
WOW!
A SUPER MONKEY!
HI BEPPO!
I'M BEAST BOY!
POP
EEP!
NEXT, LET'S WELCOME
BLUE BEETLE...
...AND HIS COLLECTION OF...
STEP
MMRROOWWW!

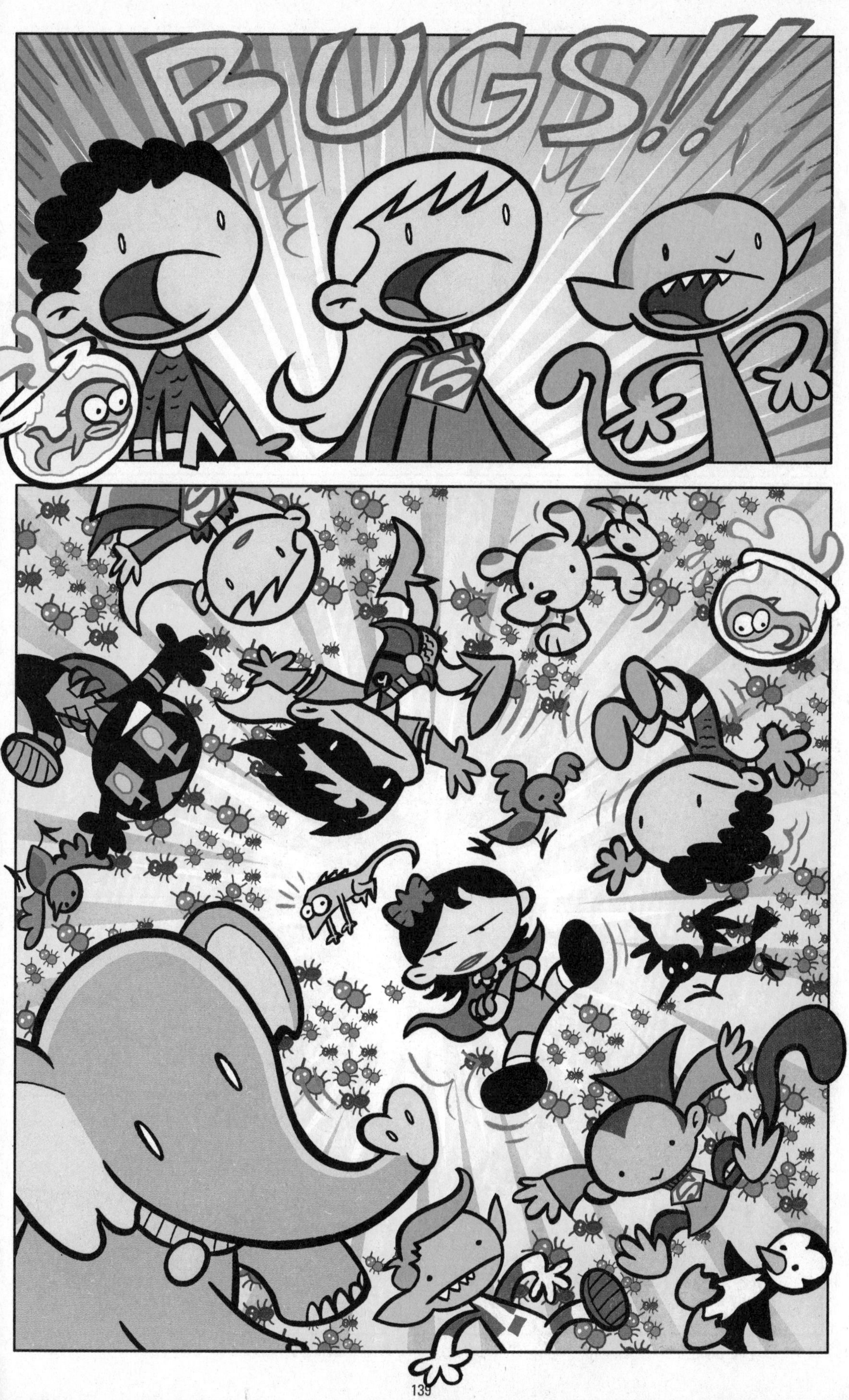
BUGS!!

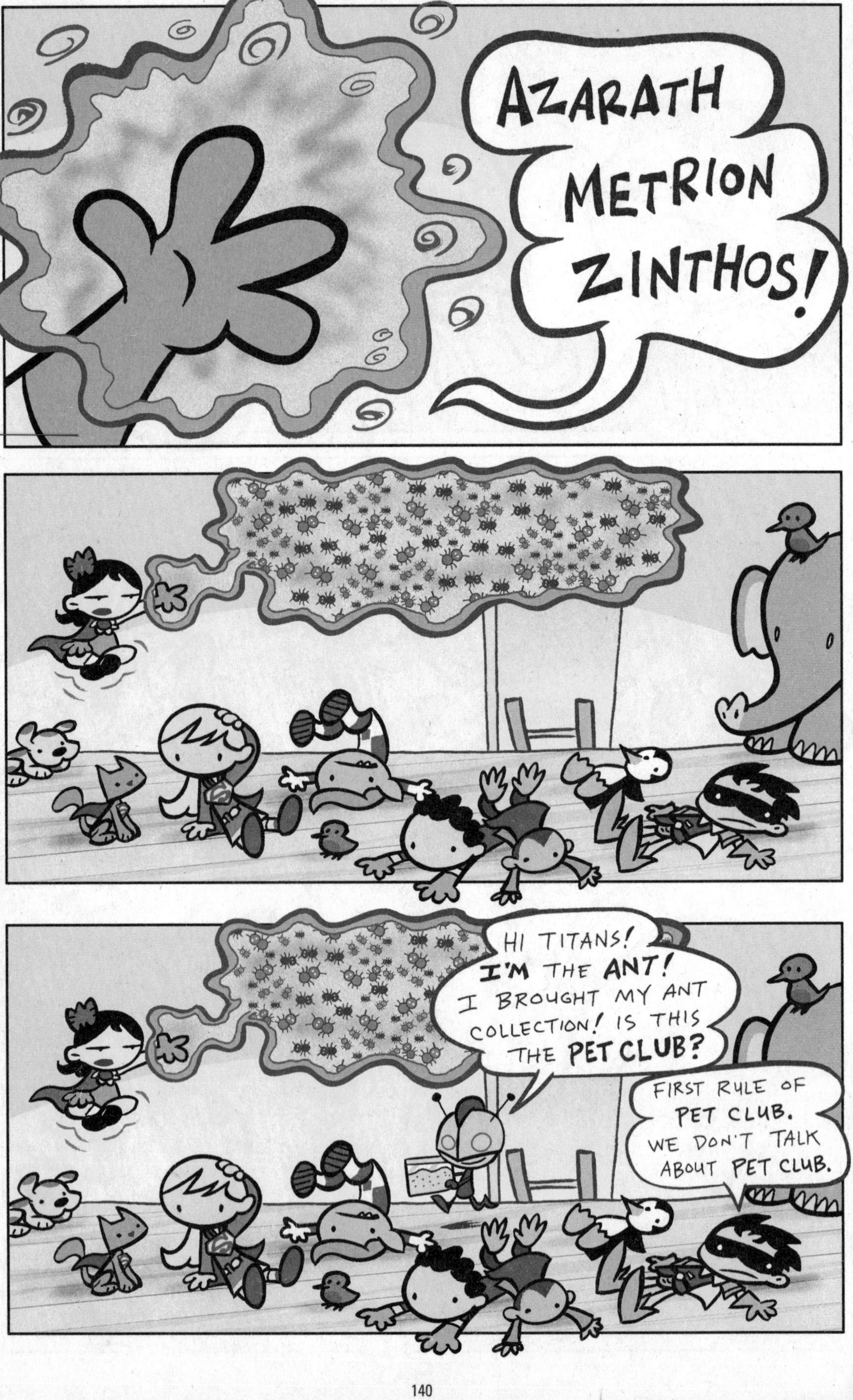
AZARATH METRION ZINTHOS!
HI TITANS! I'M THE ANT! I BROUGHT MY ANT COLLECTION! IS THIS THE PET CLUB?
FIRST RULE OF PET CLUB. WE DON'T TALK ABOUT PET CLUB.

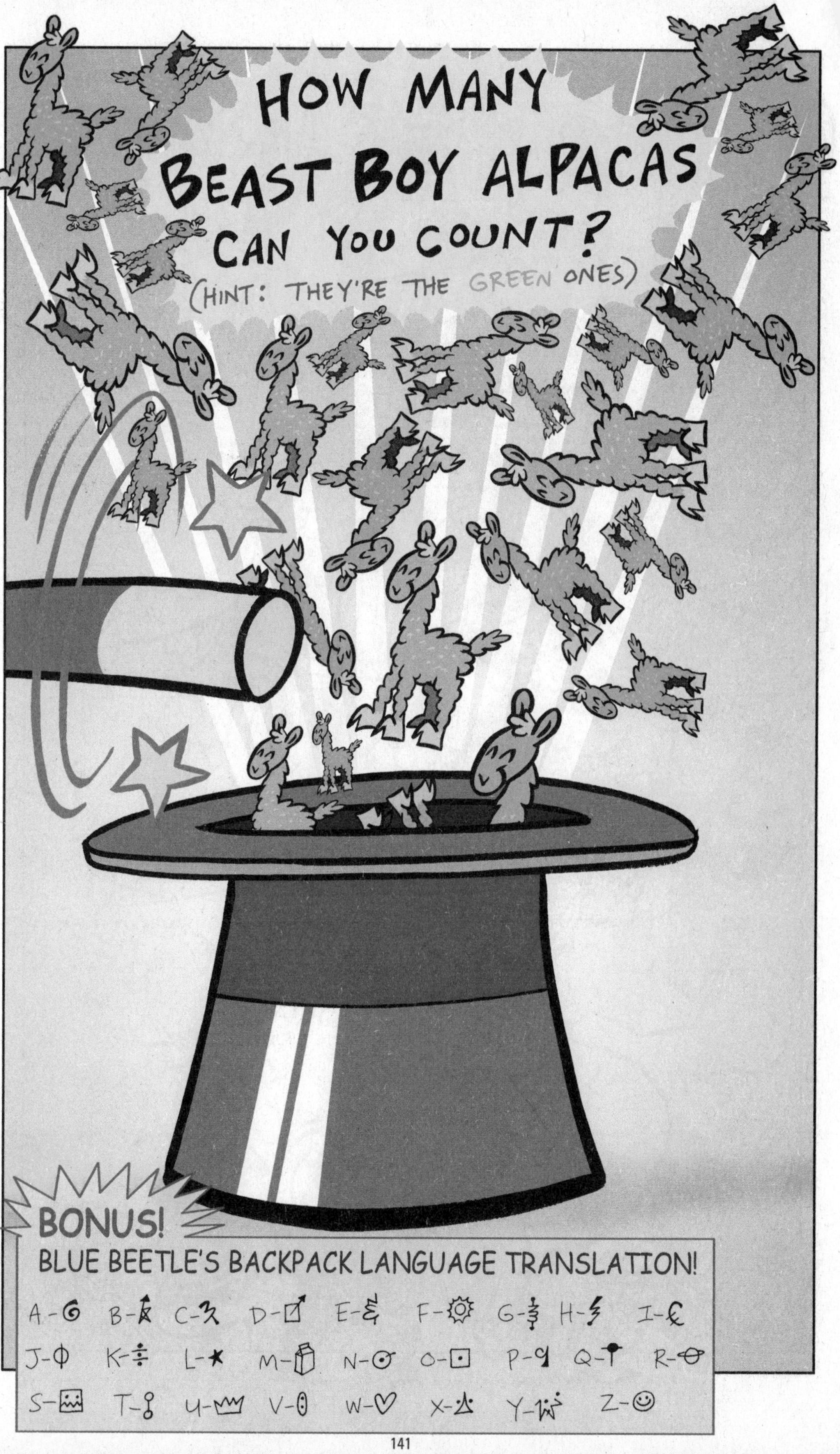
HOW MANY
BEAST BOY ALPACAS
CAN YOU COUNT?
(HINT: THEY'RE THE GREEN ONES)
BONUS!
BLUE BEETLE'S BACKPACK LANGUAGE TRANSLATION!

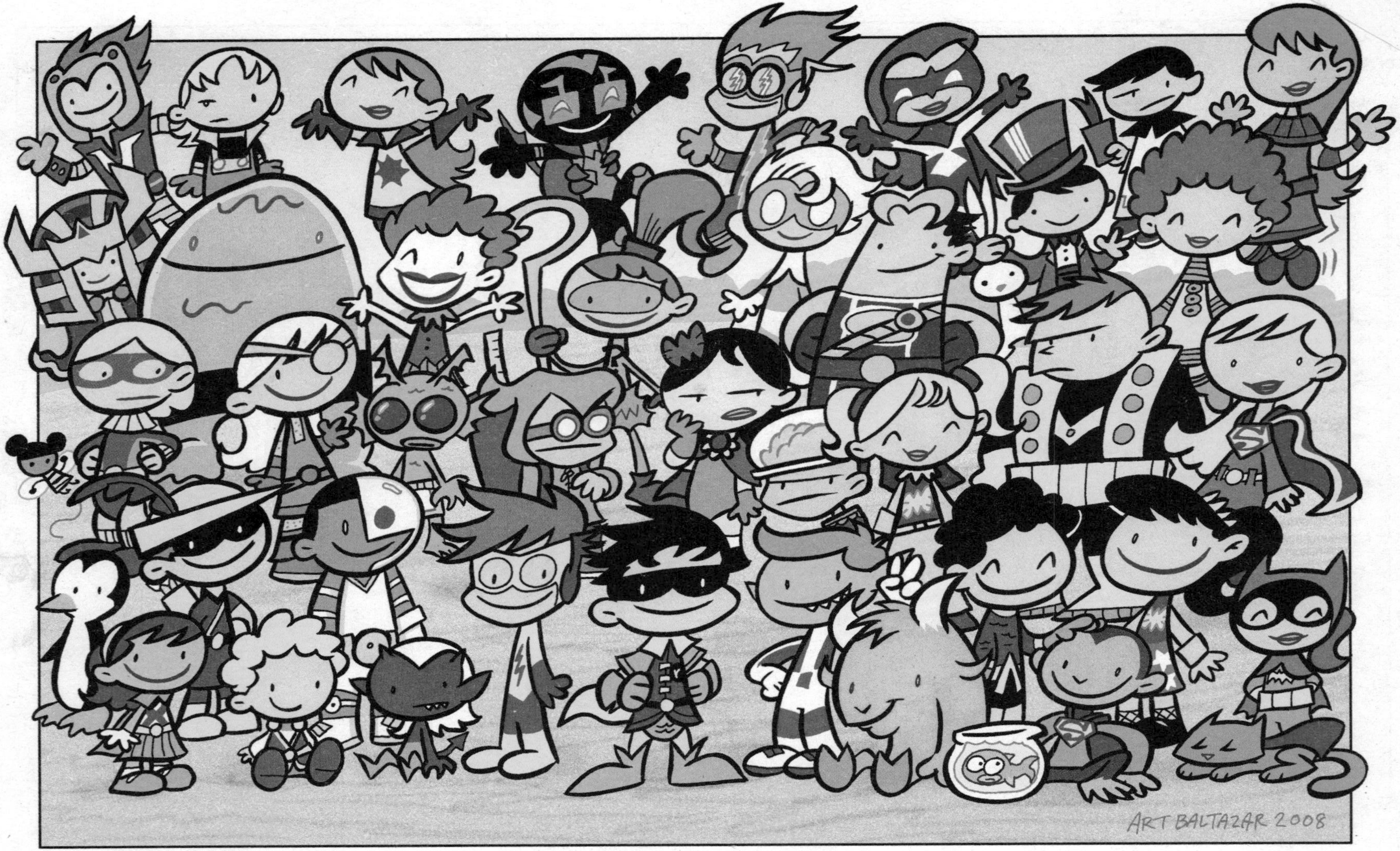
ART BALTAZAR 2008

the tiny titans of sidekick city elementary

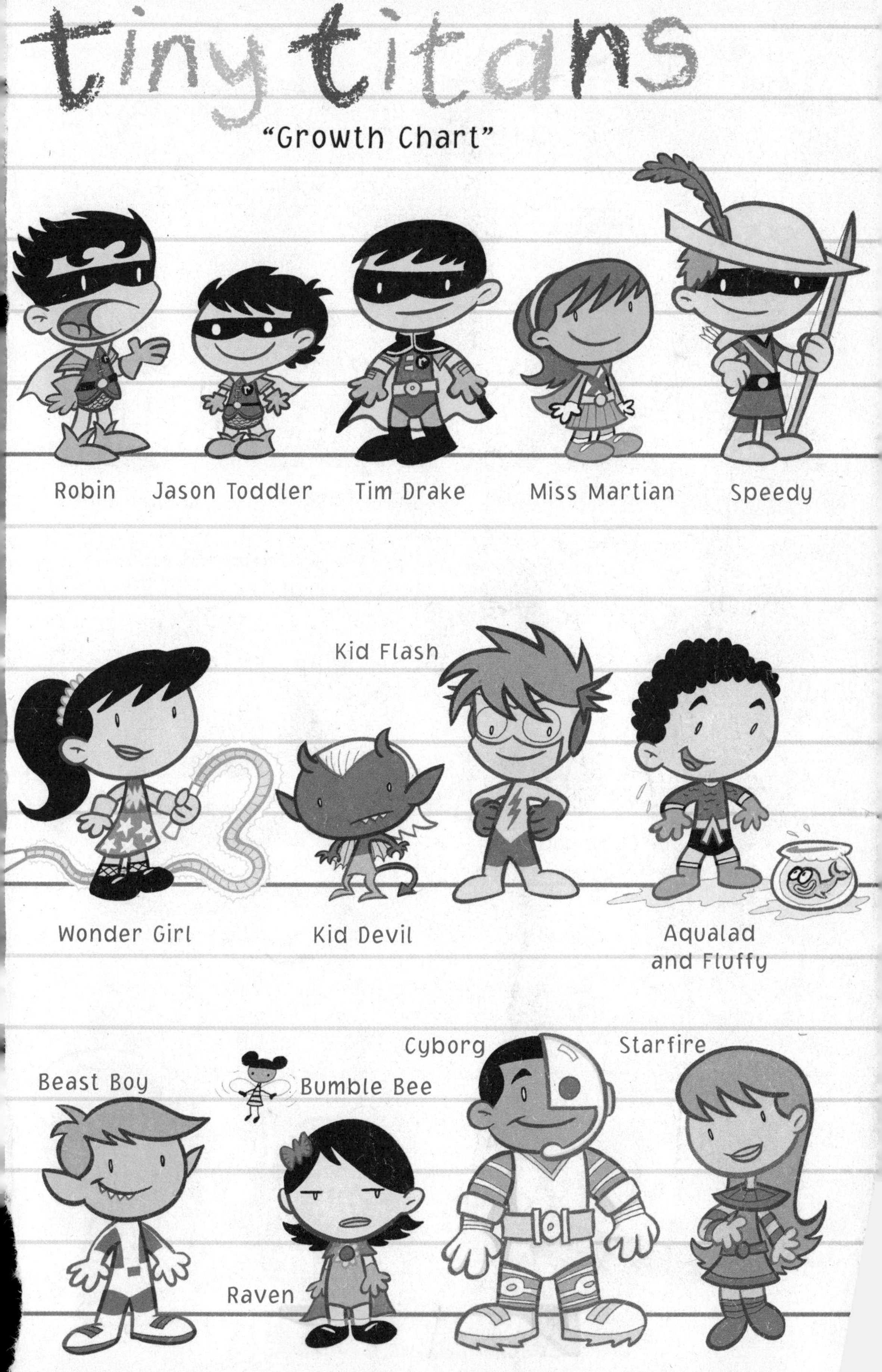
tiny titans
"Growth Chart"
Robin
Jason Toddler
Tim Drake
Miss Martian
Speedy
Kid Flash
Wonder Girl
Kid Devil
Aqualad and Fluffy
Cyborg
Starfire
Beast Boy
Bumble Bee
Raven

tiny titans

"Growth Chart"

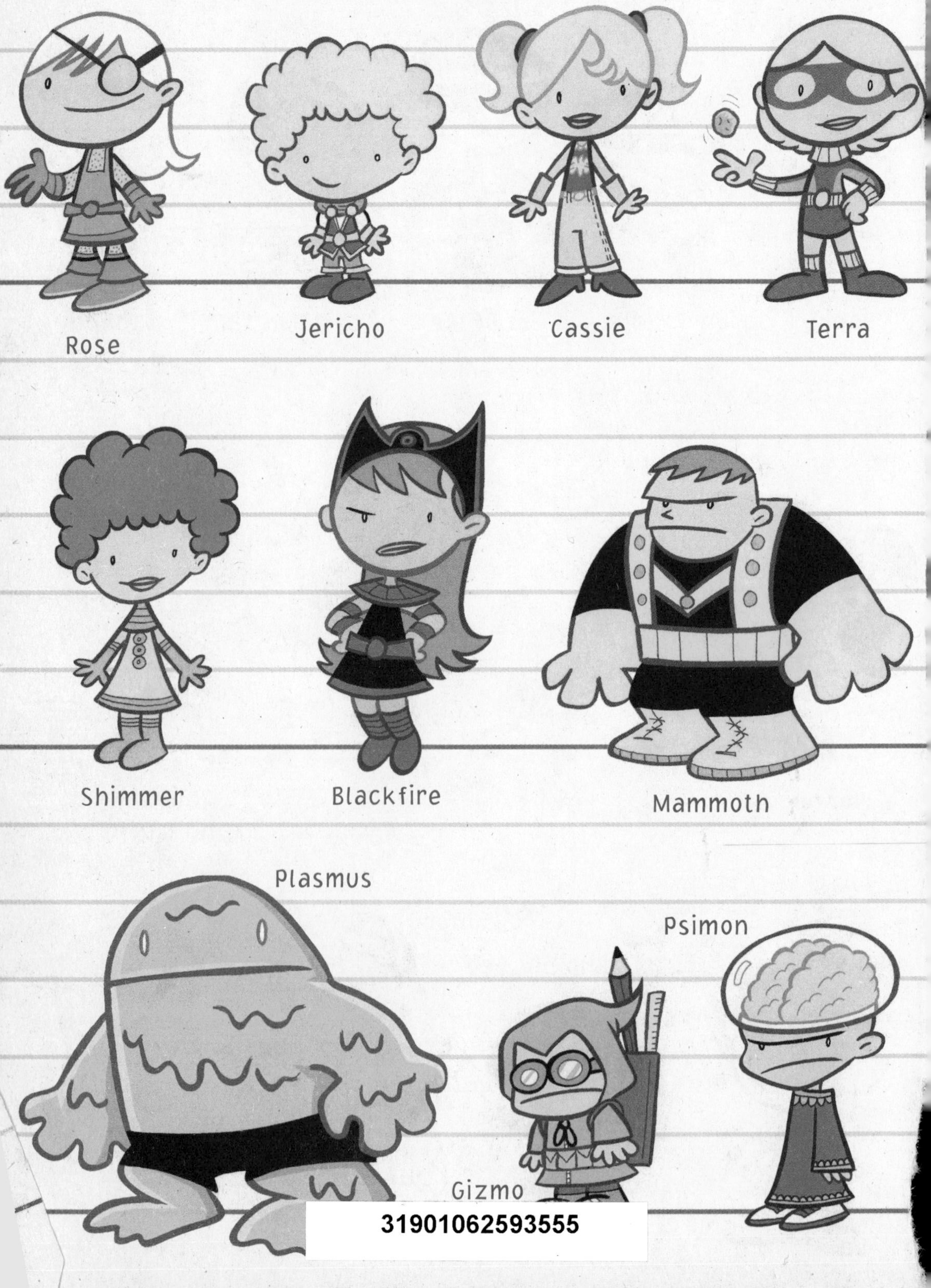
Rose
Jericho
Cassie
Terra
Shimmer
Blackfire
Mammoth
Plasmus
Psimon
Gizmo